The Spy Bazaar

Michael Alcroft

E-pub ISBN: 9780957407626
Version 1.0

Published by Craignish Publishing 2012
Fife, Scotland

First published in Great Britain in 2012 by
Craignish Publishing

For my parents, Carol and Charles

War is a part of God's creation.
- Helmuth von Moltke

Prologue

Heidelberg, Germany. May 1909.

Flesh torn by steel, a face marred forever. How they all loved their own precious scars.

The size of the wounds varied widely among them, from barely visible nicks to utterly hideous gashes. The jagged tissue on the larger cuts looked especially grim, on such young and otherwise pure faces. Those kinds of scars were loved most of all, of course; the long vicious marks carved along one's cheek or chin or forehead.

For it was the faces that always suffered such punishment. Except for hard rubber eyepieces, faces lacked adequate protection from the blades. Faces were easy targets compared to the rest of the body. And the scars were grisly badges of honour. The glory of a vivid Schmiss on a young man's face, for life.

The slight curve and sharp point of the sabre they used made it equally well suited for stabbing or slashing. Against such weapons, even the heavy leather and padded canvas protection worn by the duellists could not always prevent the occasional punctured lung. Anxious about coping with yet another student gored in the chest, University of Heidelberg administrators increasingly frowned upon Mensur duels among their students.

The Church and the military, however, continued to condone the tradition. And so, the carnival of scarring.

Horst Trommler, a student in his final year at Heidelberg, was not concerned with the fears of university officials. As his opponent struggled to fit his protection into place, Trommler suppressed a smile and confirmed again the heft and balance of the Korbschläger in his right hand. This was the sabre preferred by his own Studentenverbindung, or student corps. Trommler was eager to fight and he wondered how much damage to inflict upon his novice opponent. He was counting on the fact that his 'guest', a decade older than himself, and an Ausländer no less, would not want to embarrass Trommler in front of his friends, and would stay on the defensive.

Flushed with excitement and alcohol, and the curious presence of Trommler's foreign guest, a few dozen other students crowded around the two duellists. They sported brightly coloured caps and, on some, a sash to identify the corps to which each student belonged. With sloshing beer steins and smouldering cigarettes in hand, they took great delight in mocking the older foreigner. Opa, they called him. Granddad.

"Don't lose your balance, Opa!"

"Hey Opa, it's not too heavy for you, is it?"

Trommler stood abruptly, his sword ready, with two friends from his own student corps – wearing blue caps - close behind him. Alone at first, the foreigner, Opa, stood at the other side of the room. Then two students from a rival corps – the red caps – joined him. To Trommler's annoyance, they whispered in Opa's ear, words of encouragement no doubt, and a few other red caps sidled over to Opa's new 'team'. Each combatant also had a personal assistant to monitor the duel and step in to stop it if a strike was suspected.

Despite the size of the room, the battle would be fought very closely; Mensur fencing demanded tight proximity and vicious jabs at the face. In this contest, brutal thrusting was the preferred tactic, rather than prancing back and forth like a couple of Frenchmen. Traction would be difficult with all the sawdust on the floor, though it would also help soak up the beer and blood. Nothing could be done about the thick cigarette smoke or the heat, as the small windows in the room could not provide adequate ventilation.

When the two duellists were ready, the student referee took his place in between them, and raised his hand. They also needed a surgeon on these occasions, and he, too, was ready with his heavy leather bag of bandages, drugs, and instruments in case the match became too violent.

Now it was time.

After quick salutes by the duellists, the referee's raised hand chopped downwards. Trommler immediately hacked at Opa with all his might. The younger German, with his fuzzy Kaiserbart and leather trousers, was surprisingly quick despite his bulk. The sound of clanging Schläger filled the room as Trommler and his opponent viciously slashed at each other, forcing the other students to scramble out of the way. Trommler clearly had the upper hand; Opa seemed only to cower with fear and struggle to keep up his guard as the blows rained down upon him.

It was all over in just a few seconds.

One of Trommler's strikes caught Opa just above his right eye, and with a cry of *Halt!* from the referee, the two assistants stepped forward to stop the match. Dark blood was already flowing freely down Opa's face, and the surgeon sat him on a wooden stool to dress the wound. Thanks to his quick intervention, the cut would likely heal into a perfect Schmiss and Opa should have been very proud to wear such a badge of courage. If only he had been German.

Trommler smiled broadly as his fellow corpsmen cheered his victory. After waving to his mates, he stripped off his protective eyepieces; their black metallic netting prevented him from seeing Opa more clearly in the older man's moment of defeat. Everyone in the room knew that head wounds bleed especially profusely and they all looked on, cold-eyed and silent, as the surgeon taped a leather bandage over the wound and wiped the blood from Opa's face.

Trommler turned back to his friends to accept the beer they offered and was as surprised as they were when they heard Opa say, quite clearly, "*Noch einmal.*"

Another duel? Trommler thought of rejecting the invitation but he could not back down in front of his friends. He replaced his eyepieces and lifted his Schläger again, taking care to wipe the blood from its tip.

"As you wish," he said, in the foreigner's own language.

The duellists faced each other again, and the entire room went silent as the referee and the two assistants stepped forward.

Once again: the salutes, the dropped hand, and the slashing and clanging and cheering.

This time, Opa took the offensive. He forced Trommler outside the circle of students and backwards along the long side of the room, maintaining his attack. Trommler drove Opa backwards a handful of times, but not for long; the blows simply came too hard and too fast for Trommler to do little more than to keep the blade away from his face each time.

Back and forth they fought, grunting heavily with each blow. At one point they slammed into the wall of cheering students around them, causing them to collapse in a tangled heap of sweaty arms and legs. Another spectator was pushed into a table and his beer stein crashed to the floor in a spray of glass and foam. Even the referee seemed to lose interest in controlling the action he saw before him. And for a moment, Trommler seemed to gain the edge as Opa allowed himself to be pushed back to the far end of the room, almost to the wall.

Trommler's advantage was brief, however, and he still could not reach the older man's face with his blade. After a series of especially hard strikes, Trommler had to back off for just a moment – a split second - to catch his breath and improve his grip.

Opa took advantage of this opening. He slashed back at Trommler from side to side, causing the young man to parry each thrust from left to right to left again, all the while moving backwards. Faster and stronger Opa's blade came at him until Trommler, too unsteady on the dusty floor, ever so briefly glanced down behind himself to check his footing.

That was it. Opa struck his final blow now, but not with his blade. He dropped down slightly on one bent knee and lashed out with his right foot. He swept his foot just above the floor until it caught Trommler's Achilles tendon. The blow sent a sharp spike of pain up Trommler's leg, and he cried out in surprise. It also upended him in an embarrassed heap on the dusty floor.

Before the assistants could intervene, Opa put his foot on Trommler's sword hand, pinning it to the ground. Trommler froze in fear as Opa stood in victory above him and placed the sharp point of a Schläger in his sweaty face.

Opa pressed the point of his own sword against Trommler's unblemished left cheek; the right one already bore a nasty Schmiss. Then, ever so slowly, Opa scratched a line down Trommler's face, just deep enough to draw blood.

The room fell silent, but just for a moment before the red caps erupted in cheers. They surrounded Opa, laughing and patting him on the back. He had broken the rules, but so what? What a show! One student even put a red cap on Opa's head, and the older man's face, his foreign face, broke into a wide grin.

Opa put down his Schläger and removed his goggles before reaching a hand down to help Trommler to his feet.

He waited, with an outstretched hand, as Trommler, on his back still, and flushed in the face, considered how to respond…

PART ONE

Chapter 1

Alexandria, Scotland. January 1910.

Major General James Grierson had arrived in Alexandria in civilian clothes, yet his military bearing was almost certainly obvious to all those passing him on the quiet streets of this small town. The old gentleman who kindly directed him to his final destination in Alexandria had practically saluted him, and Grierson hoped few others would take notice of his presence today in West Dunbartonshire, to the northwest of Glasgow, Grierson's hometown.

At this time of day, Alexandria was full of chattering townspeople in search of lunch at home or in one of the tearooms and pubs along Bank Street, Main Street, and beyond. After a short walk from the railway station through the centre of Alexandria, Grierson soon heard the high-pitched roar of a petrol engine in full throttle. He tightened the belt on his overcoat and walked on, following the engine sound to the grounds of the huge Argyll Motors factory, the largest in Europe. Grierson was greatly impressed by the size of the place, with its red sandstone walls, green and gold iron railings, and high central clock tower, capped with a dome encased in gold leaf.

As instructed, the general made his way to the test track at the rear of the main building. The place was eerily empty and virtually lifeless except for an increasingly loud engine noise, the source of which was now obvious to Grierson: a red Norton motorbike. Grierson shook his head in awe at the speed of the machine as it raced around the track; it was much faster than any automobile he had ever seen. He waved to the rider as the bike sped by, and the man commanding the machine acknowledged Grierson with a quick salute as the bike passed where he stood.

After another pass around the track the bike decelerated abruptly and skidded to a halt a few feet away from Grierson, throwing off gravel and a small puff of tyre smoke. The rider stepped off the bike and, smiling broadly, walked quickly over to the general.

"Sergeant Walsh, I presume...?" Grierson extended his hand with a broad smile and the two men shook hands like the old friends they were.

Walsh laughed at that, shaking his head. "Not any more, general! So it's Nicholas now, or just Walsh."

Grierson clapped the younger man on the shoulders with both hands. Walsh was nearly thirty, two decades younger than Grierson, yet he showed a child's delight in having the general greet him so affectionately.

"Yes, you're back to civilian life now, aren't you, my boy?"

Walsh nodded. "Very much so, sir. Finally."

The two men walked back towards the factory, as Walsh wheeled his motorbike alongside them. He was careful to avoid the hot metal sides of his well-kept 1909 Norton Model One – or the 'Big Four' – with its huge 633cc engine.

Grierson kept a firm hand on Walsh's shoulder as their feet crunched along the gravel path. "And liking it? Not too boring for you?"

"Boring? You know me better than that. Just climb on this motorbike with me and let me show you how boring it is!"

Grierson raised his free hand in mock protest; his preferred mode of transportation had always been the four-legged variety. "No thank you, young man! But that wicked contraption isn't yours, is it?"

"Yes, it is. All mine."

"Yes, I heard you...came into some money recently. I'm sorry about your uncle."

They arrived at a small storage shed, which Walsh opened as Grierson steadied the bike.

"Thank you, general." Walsh wheeled in the bike and propped it against a wall. "He had a good life. He was kind to me."

Grierson looked around at the massive factory, standing long and silent in the grey winter light, then back to Walsh as the younger man locked the shed.

"I thought this place went out of business," Grierson said. "It certainly seems dead enough."

Walsh nodded. "It did fall on hard times, a couple of years ago, but it's re-opening soon. New financing, I hear."

"Hmm. Same name as before?"

"Well, now it's Argyll Ltd instead of Argyll *Motors* Ltd."

"Hmpf. I'm sure that will improve business for them. And they hired you on as a test driver?"

Walsh shook his head as he beckoned Grierson to follow him up the path back to the factory entrance. "Not exactly. I'm just helping with the engines, but I'm sure I'll find a way to test some of the new models once I find my feet around here."

"So you ended up in mechanics after all. An apprentice engineer. I'm pleased for you, lad"

"Yes, finally." Walsh smiled again, and Grierson gave him an odd, almost regretful, look. But he smiled as well.

"Well, that's good for you, Nicholas. Yes." Grierson paused for a moment. "Now, how about some lunch?"

Ten minutes later they waited for lunch to arrive at a pub around the corner from the railway station, with a half pint of Tennent's lager in front of Grierson and a mug of tea in front of Walsh. As the factory was still closed for business, they practically had the place to themselves. Grierson was pleased about that; fewer ears in the immediate vicinity to hear their conversation.

After the barman moved off, Walsh broke the silence. "You didn't come all the way up here just to see me, did you?"

Grierson shook his head. "Not exactly, lad. I was up to see the family for Hogmanay and I heard you were in the area."

"Yes, a belated Happy New Year to you."

Walsh raised his battered tea mug and Grierson smiled again as he clinked his beer glass against it.

"And to you. It's good to see you again, Nicholas."

Walsh nodded and took a sip of tea. "And you, sir. It's been a while, hasn't it?" A pause. "But we're not exactly in the vicinity of Glasgow, are we?"

Grierson smiled again. "No bother. An easy enough railway journey."

Walsh's face darkened. "Well, then, out with it, if this isn't a social visit."

"It *is* a social visit. Mostly. And let's wait until after lunch. I'm starving, as always!" Grierson attempted a smile, knowing it was no use pretending now.

Walsh slowly shook his head. "No, I'd rather we didn't. If you don't mind."

"All right, lad. If you insist." Grierson leaned in closer, and made sure no one was listening. "There's been some interesting changes back at the DMO, if you haven't heard already. I think you should be aware of them."

The DMO was the Directorate of Military Operations in the War Office, responsible for military intelligence, among other things.

"I thought you were at Aldershot now," Walsh said.

"I am. But I'm here on an errand."

"Not to see me?"

"Yes, in fact. You *are* the 'errand.'"

Walsh raised an eyebrow. "How comforting."

Grierson pursed his lips and pressed on. "They're putting together a proper foreign intelligence service, both the War Office and the Admiralty. A joint intelligence service, mind you. Both forces working together now. It's been agreed completely by the Committee on Imperial Defence, just last year."

Walsh looked dubious. "A foreign military intelligence service? And where do I come in?"

"It's not Africa," Grierson said quickly. "It's not even colonial."

Walsh considered that for a moment. Then he simply said, "Germany."

"Precisely. Have you been keeping up with developments?" Grierson paused as lunch was set before them. Two steaming bowls of Cullen skink and fresh bread. The barman moved off and they continued.

"Only through the newspapers," Walsh said, taking a sip of his soup. "Whatever one can make of them, that is."

Grierson picked up his spoon and pointed it at Walsh. "We're finally getting serious about them."

"Not all that spy nonsense I've seen lately?"

"It's not all nonsense. The CID is certainly taking it seriously. And better to confirm the situation rather than rely on...innuendo, don't you think?"

"And are you coming back to the DMO?" Walsh smiled at Grierson. "Have you redeemed yourself for them?"

Grierson shook his head. "No, I'm afraid not. Ewart is running that show now. And Macdonogh is heading up intelligence under him. At MO5."

MO5 was the tiny 'Special Section' within the DMO at the War Office. It handled ciphers and codes, protective security, postal censorship, and other sensitive matters.

Walsh smiled at the mention of Macdonogh. "Good old Blitz. How is he?"

"He's doing well. He's working with Bethell to get the Secret Service Bureau up and running as soon as possible."

"A new Secret Service Bureau? Is that what you call it? And with the Admiralty and War Office cooperating? I still don't believe it. And who's Bethell?"

"He's the Director of Naval Intelligence."

Walsh nodded his head. "So why come all this way to see me?"

"They need help. They need people with experience, and your name came up." Grierson tilted an eyebrow at Walsh. "New measures demand new men, correct? And they do agree that the priority is Germany, above everything else now."

"That's very encouraging, considering what they did to us, to you, a few years ago regarding Germany."

Grierson frowned in irritation. "Now stop that this instant! I know you were a wee bit scunnered after what happened before. And so was I, truth be told. I was as shocked as you were about it. But we were only doing our jobs. The point is, I'm still in the game, even after all that trouble in Paris. So listen to me, will you?"

Grierson wiped some soup from his moustache and stared directly at Walsh before he continued. "If Germany is serious about war then we need good people, reliable people, to measure their intentions and devise a response." Grierson pounded his index finger on the table. "Would you disagree with that? Hmm?"

"No...but I don't..."

"Nicholas, did you know that during our own naval exercises a while back a small contingent of British sailors played a little game with us? They managed to evade the main fleet, completely evade them, and then land in the north of Scotland. Without being detected!"

Walsh shook his head.

"Well, it happened, and we still haven't heard the end of it from the CID. So it can be done, my boy. Maybe not a full invasion, but Germany could certainly put a sabotage or espionage force ashore here. And that's easily enough to do some serious damage. They could reach railway lines, shipyards, arsenals, you name it! All completely vulnerable right now. So just have lunch with these folk, will you please? It's a free meal, isn't that right? And who knows, they may even decide you don't have the right skills for this."

Both Grierson and Walsh smiled at the mention of a free meal; Grierson had said many times that he had fought his best battles with a knife and fork.

Walsh dipped some bread into the remains of his soup. "So who is in charge of this new outfit? Someone I know?"

"A man named Cumming. Captain Mansfield Cumming."

"Never heard of him."

"Why would you? He's navy. Besides, he hasn't been on active duty at sea for quite some time. Word is that he gets seasick on the high seas."

Grierson knew that Walsh could appreciate that, as the young man also was not a fan of the sea, and had been sick as a dog during his first long voyage, nearly three weeks to Capetown. The RMS *Kildonan Castle* might have been a fine example of Glaswegian shipbuilding, all 9,652 gross tons of her, but when crowded with boastful soldiers, all washing down terrible food with cheap liquor smuggled in by some of the stewards, it was something else entirely. And did those damned Taffies really need to bring along their regimental goat for the voyage? The worst time of his life, Walsh once told Grierson, long ago. Until he arrived at Capetown, that is.

Walsh pushed his empty soup bowl away and sat back in his chair. He wiped his mouth with the back of his sleeve and looked out the window at nothing in particular. It was growing dark already; a typical Scottish midwinter's afternoon.

Grierson waited, silently.

Walsh turned back towards Grierson but didn't look him in the face as he spoke. "I wasn't intending to go back into service. You know that."

"Yes, I remember." Grierson's eyes bored into Walsh's face until the young man looked up at him again. "But you also never really expected to be asked to come back, did you? And do you also remember the advice I gave you just before we last parted? *Both* pieces of advice?"

Walsh was silent for a moment. He smiled again, looked up at Grierson, and lifted the hair from his forehead, revealing a scar over his right eye.

"What happened there?" Grierson said, looking confused.

"I got it in Heidelberg, last year. Or *letztes Jahr*, I should say."

Grierson put down his spoon. Ever the warrior, he sensed victory.

"You've been learning German, Sergeant Walsh? And travelling in Germany? Well, I think I'd like to hear that story, if you please!"

Chapter 2

Leipzig, Germany. January 1910.

Klaus Retzlaff stared out the window of the opulent study in the sprawling Hesse estate outside Leipzig. It had to be the most sumptuous private room he had ever been in. Heavy silk curtains, dark panelled walls, and gilded picture frames surrounded Retzlaff and the large man seated behind an even larger desk, Heinrich Hesse. A huge elk antler chandelier with electric lights hung above their heads, and the fireplace behind Retzlaff seemed larger than some of the flats he had been in. The esteemed Herr Hesse had made his fortune in banking, helping to fund Germany's rise as an industrial power, and his residence was a monument to his success.

It was not always wise, however, to demonstrate such wealth. At least, not to every visitor. With some guests, in fact, it was far better to remain 'hälinge reich', as a Swabian would say – secretly rich. For now that Retzlaff was more aware than ever of Hesse's vast resources, only one thought rattled around in his lively mind: *squeeze them.*

Behind him, Hesse's gruff voice, slightly irritated. "Well, *Herr* Retzlaff, can you help us or not?"

Hands clasped behind his back, Retzlaff turned toward Hesse, as slowly as possible without appearing disrespectful. Retzlaff made sure his face was etched with worry and he pursed his lips before answering. He forced himself not to take a closer look at the beautiful gilded carriage clock perched on the bookshelf next to him. Was it a genuine Breguet or just a skilled reproduction?

"This is a most difficult task, *Herr* Hesse. *Most* difficult. Are you absolutely sure it's not a kidnapping?"

"As sure as we can be at this stage. How do we know anything? We've had no contact from Ernie nor any ransom note. No contact whatsoever since he disappeared."

"So no leads then? No obvious place to start?"

Retzlaff sat down in a leather armchair in front of Hesse's desk. He picked up a small porcelain cannon near the edge of the desk and tried to catch a glimpse of the registration mark on the bottom. Was it Dresden or Meissen? Crossed swords, must be Meissen.

"No, none other than what I've told you," Hesse said. "And would you please put that down?"

Retzlaff did as he was told. "Yes. Yes you did. And they disappeared at exactly the same time?'"

"Yes, we believe so."

"You *believe*, but are you *certain*?" Retzlaff took care not to patronize his prospective patron. "You've spoken to his family?"

Hesse sighed with impatience. The lack of hair on his head was more than compensated for by the thick whiskers on his chin, and Retzlaff could just make out the movement of Hesse's thin lips behind all the facial fuzz.

"Yes, of course," Hesse practically hissed. "Of course we did. A few days ago."

"And?"

"And nothing. Nothing! They don't seem especially concerned about their son's whereabouts. You know how they are, don't you? Who can believe what they claim, anyhow? Ernst, on the other hand, has a bright future ahead of him. A very bright future. If he returns in time."

"Yes, if he returns." Retzlaff pretended to make some notes on a small pad on his lap. He wondered how much the huge desk separating him from Hesse had cost. "If he returns. And he could be anywhere. Anywhere in the world, really. I hardly know where to start."

"Please, *Herr* Retzlaff, there is a time element here. Ernst must return before the next term starts. If he fails to do so, his place will be lost. And I expended considerable energy to secure that place for my son. Considerable energy. Do you understand?"

Retzlaff considered the tips of his fingers. Did his nails need trimming just now? "I should need at least a month, I think. Perhaps six weeks."

"Out of the question. We need him home now."

"Three weeks, then. I have other cases to attend to. This period is a very busy time for me, you know. Very busy." Another lie. Who had the time or money to hire a private investigator at this time of year, when the Christmas bills came due?

"Two."

"I shall give you a...a preliminary report, in two weeks. Then we can decide how to proceed." Retzlaff could sense Herr Hesse reaching his limits.

"Fine, two weeks at the most," said Hesse in defeat.

"And my daily fee plus expenses, of course."

"I want a full accounting of your time on this."

"The same as I provide all my clients, *Herr* Hesse. They have never complained."

Hesse sat back in his chair, the negotiation complete now. "Where will you begin?"

"I would like to speak with your other family members, your wife and..." He consulted his notebook again. "...The one daughter, is it? Maria?"

Hesse shook his head. "Out of the question. There is no need to concern them."

"Are you sure? Perhaps they could be helpful, *Herr* Hesse..."

"Yes, I'm *certain* of it." Hesse was a powerful man and accustomed to getting his way. Retzlaff decided not to push the issue for now.

Retzlaff smiled. "Fair enough. Perhaps you are correct." He paused for a moment. "Then I should like to begin with the Stern family. Unless you object?"

"No, certainly not. Perhaps you will have more success with them than I."

"Perhaps."

Chapter 3

London, England. January 1910.

The Royal Automobile Club at 119 Piccadilly West was situated near Mayfair in central London, between Green Park and Hyde Park. Cumming arrived there early for his luncheon appointment and was surprised to find Walsh already waiting for him at the entrance to the dining room. Cumming had hoped to assess Walsh a little before he allowed him into the club, but it was too late for that now.

"Mr Walsh, I presume?" Cumming said, extending his hand.

"Yes. And you are Captain Cumming?" Walsh shook Cumming's hand.

"Yes. Mansfield Cumming. And a retired captain, I should say. It's a pleasure to meet you, finally."

Walsh nodded and quickly drained the remaining liquid in his glass. Cumming hoped the young man wasn't drunk, not yet knowing that Walsh tended to avoid alcohol.

"Shall we take a seat for lunch?" Cumming said.

"Of course. That's why I'm here."

As they walked to the table, Cumming calmed himself and took note of the younger man's dress and bearing to gauge his mood; Grierson had warned him that this deal was not yet finalized.

Walsh did not appear especially imposing physically, but he certainly looked like he could handle himself. His dark hair had grown beyond service regulation length and his equally dark eyes seemed exceptionally alert to Cumming. He could be considered handsome except for the small scar above his eye and his slightly flattened nose, a consequence of too many boxing matches. And did his lower lip seem a bit puffy, from scar tissue on the inside perhaps?

He certainly was not polished enough for officer material, at least not in Cumming's Navy. Walsh was, however, a solid marksman with revolvers and rifles, as well as an expert scout thanks to his time in the South African veld. Grierson had been very specific about those skills. And at least he was clean-shaven, like Cumming.

As they arrived at the table, Cumming asked Walsh if he had ever been to the RAC, then regretted the words as soon as they left his mouth.

"No, this is my first time," Walsh said. He appeared to be distinctly unimpressed with the place. "I wasn't even aware there was such a club."

"Oh yes. I've been a member since 1902." The two men sat down. "Of course, back then it was the Automobile Club of Great Britain and Ireland."

"Is that so?" Walsh said, as a waiter appeared and placed napkins in their laps. A second waiter poured water for them. "Not a lot of private clubs where I live."

"No, I suppose not. I'm just very keen on motorcars, you see. Kind of an obsession of mine, if I'm truly honest. I drove a Wolseley in the Paris-Madrid race in '03, in point of fact. Or should I say, 'crashed' a Wolseley!"

Cumming's face lit up at the memory of that exciting incident, although several spectators and racers had died during that race. The eager crowds had been ignorant of the hazards of standing too close to the route.

Walsh nodded in sympathy. "Too bad for you."

"Do you like fish? The plaice is especially good here," said Cumming as the waiter returned. "I'll have that."

Walsh handed his menu to the waiter. "I eat enough fish in Scotland," he said to Cumming. Looking at the waiter, he continued, "Fillet of beef for me. And bloody rare, mind you."

"I must say, Mr Walsh, you don't sound much like a Glaswegian," said Cumming, once they were left alone again.

Walsh shook his head. "That's because I'm not. I'm from Perthshire. And then I stayed in Fife, after I left primary school."

"Ahh, now I see why I can understand you!" Cumming smiled again. "And Grierson tells me you are with Argyll Motors now?"

"Yes, I was supposed to start this week. Until this came up."

Cumming registered that comment and pressed on. "And you have some experience with motorcars, in addition to your army service? With mechanical equipment?"

Walsh nodded slowly. "As a hobby at first. I actually prefer motorbikes. But I picked up some skills with motorcars in Germany the last few years."

"Yes, Grierson said you were in Stuttgart for a while. Quite recently, was it?"

Walsh nodded. "Yes, I found some casual work in the wee shops servicing the Daimler works for a couple of years. They were outfitting a new factory at Untertürkheim after the one in Cannstatt burned down. My uncle helped to arrange it. I never meant to stay too long. They needed joiners who could do detailed woodwork, saddlemakers, leatherworkers, all kinds of skills. After they began to expand with the Mercedes Simplex."

"A fine automobile."

"Yes, it is. It won the Frankfurt Circuit a few times, I think. Anyhow, I learned a lot there, after I was allowed to work on engines, and spent my final months in Germany at the Daimler works itself. Then my uncle passed away, and I came back home."

"Yes, Grierson told me. Sorry about that. And so you are comfortable with weapons and machinery?"

"I guess you could say that. I started by working on bicycles when I was younger." Walsh looked Cumming directly in the eyes, before adding, "At the industrial school."

Cumming hid his surprise; Grierson hadn't mentioned Walsh's time in the reformatory. The lad must have gone in sometime after his mother died. What else did Grierson fail to tell Cumming about this serious young man?

"I see," Cumming said. "Yes. Well, my father gave me my interest in mechanics. He was an engineer, in point of fact. With the Royal Society."

"My father wasn't so…generous. So my skills don't extend that far. I didn't study mechanics at school. But I know a wee bit about engines. And weapons of course."

"Of course. And you picked up language skills as well."

"Yes."

"And some French?"

"Yes, very fluent in French. Almost so with German. My father was from Alsace, originally. He changed his name after arriving in Scotland, but still spoke French at home much of the time. He left after the Germans, or should I say Prussians, invaded in 1870."

"A difficult time, I can guess."

Walsh shrugged. "He managed."

Cumming noted several gentlemen at the bar, brandies in hand, looking at Walsh. They were not friendly looks. Cumming knew what they were thinking and did his best to ignore their stares. Time to get down to business.

"Well, I'm grateful *you* managed to come all this way to meet with me," Cumming said, as pleasantly as he could manage. "Very grateful."

"I owe Grierson a lot."

"Yes, he speaks quite highly of you. Which is, of course, why you're here."

"So why am I here, exactly? Grierson left out some of the details." Walsh's eyes looked directly into Cumming's own. "All of the details, I should say."

Cumming glanced around the room, again, and lowered his voice now. "I imagine he told you about the new Secret Service Bureau?"

Walsh nodded. "Just a little."

"Well, I'm heading up the foreign department."

"So you deal with military attachés overseas?"

Cumming shook his head. "Not exactly. They are still under our standing naval or military intelligence departments, as the case may be. And officially attached to our embassies."

"So then?"

"Mr Walsh, what I'm about to tell you must be kept in the strictest confidence, you understand. Especially if you...if you choose not to work with us."

Walsh nodded. "I understand. That's no bother." He then leaned forward slightly as Cumming spoke and paid close attention now.

"The Bureau has three basic tasks," Cumming began. "First, to act as a screen, of sorts, between the Admiralty and War Departments on the one hand and the world of espionage on the other. Second, to conduct inquiries and investigations regarding flows of strategic or military information coming into these departments. And third, to correspond with paid agents and other persons able to provide secret information on our adversaries. Specifically, Germany."

Walsh nodded at that. "And where do I come in? Conducting investigations?"

Cumming shook his head. "No, with the third task."

Walsh frowned. "Dealing with agents? But why can't the attachés do that? And what about the diplomatic service?"

The waiter returned with their food, causing Cumming to pause again. The two men sat in silence as the plates were placed before them. A moment later Cumming continued, as he forked into his plaice.

"Because His Majesty's Government does not want the outside world to know that we engage in espionage. So the attachés will continue to liaise with their official counterparts in foreign capitals, as will the diplomats and consuls, all above board, while *we* will deal, behind closed doors, with the scoundrels who are increasingly coming out of the woodwork here and there to sell foreign military secrets to us."

Walsh hacked at his blood-rare beef. "What kind of military secrets?"

"I'm sorry; I can't be more specific until I have more of a commitment from you."

"So you want me to deal with foreign agents?"

"Yes, deal with them, and recruit them if possible."

Walsh raised an eyebrow. "From London?"

"No, I have something else in mind."

"Germany then?"

"No…but I can't say any more until we are agreed on your commitment."

"I'm not sure I'm ready to give a commitment just now." Walsh shook his head in irritation. "Frankly, Captain Cumming, I was very happy to give up this intelligence business a few years ago. It all seemed to be a colossal waste of time. Grierson must have told you that."

"Yes, he did. He did. I know something about what happened in Paris. And we all agree that it was a mistake, what happened to Grierson. But he also said you were very dependable. And that you might be willing to return when the time came." Cumming paused. "That time is now, Mr Walsh."

"Well, I do agree that Germany might require more of our…attention now, but I need to know exactly what you are asking of me before I give up the plans I've been making for the past three years. I have my own commitments, you understand. And how much time are we talking about?"

"This may be an…open-ended assignment."

"Then my answer is no. I'm sorry. But my uncle left me a little money and I'd like to open my own business soon, once I get some more practical experience."

"Please, Mr Walsh." Cumming's face was distraught. "*Please.* This has taken some effort on my part. Serious effort. I've already worked out some of the details about..."

"Then let's hear them. Now, if you please."

Cumming put down his cutlery and conceded defeat. He could not afford to waste any more time. His first six-month report was due in April, just a few months from now, and he had practically nothing to show for his efforts. Nothing at all, in fact. He had no official status in the government, and few people were even aware of the Secret Service Bureau. Therefore the phone in Cumming's office did not ring, and he was tired of waiting for the intelligence to come to him.

"Mr Walsh, it's very simple, really. I want you to go to Brussels."

Walsh frowned in confusion. "Brussels? Why?"

"Three reasons, for a start. First, we need someone to build up some useful contacts in the event of a war with Germany. I'm sure you know their likely invasion route to France is through Belgium. Hopefully the Germans will preserve Belgian neutrality, but if not, and if we can't hold them off, then we need a stay-behind network in place. The sooner we can organize that, the better."

Walsh put down his cutlery. "So you are already planning for war."

Cumming smiled, but without humour this time. "Military officers must always plan for war, Mr Walsh. I'm sure you know that."

"And the other two reasons?"

"We understand that a great deal of military intelligence, of all types and from a remarkable range of sources, is funnelled through Brussels these days. So we are finding it very hard to...to discriminate among various pieces of information. Spying is not illegal there, as long as you don't spy on the poor Belgians, of course!" Cumming brightened up again, hoping Walsh was on the hook now.

"In Brussels? I never would've believed it."

"Oh yes. Absolutely. I'm getting offers of information from there on a daily basis, almost. And you can see advertisements in Belgian newspapers for secrets for sale.

Espionage in the *petites annonces*! By freelance agents, all over the place! Would you believe that?"

"No."

Cumming waved to the waiter for the bill, then turned back to Walsh. "Baden-Powell calls it a kind of 'international spy exchange.' A couple of years ago in Brussels he even acquired a plan for a German invasion of Britain. The invasion was to be launched on the August bank holiday, to catch people off guard. So if you need secret information of any type in Europe, Brussels is your first port of call. And I'm sure you know Baden-Powell's reputation?"

Walsh didn't answer that. "And the third reason?"

"Well, we *also* believe that Germany directs its network of agents in Britain from Brussels."

"A 'network of agents' in Britain? Like all that nonsense in the *Daily Mail* about German waiters and barbers spying on us all? Are you sure?"

Cumming nodded. "Quite sure, Mr Walsh. They are directed from Berlin by a man named Steinhauer. Gustav Steinhauer. He heads the British section of the *Nachrichten Abteilung*. But we have reason to believe that Steinhauer has a man in Brussels working against Britain."

Walsh cringed slightly at Cumming's German pronunciation. "The NA. The intelligence department of the German Admiralty."

"Precisely."

"And you believe the NA is running agents in Britain? And from Brussels?"

"We know it is. We have firm evidence of that, in fact. I could give you more details if you like, some other time. So *we* are not the only ones planning for war." Cumming stood up abruptly, but then leaned down closer to Walsh's ear. "*Now*, do you understand the nature of the threat, Mr Walsh?"

Walsh stood up and nodded. "It's becoming clearer, I suppose, Captain Cumming."

Cumming smiled and leaned down to sign the bill on the table as he spoke. "I'm glad to hear that, Mr Walsh. Very glad. It looks like Grierson was right about you. And you may call me Cumming, or simply 'C'. Now, my boy, let's take a little walk."

Chapter 4

Leipzig. January 1910.

Retzlaff's two weeks working for Herr Hesse were nearly up and he had learned nothing. He also had attempted nothing. Or at least, not very much.

The Hesse boy had left only a cryptic note for his parents, on his personal stationery embossed with gold leaf. In his short message, he apologized to them for leaving and said he would be in touch as soon as he could. He also said some things were more important than one's studies, and he hoped his parents would understand.

That was all.

Ernst Hesse was an adult and had left home by his own free will, or so it seemed to all concerned. Therefore no crime had been committed, except possibly for the minor offense of failing to report one's whereabouts to the police after changing a residence. If he was still in Germany, that is. So Retzlaff was reluctant to use his contacts in the Leipzig court system for this. At least, for the moment. If Ernst had left the country, a border office would have a record of his departure, but Retzlaff lacked the time and authority to check on this without a clearer indication of where Ernst might have exited Germany. The young Hesse undoubtedly had taken some money with him, but his father was unsure of the amount, and did not claim that his son had stolen from him.

Clearly the father was equally eager to find his son and to keep this problem away from the authorities, given their attitude towards not just Catholics but political undesirables more generally. Retzlaff also understood that attitude all too well after nearly two decades in the Leipzig Staatliche Beamtenkorper, or the state police. Although Germany's police training methods were among the most advanced in Europe, and although Retzlaff made as much as he could of the limited opportunities afforded to him and his fellow patrolmen, he had quickly grown bored and frustrated with official police work. Germany's police forces were highly regimented, if not fully militarized, and Retzlaff's tendency to question their sacred working methods produced mistrust amongst his colleagues and superiors. He also had virtually no chance of rising to the level of a police commissioner as he did not come from the Junker aristocracy, did not have a university education, and had not served as an officer in the military.

Equally discouraging was the fact that merit-based promotions from the lower ranks to higher police officer positions were practically unheard of, and Retzlaff spent much of his time working on administrative tasks. He was promoted, finally, to the Kriminalabteilung, the detective force, in 1904, but by that time he was completely fed up with handling such critically important and utterly fascinating matters as public toilets, theatre regulation, game laws, the civilian registration – or Meldewesen - system, and the most common crime of all: theft of firewood.

Retzlaff looked for an exit strategy from the state police, and found one after spending his limited free time nosing around the Leipzig court system, particularly its higher jury court for felony offenses, and the Imperial Supreme Court, also located in Leipzig. Retzlaff soon learned that those unfortunate enough to stand accused before any German criminal court would almost certainly be found guilty; appeals were limited and the 1879 Code of Criminal Procedure, or Strafprozessordung, made sure that trials were usually over in one session with the same result in most cases: a guilty verdict. No rational German citizen, therefore, looked forward to having his day in court, if a *prima facie* case could be made against him – or her.

Retzlaff also learned that Germany's public prosecutor's office conducted many of its investigations in secret; it did not need to inform the accused that an investigation was under way, until an indictment was ready. So he cultivated relationships with as many clerks in the court system as he could: coffee with this one, a beer with that one, lunch with the other one, and on and on. Eventually these minor bureaucrats agreed to provide him with the names of those under investigation before they could be indicted or removed from under suspicion.

These names, in turn, were cross-referenced with Retzlaff's other sources in the Meldwesensystem, which helpfully documented not just home addresses but also occupational histories, social standing, and overall material wealth. Those unfortunate enough to face investigation for an indictable offense but fortunate enough to possess serious financial means eventually found Retzlaff at their door, offering to help them navigate the complexities of the Strafprozessordung in order to, hopefully, avoid an indictment. Such assistance as only Retzlaff could provide was offered secretly, and required a handsome fee, of course.

After a few years of moonlighting as a private detective, Retzlaff felt secure enough to strike out on his own, and his imagination produced a bigger goal; a dream, even. He wanted to become the Pinkerton's of the Kaiserreich. Retzlaff even carried with him, at all times, his favourite photograph as a source of inspiration. It was an image he could hardly believe the first time he saw it: Mr Allan Pinkerton, standing next to President Abraham Lincoln himself and Major General John A. McClernand, taken during the American Civil War. With this inspiring image, Retzlaff dreamed of his own branch offices in all major German cities, and perhaps beyond, all of which would pay him a percentage of their revenues. He paid especially close attention to potential clients among politically vulnerable and high profile groups, such as rich Catholics, Poles, and Jews, and his reputation gradually spread among these communities.

And so it was that Retzlaff's business card ended up on the desk of Heinrich Hesse, whose missing son Ernie was beginning to annoy him. The trail was turning cold, and despite all his skills, Retzlaff was not especially experienced at finding missing persons. Especially if, as in this case it seemed, they did not want to be found.

As his time was running out, Retzlaff made his way to the University of Leipzig, where he learned that Ernst's PhD supervisor was on holiday in the south of France and could not be reached at the moment. Smart man, thought Retzlaff.

In his other inquiries, Retzlaff found that Herr Hesse had been correct about Tobias's parents. Retzlaff had spent nearly a full day travelling to and from the Jewish quarter of Leipzig, around the Brühl. Herr Stern the elder worked in the fur trade that dominated the area, and Retzlaff had admired the bear, rabbit, and many other, less identifiable, pelts decorating the shops along the Brühl while he searched for the Sterns. He practically had to hold his nose at the rancid smell of skins, sweat, dyes, alum salts, and other noxious odours in Stern's filthy workshop. His only reward for this torture was the knowledge that the elder Sterns were not especially concerned about their son's whereabouts, and even seemed almost pleased that he was gone. Herr Stern's only comment was "Tobias is Tobias," as if that settled the matter.

Today Retzlaff found himself back at University chemistry lab, where Ernst had conducted his PhD research before disappearing. The term was finished and the laboratory was quiet, except for a few dedicated doctoral students here and there. Retzlaff attempted to act casually as he asked around for information about Ernst, yet he knew perfectly well that he appeared like just another police inspector to these ignorant, coddled students.

After a few inquiries in various rooms, he managed to find two of Ernst's labmates working with equipment and materials he couldn't possibly hope to understand. The clothing under their laboratory smocks looked poor to Retzlaff, so he removed the leather wallet from his coat and thumbed through a few bills.

"Are you quite sure you don't know where Ernst might have gone?" Retzlaff asked again.

The taller of the two students, Markus, a thin boy with wire-rimmed glasses and several day's worth of beard stubble on his cheeks, shook his head. The shorter one, Tomas, who evidently ate better and groomed himself more often than his companion, was adamant.

"We really weren't close friends with Ernst, *Herr* Retzlaff," he insisted. "Not friends at all, in fact."

"Yes, but you might have heard talk about him, here and there." Retzlaff paused for effect while the two students looked at his wallet with interest. "Helping me might be very…beneficial to you." He put the wallet back in his coat, having made sure they got a good look at the money.

Markus spoke up. Perhaps *he* was hungry. "He wasn't doing very well here, if you must know. With his studies, I mean."

"What was the problem?"

"He couldn't focus on his research. He was…just playing about here. Or so it seemed to me."

"What do you mean, 'playing about'? What was his research?" Retzlaff hoped the answer would not be too technical.

"He was supposed to be working on refinements to the Ostwald process, under one of the big man's own students, but he kept getting off track."

"How?"

Now Tomas answered. "Ernst was an idiot. He has a chance to work here with someone linked to a Nobel-prize winner and he just plays around with fermentation techniques and other nonsense."

Retzlaff smiled. "Fermentation? Maybe he just likes beer."

Tomas glared at Retzlaff. "Are you serious? We are doing important work here. Ostwald is a *genius* and any chemistry student in the world should be grateful to work with anyone who studied with him. But Ernst wants to throw that away."

"Do you know anything about his friend, Tobias? Tobias Stern?"

Markus and Tomas exchanged a glance. Retzlaff caught it, and smiled to himself with satisfaction.

"He was around here, sometimes," said Markus.

"Was he helping or distracting Ernst?"

The two students shifted uneasily and glanced around the room.

"*Helping* or *distracting*, boys? Which is it?"

Again, Markus: "Distracting."

"In what way?"

"Filling his head with political nonsense." This from Tomas.

"What kind of political nonsense?"

"Communism, socialism, worker's rights, the world socialist revolution, that kind of nonsense. You know the type." Tomas looked Retzlaff in the eyes, and the detective understood immediately.

Retzlaff stared at them. "And what was Tobias after? Did they go to meetings? Did they mention the names of other comrades?"

"No, nothing like that. We only saw Tobias a few times," Markus insisted.

"Please boys, I'm not a policeman. I just want to help young Ernst. His family is worried for his safety. If he is mixed up with...undesirable influences then someone needs to look out for him."

The two students exchanged another glance.

"I heard Tobias mention something about Switzerland," said Markus.

"What about Switzerland?"

"Nothing in particular, I *swear* it. Just the name came up when I was walking by them. That's all."

"Fair enough. Perhaps that will be enough to go on, for now." Retzlaff picked up his cashmere overcoat and shrugged himself into it.

Tomas spoke up. "What about the reward?"

"Only once I find him, of course. Unless you have something else to share now?"

Markus and Tomas turned away in defeat.

"*Tschüss*, boys. Until next time."

As Retzlaff strode toward the building exit in triumph, he heard a male voice call out to him: "Hey, *Kommissar*."

Three younger students were working in a smaller, shabbier lab than the one he had just left. They beckoned him to come in.

Retzlaff wandered over to them, wary as ever. "Yes?"

The students were grinning like idiots. Were they drunk?

One of them held up a vial to Retzlaff. "Johan bet me that you wouldn't be able to identify this. I think you can do it. Care to try?"

Retzlaff backed away, just slightly. "I'm not going to drink that."

"No, just smell it. It's not dangerous, I promise." He removed the cap and held it out.

Curious now, Retzlaff leaned closer and took a gentle sniff of the liquid. He immediately began to retch and staggered backwards, struggling to force down the bile rising in his throat.

Of course he recognized the odour, though he had never encountered it in such a strong form. Anyone with a functioning sense of smell would recognize it. It was highly concentrated butyric acid, which, among other things, helps to give vomit its distinctively unpleasant odour.

The three students began to laugh as Retzlaff coughed and waved his hand in front of his nose.

"It looks like he did recognize it!" one of the boys said. "You lose, Johan!" They continued to laugh at Retzlaff, who put a finger to his nose and forced air out through his nostrils, one then the other. Wasn't this just hysterical?

Retzlaff quickly regained his composure and stood up. In a sudden move, he slapped the student who had offered the tube to his nose. The blow had nearly as much force behind it as a punch, and the stunned boy fell backwards against a lab table. He dropped his test tube with a crash of glass on the floor.

The acid spread all around them, releasing its fumes. The two other students stared at Retzlaff in shock, frozen in place, and afraid to help their stricken friend to his feet. The noxious odour of the acid began to fill the room, and the three boys coughed and covered their own noses.

"You forget your manners," Retzlaff snarled, before storming out.

Chapter 5

Brussels. January 1910.

Albert I, third king of the Belgians, assumed the throne on 23 December 1909, one day after the funeral of Albert's uncle, King Leopold II. Like Leopold's funeral, Albert's coronation was a quiet affair, as Belgium did not require a formal and lavish ceremony to mark the occasion. Even so, enthusiastic and loyal crowds turned out to watch the royal family proceed in their ornate estate coaches along rue Royale to Albert's oath-taking ceremony. During his coronation speech at the Belgian parliament building, the Palais de la Nation on rue de la Loi, the new king, only thirty-four years of age, swore to himself and to Belgium to "fulfil my duties, and to devote all my strength and all my life to the service of the country."

Less than a month later, two servants of the Belgian royal family sat in a large, comfortable office within the Royal Palace in central Brussels and pondered the kinds of obligations young Albert's oath might soon entail.

The office belonged Ivo Massaert, a senior administrative aide to the Belgian royal family. Among other things, he was responsible for arranging the king's travel and appointments schedule. Massaert wore a stylish waistcoat and a boldly coloured silk necktie but still looked old for his age, at forty-two now, and had gone prematurely grey a decade earlier. A consequence, he often thought, of having to deal with the controversies surrounding Leopold's final years - controversies about atrocities in the Belgian Congo.

His slightly older colleague in the room was Martin Dewulf, a special inspector with the Belgian state security service, the Sûreté de l'État, modeled on the original French version of the same bureaucracy. Although two brigades of the Belgian Gendarmerie protected the royal Family - a Special Brigade at the Royal Palace, and a Security Brigade for the Royal Estate at Laeken - one of Dewulf's more sensitive duties was to act as liaison with Massaert about potential threats to the Belgian state in general and to the royal family in particular. Following his military service in the Belgian Congo, Dewulf had served as a member of the Special Brigade security detail and this experience put him in a prime position for assuming the liaison role after he moved to the

Belgian Sûreté in 1904. Dewulf had even witnessed the botched assassination attempt on Leopold II on 15 November 1902, when the Italian anarchist Gennaro Rubino had fired three pistol shots at the king as he was riding in a royal cortege for the funeral procession of his wife, Marie Henriette of Austria.

Both Dewulf and Massaert, therefore, were acutely aware of the threats facing the royal family, especially in light of the Congolese problems and growing unrest among the radical-socialist parties in Belgium.

Massaert poured some coffee for his companion and settled into a chair opposite him at a small table in front of his desk. As always, Massaert's rooms were exceptionally tidy, thought Dewulf, especially when compared to his rat's nest of an office at the Justice Ministry. Massaert undoubtedly benefited from an army of assistants and cleaners to keep everything in its place. How the other half lives…

"Things could be worse," Massaert was saying. "The socialists seem to have lost some of their…animosity to the family compared to this time last year. And the press is behind him."

"For now," Dewulf replied, as he stirred some milk into his coffee.

"Yes, for now."

"And as long is he is sympathetic to their idea of extending the franchise. They won't accept anything less."

"I would suppose so," Massaert agreed. "But the Catholics will fight it, and put Albert in a difficult position."

The Catholic Party, which had governed the nation since 1884, was facing increasing competition ever since a special franchise, the 'vote plural', gave additional votes to fathers of families, beginning in 1893. This had reduced the Catholic Party's majority over the two main opposition parties, the Socialists and the Liberals, to just six votes in the Belgian Chamber of Representatives. Universal suffrage would accelerate the decline of the Catholic Party, an unbearable thought to Catholics after a generation in power. And King Albert himself was a Catholic, which put him in a difficult position among these factions.

"But I think he will manage once this education bill controversy is over," Massaert continued.

"His first big test."

"Yes, I suppose it is."

"So yes, my friend, things could be worse. But does he really insist on doing this?" Dewulf held up a small file in front of his host.

"I'm afraid so. We can't convince him otherwise. And believe me, we've tried! Of course, Leopold had planned to be there, but obviously that option no longer exists." Massaert offered a rueful smile. "So the task falls to Albert now, and he thinks that if Leopold was willing to attend, then so should he."

"You've tried to reason with him? Considering the situation here lately?"

"Of course. But our new king believes he needs to be as visible as possible and as soon as possible, especially during his first year. So there's no question that he wants to attend."

Dewulf sipped at his coffee. As usual, it was excellent; well worth the cold walk he endured to make his occasional meetings here. "That's understandable, certainly. And how is the Special Brigade responding?"

"Overworked, as usual. Even before this."

Massaert smiled at Dewulf, aware of his previous service with that unit. And of Dewulf's relief at being able to leave the gendarmerie for service in the Sûreté, thanks to a personal intervention by King Leopold himself.

"But this" – Massaert indicated the file in Dewulf's hand – "is going to require some additional help."

"Which is why I'm here."

"Exactly."

"But you know as well as I do that we lack the manpower to protect him there. At least, not very effectively. The place will be an absolute circus, impossible to patrol or monitor with any confidence."

"Yes, of course. Of course. We'll do what we can about that when the time comes. But in the meantime I had something else in mind for you."

Dewulf looked at his old friend with interest. "Such as?"

"You know how the gendarmes handle these types of tasks. It's not what they do best, wouldn't you agree? Especially in this case, considering how important it all is to us. So perhaps you could just pay…pay special attention to movements of anarchists and other, shall we say, undesirable elements throughout the capital."

"Without attracting attention."

Massaert smiled. "Ideally."

"We wouldn't want to embarrass the new king with...unfounded suspicions." Dewulf smiled back.

"Of course not."

Dewulf looked out the window at the Park Royale across the street, towards his own office in the Justice Ministry on the other side of it. The trees were bare and he had a clear view across the park.

"Fair enough," he said. "So what's he really like? Albert? I've only met him a few times, years ago."

Massaert thought for a moment to find the right words. "Earnest. Committed. Very bright. But also very...careful. He's been preparing for this job for years. He knows what's expected of him, you can be sure of that! And he knows his own mind once it's made up, but is willing to take advice until then."

Massaert didn't need to add that serving Albert was already turning out to be a wonderful change of pace after his past decade working for Leopold.

"That's very admirable, very admirable indeed, but can he hold the country together?"

Dewulf referred to the Belgian king's most important role: moderating differences between the reform-minded Liberals and the more conservative Catholics.

"Yes, I think so." Massaert paused again. "But frankly, Martin, I think he is more worried about external threats. And not to himself; to the country as a whole."

Dewulf frowned at his friend. "Such as?"

"Well, I've been meeting with him quite regularly, you know, well before Leopold died. Leopold was convinced that the Germans are going to violate our neutrality in the event of a war with France."

"Yes, I've heard the stories."

"But did you know that the Kaiser *himself* asked Leopold for permission to use our territory in such an event? And not in an implicit fashion, mind you; the Kaiser simply looked Leopold in his face and asked him."

"No, I didn't. How did Leopold respond?"

Massaert leaned forward and made sure he had Dewulf's attention. "He refused. Outright. He said that neither his ministers nor his parliament would permit such a request even if Leopold himself supported it."

In fact, Massaert knew only part of the story, thanks to the limited information Albert had chosen to share with him. In 1904 the Kaiser had actually offered to help Leopold create a new Belgium, if it would support Germany in a war against France. The new Belgium would receive portions of Artois and French Flanders around Lille, as well as the French Ardennes, if only Leopold would cooperate.

In the formidable struggle which will take place, the Kaiser had insisted, *Germany is certain of victory, but this time you will be obliged to choose. You will be with us or against us. If you are with us, I shall give you the Flemish provinces which France took from you, in defiance of all right. I will create again for you the Duchy of Burgundy. You will become sovereign of a powerful kingdom. Think of what I offer you and what you may expect.*

These words had rattled around in Leopold's mind for five years before his death, and now echoed in Albert's head as well.

"Good for him," Dewulf replied. "But…tough for us."

Dewulf already began to regret his decision to help Massaert with secretly monitoring the 'undesirables', and he hadn't even left the Royal Palace yet.

"Yes, indeed," agreed Massaert. "And for Albert, especially, if he truly has to choose one day."

Chapter 6

London. January 1910.

After their lunch, Cumming and Walsh strolled through Green Park to work out the details of Walsh's assignment. The afternoon had turned quite mild and the two men enjoyed the fresh air after the stuffiness of the RAC. They noticed a small group of young women huddled around a bench, passing a cigarette around in their white gloves. One of the women saw them looking and stuck her tongue out at them, provoking giggles from her companions.

Cumming shook his head at the sight but it brought a grin to Walsh's face.

"Before this goes further, I need you to clarify a few things," Walsh said.

"Such as?"

"You want me to recruit and run agents in Brussels, but you also mentioned counter-espionage. I don't think I can do both at the same time in the same place."

Cumming turned his head to look at Walsh. "Why not?"

"Well, to purchase or solicit secret information, I need to demonstrate credibility with potential sources and therefore act as a trusted agent of our government."

"Or as an intermediary."

"Yes, of course. An intermediary. But the best way to approach counter-espionage is to act in precisely the opposite manner, as a disgruntled or former agent of our government. I can't play those two games at the same time in the same place."

Cumming considered that for a moment. "No, I suppose not."

"Unless I have my own agents to conduct counter-espionage or other tasks, which would then put us at much greater risk of exposing one or both parts of the mission. Especially if the *Nachrichten Abteilung* is nosing around."

"What do you suggest then?"

"I need to know your priorities, and will attempt to recruit agents or solicit information based on those priorities. If Brussels is as...as complicated an intelligence marketplace as you say it is, then we can succeed only if we stay focused on a particular target. Otherwise I would spend my time chasing all kinds of phantoms and false leads, and increase the likelihood that I would be exposed as a British agent. It would also result in a waste of money. And I would prefer to act alone unless absolutely necessary."

"That makes sense." Cumming was pleased that Walsh seemed to appreciate the need for cost-effectiveness in this enterprise. And he had little money to hire additional agents for Brussels, even if he could find willing recruits to help Walsh.

"I'm glad you think so." Walsh smiled. "So then, C, what's the priority for you?"

Cumming motioned them to a bench away from other passers-by, and they sat in silence for a moment while Cumming considered the question. Was this really going to happen, finally? A secret British agent of his own on the continent, to do whatever he asked? Cumming struggled to contain his excitement. He needed to think carefully.

"My priority is any information relating to preparations for, or early warning of, an attack upon Great Britain," Cumming began. "Other matters are secondary, but would include information about new weapons systems or other capabilities, especially those that would facilitate a surprise attack. Or any evidence of a concentration of forces."

Cumming reflected for another moment. "Anything on German mobilization plans would be very valuable," he added.

"So some kind of early warning system targeted at German intentions?"

"Yes, that would be ideal." Cumming smiled broadly at the thought, and slapped his hand on his knee. "Heavens, Walsh, that would be excellent!"

Walsh nodded. "And you are more interested in naval capabilities? An invasion by sea?"

Cumming thought for a moment, then shook his head. "Not necessarily. At least, I suppose not. The Germans have improved their rail network on the Belgian border and around Alsace-Lorraine, so you should be on the lookout for movements by land or sea."

Cumming was simply guessing about the priorities of his War Office counterparts; in fact they were not entirely agreed with the Admiralty on the chief priorities of the SSB. No need to burden Walsh with that information just now.

Walsh nodded again. "Aye, that's no bother. No bother at all, I should think; it certainly widens the net we can cast over there. So, then, information about army and navy plans. Fair enough."

"Yes, for a start, at least. But bear in mind, won't you, that we get offers of this type now and again and they usually turn out to be useless. So it must be credible information. And, of course, you can keep your eyes open for anything else you think we should know, once you get a feel for the place."

"Yes, who knows what I might find?"

Walsh gave Cumming an odd look, and Cumming couldn't determine if the younger man was merely bemused or downright sceptical about all this espionage business.

"And what kind of...inducements can I offer to our sources?" Walsh continued. "Assuming I can find any who will cooperate?"

Cumming thought about his limited budgetary resources for a moment before answering. He had to be careful not to over-extend himself.

"Well, I suppose we could pay from ten or twenty pounds per item for good information along those lines," he said. "Also for information relating to new weapons systems or other unique German capabilities, if the information is very important or detailed."

Another odd look from Walsh; this one was definitely sceptical. "Up to twenty pounds? That's it?"

"I'm working within budgetary constraints. And you must be careful in...in discriminating amongst these scallywags. They will offer to sell just about anything but then fail to deliver the goods once paid. Or the information will turn out to be out of date or unverifiable."

"Well, then, that's all the more reason for me to nose around on my own to find good sources, and go after them on my own terms rather than simply respond to whatever offers happen to come in. Don't you think?"

"Yes, indeed."

"And yet I'm not supposed to have any official cover whatsoever?"

Cumming nodded. "That's not my desire, Walsh; it's being imposed on me. I'm not supposed to have any contact with the diplomatic service, including naval or military attachés who are temporarily attached to it. I'm also not supposed to recruit personal business acquaintances of mine who might be located on the continent at the moment. I've asked about that. And I can't make use of active-duty naval or army officers for these tasks. *And*, I'm not even supposed to make formal requests of police or constabulary forces in Britain or abroad, unless as a last resort. Nor can I get you a position with any newspapers or ask them to work with you. So you see, I'm operating under severe constraints here."

Walsh nodded in sympathy. "I can see why I'm here now."

"Perhaps these conditions will change, but not that the moment. However, I do have some partly-official support, which should facilitate your task."

"And what is that?"

"We can discuss that before you leave for Brussels, along with other arrangements for communicating and whatnot. If you are agreed on this…this special task, that is."

Walsh was silent for a moment; his eyes scanned the world around them for nothing in particular. Signs of life were all around them in British capital even in the dead of winter, and here they were sitting on a park bench, planning for a war with Germany. Then Walsh looked directly at Cumming, with an almost mischievous grin.

"I have to admit I'm intrigued, but only to the extent that Germany presents a real threat in the very near future," Walsh said. "I'm tired with jobs that are too…indeterminate and unending. Too speculative, if you know what I mean."

"What do you propose?"

"Suppose I agree to six months, to see how things develop over there?"

This would put Walsh's efforts beyond Cumming's first six-month report, due in April. Hopefully they would have something to show for the effort then. "Agreed," Cumming said.

"And I need some discretion to make decisions in Brussels about which sources to pursue. I can't keep potential sources waiting for too long while someone is second-guessing me in London or elsewhere."

Cumming smiled at that. "Don't worry about that. One benefit of having no official connections to the rest of the Government is that we are free to conduct business as we see fit."

40

"Easier to beg forgiveness afterwards than to seek permission beforehand, you know," Walsh said.

"Yes, so it is! So it is! I like that, Walsh! But, we still must act within our normal budgetary constraints, of course. His Majesty's Treasury is not a bottomless pit, you know."

"Of course. And what are those constraints?"

Cumming stood now and motioned Walsh along with him. "We'll discuss that before you leave. Now when can you start?"

Walsh stood up and leaned in close to Cumming. "Quite soon, I should think. I just need to take care of a few things back home."

"Excellent, my boy!" Cumming flashed his smile again, and slapped Walsh on the back. "Glad to have you with us. And this is going to be great sport, Walsh, believe me. Great sport!"

Chapter 7

Paris, France. January 1910.

As the French had suspected for years, the Germans mobilized their armies in a vast line stretching from the area between Belgium and the Rhine in the north to the area between Metz and Strasbourg in the south. In a massive offensive wave of men and machines, the German army marched westwards and attacked the Belgian fortresses at Liège and Namur and the line of French fortresses stretching from Verdun down through Toul, Épinal, and Belfort, near the Swiss border. Extensive new railway lines enabled the Germans to move heavy artillery into place to demolish and overwhelm the forts, opening the way for the infantry to seize control of enemy territory across southeast Belgium.

The French, however, had chosen to concentrate their forces for their own offensive attack towards the southern end of the German line, in an effort to recover the lost provinces of Alsace and Lorraine, rather than bolster the far left wing of their troops on the Belgian frontier. This unfortunate deployment allowed the Germans to move swiftly through Belgium, then turn southwards in a grand outflanking pincer movement aimed directly at the heart of the Third Republic: Paris.

Fortunately, however, these movements were being played out with model armies on a large wargame map of a hypothetical western front rather than with real armies across the fields of Belgium and France. This fact did little to comfort Commandant Didier Marchand, who stood over the map with a frown, staring at his imagined defeat of France. He had played out this scenario countless times and the results left him frustrated, every time. At some point he was going to have to admit the problem to his colleagues. And to his superiors.

Plan Sixteen was not going to work.

Although he was a senior member of the German section of the Deuxième Bureau de l'État-major general, or the foreign military intelligence division of the French army's general staff, Marchand was not the author of Plan Sixteen. That had been the responsibility of Generalissimo Henri de Lacroix and his colleagues on the general staff. Like all good intelligence officers, however, Marchand always attempted to focus his efforts on what he thought his superiors should know rather than simply on what they asked for. And what they *should* know, he realized again and again lately, was that Plan Sixteen, finalized less than a year ago, was still not able to counter the expected German advance through Belgium, if his assumptions were correct.

From the other side of the table in the large map room in the Hôtel de Noirmoutiers on rue de Grenelle, the HQ of the general staff, Marchand's exceptionally efficient adjutant, Lieutenant Guillaume Lefevre, gamely attempted to improve his superior's mood. Lefevre reminded Marchand of a goose, with his long, thin neck, pointed nose, and beady eyes, so if anyone could put a smile on Marchand's face today, it would be Lefevre.

"Did you hear the Army is going to receive its first warplanes next month?" Lefevre said, his voice tense with excitement. "Isn't that magnificent, commandant? Do you know anything about that?"

"Yes, lieutenant. I've heard all about it. And I also know that the Cavalry has refused to volunteer any of its men for flight training." Marchand spared a glance at his companion across the table. "So who will fly the magnificent planes, Lefevre? Hmmm? The Foreign Legion, perhaps? Or will *you* volunteer?"

Lefevre shifted his feet; he did not have an answer for that.

Marchand kept his focus on the map, leaning over it, almost on top of it, with his hands spread out on the surface. Marchand and his precious maps. Maps in his office, in his home, in his officer's valise, and when he'd had enough of those, he would visit his favourite maps of all: the Plans-Reliefs museum at the Hôtel des Invalides, where he could study large three-dimensional scale models of dozens of fortified positions in France and beyond, from Mont Saint-Michel to Brest to Saint-Martin-de-Ré to Lagarde and on and on.

"Is your building still under water?" Marchand said, in his own odd attempt to change the subject from his perennial concern.

Lefevre nodded. The recent flood, soon to be known as the Great Paris Flood of 1910.

"Some of it," he said. "Most of the basement is still flooded, but no one lives down there. You wouldn't believe the stench, coming up through the rest of the building. So I moved in with my sister two days ago."

Marchand smiled. "At least you didn't have to take a boat to work today."

"*C'est vrai*, commandant. It could always be worse." Lefevre handed a cup of coffee to Marchand, who took it without a word, his blue eyes still glued to the map.

As Marchand sipped his café au lait, Lefevre walked to the other side of the table and took a close look at the map spread out upon it.

"Perhaps the Germans really will concentrate only on the southern tip of Belgium, near the Stenay Gap," Lefevre said, pointing to the gap just east of the river Meuse near Verdun. "They won't want to violate Dutch neutrality as well as that of Belgium, so it doesn't make sense to squeeze so many forces through that gap."

"Unless they do intend to outflank us from the north, which is not so protected compared to the line south of Verdun," Marchand replied. "In which case they could attempt to squeeze an extra army or two through the Ardennes, spread out across all of Belgium, even in the north, and then overwhelm us from above."

As he spoke, Marchand reached over the map and swept his right arm in an arc with his elbow pivoted at Verdun; his hand moved from Antwerp down towards Ypres and Lille, further into northern France, and then closed into a fist directly on top of Paris.

Thanks to secret documents purchased in 1904 from a German general staff officer, Marchand and his colleagues had known, or at least strongly suspected, that Germany's mobilization plans explicitly called for violating Belgian neutrality, and possibly that of the Netherlands as well, in the event of a war with France. The only question then, really, was how to meet the threat on the Belgian frontier. Or so Marchand believed.

Lefevre again consulted the document in his hands and looked at the map. "The plan is assuming fifty-nine divisions for the German offensive on its western front…and Plan Sixteen calls for a response of exactly the same size."

"Yes, of course, but look at the details, lieutenant, the *details*. The estimate includes a combination of German active and reserve classes, but also assumes that the reserves will be used only for siege or garrison duties, not for offensive field operations. If the Germans fully incorporate their reserves into the offensive, then our response of fifty-nine divisions will not be able to counter it."

"Because our plans will not make the same use of reserves as the Germans will."

"*Exactement*. And it will be major stretch for us to make up fifty-nine divisions, even with reserve forces. Our reserves are not as well-trained as theirs, either. Or as young."

Besides, Marchand might have added, the French general staff was still uneasy – if not completely opposed to – the idea of relying so much on the use of reserves rather than professional soldiers. And de Lacroix seemed to be assuming that the Germans thought as little of their reserves as the French general staff thought of their own. Which might not be the case.

Marchand walked to Lefevre's side of the table and stood next to him. Up close now, Lefevre could see his boss's teeth clenching, involuntarily, they way they always did when Marchand became agitated. Marchand's skin was pale as well these days; the 'map room complexion,' they called it.

"But it could be worse than that. Much worse," Marchand continued. "Even if we used our divisions in the same way the Germans plan to, that is not enough for victory, only a stalemate. And if the Germans use *more* than fifty-nine divisions, especially on their right wing through Belgium, then..." Marchand raised an eyebrow and looked up at Lefevre.

"Then we are defeated."

Marchand nodded in agreement. A lock of his hair fell onto his forehead and he brushed it away in irritation. "And remember the details we acquired from the 1906 German war game? There's your evidence, lieutenant. The Germans put thirty divisions through Belgium alone, between Namur and Verdun. *Thirty divisions*, and not including their reserve forces!" He shook his head in disapproval and grew more agitated. "Yet *we* are still assuming only sixteen to twenty German divisions in that sector!"

Lefevre would not be defeated so easily. "And you don't think the Belgian forces are enough to hold them off? When combined with ours? And what about the British?"

Marchand offered a wry smile and put his hand on Lefevre's shoulder. "Have you ever been to London, lieutenant? No? Then let me tell you something. If you step on an Englishman's toes, he will apologize to you! So they're not ready to fight, believe me. I tried working with them on that a few years ago, and it didn't end well. And the Belgians have no army to speak of. They are not even worth considering in our plans, make no mistake about that. No, Lefevre, you are assuming too much, and so is our blind general staff. You are assuming that the poor chicken-eaters up north will fight back, and that the polite roast-beefs across the channel will send a large enough expeditionary force in time to make a difference. Do you really want to entrust the security of France to those assumptions, lieutenant?"

Marchand looked at the map again. "At best, we could count on five or six Belgian divisions and maybe four British divisions. At best! But even those numbers, if we have them, would be delayed until after the fighting starts, and would be too little to counteract a German force greater than sixty divisions on the western front. So if the Germans can make it past this line" – he pointed to the gap between the Somme and Aisne rivers on the map, guarded by the fortresses of La Fère and Laon – "before the British arrive and the Belgians can re-group, then we'll be lost."

"But are you really so sure they will attack through Belgium? General Brugère thinks…"

"General Brugère is too concerned with his battle to the south. And our reserve forces will be no match for a major German offensive through most of Belgium."

General Henri-Joseph Brugère was de Lacroix's predecessor as Generalissimo of the French forces, and the man responsible for Plan Fifteen, which envisioned the main battle in Lorraine with the majority of the French forces. This view continued to inspire Plan Sixteen, to Marchand's growing frustration.

"It would be pointless for the Germans to focus on our eastern fortresses and hope to defeat us there before the Russians can mobilize," Marchand continued. "They know those fortresses have been modernized enough to withstand melinite explosive charges. The northern forts have not been modernized and will be more vulnerable. And the Germans have improved their rail lines near the Belgian border over the past decade, with new disembarkation platforms. And *those* platforms are far too extensive for civilian needs in that sector."

Marchand leaned across the table again. "No, lieutenant. In Germany's eyes we are the *Erbfeind*, the hereditary enemy, of all Germans. Their arch-enemy. Did you know that? So these facts do not lie. The Germans will attack, and they must go through Belgium. They *must*."

"So what do you suggest? Are you going to confront de Lacroix about his plan? And so soon after it's been released?" Lefevre smiled, but only just.

Marchand looked up from the table at him. They both knew the answer to *that* question.

Lefevre pressed on. "Perhaps we'll know more after the Picardy manuevers later this year."

"Perhaps, perhaps. *Alors*. We'll just see what we can do about this, my dear Lefevre. Yes. We'll see what we can do."

Chapter 8

Leipzig. January 1910.

Maria Hesse felt the eyes of the waiter on her low neckline as he slowly cleared the dishes away from in front of her. Too slowly, Maria realized with some irritation. She had grown increasingly uncomfortable with so much attention from men these past few years, but she supposed it was partly her fault. Nineteen years old, and encased in a fine Parisian ensemble that did not require a corset but still hugged her slim figure, she and handsome Hans Bruner had put on something of a show for the staff of the Café Hennersdorf. Now she was paying the price for it; over the past hour nearly every waiter in the place had found one reason or another to linger near their table.

"I need to go now, Hans. Please," she pleaded, but not very convincingly. She snubbed out her cigarette and fished in her purse for some chewing gum; her father would be sure to smell her breath when she returned home.

Hans had his arm around her waist again before she could get up. "But what about the concert, Maria? You haven't said yes or no. Next week?" The Thursday-evening concerts at the Gewundhaus, the Hall of the Foreign Cloth Merchants, were a major attraction in Leipzig throughout the winter.

Maria allowed him to pull her close once again. Just one last time. "I'll have to see, Hans. I don't know if I can get away that night. You know my father."

"Will that be all, *Fräulein*?" Another waiter this time, one who didn't ogle so much. Or so she thought.

"Yes, please. We'll take the bill now." Maria opened her purse again and began to poke around the lost world inside. The waiter put the bill before them on a silver tray and waited, hands clasped behind his back.

"I can get this." Hans made a move to retrieve his wallet.

Maria smiled at him and spoke too soon. "With what, my darling?"

Hans backed away from her, just slightly. "Now, that's not fair. I do have some money, you know."

"Yes, of course. I know you do. But you need it to live on for now. Until you find something."

Hans was making the rounds of the many publishing firms in Leipzig, hoping to find work as an editor, or proofreader, or assistant editor, or assistant proofreader, or *something*. Slow going, despite the presence of over one thousand publishers, printers, and booksellers in the city. Perhaps he was just unlucky lately. Poor Hans, and his sad little dreams.

Maria slid closer to him and put her lips near his ear. "So let me take care of this," she whispered. "It's my treat for you."

She pulled his warm cheek close with a gloved hand and gave him another peck on it. This helped to erase Hans's frown.

"If you insist," he surrendered, again. "But I shall pay for the concert tickets."

"Of course, darling. *If* I can get away."

Maria hoped she wasn't promising too much. Her father was becoming more agitated, and watchful, ever since Ernie had disappeared.

She paid the bill and stood up abruptly, before Hans could get another grip on her. A quick look in the mirror confirmed that her jet-black hair was out of place thanks to their cuddling, and she attempted to smooth it as best she could before putting on her plain woollen hat. It did not exactly measure up to the rest of her outfit but it would help insulate her against the cold outside.

Hans stood up and they kissed again, this time on the mouth.

"Good-bye, my darling." He held her fur-lined coat open so that she could snuggle into it. Such a gentleman. Such kindness. Too bad he was so poor.

Maria buttoned her coat and smiled at Hans while he waited. Another glove on his cheek, then a gentle squeeze of his chin. "Until next time," she said, before moving off.

"Wait, don't forget your bag!" He held out the small brown sack from Renninger's to her; this was supposed to be a shopping excursion, after all.

Maria reached back across the table and accepted the bag with another smile, then swept across the crowded café towards the door, turning just once to wave back at him. He blew a kiss to her. She smiled back at him, and returned the kiss.

Through the glass door and into the cold again, for the long tram ride home.

She breezed into the street, with a heart full of warmth, and Retzlaff was there.

He smiled at her, and offered a slight bow. "Maria, isn't it? Maria Hesse?"

"Yes, that's right." Maria struggled to retain her composure. Where did he come from? How did he know she was out today? "And you are?"

"Retzlaff. Klaus Retzlaff. We met at your home, just a few weeks ago."

"Yes, of course. I remember." Maria tried to avoid looking into his eyes, even though she knew this would raise his suspicions. Those damn suspicious eyes of his, black and cold, like a rat's eyes.

"I'm looking into the disappearance of your brother," Retzlaff said.

She began walking down the street. "Yes, of course."

"Isn't your…companion coming?" Retzlaff motioned back towards the Hennersdorf.

His smile was odd, Maria thought. He remained in place, and she had to hold back as well.

"No, no, he's…just a friend. Someone I knew in school." She could barely get the words out.

"Of course. A friend of the family."

He stood there, frozen like a statue, a statue with a long double-breasted cashmere overcoat, an umbrella, and a well-manicured Van Dyke beard, flecked with grey. But his eyes were alive with interest. Interest in her.

"How nice that you can stay in touch," he added.

"Yes…yes, I suppose so. *Herr* Retzlaff, I don't mean to be rude, but I need to catch a tram…" Maria began sidling away from him.

He caught her arm, but gently. "*Fräulein* Hesse, please. If you will permit me. I need to speak to you. I have some information about your brother. It's very important, you understand. And I need your help."

She hesitated, then her resolve broke at the thought of Ernie. Lost Ernie, her damn fool of a brother. Her family did not need another crisis, and she recalled her mother's distress when she discovered the note left on his desk. And the terrible fight her parents had had afterwards, thinking that she was out of earshot. Or perhaps they didn't care if she heard.

"Certainly, *Herr* Retzlaff." She looked back towards the Hennersdorf. "Can we...I..."

"I'll walk you to the station."

Retzlaff crooked his arm for her, and Maria was surprised to find herself taking it. They moved off down the Gewandgäßchen, arm in arm. If only Hans can stay at the café long enough for them to get away...

Retzlaff continued, keeping a grip on her forearm with his free hand. "You know, your brother is very lucky to have a sister. Very lucky indeed."

"Why do you say that?"

"To look out for each other. Your parents will not be around forever, you know. And having a sister can help a young man appreciate the...womanly point of view about certain things. Especially as he gets older."

A look crossed Maria's face. It might have been followed by a smile, in other circumstances. But not today.

"I'm not so sure about that," she said. "Ernie doesn't pay much attention to me."

"Yes, he does. I'm sure he does. You just might not be aware of it. I have two sisters myself, you know. And a brother. We all fought like cats and dogs, but we also stood together when times were difficult."

"Is that so?" They turned down Universitätsstraße now, left towards the Hauptbahnhof.

"Absolutely. We took care of each other. Still do, in fact. We kept all kinds of secrets for each other."

"*Herr* Retzlaff..."

"I spoke to Ernie's colleagues at school, *Fräulein*. Did you know that? Yes, we had a most interesting conversation. And you know something? They seem to think he has left the country. For Switzerland."

"Switzerland?"

He shrugged. "This is what I hear." Silence from her, so he continued. "Do you know what I think?"

"No."

He leaned close to her before speaking. Very close. "I think you might know where he is."

Maria frowned and thought about breaking away from him, but knew she couldn't get away if he didn't permit it. "Me, *Herr* Retzlaff? But why would I...?"

Retzlaff stopped and turned towards her. He took her hands in his own; she could feel the strength in them. He looked down into her eyes and shook his head just slightly. It was no use resisting.

"Maria, please stop pretending. I am a professional. I know what I am doing. Now, Ernie's friends also mentioned his...political views. Dangerous views, you understand. Views that could get him into trouble if he is not careful."

He moved her away from the centre of the street towards the wall before continuing.

"Now, what do we know about this Tobias, hmm? Is he capable of looking after Ernie?"

"I don't know...*Herr* Retzlaff. I can't tell you anything. And I promised my brother..."

"Yes, you did. I understand. But you also have an obligation to look out for him, don't you? He is your brother, your blood. Tobias is *not*. If Tobias has misled, has *deceived* him into something political, some kind of scheme, then you must tell me about it."

Maria glanced up and down the street, hoping Hans would not appear. "I don't know of any scheme..."

"Maria, he could be in danger now even as we speak. Do you realize that? And do you know what your parents must be going through?"

This thought nearly crushed her; Heinrich and Elizabeth Hesse had lost their first child, a son, to diphtheria at age two in 1887 at the family's original home in Frankfurt. Her mother, it seemed to her, had never recovered from the loss. Her father simply threw himself deeper into work even after a second son, Ernie, arrived a year later, followed by Maria two years after that. Ernie had been named after the eldest son of Louis IV, Grand Duke of Hesse. The family – actually, Elizabeth - liked to think there was a blood connection to the royal Hesse family but none could be proved.

Heinrich, however, had opposed the name Ernst, especially after his namesake's alleged homosexuality became more widely known, but gave in to Elizabeth in consolation to the loss of her first-born son. Then, and despite Heinrich's success with the House of Rothschild, in 1901 the Frankfurt office of the firm closed abruptly, throwing him out of a job. Heinrich was fortunate to land an equally lucrative job with the new Leipzig office of Deutsche Bank later that year, but little Maria and Ernie were forced to abandon their friendships in Frankfurt for a new life in Leipzig.

Now, to think of gentle Ernie in trouble, or in prison, or worse...and after the death of Heinrich junior...it was too much for Maria to bear. Ernie's troubles could tear her family apart, if she let them.

"He never wanted to study chemistry, you know," Maria said, in a small voice.

"But your father pushed him into it."

She nodded. "He insisted. Most forcefully. He says chemistry is the future of this country. Steel, engines, and chemistry."

They were nearly at the Hauptbahnhof, and Maria needed to finish this conversation. Her parents would be waiting. Her father.

"Maria, please," Retzlaff said. "I'm not a policeman; my job is to help Ernie. I'm here to look out for him, just like you must. So I want you to ask yourself a question. A very simple but also very important question, do you understand? Just one question. And you must think carefully, very carefully, before you answer the question I'm about to ask. Can you do that for me, please?"

Maria nodded, almost against her will. But her power to resist this man was slowly ebbing away. And she knew that he knew it.

Retzlaff took her two hands into his own, and stared directly into her eyes, again, before he spoke. "Maria, how would you answer this question, as truthfully as you can: do you trust Tobias Stern with your brother's life?"

Maria now shook her head, as they both knew she would.

Retzlaff shook his head as well. "Of course you don't. Nor should you, based on what I know. Good for you. And for your missing brother. So now you understand me, don't you? So you can tell me, please Maria, where have they gone?"

"*Herr* Retzlaff, you must promise not to tell anyone I told you this. Not Ernie, and not my parents. Please."

Retzlaff nodded, very slowly. "Yes, of course, of course. Where is he?"

She sighed the words. "He said he was going to Bern. But I don't know why, honestly I don't. I promise."

"*Where* in Bern, Maria?"

"I don't know. He said Tobias knew some people at the university there. I imagine they are involved in…socialist politics. That's all Tobias cares about. But I don't have an address. I swear it."

"Is Ernst going to contact you?"

"Possibly."

At the train station now, busy with travellers on this crisp winter's day, rushing with their packages and briefcases. Retzlaff waited as she purchased a tram ticket at the kiosk.

"If he contacts you, would you please contact me?" he said.

He held out a business card to her; she slipped it into her bag.

"Yes, of course. But…"

"Yes, Maria?"

"*Herr* Retzlaff, you won't mention my…companion to my parents, will you?"

He smiled at her again, that odd, knowing smile that conveyed sympathy but somehow lacked warmth.

"Of course not. It's our little secret."

Chapter 9

Aldershot Military Town, England. February 1910.

"You're taking the ferry to Ostend, I presume?" Grierson said, as he and Walsh sat in leather armchairs in the general's comfortable office at the HQ of the British First Army Division at Aldershot Command.

Walsh nodded and reached for the cup of tea in front of him. "Tomorrow morning, early. So I need to be back in London tonight."

Grierson smiled at the young man; he was not used to seeing him in a business suit. A dapper young gent, off to drum up some business with those daft Continentals.

"Three hours across the channel," Grierson said, still smiling. "Will your poor stomach handle that?"

Walsh shrugged, and sipped at his tea. "My poor stomach has no choice in the matter. Nor do I, I suppose. I'll sit outside, on the rear deck. That should help."

Grierson shook his head. "Of course you have a choice, lad. You're a free man now. You could've declined Cumming's offer."

"I know," Walsh said. "In fact, I was close to saying no when I first met Cumming. He's an odd sort, don't you think, with that monocle and his way of shifting so quickly between a frown and a smile. You should've seen the look on his face when I told him about my time in the industrial school!"

Grierson smiled and nodded.

"But he does seem very enthusiastic about this work," Walsh continued. "And I have to say, I am intrigued about the idea of working on my own in Belgium. I may never get the chance to do something like this again. And the factory will always be there."

"That's encouraging, Nicholas, but has Cumming sorted out a story for you over there? An official story?" Grierson paused, then lowered his voice slightly. "You know, I've asked around about him, discreetly, and I suppose you must know he has little experience in intelligence. Almost no experience at all, in fact. He's been working on our boom defences for a number of years, but no intelligence work."

Walsh put down his teacup, leaned forward, and spoke quietly. "We met the day before yesterday, again. About all the details for this assignment. He's managed to arrange a kind of...informal position for me with our Board of Trade. A kind of 'travelling representative' for the Board in Europe, is how he put it. So I can look into markets for heavy manufacturing, vehicles and armaments, and so on. Also commodities and foodstuffs. Whatever turns up over there."

Grierson frowned in confusion. "The Board of Trade agreed to *that*?"

"That's what Cumming said. He agreed to it in person at the Board, with the new chief there. Churchill."

"Churchill is involved with this plan?"

"As far as I know. Cumming said he is very keen to cooperate with us."

"Well, just watch yourself, lad. You know how reckless he can be."

Walsh nodded in agreement.

Of course, every British soldier involved in the Boer War had known about Churchill, after he had escaped from the Boers and published a book about his 'triumph'. Admirable indeed, but both Grierson and Walsh had their doubts about the man. Spying as a civilian reporter in what quickly had become a guerrilla war zone? Nothing but a good way to get executed.

"And how will you communicate? Has Cumming given any thought to that?"

"That's been arranged as well, apparently. We'll test the system when I get settled there."

This 'system' devised by Cumming involved a cover firm arranged in London for transferring messages: Rasen Falcon & Co, shippers and exporters, in the London post office directory. Cumming had also set up two telegraphic addresses: 'Sunbonnet London' for normal messages, and 'Autumn London' for emergencies, which would also be copied to the Admiralty.

"See that you make sure it works, and that it's secure," Grierson said, pointing his finger at Walsh. "As soon as you get to Brussels, mind you. And I suppose you know about the sensitivities in the FO about all this spy business?"

"Cumming mentioned that. But at least everyone seems agreed on the need to concentrate on Germany, as you said."

Grierson frowned again. "Well, up to a point, that is."

"How do you mean?"

"You've been out of the game for a few years, lad. So listen, before you leave I want you to be aware of some things. The main point is for you to know that there is still some...*some* disagreement about all this German invasion talk. In the FO, that is."

Walsh put down his teacup on the table with a clang. "Bloody hell, general! I thought..."

"Now hold on a minute, young man, this is precisely why we need someone like you over there to sort things out for us. I was only going to mention that the FO is still debating this problem, internally. Do you know about the Crowe memorandum?"

Walsh shook his head.

"It came out in 1907, soon after you and I...abandoned the Paris operation."

Walsh smiled at the word 'abandoned'. That was one way of putting it.

"Nicholas, forget about Paris, will you?" Grierson continued. "Times have changed since then. In fact, I was with the French army on manoeuvres just last summer. So things *are* moving forward on that front. Slowly but surely."

"Fair enough. And so who is Crowe?"

"And so, Crowe is Eyre Crowe, head of the Western section of the FO. He's been following the arms race, you understand. He's a demon for facts about Germany. Has them all at his fingertips, in reams of files in his office. His mother's German, in fact, and so is his wife. He lived there until he was seventeen."

"So the man knows Germany. I understand."

"Absolutely. Anyhow, he wrote a letter to the foreign secretary, stating quite conclusively that the Germans must build a navy, a powerful navy, to protect their growing interests around the world. And that this navy will eventually challenge our own global interests. It is inevitable."

"So then Germany is a threat, isn't it? The main threat. Which is why I'm going to Brussels, correct?"

"Not so fast. You see, Crowe's memorandum inspired *another* FO man, Sanderson, to write his own assessment of the situation. Which he gave to Secretary Grey a month after Crowe sent his. Just before Sanderson retired, in point of fact."

"All right then, I can guess: Sanderson disagreed with Crowe."

Grierson nodded. "Absolutely. He said Germany will always be a challenge, and is a tough bargainer when she has to be, but is just 'oversensitive'. He thought it would be mistake to adopt a general policy of antagonism against Germany."

"So where does that leave me?"

"Well, Sanderson is out and Crowe is still with the FO, and Grey is tending to lean toward's Crowe's views. And we have our attaché in Berlin, Colonel Trench, who also tends to support Crowe's thinking. He's been there nearly four years now, and probably knows Germany as well as Crowe does. Or even better, possibly; he went to Geneva University and spent time with German forces as a military observer, in Southwest Africa, before going to Berlin. They even gave him a campaign medal for it, a *German* one!"

A flash of recognition crossed Walsh's face. "Is he the same Trench who wrote *Manoeuvre Orders*?"

"Yes, he did." Grierson smiled. "Good lad. And he's met the Kaiser personally, and gets along with him much better than our previous man there. Gleichen, Colonel Gleichen, it was. So Trench's views are important around here, but we can still use all the confirmation we can get. Which is precisely why the SSB has been set up. But just bear in mind that we, Britain that is, we are still discussing the best policy towards Germany. The best general policy, mind you, military, economic, whatnot. So what you turn up over *there* could be very important to us over *here*."

Walsh nodded and put down his teacup. "Fair enough. Thanks for the warning."

Grierson stood up. "It's not a warning, lad, just…just part of the picture you'll be filling in for us."

Walsh stood as well. "Well, thanks for looking into all this for me."

Grierson nodded. "It's the least I could do, considering that it's my fault you've been drawn into this. But not drawn in completely against your will, I hope?"

"No, I have a stronger will than that."

"I know you do. You certainly do. And I know you need to get going," Grierson said, moving back towards the bookshelves behind his desk. "Just one other thing."

"What's that, general?" Walsh walked over to stand near his old friend.

"Just a little gift for you." Grierson took two leather-bound volumes down from his shelves and handed them to Walsh.

Walsh looked at the title of the set: *Stonewall Jackson and the American Civil War*, by Colonel G.F.R. Henderson.

"I hope you don't have it already," Grierson said. "An old acquaintance of mine wrote the foreward to it."

Walsh accepted the volumes with a smile. "No, I don't. Thank you very much, general. This looks very interesting."

Walsh put the volumes in his bag and the men walked to the door of Grierson's office.

"I'm almost jealous of you. I still remember my time in Berlin with great fondness. Some of the things we used to do there!"

Indeed, Grierson's service as military attaché in Berlin, from 1896-1900, was a decisive experience in his life, as Walsh knew. Even now, Grierson took great pleasure in poring over his German military publications like the *Militärwochenblatt*, which specifically mentioned putting sabotage agents in place in an enemy's territory before invading.

"Goodbye, sir, and thanks again for your help."

"Good luck to you, lad. And remember, even if you find nothing useful in Cumming's spy market, you can still be of service to us. Walk the terrain. And study the maps. They might tell you more than any spy could!"

Walsh smiled at those words. Someone, years ago, had once told him that you could show a military button to Grierson from any battlefield in Europe and he would be able not only to reconstruct the button-owner's uniform but also describe the exact role his unit had played in the battle. Walsh could only hope to become as adept at reading the terrain as the old general.

"Yes, sir." They shook hands. "I'll keep that in mind."

Grierson lowered his voice as he opened his door. Walsh walked through it to the adjoining office outside, pausing for a final moment.

"At least spying is not illegal in Belgium, in case you do come up with something over there." Grierson patted Walsh on the back as he left the office.

"And it's not a war zone," Walsh added.

Chapter 10

Brussels. February 1910.

Inspector Dewulf had a clear schedule for once on a Thursday afternoon, so he took the No. 1 tram down stately Avenue Louise. It passed the grand private homes on that busy thoroughfare, and the small aquarium at No. 525, before arriving at the Bois de la Cambre. From there it was a short walk along the new Boulevard du Bois de la Cambre to the busy construction site. Dewulf could hardly miss finding it; the works were enormous. In fact, they were growing much larger and more complicated than he had ever expected, and he found himself regretting not coming out here more often since construction had begun at the tail end of 1907.

The Bois de la Cambre, the most popular park in Brussels, was over a mile long and normally busy with pedestrians, cyclists, carriages, and vendors throughout the spring and summer. Now, in late winter, it would have been dead quiet but for the thousands of workers involved in the creation of new gardens, pavilions, exhibition halls, pathways, roadways, tramways, information signs, direction signs, and countless other projects. Dewulf wandered among the workers in silent admiration, moving closer to his main target, the central Grand Palais, which was nearly complete.

The Exposition Universelle de Bruxelles of 1910 was to be held on this site from Saturday, 23 April, to Tuesday, 1 November. King Albert had volunteered to launch the festivities himself with a speech on the opening day. This was the first exposition to be held in Belgium since the Liège Exposition of 1905, and the first in Brussels since 1897. The small country had spent nearly three million francs on the effort so far, and everyone involved was hoping to exceed the expectations of visitors and exhibitors alike. This would require considerable effort, as the organizers were hoping that over ten million visitors would attend. Ten million visitors, in a country with less than eight million citizens!

Dewulf had acquired a general plan of the exhibition from the organizers, as well as a summary of the major exhibitors expected to contribute. Spread over two hundred acres, the event was organized into twenty-two divisions and over one hundred sub-divisions, from education to artworks, from agriculture to food, from mining to textiles, from chemistry to hygiene, and from commerce to sports.

The main theme, however, was industry and engineering, and the Exposition included exhibits devoted to mechanical engineering, electricity, and transport, including some exciting new examples of modern technology in the aeronautics class. Military technologies were represented as well, for the benefit of both armies and navies; in this group visitors could marvel at ordnance and artillery equipment, hydraulics, torpedos, hydrography, cartography, and related martial equipment for the modern warrior.

So far over twenty-seven thousand different exhibitions were scheduled to appear across the venue, representing twenty-five different countries, plus the host country. As the host, Belgium was proud to serve as one of the largest participants, with nearly six thousand exhibitors. Even so, France still beat her with over ten thousand exhibitors, while America had disappointed the organisers by sending a paltry one hundred and twenty-five exhibitors, all from the private sector.

At the Grand Palais, a massive neo-classical structure at the heart the complex that housed the central gallery of the Exposition, Dewulf surveyed the large stage where Albert would deliver his opening address. The novice king did not want an oppressive security detail to overshadow the occasion, so Dewulf and his colleagues needed to be as unobtrusive as possible. They planned to locate spotters around the arena to monitor the crowd and, using a system of hand signals, they could swiftly deploy officers to any section of the audience as the entire space had been organized into a grid system.

There had been no specific threat to Albert since he took the throne, yet Dewulf and his colleagues were taking no chances. Various heads of state, past and present, were scheduled to visit the Exposition, and an assassination attempt, successful or not, would severely damage Belgium's reputation as the country worked to improve its position on the world stage after the last unfortunate years of Leopold II's reign. Dewulf himself was especially looking forward to a visit by former US President Teddy Roosevelt; King Edward of Great Britain and Kaiser Wilhelm of Imperial Germany, among other dignitaries, also were expected to attend at some point.

Fortunately, Albert's series of official visits to Berlin, Paris, Vienna, Luxembourg, and the Hague was continuing with no major problems, and the calls by some Socialists for another series of disruptive general strikes, like those of 1886, 1887, 1891, and 1893, went unheeded so far. Albert also had been taking special care to moderate differences between the Flemish-speakers in the north and the French-speaking Walloon communities in the south; members of these communities could be found in both the Catholic and the Socialist parties so the effects of their linguistic disputes were somewhat moderated in light of larger political concerns.

As Dewulf reflected on these complications, while wandering among the exhibits under construction, he also made a decision to request an increase in surveillance among the hotels and guesthouses of Brussels. The police in the capital might complain at first, yet Dewulf hoped that by confining his request to the Brussels region alone he would avoid further complications with the rural police. Both forces, city and rural, were used to visiting hotels to collect names of guests and pass them on to the Sûreté, yet they were usually instructed to focus primarily on French visitors.

Now, Dewulf thought, it might be a good idea to start collecting the names of other foreign visitors as well, at least temporarily. These names could be matched against lists of anarchists, revolutionaries, and other potential threats to the Belgian state; such lists were regularly circulated among the major capitals of Europe. As usual, manpower would be a continuing headache throughout the Exposition, but Dewulf was not quite ready to request assistance from resources beyond his direct control, particularly the more militaristic gendarmerie force headquartered in the capital. Those thugs would be far more trouble than they were worth.

Chapter 11

Walsh arrived in Brussels well after dark on a February evening. The Belgian capital was miserably cold and wet, or 'dreich,' as the Scots would put it. He took a cab from the Gare du Nord station and promptly checked into the Hôtel Cecil nearby, where he had already reserved a week's accommodation. His channel crossing, on the SS *Queen*, had been much smoother than he had anticipated, and he was able to distract himself with volume one of the Henderson book Grierson gave him. Reading about Jackson's early campaigns, at Chapultepec, Contreras, Mexico City, and Veracruz, helped to motivate Walsh about the potential importance of his mission in Brussels, especially in terms of how important it can be to permit military leaders in the field to use intelligence, and make decisions, with far more discretion than their commanders back at headquarters might otherwise prefer.

Walsh also spent much of the time thinking about his previous crossing in this direction, on the way to Germany, nearly four years ago now. He remembered his long time with Herr Kaspar Trommler and his family, a trip arranged so that he could learn something about German mechanical engineering. He also learned more than he cared to admit about the German way of life. In fact, the first word he learned on arrival was 'Verboten'; it was plastered everywhere but did in fact help Walsh navigate his three years in the most regimented society he had ever encountered. Armed policeman were all over the place and nearly every public square seemed to honor some obscure general or soldier. The Germans had also banned behaviours that Walsh didn't even recognize as a crime; in Stuttgart he even faced a policeman once for appearing to fall asleep in a restaurant. Fortunately the policeman was more forgiving of Walsh, as an Ausländer, than the restaurant owner who reported him, and he was given only a polite warning. Despite this minor embarrassment, Walsh had to admit that the streets were safer and more orderly than those of Glasgow or Edinburgh. Cleaner, too, and they didn't smell so damned noxious.

Two weeks after his arrival in Brussels, Walsh was ready to begin his mission. His first priority, accommodation, had been handled most effectively after a visit to the British Chamber of Commerce on rue de la Bourse on his third day in the city. The helpful staff there had provided him with a list of rental agencies that catered to expatriates, particularly those from Britain. Hotels were too expensive given Walsh's budgetary situation, and the staff of most hotels were known to share, if not sell, information about new guests to anyone who asked. Hotels frequented by business travellers were especially prone to this problem, and Walsh could do without that kind of attention.

After a week of searching he had secured a small flat on rue Souveraine, in the Brussels commune, or district, of Ixelles. This was a largely French-speaking commune, which suited Walsh's own language abilities; he had been blissfully unaware of the linguistic complexities between the speakers of French and Flemish who shared the nation's capital, until the owner of the rental agency set him straight on this issue. Walsh's two-room flat was sparse and the drains stank after a rain, which meant they stank nearly all the time, but it benefitted from a balcony almost as large as the flat's interior. From here Walsh enjoyed a view of the imposing bulk of the Palais du Justice and, beyond it, the Gothic spire of the Hotel de Ville on the Grand Place.

Walsh and Cumming had made arrangements for his financial needs through the Brussels office of Thomas Cook & Sons, on rue de la Madeleine near the Grand Place. As Grierson had suggested, he also visited his local post and telegraph office on Chaussée d'Ixelles to send a test telegram to Cumming in London, using the 'routine business' address had he been given: Sunbonnet/London. Cumming's reply indicated that all was well and that he would be visiting Brussels very soon.

In the meantime, Walsh enjoyed exploring his environs and laying the groundwork for his time in Brussels. Ixelles was a pleasant enough neighbourhood, neither too poor nor too rich, and was well-located without being as expensive as accommodation at the very core of the city. He could reach central Brussels with an easy walk downhill, and was well-placed to reach the Gare du Luxembourg and the embassies clustered around the Royal Palace. He also had quick access to the tram lines on Avenue Louise, which could take him throughout the city centre or well outside of it, depending on which direction he chose.

Ixelles also boasted numerous shops, small restaurants, cafés, and brasseries, all of which encouraged Walsh to spend as little time in his flat as possible. Like his experience with German food, Belgian cuisine was a revelation after his years of neeps and tatties on his uncle's farm, and he had to force himself to avoid wasting his monthly stipend from Cumming on food and drink in various establishments. The salary Cumming paid was not exactly generous, and Walsh did not want to make a habit of dipping into his personal funds from the inheritance left by his uncle. He was already regretting his impulse purchase of the Norton last year, and he hoped his three male cousins back on the farm would not abuse the vehicle too much while he was away.

Still, he had to eat and drink, didn't he? And he much preferred being out in the city than sitting alone in his cramped and smelly flat. So Walsh explored his neighbourhood as much as possible, and was very happy to find the welcoming Café Regina nearby, on Avenue de Marnix near the Porte de Namur, with its excellent plats du jour and coffee. He was somewhat put off, however, by the occasional appearance of smoked horse meat, or pièreju, on the menu; his early years on his father's horse farm had given him too much respect for those hard-working animals to consider them as a mere food source. Walsh did enjoy sampling the Nürnberger sausages and spaetzle at the Old German Wine Room on Avenue de la Toison d'Or, also a short walk from his flat. The Old Tom Tavern on Chaussée d'Ixelles also became a favourite drinking spot, and he was happy to spend several hours each evening there with a steaming hot cup of coffee or tea, working his way through his newspapers.

As Cumming had mentioned, spying did indeed seem to be a major industry in Brussels, and he found small advertisements on a regular basis in nearly every major newspaper published in the Belgian capital: *Le Temps, Le Courrier de Bruxelles, Le Journal de Bruxelles,* and *La Réforme.* Even the weekly newspaper associated with Belgian interests in the Congo, *Le Mouvement Géographique,* had the occasional petite annonce offering services, or knowledge, relating to military affairs.

Most of these items were placed by those with a military background, or so they said. Information about weapons was the most common item on offer, followed by information about fortifications, new harbours, and railway lines. And, occasionally, the offer of mobilization plans or details of the order of battle for one country or another. Walsh knew perfectly well that many of these offers were completely bogus, yet he was still amazed at the optimism reflected in the efforts of these desperate souls to sell such information. He began making lists of the information offered, and the newspapers in which the offers appeared, to discuss with Cumming during their next meeting.

Walsh had plenty of time to notice other items in the recent news, mainly the British elections which returned a Liberal government to power in coalition with the Irish Nationalists, with H.H. Asquith remaining as prime minister. He hoped this meant the SSB would remain on a relatively secure footing while he was in Brussels. In Paris, heavy rains had caused the Seine to flood and put the city in darkness when electrical power stations suffered from short-circuiting. Beyond Europe, Walsh read that Glenn Curtiss had tested the first seaplane in America, at San Diego Bay, and he made a mental note to ask Cumming if he would be interested in German air warfare capabilities. America also took the initial steps of changing the status of Arizona and New Mexico from territories to US states, although there were still heated debates in Congress about whether the indigenous peoples of these regions were truly assimilated into American culture.

Walsh also began making the rounds of the British expatriate community in Brussels, once his accommodation and financing were sorted. A weekly English newspaper, the *Belgian Gazette*, was most helpful in this regard. It served an expat community of about two thousand residents in Brussels, mostly clustered around Walsh's commune, on Avenue Louise and the Quartièr Leopold. In addition to regular visits to the British Chamber of Commerce, he also visited the Union Club for American and British expatriates, where a member suggested that he also call in to the American Chamber of Commerce at Place de Brouckère. He didn't expect to glean any useful information from American firms but he introduced himself at their Chamber nonetheless. Walsh also stopped by the Brussels Cricket and Lawn Tennis Club, although he despised both sports, and the Royal Golf Club in Tervuren, which was somewhat closer to his own interests.

As Cumming had instructed, Walsh introduced himself everywhere as a travelling representative of the British Board of Trade, on a mission to help explore new markets for British firms seeking to do business on the continent. His chief focus would be on manufactured goods, particularly transport and armaments; a visit to the Automobile Club de Belgique was most informative in this respect. Their office on Avenue de la Toison d'Or, like that of the Union Club, was practically in his back garden. He was surprised to learn how extensive Belgium's automobile industry had become in just a few short years, thanks to the creative efforts of firms such as Auto-Mixte, Excelsior, Impéria, Métallurgique, Minerva, Pipe, Springuel, and Vivinus. At least one of these firms, Nagant in Liège, had had previous experience in the small arms industry as a supplier to the Russian army, and Walsh decided to visit their operations at some point, if he could get away. Several British firms were also present in Brussels, and Walsh made plans to seek out the Brussels representatives of Armstrong Mitchell and Vickers, for a start.

Pleased with his preparatory work so far, Walsh looked forward to his meeting with Cumming in Brussels on the twenty-first of the month. On that Monday, he secured a quiet late-afternoon table towards the rear of a fairly new place near the Bourse: Falstaff, on rue Henri Maus. Walsh was admiring the strange décor of the place, all sinuous ironwork and elaborate stained-glass installations – 'Art Nouveau' they called it – when Cumming breezed in, looking extremely harried. Walsh was amazed to see that Cumming was wearing, in addition to his normal gold monocle, what seemed to be false moustache; it looked faintly ridiculous on him.

Cumming sat across from him and began mopping his brow, although it was only four degrees Celsuis outside. Hopefully the moustache would stay put despite his perspiration, Walsh thought.

"Something the matter, C?" Walsh asked.

"No, just a little rushed today, that's all. I've got to get back up to Antwerp in a few hours."

Walsh thought it best not to ask. It was no business of his, after all. But Cumming filled in the blank on his own.

"I'm meeting with another source there but he failed to turn up yesterday," he said. "So I've got to go back to try again."

"That must be annoying." Walsh took a sip of his coffee. "Would you like anything just now?" He motioned to the waiter.

"No, that's all right, my boy. Not enough time. But thanks." Cumming calmed himself a bit and then got down to business. "I must say, I'm very pleased to see you're alive and well, Walsh."

Walsh frowned. "Why would you say that?"

"Because of that English chap who was killed here a few days ago. Surely you've read about it?"

"Yes, but it didn't concern me. I thought it was just a robbery."

"Well, I thought it might have been you!"

"No, C, I am quite fine. Obviously." And I'm not English, Walsh might have added, but didn't.

"Of course you are. Good for that. But, you might give some thought to arming yourself while you're here. Just in case, you understand."

"That thought had occurred to me."

"But, of course, we can't pay for that. Sorry, old boy."

Walsh nodded, with an amused look. "That thought had occurred to me as well. But I might look into it, since I'm going to be here for a while."

Cumming smiled back at him, then seemed to relax a little more. "See that you do, my boy. Now, given that you are still alive, how are things on this end?"

Walsh relayed his movements over the past couple of weeks and highlighted a couple of possibilities gleaned through his newspapers: information about a German Mobilmachungskalendar, or mobilization calendar, for the Kaiser's force deployment in the west, and plans for several new Zeppelin engines from someone associated with Luftschiffbau Zeppelin, near Friedrichshafen.

"I've also heard about an offer for French railway-march timetables, but I assume you don't want information about that, do you?" Walsh said. "I could try to get more details, if you want."

Cumming thought for a moment. "No, no, that doesn't interest us, not at the moment, I don't think. But the German information could be useful. Have you contacted these individuals?"

Walsh shook his head. "I wanted to speak with you first, in case they ask for more money than we can offer."

"If the information is credible, if you personally see the items, then we can certainly go above twenty or thirty pounds depending on how useful it is. Maybe even as high as fifty pounds. Remember, we are paying for results, not to keep agents on a retainer basis, so to speak. If we can avoid it. Our budget simply can't handle so many long-term salaries if results are not forthcoming. So by all means look into this, will you?"

Walsh nodded. "Of course. And one other thing, C."

"What's that?"

"It occurred to me that having a camera could be useful. They have Kodak Brownies for sale here, the new folding ones that don't take up so much space. Could I purchase one here, or can you supply one for me?"

"Yes, indeed, indeed. I hadn't thought of that. They aren't too expensive, are they?"

"No, around two or three pounds. For a new one."

"All right, go ahead and purchase one, and keep the receipt. I'll wire funds to reimburse you once I have the receipt."

Walsh nodded again, and took a sip of his coffee. A waiter lingered next to them for a few moments, wiping off a table, and they waited until he left.

"Now, listen carefully, Walsh, I have some...some news for you as well." Cumming leaned forward and looked down at the table.

"What is it?"

"I can already see it will be useful to have you here. Very useful, and good work, that was, with looking into these sources so quickly." Cumming paused, then looked up at Walsh again. "Good work indeed. But, I'm...I'm afraid things have become slightly more complicated regarding your cover story here. I suppose that's the best way to put it."

"What do you mean, 'complicated'?" Walsh's tone was measured.

"Well, it's all a bit awkward, I admit. Certainly not good timing for you! But it seems…it seems that Churchill has moved on from the Board of Trade."

"And so?"

Cumming hesitated. "And so, it also seems that the new head of the outfit is not so keen with our mission here. In fact" - Cumming attempted a smile - "he was quite adamant that we do *not* use the Board of Trade name to support our work. In any capacity. He was quite adamant about it, you understand."

"I don't believe it." Walsh leaned back in his chair. "What the devil happened to Churchill?"

Cumming avoided his gaze. "He's just become the new Home Secretary."

Walsh leaned close to Cumming. "Do you know I've just spent the last two weeks spreading my name and contact details all over this town, using the same cover story that *you* provided? Two weeks of work!"

"Yes, well, I'm sorry about this, Walsh. Really I am. But it's out of my hands, you see. I've met with the new chap, Buxton, and he refuses to have anything to do with us."

"Can Churchill have a word with him?"

"I've tried that too, but Churchill is now far more interested in the domestic situation. He is Home Secretary after all. So his priorities have changed. And he thinks you can carry on your work in a more…private capacity."

"Oh, he does, does he?"

"Yes, like he did as a journalist. In South Africa. But in a freelance capacity, of course; we can't have you officially linked to any British newspapers. It wouldn't look good for us, you see."

Walsh shook his head. "Well, I don't think that's an option, C. I'm not a writer like he is. I don't plan to sell stories to the papers. I wouldn't even know where to start with that. And I don't plan to get imprisoned like he did."

Cumming brightened a little now. "Yes, good point. Speaking of which, a German spy was just convicted in France. In Rheims."

"Is that so?"

"Yes, so they are clearly up to something. And this game is becoming more complicated. So we've stepped up our reconnaissance of various German ports, Konsor, Kiel, Burnshuttel, Bremerhaven, and so on."

"Have you learned anything useful?" Walsh said, without much interest, given this unwelcome news about the loss of his cover story in Brussels.

Cumming shook his head. "Well, not yet; we're only just starting to send officers over there. But as they begin to do their work, the Germans are likely to get nervous about it. And pay more attention to the situation *here*." Cumming stabbed his index finger on the table.

"And hopefully none of us will end up like those German spies in Rheims."

"Yes, we hope not. So look out for yourself here, mind you. But listen now, Walsh, there might be a ray of hope here. Just a small one. I've spoken to Grierson again and the word is that a new attaché is coming to Brussels next month."

"I thought the attachés were not willing to help us?" Walsh said.

"No, not normally. But Grierson has been attempting to…to move things along on that front. All of the other attachés are comfortable with dealing with agents of one sort or another. The French, the Russians, and certainly the Germans."

"So how does that help me?"

"Well, he's going to be new in town and could use a leg up. So he is willing to meet with you and send any offers of information your way. If he gets any, that is. He'll keep an ear to the ground."

Walsh refused to believe this, but asked anyway. "Should I contact him at the embassy?"

Cumming shook his head. "No, not just yet. Absolutely not, do you understand? That could ruin everything for us. But he'll be in touch with you, after he arrives here. In a few weeks at most, I would think."

"What's his name?"

"Bridges, Major Tom Bridges."

"Fair enough, I'll wait to hear from him. I assume he has my contact details?"

"Yes, we'll get that to him when he arrives."

"And what about my new cover?"

Cumming looked down at his watch, avoiding Walsh's gaze. "I'm afraid you're on your own at the moment, my boy."

Walsh had already guessed as much. What a surprise. But he had also been considering one or two other possibilities since his arrival in town, and now would have to follow them up. Obviously, he had no choice.

Chapter 12

Troyon-sur-Meuse, France. March 1910.

Marchand removed his boots with a loud groan of relief. What a day! Normally the occasional staff visits he made to France's frontier fortifications were moderately tolerable, and even pleasant once in a while. They usually concentrated on only one or two locations during each trip. Review the troops, inspect the guns and communication systems, confirm the availability of supplies, look over the nearby railheads, if any; the usual drill. He had done it dozens of times before. But this time Marchand was being dragged from one site to another over a much wider territory, and for an entire week, from Verdun to Toul.

Generalissimo Henri de Lacroix and his colleagues on the general staff were eager to verify their assumptions behind Plan Sixteen, and Marchand was paying the price for that attitude. Of course, the generalissimo *himself* could not be bothered to visit the frontiers. He had stayed behind, warm and comfortable in Paris.

Now in Troyon, on the bank of the river Meuse, Marchand looked forward to an evening of good food and drink with his colleagues after a long day on his feet. This hamlet was little more than a crossroads on a map, but there was a decent country bistro here, the Café du Minke, which would have plenty of Alsatian wines available, cheap and tasty.

A knock at the door, and Lefevre poked his head in a moment later.

"Ready, commandant?" This was Lefevre's first visit to the frontiers and he was a little too eager to join in the amusements after each day's work.

"*Un instant*, if you don't mind, lieutenant. Come in for a moment."

Lefevre waited at the small window while Marchand removed his socks, dried his aching feet, and rubbed them vigorously.

"So what did you think of today's spectacle?" Marchand asked. As always, the fortress commander had done his best to impress his visitors, but to Marchand it all seemed a waste of time. The only question here was how long the forts could hold out under the bombardment of heavy German guns.

"I don't know, sir. Duty out here seems kind of...well, boring."

"I'm sure it is, lieutenant. Until the *Uhlans* appear, that is." Marchand put on a fresh pair of socks and stepped into his boots.

"But now that I've seen these preparations, I understand your point about a possible invasion. It doesn't make sense for the Germans to attack us directly here. These forts are too close together to penetrate easily. Besides, the Germans prefer flanking maneuvers, so they are likely to simply go around these positions."

Marchand stood up, ready now. "Well, let's just see what our colleagues think, shall we?"

Two hours later, fortified by generous helpings of potée Lorraine, andouille sausages, and nutty Brouère cheese, all washed down with a decent local Pinot Gris, Marchand casually sidled around the table to sit next to Commandant Gérard Dupont, his counterpart in the Troisième Bureau, or the Operations Bureau, of the general staff. The officers in the Troisième Bureau produced their own intelligence estimates, of course, and Marchand needed to know their thinking ahead of the upcoming staff meetings to plan the Picardy maneuvers. Dupont was pleasantly intoxicated, enough to be truthful but not enough to be incoherent. Perfect for Marchand.

"So tell me Gérard," Marchand put a comradely arm across Dupont's bony shoulders. "Are they keeping you busy over there?"

"Only too much, too much! These Picardy maneuvers, you know. Now they want sixty thousand men involved. Sixty thousand men, Didier! Plus the airships as well. So how can we coordinate *flying machines* in a military exercise? Can you tell me that, please? It's trouble enough to coordinate men on the ground!"

"I haven't a clue, my friend." Marchand shook his head and took a sip of wine. "But this is why we have exercises and manoeuvers and plans."

"Yes, yes, something to do while we are not at war." Dupont gulped another measure of wine after he spoke; Marchand was amazed that his colleague was still on his feet. Dupont was thin as a rail physically but thick as two planks mentally, or so Marchand often thought. But Dupont's uncle was currently serving as a deputy in Prime Minister Briand's cabinet, under foreign minister Stéphen Pichon, and he knew how to take care of his family. And so it goes...

"And your bureau is pleased with Plan Sixteen?"

"Well, to be honest, I really didn't see any problems with Plan *Fifteen*."

Damn. Marchand almost swore under his breath but caught himself; Plan Fifteen was even more focused on Lorraine than Plan Sixteen. Then he said, "But you do agree there is an argument for focusing slightly more on the Belgian frontier, don't you?"

"Well, de Lacroix seems to think so. So who am I to argue?"

Before Marchand could reply, Lefevre joined them at their end of the table, along with Dupont's own adjutant, Lt. Paul Morel. Unlike Dupont, Morel had a keen mind for strategy and enjoyed debating it. He was as polished and proper as Dupont was coarse and offensive. Morel still sounded like a Breton, though, which could put him at a disadvantage in discussions with his more urbane colleagues.

Lefevre waded in first. "The Germans would be mad to waste their time against these fortresses. We could hold out for days, weeks even, all the while the Russians will be moving against them on the Eastern front. It makes more sense to come in through Belgium."

Marchand completed the argument. "They've already improved the railroads on the Belgian frontiers. And there are new disembarkation platforms as far north as Aix-la-Chapelle." Or Aachen to the Germans. "What other purpose would they serve, other than helping to move the German First Army into Belgium?"

"It could be a ruse." This from Morel, who looked to his superior for confirmation and found none.

Marchand turned on him. "All of that expensive new construction is just a ruse? Do you really believe that?"

"Yes, to divert our forces to the Belgian frontier, away from the real objective, here in Lorraine." Morel again looked to Dupont for help. "The Germans must assume that we will want to take back Alsace and Lorraine, so they know we will attack here. So they must reserve the bulk of their forces to defend that attack. Otherwise they would be vulnerable to our offensive."

Dupont spoke, finally. "And they have improved their railroads in Lorraine as well. So what are they for, if not an offensive here? Besides, it will take them too long to move through Belgium, if they attack there. *If* they attack there. Weeks even. They have to get through Liège and Namur. So we can easily hold them off up north with eight or ten active divisions, plus another eight in reserve. Between Mézières and Stenay. By that time we will have defeated them in Lorraine, and we can then move our forces to reinforce the Belgian front, if necessary."

Marchand turned towards him. He was not ready to give up. Not ready at all, in fact. "Suppose they push further west than Mézières? Towards Maubeuge or Lille even? And with more troops?"

"Why would they go so far?" Dupont was confused now. Was it the alcohol or simple stupidity?

"To take *Paris*, my friend. Lorraine will be theirs in the end, no matter what happens there, if they take Paris while we sit here in these fortresses. They could simply hold us off in Lorraine, behind their own fortresses at Thionville and Metz." Marchand began to grow agitated. "And then attack from behind out here once they've taken Paris."

Dupont and Morel exchanged a look.

Marchand leaned over the table and gathered up empty glasses, bottles, and cutlery. He began lining up these items on the table as he continued to speak. "*Look* at the map, gentlemen! Verdun, Génicourt, Troyon, Les Parroches, Camp des Romains, St. Mihiel, Liouville, Gironville, Jouy-sur-les-Côtes, Toul, Nancy, Manonviller, Epinal, Arches, Parmont, Chateau Lambert..."

"You forgot Rupt," Lefevre interjected. From the other end of the table, a few other officers took an interest and moved closer to the source of the arguing.

Marchand shot him a hard look, then smiled. "Sorry, *Rupt*, then Chateau Lambert, Ballon de Servance, Giromagny, Belfort, Montbélliard, Le Lomont. Then SWITZERLAND!"

He grabbed a huge wedge of cheese and stuck it at the end of his line of glasses, bottles, and cutlery. Neutral Switzerland at one end, neutral Belgium at the other. France in between, protected by the long line of fortresses constructed after its humiliating defeat in 1871 and designed by the French engineer Séré de Rivières.

Everyone erupted in laughter. *Viva la Suisse!* Except Dupont, who got to his feet, still unsteady. But committed now.

Marchand continued his little lecture, staring up at Dupont. "Now why would any attacking force attempt to breach this line when there is an easier route through the north?"

"They don't have enough manpower to invade Paris through Belgium and hold us off in Lorraine *at the same time*, Didier!" Dupont said, his voice not so slurred now.

"They do if they use their reserves!" Marchand stood up as well.

"What reserves? They always say 'No husbands and fathers on the frontlines,' don't they? Hmmm? So their reserves will stay behind, just like ours. Besides, they don't have enough officers to command so many reserves in an offensive action!"

Dupont glared at Marchand in triumph. His supporters around the table nodded their heads in agreement.

Marchand shook his head. "That problem can be solved only too easily...and we have intelligence from our attaché in Berlin that the Germans are forming mixed divisions with actives and reserves in their field army!"

Indeed, France's very effective military attaché in Berlin was fortunate to coordinate closely with his Russian counterpart on a regular basis now thanks to the formal Franco-Russian alliance. The Russian attaché had recently provided this useful information for the benefit of his French allies.

"They didn't go through Belgium in 1870," said someone else from operations, whose name Marchand didn't care to learn. "The First Army came down just south of Trier. They didn't even go through Luxembourg."

Lefevre glared back at the operations contingent as he said, "They didn't *need* to go through Belgium in 1870 because we didn't have so many fortresses out here. Now we do. Now we are protected out here."

Marchand continued the thought. "And that was a different war! We were isolated then, and Prussia was only interested in unifying Germany. A *small* war for them, just like those against Denmark and Austria. Next time they will have

Russia to contend with, and they must achieve a quick victory here in order to move their forces to the Eastern front before the Russians can mobilize. Now why would they risk tying themselves up against this line of fortresses when they can simply go around them to take Paris, the main objective?"

Dupont smiled at Marchand and slowly walked around the table towards him. "You are building castles in the air, my friend, while we have a strong defence already in place here. German reserve divisions on the front lines, conjured up by magic. Trained officers to lead them into battle. Magic. Guns portable *and* large enough to defeat Liège and Namur. Magic! Infantry who can march hundreds of kilometres across Belgium to Paris and still be ready to fight when they arrive. Magic!!"

Dupont was in Marchand's face now, and their subordinates around the table watched the two men with fascination.

"So are you a magician or an intelligence officer, Marchand?" Dupont finished, provoking laughter all around. "Answer me that!"

Marchand faced him. "This isn't 'magic,' you fool! And the German force meant for Belgium is not just a feint. They *do* have the capabilities to mount major offensive operations in both sectors, at the same time. And they *are* improving their forces all the time. It's all spelled out in the German war plans! So you need to start thinking like a German!"

"And you need to start *acting* like a Frenchman, and trust your general staff officers!"

At this, Marchand was just about to strike Dupont when Lefevre grabbed him and held him off.

Back at their inn, Marchand and Lefevre smoked outside before turning in. The evening air was calm and cool but Marchand was still churning inside.

"Well, now we know," said Lefevre.

"I already knew." Marchand took a long drag from his Gitanes. It was a new brand of cigarette and he wasn't sure if he liked it yet. Right now Marchand didn't care what he was smoking; it could have been a cowpat for all he was concerned. "I just wanted them to know that there are other points of view," he added.

Lefevre nodded and leaned on the wooden railing next to their rooms. They could hear the ring of cowbells from somewhere across the fields, along with the singing of a farmer. Or perhaps it was another drunk soldier.

Marchand looked around as if he could see the peaceful countryside in the dark. "My father was out here, you know. In 1870."

"Really, sir?"

"Over at Gravelotte." Marchand nodded his head towards the east.

They exchanged a look. Lefevre knew what that meant.

"He survived," Marchand continued, answering the unspoken question. "Ended up in a prisoner of war camp."

Marchand didn't need to share the rest with Lefevre, but over the years he had gently coaxed the details of the battle from his father whenever he could, long after the old man's nineteen months in captivity. The rout of the French was so badly disorganized that they had to use a new word for it: a 'dégringolade.' A rapid decline or tumble. A collapse. And it certainly was, in the end. Over four thousand prisoners of war and nearly eight thousand dead on the French side, and that idiot commander Marshal Bazaine still tried to claim it as a victory. How blind and arrogant do you have to be to equate a collapse with a victory?

Marchand had been born soon after his father left to fight. And throughout his youth Marchand would be ridiculed about how much he looked like the milkman. Or the baker. Or whatever.

Enough of those memories. There would not be another Gravelotte if he could help it. Not on his watch.

"You did well back there," said Marchand. He tapped the ash from his cigarette and stared at the lit end of it, turning the butt slowly in his fingers.

"Thank you sir."

Marchand looked Lefevre in the eyes. "But do you really believe my argument, lieutenant? Or are you just being a loyal officer?"

"It does make sense, sir. But..."

"But what, Lefevre?"

"But, only if they use reserves in the way you suggest. I don't think they would leave Lorraine to itself in case we mount our own offensive there. It would be far too risky for them. They have to have enough manpower to serve on both fronts, simultaneously."

"And we do still plan to mount our own offensive here, apparently. Those damned 'lost provinces'." Marchand practically snarled his words. "They may prove to be far more trouble than they're worth, in the end."

"And the Germans probably know that, just as we know their current war plan. So they must have forces strong enough to hold off Lorraine while another force moves through Belgium, and quickly enough to threaten Paris long before Russia is ready."

"Which means, lieutenant, the use of mixed forces in field operations to give them enough offensive manpower."

"So we need to know about their reserve situation. And quickly."

Marchand nodded. "That's absolutely right."

They crushed their cigarette butts on the ground and turned to go back inside the inn. Marchand put a comradely hand on Lefevre's shoulder.

"*Vengeance* is not the same as *defence*," Marchand said, in a small voice. A small but deadly serious voice. "Never forget that, lieutenant."

Chapter 13

Bern, Switzerland. February 1910.

It took less than a week in Switzerland for Retzlaff to discover the final destination of Ernie and Tobias.

After reporting his initial findings to Herr Hesse, he had been allowed to visit Bern to pick up the trail based on the information provided by Maria. Retzlaff had kept Maria's name out of the conversation, as he had promised, but Herr Hesse apparently couldn't care less about Retzlaff's working methods once he learned that political intrigue might be involved.

Socialists! Jewish revolutionaries! Perhaps even an anarchist plot against some foreign government! There is no time to lose, Herr Hesse!

Hesse had put Retzlaff on a much longer leash, with a more generous expense account and some supporting documents provided by Herr Hesse to assist with his task. With these resources, Retzlaff had spent a pleasant few days in Bern searching around the university district for Ernie and Tobias. He was pleased with the way he had used the Meldewesen records to learn of the Hesse family tragedies in order to make Maria talk. It was only too easy for him to imagine how the sad tale of a dead child, a job lost, and a young family dislocated might inspire the young Hesse girl to help him 'save' her lost brother. As indeed it had.

Switzerland relied upon its own Meldewesensystem to keep track of its citizens, but Retzlaff knew it would be fairly useless against foreigners, especially if they slipped across the border undetected. If Tobias and Ernst had stayed in a hotel or inn, they would have been required to provide identification documents for the hotel register, which then would have been checked by the local police. Retzlaff assumed they would not be careless enough to do that, if they were attempting to travel as secretly as possible.

So he had had to rely on old-fashioned methods: showing Ernie's photograph around the rooming houses near the University of Bern, and asking about him at various university offices and student organizations. After three days of systematic searching, his efforts had led him to a ramshackle boarding house in the warren of tiny streets off the

Nydeggstalden in the old town. There he managed to charm an old landlady by feigning terrible sorrow at the lost young man smiling in the photo he clutched to his breast.

His parents are searching for their missing son. They are distraught...his mother and young sister cannot sleep or eat. Can you please help this poor family? I just need to get a message to the boy, so they can contact him.

Of course she would be only too glad to help. Dessicated and poor she was, but still very eager to be of service, the landlady kept her bony hand on Retzlaff's forearm as she spoke. The older boy – Tobias his name was? – had a loud voice. *Quite* a loud voice, she insisted; you know how his kind can be, don't you? In fact, she thought she remembered some of her other tenants had complained about it. Yes, indeed they had complained, so she was forced to pay closer attention to them, just to calm everyone else in the building. So she didn't *mean* to listen in on their conversations, but she had to keep track of everyone under her care, didn't she? And she remembered that they had argued once or twice, and perhaps she happened to hear a few words from behind their cracked wooden door. She couldn't be absolutely *sure*, of course, but during one of their arguments Tobias had mentioned the name of a city, one she had never been to but whose name she recognized most clearly. She would be happy to pass this name to Retzlaff, to aid his search for the poor missing boy.

It was Brussels.

Chapter 14

Brussels. February 1910.

With the loss of his link, such as it was, with Britain's Board of Trade, Walsh felt somewhat adrift, but not for too long. It quickly dawned on him that the lack of official cover actually freed him from many constraints, except perhaps for financial ones. Spying was still legal in Brussels, and he would essentially be acting as a private citizen here - just one who happened to be in a position to give useful information to the British military establishment. He assumed that other SSB operatives were in a situation similar to his own in other European capitals, without any official cover, and they must be able to find what they need. So would he.

Still, Cumming's inability to follow through with Walsh's cover story as promised, and so soon after he had arrived in Brussels, was extremely annoying. Hopefully such incompetence would not become a regular occurrence. Walsh had had enough of that when he first entered the military, over a decade ago. But at least he was a civilian now, and working on his own rather than under a rigid chain of command.

So, a fresh start. But where to begin? After several hours of thought on the subject, Walsh purchased a Kodak Folding Brownie, Model 3A, from a shop in the warren of streets between the Grand Place and the Gare du Nord. It came pre-loaded with a roll of film and he purchased three additional rolls of size 122 film for the camera. He also purchased a small pair of field glasses in a leather case. Next he located a stationery shop and had a set of name cards made, with a new title for himself and his contact details in Brussels. Once these were ready for him, he made plans for a second round of meetings and visits to build upon those he had made earlier in the month.

Fortunately, and even before Cumming had set him adrift, Walsh had noted one potential goldmine of sources in the form of a large poster he spotted near the Grand Place. It announced the upcoming festivities associated with the Exposition Universelle et Internationale de Bruxelles. As he had never been to such an event, the thought of exploring the Exposition on his own for several months, and of being paid to do so, gave him more to look forward to than he could remember in a long time. The transportation and military exhibits would be especially illuminating, even if he didn't manage to discover any secret German war plans.

Walsh did have several weeks to wait before he could start poking around the Exposition, so perhaps it was time for a little reconnaissance beyond the city, as Grierson had suggested. If the Germans indeed planned to invade France through Belgium, then their first major Belgian obstacle would be Liège, so Walsh stopped by the Thomas Cook office and had them reserve a room for him at the Hôtel de l'Universe near Guillemins station in Liège. At the same office he picked up a small *Guide Sommaire* and spent a pleasant afternoon at a quiet brasserie on the Sablon, sipping a cup of tea and perusing the timetables. Belgian railway timetables had just recently introduced continental time, or the 24-hour clock, so it took a few moments for Walsh to work out his options. At least the *Guide Sommaire* was easier to read when compared to the cramped printing of the *Bradshaw's* timetables in the UK.

After his tea, Walsh booked an unreserved second-class ticket to Liège on one of the wagons-salon, but paid a small supplèment as well so that he could sit in the saloon carriage along with the other first-class passengers. He was sure Cumming wouldn't mind this small luxury, especially if he didn't know about it. To complete his preparations, Walsh stopped at the Touring Club de Belgique on rue Royale and purchased a suscription for foreign members for 3½ francs; the Club also sold him a Carte de la Belgique, a detailed map published by the Military Cartographical Institute. The map would be very useful for motorists and cyclists. And spies.

A week later Walsh's train left the Gare du Nord and soon passed through Louvain, followed by sixty more kilometres of peaceful Belgian farmland, misty and still in the late morning light. Walsh caught a glimpse of Park Abbey just after Louvain, then he relaxed with his guide books and maps as the train chugged through Tirlemont, Landen, Gingelom, and Remicourt, before descending further into the Meuse valley. It stopped, finally, at Liège, less than three hours after he had departed. From Guillemins station, on the left bank of the Meuse, it was only a short walk to his hotel, where he dropped his luggage and cleaned up after the day's journey. Afterwards he made a few inquiries at the concierge desk before a drink and dinner nearby.

After breakfast the next day he made his first stop: a gun dealer near the Fabrique Nationale headquarters on rue Louis Demeuse. Thanks to his earlier experience in the army, Walsh was well aware of Liège's reputation in the arms industry, and he was eager to see what was available in the actual city where the FN was based.

A few inquiries had led him to this location, where the very knowledgable shopkeeper, a Monsieur Evrard, proudly showed him several pistols designed for the FN by John Browning, the American. Evrard, a shrivelled but vigorous old man with gnarled hands and a bushy moustache, was happy to relate the story of how Browning had offered to work with the FN on some new designs after his US manufacturer, Colt Firearms, refused to cooperate. Obviously the very talented Browning must have been aware of Belgium's craftsmanship in this area; Evrard therefore insisted that one could certainly trust anything produced by the FN.

Although Walsh had set out to purchase a revolver, and in fact there was a nice Colt .45 model in the display case, Evrard was eager to show him something very new, and very special, that the FN was just starting to produce. It was not even available outside of Belgium at the moment. Or so Evrard claimed.

The weapon was the FN Model 1910, a type of semi-automatic that Walsh had never seen before. He had had some experience with a Mauser Model 1896 – the famed 'Broomhandle' - in Africa, and had once fired a Borchardt C-93 in France, but those semi-automatics seemed heavier and much less refined than this one. Evrard expertly dismantled the M1910 for Walsh and showed him the spring mechanism that pushed each round into the firing chamber, the smooth working of the slide, and the unique 'triple safety' devices on the weapon: a grip safety, a magazine safety, and an external safety lever. The weapon would not fire unless a magazine was inserted, the grip was squeezed, and the external safety lever was disengaged.

Evrard re-assembled the gun and handed it back to Walsh, who took it and wiped the weapon with a cloth lying on the counter before inspecting it. Evrard peered up at Walsh over the rims of his steel eyeglasses.

"So you see, *monsieur*," Evrard continued, "This is much more...*elegant* than anything else on the market today. Accurate, reliable, and safe; it will not jam on you like the shoddy Mausers or Lugers made across the river." Evrard jerked his head towards the east: Germany. "I would stake my reputation on it!"

Walsh doubted that, but there was no denying the reassuring feel and balance of the weapon in his hand. And it was small enough to be carried easily under a coat, or even slipped into a large trouser pocket.

As Walsh worked the slide and checked the weight with a full magazine, Evrard pulled another model from the case.

"I have also an older model of Browning's, the Model 1900, in 7.65mm calibre, if you prefer something a little more...affordable, *monsieur*."

Walsh looked over at the M1900, also an attractive weapon but just a little bulkier than the M1910. It also had more contours on the body as compared to the smooth, modern lines of the M1910. He returned his attention to the M1910. "And the 1910 is available in which calibres?"

Evrard smiled again. "I have the 7.65mm calibre, with the seven-round magazine, as you see here, and the 9mm with the six-round magazine, if you prefer something a little more...*convincing*."

Evrard pulled a slightly larger M1910 from his case and handed it to Walsh. It too was a very handsome weapon, and bore the large 'FN' badge on its side like its slightly smaller brother.

Walsh weighed both in his hands and admired them, to Evrard's delight. The 9mm seemed only a few ounces heavier, and it was not much bulkier to carry, especially underneath a suit jacket.

"Either one would be a fine addition to your collection, *monsieur*. I only hope I still have them in stock when you are ready to make your choice." Evrard frowned and looked up above the rims of his eyeglasses again.

Walsh smiled at the old man, who gazed at him expectantly.

"How easy is it to load the seven-round magazine on the 7.65mm?"

Evrard hesitated, and his smile became a little strained. "Uh, it can be a little, just a little tight, *monsieur*, you understand. The extra shell casing, you see..."

Walsh nodded. "I'll take the 9mm, if you please. With ten boxes of cartridges for it. And two extra magazines."

Like all good salesmen, Evrard was wise enough to shut his mouth after closing the deal. He merely nodded and began collecting Walsh's purchases together, including another new item on the market: a leather shoulder holster. The holster even had a slot for an extra magazine on the front of it; very useful.

Afterwards he directed Walsh to a small shooting range in the backroom of a gunsmith nearby, a close acquaintance of Evrard's. Despite the apparent dominance of the FN, hundreds of individual armaments craftsman still maintained private workshops throughout Liège, most of which were located between the Quai St. Léonard near the cannon foundry and the FN factories in Herstal. All the heavy industry next to the river reminded Walsh of the River Clyde in Glasgow, which was devoted to shipbuilding rather than armaments. No matter what the purpose, the activity always assaulted one's eardrums on a workday such as this one. And so, thanks to the racket from all the heavy machinery in the neighbourhood, Walsh was able to practice with three boxes of shells without so much as raising an eyebrow to any passers-by on the street outside. The new weapon felt very good in his hand.

On Walsh's second day in the city, it was time for a little recce, the second purpose of his trip to Liège. Walsh left the pistol in his hotel room for his next excursion, across the river to the eastern fortresses. At Guillemins station he rented a bicycle for the day, and purchased a rail ticket for himself and his machine to a destination on the right bank of the Meuse, at Fléron. If the Germans did invade Belgium, they would first have to contend with six fortresses on the right bank of the Meuse, then cross the Meuse and take six fortresses on the left bank before proceeding to Namur and then into the Belgian interior.

Consulting his maps, Walsh could see that of the six fortresses on the right bank – Barchon, Evegnée, Fléron, Chaudfontaine, Embourg, and Boncelles – only two, Fléron and Chaudfontaine, seemed to be located on railway lines leading into Liège. From each of these locations their individual west-bound lines converged at a single point on the southern end of Liège and there, after merging with another line running down the right bank of the Meuse from Maastricht in the Netherlands, crossed the Meuse over a railway bridge.

This was the railway gateway into Belgium, and the Germans would have to control it to move their forces safely by rail into the interior. The fortresses at Fléron and Chaudfontaine would have to be taken quickly so that the Germans could protect the railway line into Liège, across the river, and beyond. Fléron, and the fortress above it, at Evegnée, were particularly critical as they protected main railway line from Aix-la-Chapelle into Liège, the railhead that would facilitate any major German advance into Belgium. They also protected the Route de Hervé, the main road into Liège.

Walsh intended to visit two or three fortresses on his second day in the region, and the bicycle ride from Gare Retinne at the edge of Flèron to the large fortress in the center of the village was a quick one. And he could hardly miss the place. Walsh rode around the hulking concrete mass of the large triangular fortress, taking note of what he saw. From his initial point of view, it seemed as if the massif was raised just a few metres above the groundline, but upon closer inspection with his field glasses Walsh could see that it was at least ten metres high at its lowest point. It reminded him of a large tortoise shell, set close to the ground with only a few protusions visible on the top of it – sunken gun turrets.

The rear of the fortress faced westwards, towards the railway line nearby, and contained the main entrance to the complex. Walsh had no idea how many men were garrisoned behind the barbed wire surrounding the fortress, nor how many large guns the complex contained, but the place seemed virtually impregnable. And this was just one of twelve such fortresses surrounding Liège, like the numbers on a clockface, with Fléron at about the three o'clock position. Further bicycle rides down small lanes to the north of the village revealed smaller redoubts surrounded by barbed wire and what looked like trenches as Walsh sped by. He also noted an artillery position to the northwest of Fort de Fléron, on the other side of the railway and obviously intended to protect it, as well as guard the rear entrance of the fortress.

By lunchtime Walsh had grown tired and hungry, yet he visited four different brasseries in Fléron before he found what he wanted: off-duty soldiers. The place he chose to stop was half-empty so Walsh was able to take a table fairly close, but not too close, to a table shared by four men in uniform. Or perhaps 'barely in uniform' would be more appropriate; to Walsh they seemed quite dischevelled and undisciplined, even for soldiers enjoying a few beers away from their barracks. Their dark blue greatcoats were rough and mottled, and they wore them unbuttoned in the front and in the rear skirts. Each man also had a day or two of whisker stubble on his cheeks and, most surprising of all to Walsh, they were not fit young men but looked to be in their late thirties or early forties; perhaps they were reserves or Garde Civique volunteers. He was too far away to inspect their insignia, but hoped to change that.

There is always one sure way to get soldiers, especially drunken ones, to talk: encourage them to complain. So after ordering his lunch, Walsh went to over to the table and asked if they knew anything about the garrison at the fortress. When they asked about his interest, Walsh said he was a Scotsman on holiday, bicycling in the area today, and he did not want to accidentally trespass on a military installation. And he most certainly did not want to be mistaken for an invading German, and shot on sight!

The old boys laughed at this, and confirmed that they were indeed stationed at the fortress. On hearing that, Walsh wondered aloud how his combat experience on the unforgiving open veld in South Africa a decade ago compared with their service on home territory in what seemed to be an impregnable fortress. They must feel very safe in there, surely? This provoked another drunken laugh from all four of the men: 'impregnable' indeed! They then launched into numerous criticisms about their tedious garrison life; their main concern was how the famed fortress engineer and designer, Brialmont, had located all their latrines, kitchens, and shower facilities outside of the main fortress itself, on one of the counterscarps. Obviously the troops would have to stay inside the complex if it came under attack, yet how long could they last without easy access to these facilities? Besides, the various guns inside – manufactured by Krupp, of course – all used black powder and the ventilation was terrible, so the place would most certainly fill with smoke if the guns had to be fired.

At this stage, Walsh simply sat down at a small table next to them, as casually as possible, and called the barman over to the table. A few moments later a tray of beers arrived and Walsh passed them around. Walsh raised his glass in a toast to the men and took a few sips from his glass; his new companions responded in kind. Walsh introduced himself as a former soldier now working for a small Glaswegian manufacturer of internal-combustion engines interested in breaking into the Continental markets. He was in Liège to make some sales calls to the factories and thought he would take a break today by doing some cycling in the countryside. Walsh produced a business card from his coat and showed it around the table just as his lunch was set before him.

They chatted for twenty minutes or so, and once Walsh got them talking freely about combat, it was easy enough to ask about his primary concern: how much warning they might have if the Germans lauched a surprise attack – or an 'attaque brusquée' – against Belgium. This inspired a short discussion of Fort de Fléron's signalling and monitoring capabilities. The fortress had a large sixty-centimetre diameter electrical searchlight with a range of two to three kilometres on a clear night. Obviously this was not far enough to see the German border, at about forty kilometres away, but it could be used to send signals to other adjacent forts if communications were disrupted by an attack.

Walsh was eager to continue this conversation but he feared the men would grow suspicious. One of them, who seemed to be the leader, also began complaining that they needed to get back to work. So they all paid their bills, exchanged a friendly farewell, and parted at the door.

A moment later, as Walsh lingered outside the café, watching them walk away, he heard a new voice behind him.

"Did you get everything you needed, *monsieur*?"

Walsh turned and saw a man closer to his own age, around thirty, dressed in dark civilian clothes, lighting a cigarette by the café door.

"Pardon me?" asked Walsh.

"I said, did you get everything you needed?"

The man blew out his match and threw it away, then walked over to Walsh and faced him directly. He was clean-shaven, except for a thin moustache, and far more alert-looking than Walsh's lunch companions. The man kept himself a slight distance away, and his dark eyes kept scanning Walsh's face and upper body, as if he expected a violent response.

Walsh smiled and held out his hands. "I'm sorry, *monsieur*, I don't know what you mean. I was just having lunch."

The man smiled. "Please, my friend." He blew a small puff of smoke at Walsh and slowly shook his head. "*Please. Let us not deceive one another.*"

He looked up and down the street and back at Walsh, pausing as if to make up his mind. "I know exactly why you are here," he continued. "Now walk with me for a few moments and I will enlighten you."

Walsh held out his arm, pointing his palm down the street, and the man nodded and walked ahead. His heart beating faster now, Walsh joined the stranger and waited; Cumming's comment a month ago about not spying on the Belgians themselves rattled in his head. This man had not been in the vicinity when Walsh joined the four soldiers in the brasserie, so he must have slipped in later. But when? How much did he hear? Was he about to arrest Walsh? And most importantly, should Walsh run or fight or just wait?

"There is a lot of interest in our little village here these days," the man continued, waving his cigarette hand around to point up and down the street. "We get Frenchmen, and Germans, and sometimes other...more exotic nationalities here, I can tell you. I met an Austrian just last month, also on a bicycle. My colleague over at Loncin ran into a couple of Russians once. Usually they come in twos or threes, but sometimes they are alone. All alone." He paused for effect. "Like you."

"And all here to take a look at your beautiful countryside, I'm sure." Walsh paused, extremely pleased that he did not have his pistol, or his camera, with him today. "Just like me."

"Yes, but these fortresses are not so beautiful. I think you'll agree they are quite ugly, in fact. They've been here as long as I can remember, since I was a boy even, so I guess they are part of the landscape now. And you were not talking about the countryside, back in the café. You were interested in the fortresses." The man took another puff of his cigarette. "Just like our other foreign friends who come through."

Walsh shrugged and adopted an innocent expression. "And what of it? I'm an ex-soldier, so I always take an interest in those with similar experiences."

"An ex-soldier? With the British army?"

"Yes, that's right."

"But just here on business now, and for some relaxation perhaps?"

Walsh hesitated for a moment. Was this man in a position to help him? "Yes, as I told the men at my table." He produced another card and handed it to the man. "Nicholas Walsh, from Glasgow. I can show you my passport if you wish."

The man stopped walking and looked at the card; it simply said 'Clydeside Machinery Ltd, Nicholas Walsh, Proprietor,' and gave a Brussels address – Walsh's 'Continental Headquarters' – indicating his flat in Ixelles. Walsh stood beside him and waited.

"Yes, of course. Just an innocent businessman, I see. And not yet another 'bird-watcher'."

The man raised his eyebrow as he said this, then put Walsh's card in his coat pocket before walking again, very slowly. Walsh followed him, carefully. His heart began to slow to its normal rate.

"And who are you, *monsieur*?" Walsh asked.

"My name is Delfosse." The man – Delfosse – dropped his cigarette butt and crushed it with his shoe. "Captain Marcel Delfosse, of the Belgian Army. I don't think it's important for you to know my exact unit, at the moment."

"Pleased to meet you, Captain Delfosse." Walsh held out his hand.

Delfosse smiled again and shook Walsh's hand.

"So I am not under arrest?" Walsh raised an eyebrow at Delfosse.

Delfosse shook his head: no.

"And do you have any questions about the *British* army?"

"Just one."

"And what is that?"

"Will you help defend our neutrality, if these ugly fortresses are attacked?"

"We've made a pledge to do so, haven't we?"

Delfosse suddenly grabbed Walsh by his coat lapels and pushed him against the wall. He glared into Walsh's face, then said, "But do you even understand what *neutrality* means, you idiot? Do you know that we cannot even *discuss* such matters with you in case the French or the Germans are watching?"

Walsh fought the urge to break free of Delfosse's grip and bury his knee in the man's lower ribcage. Instead he adopted a submissive stance; he didn't want to blow this opportunity. He might not get another one.

"Then how are *we* supposed to help defend *you*, if we can't even discuss it during peacetime?" Walsh said, as calmly as he could.

Delfosse looked up and down the street again; the vicinity was clear of passers-by. Before he could act or speak, Walsh added, "Let's get out of the street for a few moments. Let's try to help each other. We might not have another chance at this."

Delfosse considered that for a moment, then nodded, just slightly, and relaxed his grip. They quickly moved down a smaller street nearby, and slipped through a doorway. Delfosse led Walsh to a corner table in the backroom of the cramped, but mostly empty, bar – obviously someplace he had been to many times before. Or so it seemed to Walsh. Delfosse gestured to the barman for two glasses of beer, which arrived at the table just a moment after they sat down.

"We saw you from the fortress, riding near the railway," Delfosse said. "Then I followed you on your…your tour of several brasseries. I guess you couldn't find a menu you liked." He smiled. "In case you were wondering."

"No harm in that, is there?"

"Of course not. And you didn't learn much from your lunch companions."

Walsh smiled. "It was just a friendly conversation among old soldiers."

Delfosse nodded and lit up another cigarette. He offered one to Walsh, who declined.

"Yes, of course it was," said Delfosse. "So let me enlighten you about some other points." Delfosse lowered his voice now. "Given your…professional curiousity."

Delfosse smiled a little, and Walsh visibly relaxed.

"The fortress is connected by above-ground wires to telegraph and telephone lines in the vicinity, which would be vulnerable to enemy attack," Delfosse continued. "A central civilian operator in Liège controls the line, and the operator has to manually connect the telephone lines between the fortresses if their commanders wish to speak to each other. There are no permanent forward observation posts, and the commanders have to rely on observers located in high buildings, such as church steeples."

Walsh considered what he heard for a moment. He was not impressed. "What about observations closer to the German border?"

Delfosse shook his head. "Nothing beyond normal border checks at customs houses at the main crossings."

"So you are vulnerable to a surprise attack."

Delfosse nodded. "I suppose. Somewhat vulnerable. Certainly we would notice if troops were massed across our borders, but until they moved we could only wait in our precious fortresses. And remember, here is not the only possible crossing. The crossings at Visé and Argenteau, north of here, are not protected by the forts."

Walsh frowned and took a sip of his beer. "Why not?"

Delfosse shrugged. "No money, they said. But you see, this is not the point. The point is that the more we fortify ourselves, and the closer we get to the German border with our defences and observations and patrols, the more...*provocative* we become." He paused and blew out some smoke. "Just as we become more provocative by talking with you. Or with the French. So you see, I don't mind letting you know that our intentions are peaceful on all sides."

Walsh took a sip of his beer and considered his next statement carefully. "But if you – Belgium – expect the British to defend your neutrality, if you expect us to risk our lives for you, then shouldn't we be cooperating more?"

"*Monsieur* Walsh, you must understand our position. Neutrality is like...it is like a young woman's virginity, no?" He smiled. "Once you lose it, it cannot be restored, by any means. And your reputation changes in the eyes of others. You become...cheaper. So you cannot risk *anything* that might encourage others to take advantage of you."

"But what about helping someone who wants to protect your...'virginity' against those who might violate it?"

Delfosse blew some more smoke at him and paused while two old men passed by their table. "We cannot be sure of that," he said.

"Certainly you don't believe we would send troops into Belgium without being invited first?"

"We cannot risk *any* collaboration with *any* other nation, in matters of defence. No matter what! Otherwise we give the impression that we are not neutral, that we are not a *virgin*, and we become only another belligerent waiting to join the conflict."

Walsh shook his head. "Pardon my rudeness, Captain Delfosse, but I think *you* are being an idiot now. The Germans plan to violate your 'virginity' in the event of war, and the French are likely to do the same, even without an invitation from you. But not the British."

"You don't know that."

"Well, I will find out, my friend. And in the meantime, you need to consider whether you simply want to wait to be screwed by the Germans or the French, or both, while denying us a chance to help you quickly once they do." Walsh glared at him.

A look of anger flashed across Delfosse's face, but he said nothing for a moment. Then he leaned very close to Walsh. "So, *Monsieur* Walsh, it sounds as if you *are* more than just a simple businessman, a simple ex-soldier, taking an innocent bicycle ride in the country, no?"

"I am a businessman, and an ex-soldier. But I might be useful to you in other ways. If you would stop worrying so much about your damned reputation."

Delfosse considered that. Then he produced Walsh's business card from his coat pocket and took a closer look at it. "Are these details correct?"

"Yes, they are."

"For how long?"

"I'm here for the Exposition, in Brussels, so at least until the end of the summer. Perhaps a little longer."

Delfosse sniffed at that. "The Exposition! They can spend millions on that, yet leave Visé undefended."

"It's the same everywhere. Stupid governments, wasting money. How many Dreadnoughts do *we* need, in Britain, to fight a land war in Europe?"

"Very well. Then perhaps we can speak again sometime." Delfosse smiled and checked his wristwatch. "About our lovely countryside here. And some other matters, if time permits."

Delfosse stood up abruptly and belted his coat.

Walsh stood up as well, and extended his hand. "I would look forward to that, very much."

Delfosse shook his hand, threw a few coins on the table, and tipped his fingers to his brow in salute. *"Adeiu, Monsieur Walsh."*

Then he was gone.

After his encounter with Delfosse, Walsh decided to cut short his visits to the other border fortresses in the region; no need to push his luck and risk upsetting another Belgian officer or raise suspicions about his mission. He also decided not to visit the Nagant firm this time for the same reason. Instead, he wandered around central Liège and took in the sights around the old Citadel, which offered wonderful views of the city below and countryside beyond. He also practiced with his new camera, and captured several innocent shots of the railway bridges and the citadel, from a long distance.

After his excursion, Walsh took an early evening train back to Brussels, arriving at his flat in Ixelles around 23:00. The building was dark and quiet; no sign of the grinning concierge or his rotund wife at this time of night. Sighing with fatigue, Walsh opened his door and dropped his bag on the floor, where he saw a small envelope lying in front of him.

Inside the envelope was a short note, handwritten: "Café Mêtropole. 2.3.1910. 19:00."

Chapter 15

Sarajevo, Bosnia-Herzegovina. March 1910.

Feldzeugmeister Marijan Freiherr Varesanin von Vares of the Austro-Hungarian army looked at the calendar on the dingy wall of his office and noted the date with surprise: it had been exactly one year since he had been appointed Governor of the Austrian-Hungarian government of the Balkan provinces of Bosnia and Herzegovina.

Governor with full powers. In control of Bosnia-Herzegovina, the most unruly corner of the increasingly unstable Austro-Hungarian empire.

One year in Sarajevo, already. General Varesanin could hardly believe it. He had turned sixty-three only a month ago – where does the time go?

It had been a long journey for him, and Varesanin sensed, more and more these days, that he had reached, or soon would reach, the end of the line. The end of his long journey with the Empire. But where to go from here, after such a varied career already? Born in Gunja, a tiny village in Croatia next to the border with Bosnia-Herzegovina, and the son of an officer from the Slavonian Grenzinfantrie, he had attended the cadet institute at Fiume and then the military academy at Wiener Neustadt before entering the infantry as a lieutenant. And in 1866, no less.

Not a good year for the army of the Hapsburg Empire. The year of Austria's embarrassing defeat at the hands of the Prussians. And for the Prussians, another victory in a series of wars that led, ultimately, to the creation of Germany in 1871.

Varesanin had seen action in the north as part of the Third Army, then returned to complete his military education in Vienna at the Kriegsschule. After that his career began its steady rise, from Vienna to Lemburg, then to Agram, to Zara, and then back to Vienna, where he joined the military mapping bureau of the general staff corps. Then he left Vienna for the second time, to serve in Montenegro, then Zara again, Prague, Przemysl, Mostar, and Hermannstadt. One wretched outpost of the Austro-Hungarian Empire after another.

And now, Sarajevo.

Varesanin was a highly capable officer right from the start of his career, in a multinational, multilingual army that could draw upon martial talent from a range of traditions across central Europe. He had won prestigious decorations, such as the Montenegrin Order of Danilo, the Military Merit cross, the officer's cross of the Serbian Order of Takowo, the Prussian Order of the Red Eagle, the knight's cross of the Order of Leopold, and the grand cross of the Order of the Iron Crown. He had been authorized to instruct the young heir to the Austrian throne, Rudolf Franz Karl Joseph, in military affairs, just a few years before the sad Crown Prince, along with his mistress, had been found dead in their rooms at the imperial hunting lodge at Mayerling, a suspected suicide. General Varesanin had even been ennobled with the 'von Vares' suffix thanks to his father, the retired Hauptmann (first class) Raimund Varesanin.

Yet with all his honours and experience, Varesanin was still utterly confounded by the problems involved in governing Bosnia-Herzegovina. You might as well try governing a sack full of alley cats.

Austria-Hungary's surprise annexation of Bosnia-Herzegovina, on 6 October 1908, had provoked riots in the Balkans, and instability well beyond it. Protests in tiny Serbia, which had designs of its own on Bosnia-Herzegovina, were especially fierce. Serbian government ministers were dispatched throughout Europe to appeal for help, particularly from Serbia's fellow Slavs in Russia. But Russia had declined to commit troops, especially in light of its recent defeat by the Japanese, and Serbia was left to lick its wounds after Austria-Hungary's bold move.

Back in Belgrade, prominent Serbians – military officers, professors, politicians – met in secret to form a new organization dedicated to oppose Austria-Hungary's hegemony in the Balkans: Narodna Odbrana, or the People's Defence. This was the second new organization devoted to the cause of the Slavic peoples, following on the formation of Slovenski Jug – or Slavic South – just a few years before.

Now, seventeen months after the annexation, Varesanin was attempting to implement Austria-Hungary's latest effort to calm the Balkans: a parliamentary constitution for Bosnia-

Herzegovina. But he knew perfectly well, as did those he governed, that the constitution was a mere fig leaf. The parliament would have no real control over the administration of the two provinces, and the Austrian Emperor, Franz Joseph I, would appoint twenty out of the ninety-two members; the rest would be elected according to a very limited franchise.

Once again, protests had broken out in the region, and Varesanin realized he needed help. But what to do? He was reluctant to use force against these young people; it could easily backfire and produce even more violence than the original annexation had in 1908. Perhaps there was some other way to appease them, at least temporarily, until it was no longer his problem.

In a flash of inspiration, Varesanin had written an appeal to his aged emperor in Vienna, stating the facts as he saw them about the new constitution without directly questioning His Excellency's overall strategy, if one could call it that, in the Balkans. A delicate matter, as always, but perhaps a solution could be found. Even a temporary solution would be better than simply waiting for others to force action upon them. Varesanin cautiously suggested one.

Today, the response lay on his desk, and Varesanin opened the letter with fear in his mind but hope in his heart. He read it quickly, then the full lips under his bushy moustache broke into a rare formation for Varesanin: a broad, genuine smile. Then Varesanin slammed his hand on his desk in excitement and rang for his personal secretary. There was much to organize.

Franz Joseph I, Emperor of Austria, Apostolic King of Hungary, King of Bohemia, King of Croatia, King of Galicia and Lodomeria, and Grand Duke of Cracow, had agreed to visit Bosnia-Herzegovina between 30 May and 5 June 1910. It was hoped that the visit would help strengthen the loyalty of Franz Joseph's subjects in Bosnia-Herzegovina to the Hapsburg crown, and help to put an end to these infernal nationalist secret societies that seemed to be proliferating throughout the region.

Chapter 16

Brussels. March 1910.

Walsh sat in a corner table at the Café Mêtropole, picking at a small dish of dried meats. He had a good view of the front entrance to the street and the rear entrance into the Hotel Mêtropole itself; mirrors on every wall and pillar of the bright, high-ceilinged room improved his perspective even more. Walsh was impressed that Delfosse was able to contact him so quickly in Brussels, perhaps even before he had left Liège. The captain must have some association with Belgian military intelligence, or perhaps the Belgian Sûreté, if he is actively working on counter-espionage in the area around the frontier fortresses. Either way, obviously Walsh's comments had not discouraged the man from working with him, or at least opening a link for unofficial communications.

Walsh was just considering these possibilities when he noticed a tall man, about forty years of age, watching him from the doorway leading into the hotel. Like Captain Delfosse, he too was smartly dressed in civilian clothes. Once they made eye contact, the man wandered over to Walsh's table, looking around the room as he moved through it. On arriving, he removed his black bowler and extended his hand. His greying hair was swept back from his broad forehead, as if he had been facing a gust of wind.

"Mr Walsh?" the man said, in a hushed voice. "Nicholas Walsh?"

The voice was somewhat shaky, but there was no mistaking the language he used: an Englishman! What was this? Walsh stood and extended his palm, doing his best to keep a look of confusion off his face.

"Yes, that's right." They shook hands. "And you are?"

The man sat down, quickly, and glanced about the room. "Name's Bridges. Major Bridges. I believe you've heard of me?"

Walsh's mind raced. Bridges, Major Bridges…yes, the new British military attaché to Brussels.

"Right, Major Bridges. How do you do?"

"I'm all right, I suppose. And how are you?"

Walsh shrugged and smiled slightly. "Slightly less confused, now that I remember who you are."

"Yes, well, I'm sorry about the secret note, old boy. But Cumming told me you would be back from Liège by now. I stopped by your flat a couple of days ago and you were out, so I just slipped it under the door. Didn't want to leave my name on it in case someone found it. I hope I didn't...didn't upset any protocol you have."

"No harm done. Would you like a drink?" Walsh gestured to a waiter.

"Yes, certainly." Bridges looked up at the waiter, and loudly cleared his throat before ordering. "A whisky please, with a glass of water on the side."

Once the waiter departed, Bridges cleared his throat again, coughed into his hand, and shuffled his chair closer to the table. He smoothed his moustache a few times, crossed his hands in front of him, and uncrossed them, and then squirmed in his chair as if it didn't fit him properly. After a moment or two, Walsh realised that Bridges was waiting for his whisky before he would speak again.

Watching this display, Walsh's confidence in the SSB's prospects in Brussels weakened further.

"Been in town long, Major Bridges?"

"Just a few days now. Still finding my feet, you know."

"I am too, still, I suppose."

Bridges nodded to him. "And Cumming tells me you also have a military background? From South Africa?"

Walsh nodded back. "Yes, that's right. From the beginning of the war. I came in with the Black Watch." But didn't leave with them, he failed to mention.

"I was there as well," Bridges said. "Bloody awful, wasn't it? I commanded some of the Australian mounted towards the end of it."

The whisky arrived and Bridges was about to take a drink when he saw Walsh raise his own glass. Bridges smiled awkwardly and they clinked glasses.

"To your good health," Walsh offered.

"And yours." Bridges practically gulped the whisky down, and set the empty glass in front of him. He visibly relaxed, but only a little.

Walsh wondered where to begin. "And I suppose Cumming gave you my details?"

"Yes, that's right. Hmmm." Bridges wiped his mouth with his palm then crossed his hands in front of him again.

"Hmmm. Well, it sounds as if you have quite an interesting job here."

"I'm not so sure about that."

"Is that so?" Bridges looked around the room. "Not getting on so well then, hmmm?"

"I thought I was, Major Bridges. At first. But then I lost my relationship to the Board of Trade just after I got here. So I have no official cover, no official support from the Bureau. And it also seems that no one else in His Majesty's Government wants anything to do with me. So I struck out on my own this week, taking a look around the frontiers, where I learned that the *Belgians* also don't seem too worried about a surprise attack by the Germans. Nor do they seem all that interested in working with me. And now I'm *here*, where I thought I was going to be meeting with someone who had information to offer, and *you* show up."

Walsh took a sip from his tonic and lime. "So, Major Bridges, do you have anything to offer me? Or is this yet another damned waste of my time?"

Bridges offered a weak smile. "Yes, well. Well, that's all too bad. It certainly is. But you must understand, we – I mean, those of us at the embassies – we don't normally do this sort of thing."

"What sort of thing?"

Bridges lowered his voice. "*This* sort of thing. Deal with spies!" He practically hissed that last word.

"Is that so, major? So what the hell do you do, if I might ask?"

"We behave like gentlemen. Professionals. We meet with our local colleagues, in the open. We follow the news items in our countries. We interact with as many local authorities as we can, in politics and business and society. We report back to our government about defence-related developments, and give advice where we can. But we do *not* normally deal in secret information, bought and sold on the market like cabbages!"

Walsh leaned forward. "So why are you here? Just to tell me that?"

"Don't be daft. I promised Cumming I would meet with you once I took up my post here. So of course I know about your…situation. Your problems. I've spoken to Grierson as well. He's a good friend of mine, you know. They both seem to think very highly of you." He paused. "I also told them I would send potential sources your way, so we don't have to deal with them at the embassy."

"Yes, heaven forbid you would dare speak to someone with useful information for us, even though your counterparts in the French and German and Russian embassies do it all the time. Wouldn't want that to happen now, would we?"

Bridges frowned and crooked a finger at him. His already-ruddy cheeks were growing pinker from anger, or the whisky, or both. "Now look here, Mr Walsh. I have my instructions, just as you do. We are not supposed to treat the embassy like some kind of spy exchange. And I have my own problems, you know. Working in Belgium is very delicate. Very delicate indeed."

"Yes, I know how delicate. I heard all about that in Liège."

"No, I don't think you do. You've haven't heard it from our point of view."

"Then enlighten me, Major Bridges, if you please."

Bridges looked around the room again, then removed a pocketwatch from his waistcoat and glanced at it. "Frankly, I don't have the time just now, Mr Walsh."

Walsh shook his head, downed the rest of his tonic in a single gulp, stood up, and shrugged himself into his coat. "Perhaps some other time, then. I'll just sit in my flat and wait for you. Just slip another note under my door. And please let *me* pay for the drinks. Wouldn't want you to have to claim a spy meeting on your own expenses, you know."

Bridges stood up and held Walsh's arm. There was a firmness in his grip that Walsh respected. For the moment. "All right, then, Mr Walsh," Bridges said. "That's quite enough. I'm not here to argue. I came here to give you an invitation, you fool. Now walk me back to the embassy and I'll explain."

As they left the Métropole, Walsh asked how he had been recognized. As far as he knew, he had never met Bridges.

"I had an old photograph of you that Grierson sent me. You looked younger in it." Then Bridges affected an odd little smile.

"What is it?" said Walsh.

"He also said you would most likely be sitting in a corner table of the café. With a scowl on your face and no alcohol in front of you. And there you were."

One week later, Walsh found himself at the last place he expected to be during his time in Brussels: a reception at the personal residence of the British vice-consul in Belgium, Thomas Jeffes, on rue d'Edimbourg in Ixelles, a five-minute walk from Walsh's own flat. According to Bridges, the private reception was intended to help launch Britain's participation in the Exposition, so the reception rooms were filled with exhibitors, diplomats, military officers, businessmen, and other assorted guests from throughout Brussels and beyond. Obviously Walsh was not allowed to use his Board of Trade cover, so Bridges was pleased to know that Walsh had already arranged his own 'background' as a Glaswegian manufacturer of internal combustion engines. Vice-consul Jeffes, however, was completely unaware of Walsh's true affiliation, which was precisely how Bridges wanted it at the moment.

Bridges also kindly introduced Walsh to other guests: the heads of the Brussels offices of Vickers and Lloyd's, as well as several smaller British firms that Walsh had never heard of, plus the heads of the British and American Chambers of Commerce in Belgium. As casually as he could, Walsh raised the issue of trading with other Continental countries, such as Germany, and was surprised to learn that Lloyd's already insured much of Germany's merchant marine. The City of London was also financing around twenty per cent of Germany's import of raw materials and foodstuffs. Men from other firms reported a steady increase in their trade with Germany over the previous decade; in fact, they eagerly explained to Walsh how Germany had eclipsed France as Britain's main Continental trading partner, with no end to the growth in sight given Germany's seemingly insatiable appetite for natural resources.

After less than two hours in the room, Walsh could barely remember all the details he had heard, mostly about expanding business opportunities. This was, of course, the main point of the reception, and it certainly lived up to its billing. Walsh wished he had a more efficient way of recording all of the facts he encountered that evening, such as Germany's heavy investment in the iron ore mines of Northern France, difficulties in financing the German-dominated Baghdad Railway Company, the troubles encountered by a firm incorporated in Britain (Petroleum Wells of Germany Syndicate, Ltd) regarding its interest in the Wietze oil fields near Hanover, details of the manganese trade flowing through Trieste, the rapid success of the International Bell Telephone Company once it opened its lines to Belgium in 1903, and on and on.

Walsh's mind was still racing as he readied himself to leave in the foyer of the building, where Bridges joined him.

"Shall we take a walk?" Bridges said.

"Of course."

Outside, Bridges seemed much calmer than during their first meeting. And somewhat friendlier, on his own turf now, so to speak. Walsh also had to admit to himself that it was indeed possible to glean a great deal of information from receptions such as this one, so he had a new respect for Bridges and his work.

"Meet anyone interesting?" Bridges asked.

"Yes, in fact I did. Some very well-informed people in there. Very knowledgable, in fact." Walsh paused. "Thank you for the invitation."

"My pleasure. I'm glad you made it. So you see there are plenty of potential sources here. All willing to talk freely, more or less. And that was mostly just the Brits, mind you. Wait until you start…dealing with other nationalities. They can be tiresome, if you get my meaning, but also very useful if you pay close attention."

"Yes, I can certainly see that. But there's also a slight problem here, major."

Bridges frowned as they walked into the street. "Oh? And what is that, old boy?"

"Simple. These guests of yours, well, they all seemed more eager to sell to the Germans than to fight with them, or so I thought," Walsh said. "Which makes it highly unlikely that any of them would be willing to help my mission here."

"Well, now you know what you, what *we*, are up against."

"I suppose so."

After they turned a corner, onto Chaussée de Wavre, out of sight of Jeffes's building, Bridges put a comradely arm on Walsh's shoulder.

"Listen, Mr Walsh, we got off to a rough start," Bridges continued. "I'm sorry about that. Let me make it up to you. Can you get me a small photograph of yourself? Just the upper body, above your waist, about seven centimetres tall by six centimetres wide. Wear a nice suit for it, won't you? And no hat, mind you." Bridges nodded towards the worn wool cap on Walsh's head.

"Yes, I suppose I can do that," Walsh said, failing to mention that he was wearing the nicest suit he owned. "Why?"

Bridges smiled at him. "Just trust me, won't you? You know I don't normally work with Secret Service types, but I will try."

"Hmpf. I don't think anyone 'normally' works with us," Walsh said. "And there aren't that many of us to work with in the first place, from what I gather."

"Yes, indeed! True enough!" Bridges smiled again. "Now look here, I have a job to do, just as you do, and I face even more constraints than you."

"Such as?"

"You know how the Belgians are so nervous about protecting their image of neutrality?"

"Yes, of course."

"Well, we, those who must plan operations, that is, *we* don't have the luxury of thinking only about images. We have to make plans. Plans about how to move men and machines as quickly as possible in the event of a war."

They turned right onto Chaussée d'Ixelles, heading back towards the centre of Brussels. Crowds were thicker here and they had to weave among the passers-by.

"I mean," Bridges continued, "If we, Britain that is, if we need to defend Belgium in the event of a crisis, then we need to think about how to land troops here, correct?"

Walsh nodded.

"Well, then, where do you think that will happen, Mr Walsh? Exactly where?"

"One of the port cities of Belgium, of course. Or Calais, perhaps."

"And a *large* port, if possible, wouldn't you agree?"

"Yes, I suppose."

"Antwerp."

"That makes sense."

"Yes, but the First Treaty of Paris specifies that Antwerp is to be solely a port of commerce. A view which has been upheld in several subsequent agreements, I might add. So that's our first problem."

"But that view would change during a war, correct?" Where was Bridges going with these questions?

"Not necessarily, as Belgium reserves the right to determine whether its neutral status, and therefore that of our landing point, should change after an invasion. And you've already heard their views about that in Liège."

"Yes. More than I cared to know, in fact."

"Yes, but that's the least of our problems. Because the second problem is that access from the Channel to Antwerp is along the River Scheldt, whose banks, *both* banks, mind you, are the legal territory of the Netherlands."

Now it dawned on Walsh what Bridges was getting at, and he continued the line of reasoning. "And the Dutch, as neutrals, also reserve the right to determine if and how the Scheldt will be used during wartime."

Bridges nodded. "Yes. Of course they do! They've mentioned that view in two conventions on pilotage of the river, in 1890 and 1905. My predecessor here, Barnardiston, has confirmed this."

"Which means they could block any landing by our expeditionary force."

"Exactly." Bridges stopped walking and motioned for Walsh to stop at the intersection at Porte de Namur. Then he continued speaking.

"Obviously, we could land in France – Calais, Boulogne, Dieppe – but then we would have to use railways to get into Belgium, assuming they are not controlled already by the Germans. Or we could simply land in Antwerp or the smaller ports of Belgium and ignore what the Dutch and the Belgians think. But we hope to avoid such a scenario. So part of my job here, you see, is to…to smooth the way on this matter, if at all possible. And remember, I'm the attaché for both Belgium and the Kingdom of the Netherlands."

"And what are your prospects?"

"It's too early to tell. But I have learned, or at least strongly suspect, that this is yet another issue where the Belgians, and the Dutch, prefer to muddle through rather than formalize any commitment as to how we use Antwerp, or the Scheldt. In fact, they don't even discuss this issue between themselves, as far as I know."

"Well, I think they are being a little too naïve in how they think that this precious neutrality will save them."

"No argument there, old boy! But as long as they believe it, then we cannot make serious plans to defend them. At least, not with an expeditionary force. But I haven't mentioned problem number three." Bridges held up three fingers.

"And what's problem number three, if I dare ask?"

"Problem number three is that Britain *itself* is just as eager, if not more eager, to avoid the appearance of a firm commitment to defend this country."

"But we are pledged to do so."

"Well, not quite. Not quite. The commitment is not…it's not so automatic. The same with our entente with France and Russia, against Germany. It is merely an agreement to consult in the event of a crisis. There is no formal obligation to aid them."

"What are you telling me?"

"I'm telling you, Mr Walsh, that unless there is a drastic change in all of the facts of problems one, two, *and* three, as I've presented them, *all of them*, you and I are just wasting our damned time here."

108

Chapter 17

Brussels. March 1910.

Dewulf shifted uncomfortably in his seat across from Pieter Lokermans, Belgium's deputy justice minister – the boss of Dewulf's boss. Dewulf had no idea why he had been summoned here, but Lokermans wasted no time in getting to the point. As usual.

"Thank you for coming, inspector," said Lokermans, in a tone that sounded somewhat less than appreciative.

Lokermans was a gangly man, all arms and legs, and nearly bald, though his few remaining hairs were artfully combed across his skull in a rearguard action to protect his vanity. He wore a dark pinstriped suit, buttoned at the front, with a red satin waistcoat underneath. He always reminded Dewulf of an undertaker, though Dewulf couldn't precisely explain why.

"My pleasure, minister," Dewulf lied, but adopted the same tone. He removed his Homburg and balanced it on his bent knee. He very carefully smoothed into place his own full head of light brown hair, taking care to get…it…just…right.

"I know your time is limited, inspector, just like my own. And I expect you understand I'm not in the habit of…of personally disturbing the normal chain of command regarding the functions of the Sûreté. Unless it is absolutely necessary."

"Yes, I understand completely," Dewulf said. Another lie.

"So this discussion has no bearing on the competence of your superiors."

"Certainly, minister. So what can I do for you?"

Lokermans glanced at a file in front of him, pursed his lips, and then casually shifted a few papers on his desk before he spoke.

"I have a…a somewhat delicate matter that involves you. Or, should I say, some of your current duties."

"Is that so?" Dewulf forced himself not to frown.

"Yes." Lokermans leaned forward. "Yes. You are…preoccupied now, I understand, with preparations for the Exposition? Is that correct? For the king's protection?"

"Yes, that's correct. For everyone's protection, I would say."

"Not an easy task, I should think."

"It is a large undertaking, given the number of visitors we expect." Dewulf allowed himself to relax, just a little. "A very large undertaking, to be truthful. But there have been no specific threats against the royal family. And I'm receiving adequate cooperation from local authorities in the matter."

"I'm glad to hear that." Sure he was. "Yet we must remain vigilant."

"Of course."

Lokermans crossed his hands on his desktop, and looked Dewulf in the eyes. "Inspector, I know you have increased your surveillance of our many visitors. That is to be expected. We cannot take any chances, especially with such a...a young, and new, and popular, sovereign. And his family, of course."

Dewulf nodded, still wondering what this was all about. Though he was starting to have an idea about it.

Lokermans stood up abruptly, and walked slowly around to the front of his desk, where he rested his bony rear end on his desk. He stared down at Dewfulf, who could see the sharp crease on the minister's trousers.

"However, I'm sorry to say we've had a few complaints about these efforts," Lokermans continued.

"What complaints?"

"I can't be very specific, I'm afraid. In fact, I don't have all the details myself. I am only hearing of this through...through secondary sources. Well-informed ones. But you know the type I'm speaking of: minor foreign dignitaries, heads of industry, insignificant members of obscure royal families, that sort of thing. Some of them have been made aware of your surveillance efforts, I'm afraid, and they have complained to their embassies here. Who passed on the complaints to our foreign ministry. Who passed on this concern to me."

"And now to me."

Lokermans twisted his lips into his version of a smile. "Yes."

"With all due respect, minister, I can't very well adjust my methods unless I know who is being affected and what they specifically object to. Is it the French?"

"No, inspector." Lokermans stood again and walked behind Dewulf. "It's not the French. In fact, they are quite used to your methods. *Our* methods. After all, we all learned them from Napoleon, did we not?"

Dewulf nodded in response. Now he knew precisely what Lokermans was getting at, though – and most unlike him – in such a cautious fashion.

"So the Germans are complaining," Dewulf said.

"And the Austrians as well."

"So what am I supposed to do?"

Lokermans walked in front of Dewulf again. "Can you and your men try to be just a little more...discreet when you collect information from hotels? Not so conspicuous? And perhaps just slightly more pleasant if you need to speak directly with some of our visitors? They are *visitors* here, after all. Our guests."

"Well, some of our 'guests' are refusing to cooperate with the hotel managers. Which means they are breaking our rules. So then we must be called in to verify their information. There's no other way around that. Unless we might be allowed to read all foreign correspondence, minister?"

Lokermans glared at him. "Out of the question. We will not abandon our ideals and start reading the mail of private citizens. That is not our way." Lokermans paused. "Inspector, there is always a way. Always. Now we both know that the sort of 'visitors' who might threaten the Exposition tend to come from the lower classes of society. Ruffians and anarchists. Unwashed young men with scraggly beards and loud mouths. Would you agree?"

Dewulf nodded. "Yes, that is often the case, I suppose. But with millions of visitors we can't..."

"Inspector, please! Let us not deceive each other here!" Lokermans walked back behind his desk and leaned on it with his palms, facing Dewulf directly. "Now, I need you to cooperate with me on this matter. You and your men must show more discretion, more courtesy, when dealing with certain types of visitors here. And you know exactly the type I mean. The type who stay in *certain* hotels, who visit *certain* restaurants, and who are *not* likely to throw a bomb at King Albert!"

"Yes, of course, minister." Dewulf looked into Lokermans's eyes. "I understand completely now."

Lokermans sat down, his mission accomplished. "I'm pleased to hear that," he said. "We all need to work together to make the Exposition a great success. To make it as pleasant as possible for everyone. There's no harm in that, *n'est-ce pas?*"

"Of course not, minister." No harm until someone aims at pistol at the king.

Lockermans attempted another smile. "Excellent. That's all I need to hear." Lokermans turned his attention back to the papers on his desk. *"Bon après-midi,* inspector."

Dewulf removed the Homburg from his knee and stood to leave. "And to you, sir."

Lokermans raised his head again. "You know, inspector, the Kaiser himself is expected to attend the Exposition himself, later this year."

"Is that so?"

"Yes, of course. He wouldn't miss it. Isn't that exciting?" Lokermans continued, in the same flat tone he had adopted earlier. "Perhaps you would like to meet him, inspector?"

Dewulf gave a small nod, and left the room without a word.

Chapter 18

Brussels. March 1910.

Alone and discouraged, Walsh wandered around the Exposition construction site and tried to build up his spirits to last the remainder of his time in Brussels. He had produced nothing but dead ends so far, it seemed, and he felt there was not much interest at all on the part of the British or the Belgians in what he could learn in Brussels. So what was the point of staying for several more months?

At least there was plenty enough here to distract him, even before the formal public opening next month. Walsh had supplied Bridges with his photograph as requested, and three days later Bridges handed him his 'gift': an official Carte d'Exposant, an exhibitor's identification card, for the Exposition. It listed Walsh as part of the United Kingdom's section, and allowed him to visit the site even before it opened, and outside of normal hours when it did open to the public. The card was in Walsh's own name, however, as Bridges was not willing to provide him with a false identity that could be traced back to the British Embassy. But it was something.

Given his state of mind, Walsh decided to pursue some interests that had little if nothing to do with his official business in Brussels: engines and mechanical devices. Thanks to his new Carte d'Exposant he was able to spend a few happy hours among the automobile exhibits being set up by firms from various participating countries. The shiny new machinery on display was indeed marvellous; in fact, he had never in his life seen so many mechanical devices in one place, outside of his combat experience in South Africa. With less than a month to go until the opening, the place was a hive of activity, and no one paid any attention to Walsh as he kept out of the way and watched the staff carefully drive the automobiles into position.

So he had a close-up and privileged view of several new models that would be appearing on the market in 1910-11, many from countries that Walsh could only dream of visiting. Each one also boasted unique mechanical or design features that fired his imagination. A four-cylinder Franklin from America had an air-cooled engine, while a 12-hp Sizaire et

Naudin boasted a unique transverse spring to give its wheels more independence. Walsh also marvelled at a large Darracq C-II with its 2412cc, 15-hp powertrain. He noted that the phaeton syle was being overshadowed by the tourer and roadster styles, at least among the models on display here.

No matter what the style, however, all of the automobiles were adorned with polished brass fittings, plush leather upholstery, lustrous wooden steering wheels and dashboards, and bright glossy paintwork in various colours. These visual delights were further enhanced by the very scent of the machinery, a heady aroma composed of petrol, rubber, and leather that gradually but effectively put Walsh in much better spirits than when he arrived.

Eventually he made his way to the German section, convincing himself that perhaps he could combine business with pleasure by speaking with some of the German engineers. He was amazed to see a 1909 Benz Blitzen, the 'Lightning of Mannheim,' with its huge 200hp engine. It had been breaking speed records across Europe. Nearby, Walsh also stopped to admire the unusual curves of a Hansa C-type; the large upper body had to line up with the narrower chassis under the vehicle, under German law, so it curved inwards on each side.

As he looked on, a slight young man in grey worker's overalls was attempting to turn the steering wheel to line up the tyres of the vehicle, and seemed to be struggling with it. Walsh walked over and put his own hands on the steering wheel.

"Let me help you with that," he said, in German.

To his amazement, the voice that answered was female, also in German. "I can manage very well, thank you very much."

Walsh stepped back from her, and smiled. "My apologies, *Fräulein…?*"

The young woman kept her hands on the wheel, then looked up at him with some irritation. "Koenig. Gisela Koenig."

"Pleased to meet you. I'm Nicholas Walsh." He tipped his cap to her, and she nodded slightly in return.

"I didn't mean to offend you," Walsh continued. "My deepest apologies. Are you sure I can't offer you some assistance? It would be my pleasure."

Gisela stood up and wiped her hands on her overalls. She looked around and saw no one else in the immediate vicinity. Walsh followed her gaze with amusement. He wondered how she managed to keep her hair tucked up under her cap so neatly, while fiddling with these vehicles. Her eyes seemed exceptionally bright and blue against the dingy grey of her clothing, and the small smudge of grease on her cheek.

"Very well," she said, in excellent English. "Just help me line up the tyres, if you please." She put her hands back on the steering wheel.

"Certainly." Walsh put his hands next to hers and the two of them easily put the tyres right. "There you are. Ready to show."

"Thank you, Mr Walsh. I'm sure I can manage now." She nodded at him, then turned back to the Hansa.

"My pleasure." Walsh tipped his cap again. "Do you have any other automobiles to prepare?"

"No, thank you. Just this one for now." She offered a tight smile, then turned away again.

He took the hint. "Good day then, *Fräulein* Koenig."

"And to you too, Mr Walsh."

Walsh moved off to some other vehicles on display. On his way out, he took a moment to stop by the army/navy exhibits hosted by his fellow countrymen, in the Grande-Bretagne et Irlande section.

When he returned to his flat that evening, with tired feet and a rain-soaked cap, Walsh found another envelope waiting for him on the floor. The note inside was in Bridges' handwriting, again, and this time they met the next day at a location roughly halfway between Walsh's flat and the British Embassy, in the Quartier Léopold. A small café across from the station; just enough time for a coffee as Bridges was in a terrible hurry. He gave Walsh just the barest details: *A couple of 'walk-ins' at the embassy, offering information that 'could be useful to Britain's national defences', or so they said. Spoke German. Didn't recognize them. I can't afford to be seen with them; are you willing? Yes? Then I'll set it up...but only if you're sure. Now listen carefully...*

Three days later, Walsh found himself in the Marolles, the working-class district of Brussels, directly below the huge

Palais du Justice. He had walked past this area many times on his way into central Brussels since arriving in the city but had never ventured into it. As he wandered deeper into its warren of streets, he noted that most of the inhabitants were dressed as shabbily as any poor city-dwellers he had ever encountered. They wore layers of mis-matched clothes in a range of fabrics and colors, with holes in their gloves and stains on their trousers. He could barely understand their language; it sounded like an unhappy marriage between Dutch and French, as far as he could tell. At one point along the way he saw a small milk cart being pulled by two large shepherd dogs, both Malinois with black masks and tan coats. One of the animals growled at Walsh as he passed by, prompting a tug on the dog's leash by the owner of the cart. But no smile of apology.

The meeting was set for the Place du Jeu de Balle, in front of the fire brigade station on rue Blaes. The Place du Jeu de Balle was a busy 'brocante', or second-hand market, every morning but by the afternoon the crowds had disappeared. Walsh could easily see his two contacts lurking near the entrance to the fire station, each carrying a map of Belgium – spelled 'Belgien' - as they were instructed. They were much younger than he expected, dressed in shoddy clothing, and as he moved closer to them Walsh could see that they were very young men indeed, just out of school perhaps.

He moved close to them and felt slightly ridiculous when he feigned to notice their German-language maps and asked them the time in their own language, as Bridges had instructed.

"I think my watched has stopped," Walsh explained, holding up his pocketwatch.

"I'm sorry, I left mine at the hotel," said the shorter one.

"And I don't carry one," said the taller one.

"Then perhaps someone inside the church can help me," Walsh said, and then moved in closer to them. So this was it. Two kids! Another waste of time?

"You are Mr Walsh?" said the taller one.

"Yes, that's right. And you are?"

"Stern, Tobias Stern."

"Good to meet you." Walsh extended his hand and Tobias shook it with a slight look of surprise, even embarrassment, on his face.

"I'm Ernst Hesse," said the shorter one, and then he too shook Walsh's hand, smiling with relief. His forehead was damp despite the cold March air.

"Good to meet you. Shall we have a coffee somewhere?"

"*Ja, bitter.*"

In awkward silence, they sat at the back of a small café just off the Place, waiting for their drinks. The walls were covered in an unusual assortment of posters, probably to hide the cracks in the plaster: railway destinations, farm equipment, ocean liners, beer and liquor brands. At least they had something to look at, other than each other, for a few moments.

After they had been served, finally, the taller one – Tobias – leaned forward to speak. He wore small rimless glasses and a full beard of black hair, although it was trimmed very neatly.

"You are a friend of Mr Bridges?" Tobias said.

"An...acquaintance, from Britain. With similar professional interests, I suppose you could say." Walsh avoided the term 'colleague'; he didn't want these two to think that he worked at the embassy. Or that he worked for Bridges.

"And has he told you why we are here?"

Walsh sipped his coffee. Delicious, as usual. "Only that you have something that might be useful to us. And I'll be the judge of whether it is useful, not Bridges."

Tobias and Ernst exchanged a look.

"Can we trust you, Mr Walsh?" asked Ernst, who then cracked three of his knuckles in quick succession. Tobias glared at him but said nothing.

Ernst was a head shorter than Tobias, but probably outweighed his companion by at least a stone. He had sharp eyes and a round, almost boyish, face speckled with a few acne scars. He also seemed to be trying to grow a moustache. But it didn't suit him. At least, not yet.

"This...this opportunity is very important to us," Ernst continued.

"Yes, you can trust me," Walsh said. "Otherwise Bridges would not have given you my name, correct?"

"I suppose not, Mr Walsh," said Ernst.

He exchanged another look with Tobias, who seemed to be ready to talk.

Walsh nodded at them and leaned in closer. The room was nearly empty at three in the afternoon, and the proprietor had his large red nose in a newspaper behind the counter, but Walsh was taking no chances.

"Now, gentlemen," he began. "What brings you to Brussels?"

They exchanged another look, then Tobias said, in a very small voice, "What do you know about propellants?"

"Not much, other than that they are useful in warfare."

"Do you know anything about cordite, in particular?"

Walsh shrugged slightly, and kept his face blank. "I've heard of it."

"It is used in Britain's heavy artillery pieces, such as the guns on your Dreadnought battleships, among others." Tobias sipped his coffee. "It does not burn as hot as other modern propellants so it is safer on the gun barrels."

"And so?"

Ernst spoke up. "And so, Mr Walsh, cordite is made according to a very specific formula: 64 parts nitrocellulose, 30.2 parts nitroglycerin, 5 parts petroleum jelly, and 0.8 percent acetone. The acetone is absolutely critical despite its tiny proportion in the formula. It makes the cordite pliable for safely moulding it into the correct shapes and sizes for various guns. Cordite cannot be manufactured without it."

"Very interesting. And why should that concern me?"

"Because acetone is *very* difficult to make, and therefore in *very* short supply," Tobias said, a little too pleased with himself. "According to currently known methods, that is."

"So how is it made?"

"Normally through the dry distillation of wood," said Ernst. "Also known as pyrolysis. But this method is very time-consuming, and so expensive. And it would not be very practical during, say, a national emergency, when you might need thousands of tons of acetone."

"And I suppose you have a more effective method?" Walsh kept his voice steady and tried not to appear too eager; could these two really have something useful for him?

"Most effective, Mr Walsh, *most* effective," Ernst continued, with a proud look on his face. "In fact, my method does not rely upon distillation at all – ow!"

Tobias had cut him off with a sharp nudge, and Ernst shut his mouth.

"And you are prepared to share this new method with us?" Walsh asked.

"For a price," said Tobias.

"And what is the price?"

Tobias and Ernst exchanged another glance, and leaned in close to Walsh.

"The amount we require for our secret," Tobias practically whispered to him, before glancing around the room again, "is firm. We believe our information is worth no less than...than two-hundred and fifty thousand Belgian francs. Or in your own currency, about..."

Sinking back into his chair, Walsh finished the sentence for him. "Ten thousand pounds."

PART TWO

Chapter 19

Leon Franck, assistant general manager of the new Hôtel Astoria in Brussels, rubbed his temples and resisted the urge to request a large glass of Moortgat's beer from the opulent and well-stocked bar of his hotel. His desk was covered with paperwork related to the steady stream of new guests checking in to his two-hundred room establishment. The splendid building on rue Royale with its Louis XVI façade had been constructed at the request of King Leopold II himself, in anticipation of the Exposition.

Franck was extremely proud of the final result, yet he was feeling the strain of the job even before the Exposition had opened. Too many foreign guests with too many strange demands, that was was the problem. Invading his precious Astoria from all corners of Europe and beyond, it seemed, and from places that sounded utterly alien to him: Brazil, Guatemala, Nicaragua, on and on and on. They complained about his food, his service times, the layouts of the rooms, the quality of the bedding, the plumbing, the noise of the city, the damp and chilly weather, on and on and on. As if Franck and his dedicated but increasingly careworn staff could control every aspect of their stay in the Astoria.

The European guests could be equally, if not more, difficult, especially those from countries with antagonistic relationships against their neighbours. Just last night a fight had nearly broken out in the bar between a Russian businessman and an Austrian army officer over some silly little misunderstanding. In Franck's own hotel! A few days before, some Germans had insisted on switching rooms once they learned that their French competitors had secured more luxurious accommodation. Two weeks earlier, a guest claiming to be a baron from Moravia had insisted that a bottle of fresh goat's milk be delivered to his door every morning. One demand after another, and the Expo had not even opened yet. How was Franck going to cope with helping foreign guests during an international event that lasted for more than six months?

Forcing these thoughts from his mind, Franck shuffled the papers across his desk and wondered whether to leave some of his tasks for the next morning, when he might be in a better frame of mind. More strange guests, more administrative tasks. Especially this new special police directive to report the names and nationalities of all foreign guests. Did he really need that headache as well? Perhaps he would check just a few more names on the list, and then he would find some dinner and, finally, a drink. Or two.

Franck looked at his paperwork for the hundredth time today, or so it seemed, and checked the next name, pausing to think if he met the man on his arrival. Ah yes, he remembered, it was some strange doctor from Germany, travelling alone. A quiet man, very well-dressed and polite, for a German. But best of all, no special requests from him so far, thank heaven.

Five floors above the hapless Mr Franck, 'Doctor' Retzlaff reclined happily on his comfortable bed and considered his next steps. He certainly had no complaints about the accommodations at the Astoria. The trip from Bern had been long and tiring but quite uneventful. The papers Retzlaff had prepared before his departure from Leipzig had worked as well as he had expected, allowing him to move across the borders of several countries on his way to Brussels with his physician's bag intact. Inside the bag, among other things, was a small glass bottle of chloroform and a pair of Tower's Double Lock adjustable handcuffs, made by Union Hardware in America. He expected that young Ernst would have smaller wrists than the average man, so the more traditional Darby-type handcuffs, with their fixed size, might not be effective on him. Better to be prepared for this possibility, and so Retzlaff was.

Retzlaff hoped he would not have to use the items in his bag, but Herr Hesse had effectively given him permission to bring his son back home by any means necessary, even against his will. Perhaps the boy could be persuaded to return without resorting to force, but Retzlaff would be ready either way.

At least Herr Hesse was not concerned about what happened to Tobias. Not concerned at all. He was most adamant about that.

Chapter 20

London. March 1910.

Cumming was ready for Walsh's telephone call thanks to the telegram Walsh had sent earlier from Brussels. The message sent to the Sunbonnet-London address was cryptic, so Cumming had no idea what to expect from this conversation. There was some static on the line, but Cumming could hear Walsh easily enough if he concentrated.

"Look here, C, I've been offered some information that might be useful to us," Walsh was saying.

"Hold on, my boy, hold on." Cumming's voice was tense. "Where are you now?"

"I'm calling from the embassy here. Bridges let me use his telephone for this."

Bridges allowed Walsh into the embassy? To use his personal telephone? This must be important.

"All right, then. Go ahead," said Cumming. "Is this about the Zeppelins?"

"No, C, I'm still working on that. It's something else; came in unexpectedly. It's about the production of cordite, which requires acetone."

"Yes, Walsh, what about it?"

"Well, these two lads I've met here, they have a new method of making acetone. Or so they claim. Supposed to be cheaper and much more efficient than the methods we use."

"And what is the method?"

"They won't say just now. But their secret is for sale, apparently."

"For how much?"

Walsh paused. "Well, that's the tricky bit, C. They said they want the equivalent of ten thousand pounds."

Cumming paused. "Walsh, did you just say *ten thousand* pounds?"

"Yes, that's correct."

Cumming sighed loudly enough for Walsh to hear it. "Well, they can't be serious."

"I think they are. And so does Bridges."

"Well, who are they, anyhow?"

"A couple of Germans," Walsh said. "University students, it seems. Kind of an odd pair, not the sort who would normally be mixed up in this sort of business. If you understand my meaning."

"Walsh, did you just say a couple of *Germans*?"

"Yes, that's right."

"And how did you find them?"

"They just turned up at the embassy here. Our embassy. The guards turned them over to Bridges, who turned them over to me."

Cumming sighed again. "Walsh, assuming this is a legitimate offer, which it may not be, you realise, we can't possibly pay that kind of money for some chemical formula. Ten thousand pounds? Good Lord, Walsh, that's more than my entire yearly budget!"

"But, C, if this formula can save us hundreds of thousands of pounds, or even more, during a war, then this could be a bargain. Can't you at least look into it?"

"How so?"

"Ask around the Admiralty about how much this secret could be worth."

"Yes, I suppose I could do that."

"There's no harm in that, is there? And try to find out if there could be competing buyers for this kind of information."

"Like who?"

"Who else uses cordite? The French? The Russians?"

Cumming realized he hadn't the foggiest idea of such matters. "Yes, Walsh, I'll ask about it. But I still cannot believe we would pay that kind of money for such a secret. Especially during peacetime."

"Yes, well, just think how much more expensive it could be during wartime. When such knowledge could help us win a war."

The lad had a point there, Cumming realised. "Fair enough."

"Hopefully we are the only buyers for this kind of information. So then I might be able to bargain them down a little."

Cumming tried not to laugh. "More than a little, Walsh. Seriously, my boy, I simply don't have the authority, on my own, to spend this kind of money. At least, not for this kind of thing. We are still mainly interested in…"

Walsh cut him off. "In a surprise attack, yes, I know. But there is no evidence of that so far, C. None whatsoever.

Believe me, I've tried to find it. And the Belgians don't seem to be too worried about that either. Besides, you are forgetting something else about the acetone offer."

"Which is?"

"If these lads have some sort of connection to a German arms or chemical firm, or develop such a connection, and we make a deal with them *now*, then we have a potential intelligence source in their war industry. We already know they are willing to sell us this secret, so what else might they come up with, in time? Even if we have to...to put pressure on them, somehow, to cooperate, they might lead us to other sources, to find more information about German war plans and weapons. Don't you see?"

Cumming was stunned into silence. Perhaps Walsh really was onto something here, finally.

"Yes, of course. Of course. But you must also keep in mind that this could be a trap for us. To draw us out in Brussels." He paused. "To draw you out."

"I really don't think so, C. Not these two. Steinhauer can't be behind this."

"Then they came up with this plot on their own? Entirely? Finding a new method to make acetone, and then travelling to *Brussels*, to sell it to *us*?"

"The Exposition is about to start, you know. The town is full of buyers and sellers. All kinds of products and services."

Of course, the Exposition! Cumming hadn't seen that angle either. "Well, just be careful in dealing with these men."

"Yes, of course. I've got to go now, C. Bridges is getting jumpy outside. Now when can you get back to me?"

Chapter 21

Paris. March 1910.

General Charles Regnault, assistant chief of the French general staff, looked up from the short report in front of him and across his wide, cluttered desk to the author of the report, Commandant Marchand. Regnault was not frowning, for once, so Marchand took this as a good sign.

"Are you confident in these figures, Marchand?" said Regnault. His tone was even.

"Of course, they are only estimates, sir, based on the most recent intelligence from Lt. Colonel Pellé in Germany..."

"And Pellé's source is the Russian military attaché in Berlin?"

Marchand nodded. "Colonel Mikhelson."

Regnault sat back in his leather chair and lit a cigar. He inhaled deeply and blew the smoke up towards the high ceiling of his office. He ran one hand through his hair, and held the back of his neck with his cigar-free hand as he leaned further back in his chair. Some of his uniform buttons were unfastened and Marchand was pleased that his request to meet the general at the end of the day, at the end of the week, seemed to have been a wise idea. Relaxed and reflective, that's how Marchand wanted to encounter the general.

Marchand sat patiently, knowing exactly what was going through Regnault's mind. He decided to force the question rather than wait for it.

"I know there is room for...alternative interpretations, sir," Marchand said. "This information could be a feint of some sort, to draw us away from Lorraine. Or perhaps the Germans will not make such use of their reserves. Or perhaps they will in fact lack the officers to command reserves on the front lines."

"Life is full of uncertainty, isn't it, Marchand?" said Regnault, tapping some ash into a silver tray on his desk. "All part of the game."

"Yes, sir, I suppose it is."

"Well, it's time to place your bet today, commandant." Regnault actually smiled at Marchand. "The roulette wheel is about to stop turning."

Marchand drew in his breath. His next words could be fatal to his career, so he had to choose them carefully.

"Based on the information we have at the moment," he began, "and the details of the most recent German war plans and war games involving our frontiers, I think we need to reconsider Plan Sixteen. Seriously reconsider it, sir. I think the Germans will send the bulk of their forces through Belgium, and I think we will not be able to hold them off up there if we stay with the current plan. I think they aim to take Paris as quickly as possible, by going through Belgium, and will try to force a defeat upon us that would allow them to concentrate on the Russian front. And so I think we need to shift our entire deployment more towards the north."

"And even abandon the Lorraine offensive?"

Marchand paused for a moment. This was it! "Yes, sir."

"Mixed divisions in German offensives. Mixed divisions, Marchand!" Regnault shook his head. "And here we are, the grand French *Republique*, and we cannot do what the crusty old German monarchy can do: create a truly republican army, where citizen soldiers march into battle alongside the professionals. And not just another *lévee en masse*, that is! Do you really believe the *Boche* are going to take that path?"

"It's what all the evidence tells me, general. And it also seems to be the logical choice, if the *Boche* hope to knock us out of it before the Russians can mobilize. The Russians are their main priority, not us."

Regnault stared at him for a few moments, blowing more smoke into the air.

"And they are not so concerned about violating Belgian neutrality? And possibly bringing the British into the war?"

Marchand shook his head. "Not enough to risk defeat at the hands of the combined forces of the French and the Russians. I think they expect it to be over before the British can do anything about it."

"A *fait accompli*, as it were, to re-draw the map of Europe on their terms quickly and decisively enough to prevent anyone else from restoring the old order."

"*Oui, c'est exact.*"

Regnault closed his eyes and rubbed the bridge of his nose. "France and Russia as allies. Our glorious republic tied with a…a despotic monarchy. A tyranny! I tell you, Marchand, I never would've believed it when I first joined the army. Even when I first heard about the *Uhlan* guns at Metz, as a boy, I never dreamed we would be looking to Russia for help one day."

Marchand nodded. "Napoleon must be spinning in his grave. But times change, sir. We can't stop that, can we?"

Regnault opened his eyes and looked out the window, at the grey sky over Paris. At least the rains had stopped.

"Indeed. Indeed. And more changes mean more questions. Will Belgium be invaded? Will the Italians join in? Will the British? And can we even rely on the Russians?" Regnault turned back to face Marchand. "You, know, the Russians have an old saying, Marchand. Some Russians, anyway. 'It is better to have a whore for a daughter than a soldier for a son'. Or something like that. And here we are talking about them having to fight another war, and so soon after their defeat by the Japanese. A major war, between Russia and Germany. With us drawn into it, on the Russian side."

Marchand nodded, but said nothing.

"Interesting analysis, Marchand. Most interesting." Regnault paused again, looking down at Marchand's report. More cigar smoke puffed into the air. Then another smile, as Regnault looked up and met Marchand's eyes. "Well, guess what, commandant. I happen to agree with you."

Marchand let himself breathe again. "I'm very pleased to hear that, sir."

"Don't break out the champagne just yet, Marchand. Because there are some unpleasant truths that prevent us, prevent me, from making such a change just now."

"Such as?"

"I can't go into details about it, young man. But trust me, there are difficult obstacles in place."

Marchand suspected as much: politics. "So where does that leave us?"

"You continue to do your job: find more evidence of German plans to support this point of view about their Belgian offensive. And I will do my job, and try to pave the way so that this evidence, if you find it, will be interpreted appropriately by the general staff."

Chapter 22

Brussels. March 1910.

Walsh had some time to kill before his second meeting with Tobias and Ernst, so he made his way out to the Exposition site again. It was much quieter now on this Sunday morning compared to Walsh's earlier visit, but still busy with activity. Work on the massive spectacle was almost complete and Walsh decided to take a new route through the site to help improve his bearings. He walked towards the right upon entering, rather than straight ahead, then headed past one of the Belgian pavilions and another of the French pavilions - there were several each of these - and out to the huge German section at the rear of the Exposition. Here he noted the extensive, well-organised displays of railroad locomotives and signalling equipment, and gradually made his way towards the left side of the complex, where the German automobile section could be found.

There was no one to speak to at the Hansa automobile section, so Walsh chose to inspect some of the other German models and, hopefully, meet with some representatives of the firms on display. He chatted briefly with a mechanic working on a Mercedes Knight, a model he had never seen before. The mechanic, a cheerful man in his fifties with as much grease on his hair as on his rough hands, was very happy to talk after hearing about Walsh's time in Stuttgart. As Walsh leaned in closer to inspect the engine, the mechanic began explaining the workings of the Knight's unusual sleeve-valve mechanism. Walsh had never seen an engine of this type before, and he listened with interest.

After a few minutes, Walsh became aware of a young woman standing nearby, also listening carefully. He took a closer look and recognized the blue eyes: Gisela. Today she was outfitted in an elegant tailored suit, in lightweight wool, with a trim skirt hemmed just above the ankle. Quite an improvement on the grey overalls, Walsh thought. She pretended to be focusing on something else, but spoke up once she knew Walsh had seen her.

"That model will use too much oil," she said, with a slight wave of her hand.

"Ah, but the advantage is much greater distance between servicing," the mechanic said.

"And it runs quieter," Walsh added, with a wink at the mechanic. He had been paying attention.

"Hpmf. Who cares about noise when you are already outside, among the streetcars and carriages and people?" Gisela said.

Walsh stood up and looked her over again. Very carefully this time. He was impressed. He smiled. "Shouldn't you be in church, *Fraülein?*"

The mechanic smiled to himself, then covered his mouth. Walsh continued to smile at Gisela. His gaze was steady.

She looked him in the eye, and waved a hand around in the air. "*This* is my church, Mr Walsh."

After Walsh apologised, more or less, about the church remark, he and Gisela spent a very pleasant hour admiring, and occasionally ridiculing, some of the models they saw on display before Walsh had to leave for his meeting. He learned that Gisela was the daughter of one of the engineers for the Hansa firm of Bremen. Her parents had not been blessed with sons so Gisela, as the eldest daughter, had attempted to fill that void by taking an interest in her father's work at a young age. To her surprise, and her father's as well, she seemed to have a talent for it. And so he asked her to help out with the Hansa exhibit at Brussels. But today was her day off, and she had no intention of spending it in church.

At the French automobile section, Walsh and Gisela admired one of the handsome Delages on display. Next to it was a large Rochet-Schneider, with its double-phaeton body, built in Lyon. Walsh remembered something about the firm's link with the Schneider armaments firm but could not ask the representative about that while Gisela was with him.

A moment later they stood together next to something neither had seen before, a prototype Le Zèbre model, built in Puteaux. It was very small, with a five-HP, one-cylinder engine. To Walsh it looked cheap and badly made compared to the larger models on display.

"I've heard about these," Gisela said. "They're supposed to be for the common man. For workingmen."

Walsh took a closer look at the vehicle, with its thin sheet-metal bodywork and modest brass fittings. "Workingmen could afford this?"

"Yes, if they use mass production."

Walsh shook his head. "I don't think that would sell. People will always want to choose their own fittings and materials. They like automobiles to be custom-made for them. When you spend that much money, you want to have some choice. How is that going to change?"

Gisela pointed to a much larger Renault on display nearby. "Renault is already mass-producing its engines, Mr Walsh. So if Le Zèbre does the same with the engine *and* the chassis and body and other fittings, the cost will come down. More people can afford them."

"Mass-produced engines? Gisela, engines are complex. They require craftsmanship. Craftsmanship and passion and time. If Renault is mass-producing them then they are going to have a lot of unhappy customers. Customers broken down by the side of the road. And besides, this is much too small to be used as a family automobile. Workingmen won't like that."

Gisela folded her arms and looked at him. "Have you been to the American exhibits? They have a Model T there. It has a four-cylinder engine and can take a family. It's also being mass-produced."

"Well, let's go take a look at it," Walsh said. He checked his pocketwatch. "I have a little more time to spare."

As they walked away from the French section, Gisela said, "Workingmen should be able to afford the things they make, wouldn't you agree?"

"Well, it depends on what they make, doesn't it? Suppose they are building ships? Or trains?"

"You know what I mean," she said.

Of course he did. Odd, though, that he felt compelled to argue with her, even though he knew perfectly well that she was correct.

Walsh left Gisela at the Exposition after lunch. He had arranged to meet with Tobias and Ernst a week after their first encounter at the Place du Jeu de Balle. This time they met in Walsh's own neighbourhood, at a small café on Place Fernand

Cocq. Walsh expected the meeting to be a short one, so he was reluctant to venture far beyond Ixelles to deliver a simple message to the two young men. Nor was there any sense in lingering over a meal in a restaurant, especially if he – that is to say, the Bureau - was expected to pay for it.

The meeting was set for 14:30, when the lunch business had thinned out and the late afternoon/early evening drinkers had yet to arrive. The place was almost completely empty, except for a tired waitress and two nearly catatonic old men slumped over a table near the bar. Walsh could smell the mud on their boots.

He had arrived at 14:15 and it was now 14:40, with no sign of Tobias and Ernst. He downed the last of his small coffee and was just about to consider leaving when he saw their faces through the window.

Harried and nervous, they slipped into the café, glanced around the small room, and settled into two seats across from Walsh.

"You're late," he said.

"It could not be helped," said Tobias. "We had to make sure we were not followed."

Ernst said, at the same time, "We got lost."

They glanced at each other in embarrassment and Walsh smiled at their unease.

"Fair enough. This won't take long." Walsh leaned in close and spoke quietly. "The good news is that my colleagues in London are interested in what you have to offer."

"And the bad news?" said Tobias.

"Well, the bad news is that they think your price is a little high. Very high, in fact."

Ernst glanced at Tobias, who said, "Is that so? *We* actually think the price is quite fair, fair indeed, considering how useful this information could be to your war effort."

"Well, we are not at war, so perhaps your asking price is a little…inflated." Walsh checked his pocketwatch.

Ernst spoke up. "Mr Walsh, you must understand that this information, this process, is very difficult to develop. It could take years of effort for you to discover this secret, even with a concerted effort during wartime. And if you are not fortunate, you might not discover it at all, when you need it most."

"How can I be sure that what you have will be useful to us? In fact, let me say that another way, gentlemen. Who the devil are you, really, and how did you come by this fantastic secret, hmmm? Why are you so special? And who are you working for? I need some answers to these questions, right now, and if you expect us to pay thousands of pounds for a piece of technical information, then I need to know exactly what I'm getting before we proceed much further."

Walsh whispered these last words, but the urgency in his voice was clear, as he stabbed his index finger on the tabletop to punctuate his queries.

"It's none of your business who we are," Tobias began, before Ernst cut him off.

"We are simple students, Mr Walsh. That's all. We work for ourselves, not for the government. And I discovered this secret through my experimental work at my university, while researching for my doctorate. It's as simple as that."

"So you didn't steal it from anyone? Another 'student,' perhaps, or one of your professors?"

Ernst looked shocked. "Certainly not!"

"And you simply knew it would be useful for British cordite production?"

"Not immediately, no. In fact, this process has uses well beyond cordite. It produces not just acetone but ethanol and butanol as well. All very useful byproducts of my work. So it might be helpful for fuel production and other industrial purposes. Who knows what the future may bring? But once I made the discovery I did some research into the potential markets for this secret, and the question of cordite…presented itself."

"And why not sell this secret in Germany? To your own firms, or government?"

Tobias answered him. "Because Germany does not use cordite."

Walsh had suspected as much. "So no one else knows about this method at the moment?"

"I alone know the secret," Ernst said, with a hint of pride in his voice.

Walsh registered that fact. "So then we, the British, are your only potential buyers?"

Tobias smiled for the first time, but without humour. "Not quite, Mr Walsh. Not quite. There are many armies and navies, even among your own allies, that might become interested in cordite if they had a more efficient way to produce acetone. And that is precisely what we are offering. In fact, many of their representatives will be attending the Exposition here, as I'm sure you know. We intend to speak with some of them when it officially opens next month. Unless you are prepared to make a deal right now with us?"

Walsh considered Tobias's arguments for a moment while Ernst squirmed in his chair; it was no use pushing this point until he had heard from Cumming.

"That remains to be seen, gentlemen," Walsh said. "But how can you prove to me that your process works? And that we can duplicate it in Great Britain?"

Tobias and Ernst exchanged another glance, then leaned in close together and spoke in German. Walsh could not make out what they were saying.

"It should be simple enough to demonstrate, with some basic laboratory equipment," said Ernst. "But only after we see the money."

"Yes, the money. The money." Walsh leaned back again. "As I said, my colleagues are not likely to pay that price."

"With all the resources of the British Empire at your disposal?" Tobias shook his head. "You can build an entire fleet of modern Dreadnoughts and yet you cannot afford ten thousand pounds to help fill their guns with cordite? I find that hard to believe, Mr Walsh. Very hard to believe. And suppose we find other bidders? What then? Ten thousand pounds might turn out to be a bargain for you then."

"Gentlemen, unless a war breaks out in the next few weeks, if you can find someone to pay ten thousand pounds for your secret, then you will have my *heartiest* congratulations."

Walsh stood up. Ernie suddenly reached out and grabbed his arm.

"Wait, Mr Walsh," he said.

Walsh paused a moment and looked at him. So did Tobias, with a frown.

"Tell your colleagues in London that we are prepared to demonstrate our process at any moment, here in Brussels," Ernst said. "We will start making the arrangements. You can bring a technical expert with you, a chemist, to verify that what we say is true. It's not a problem."

Walsh looked outside the window. The sky was beginning to darken as the afternoon sun slipped towards the horizon.

"Sounds reasonable," Walsh said. "I'll pass your offer to my colleagues. But remember, gentlemen, I'm just a messenger here. This is not my money we're talking about; it's the British government's. And I'm sure you can appreciate how complicated it is to get any government to pay for anything. No matter how important it is." Walsh offered a small smile. "But I'll do my best."

Tobias and Ernst stood up as well. As Tobias shrugged on his coat, Ernst loudly cracked two of his knuckles. Tobias cringed at the sound and shook his head.

Ernst suddenly came to Walsh's side of the table and extended his hand. Walsh shook it, then deftly pocketed the small slip of paper that Ernst slipped to him. Their eyes met too quickly for Tobias to notice.

"You know where to reach us," said Tobias. Then he turned to Ernst. "*Gehen wir*, Ernie."

After they left, Walsh sat down again, reached into his trouser pocket, and retrieved the paper Ernst had passed to him. Scribbled on it was a short message, noting a place and time for a meeting next Sunday. A meeting without Tobias.

Chapter 23

Sarajevo. March 1910.

In preparation for the visit of Emperor Franz Joseph to Bosnia-Herzegovina, General Varesanin created a special task force to ensure the security of the royal party. One segment of the group focused on the details of the visit within Bosnia-Herzegovina; the other consolidated reports of threats and plots that might involve the visit gleaned from Austria-Hungary's vast network of embassies, consulates, and other sources throughout its European empire.

In addition to the anti-Austrian views of Slovenski Jug and Narodna Odbrana, of which they were well aware, the general's security team also attempted to monitor their organizational routines and recruitment tactics. Narodna Odbrana, based in Belgrade, was a potential threat; its president was a serving general in the Serbian army, and its methods involved not just propaganda but training for sabotage and guerrilla warfare as well. It developed links with shooting clubs, created a special training camp for young komitádjis, or guerrilla fighters, and built an extensive network of committees and informants throughout Serbia. This network also established an underground route into Bosnia, to shift weapons, funds, and personnel secretly between the two countries, across the river Drina. This smuggling was not terribly difficult, as the river could be forded easily when the tide was low; the darkness of night and the presence of mist on the river provided very effective cover for these excursions.

Funds to support Narodna Odbrana, and similar groups, were coming into the Balkans from throughout Europe and helped to keep the movement strong. Funds were distributed for training, for weapons, for communicating their message, for a thousand and one reasons. And the Narodna Odbrana network seemed to have an endless appetite for money. Try as they might, and indeed they tried, the Austro-Hungarian authorities outside of Serbia could not control the movements of this cash, which arrived in countless denominations and in a wide variety of containers: from expensive suitcases and valises to railway carriages, automobiles, and ox carts.

Fortunately for Varesanin, however, there seemed to be no local counterparts in Sarajevo to these well-funded anti-Austrian groups, or at least as far as he could tell. His governorship in fact benefitted greatly from the various ethnic-religious factions located within the provinces of Bosnia and Herzegovina: Bosnian Muslims, Catholic Croats, and Orthodox Serbs, among others. These factions seemed far too concerned with animosities amongst themselves to organize their people into an effective opposition force against their status as subjects of the Hapsburg dynasty. Border patrols on the Bosnian side of the river, authorised by Varesanin, also could detect no significant opposition forces massed on the Serbian side, or any smuggling networks that would indicate cooperation between anti-Austrian groups on both sides of the river.

Or so Varesanin's men thought. And so they were confident about the security they could provide for the royal visit.

As the date of the visit grew closer, and as the preparations grew more complicated, Varesanin found himself investing more of his emotional energy in his need for this event to go as smoothly as possible. He recalled his happy memories of teaching the Emperor's son Rudolf before the young man was found dead at Mayerling, a death that shocked the empire. He thought of the many other tragedies poor Emperor Franz Joseph had suffered before and after the death of his son. An assassination attempt, by a Hungarian nationalist armed with a knife, against the emperor himself during his early years, aged only twenty-two, in 1853. The sudden death of his precious first daughter, Sophie, at the tender age of two in 1857. The execution of his younger brother, Emperor Ferdinand Maximilian I of Mexico, in 1867, which caused the emotional collapse of Maximilian's Belgian-born wife Charlotte, the only daughter of King Leopold I. Rudolf's alleged suicide in 1889.

And then, most terrible of all, the assassination, by a stab wound, of his own wife, Empress Elisabeth of Bavaria, by an Italian anarchist in 1898 while the beloved 'Sisi' was on holiday in Geneva. The tragedies did not end there; even his nephew and heir to the throne, Archduke Franz Ferdinand, had suffered the birth of a stillborn son just two years ago, which added more grief to the Hapsburg royal family.

Varesanin greatly hoped that the Emperor's successful visit to Bosnia-Herzegovina would help to take his family's mind off of this most recent tragedy and ease Franz Ferdinand's worries about assuming the throne of the Hapsburg Empire once Emperor Franz Joseph passed from the earth. Varesanin would do everything within his power to make that possible.

Chapter 24

Brussels. March 1910.

Walsh spent most of his afternoon wandering around the Exposition, again, taking in the new sights as they were completed. He tried to convince himself that he was just killing time before his meeting with Ernst, but he knew perfectly well that he was hoping to run into Gisela. In the end, he had no such luck.

After nearly four hours on his feet, shuttling between the automobile exhibits and various other attractions around the Exposition, Walsh finally gave up and returned to the centre of Brussels in a foul mood. A hard rain began to fall as he made his way across the inner ring of the city, and his cap and topcoat were soaked through by the time he staggered into a small brasserie on a corner of the Place du Grand Sablon, hoping the rain outside would subside before his meeting with Ernst.

Walsh wolfed down a plate of steak and frites, followed by a second helping of frites slathered with mayonaisse and then a slab of Belgian chocolate cake. The meat was overcooked but everything else was excellent, though the meal did little to improve his temper. Walsh finished by 19:45, and motioned to the waiter for his bill. It was nearly dark now and he could just detect the outline of the high Gothic church at the top of the hill, firmly anchored in its commanding position over the Sablon. A few dim figures hurried around in the shadows cast by the church on the wet pavement, but the streets were mostly deserted thanks to the incessant storms throughout the day.

After downing the last of his coffee, Walsh stood and drew his topcoat around his shoulders, threw a few francs on the table, and plodded his way up the hill. The main entrance to the church was closed and Walsh waited there a few moments before wandering down the length of the structure on rue de la Régence. No doors were open and the place seemed to be closed for the night. It was nearly 20:00 by this time, the hour of his meeting with Ernst. Walsh assumed that the lad would simply meet him outside the church, so he walked back to the main entrance and lingered across the street from it. It was impossible to look casual now, standing outside in the pouring rain, so Walsh ducked into a café to observe the scene.

The place was empty except for the owner, who sat wearing a dirty apron at a table set against one of the long walls of the room. Still standing in the doorway, Walsh nodded at him, and the man nodded back before offering to serve him. He said this half-heartedly, and did not bother to get up.

Walsh replied that he was just waiting for the rain to let up.

The owner gave him an amused look, as both of them knew perfectly well that the rain was likely to continue pouring down throughout the evening. The owner returned to his paper, just as he muttered that he was closing up for the night in a few minutes. He rubbed his impressive sideburns with one hand as his other scratched a pencil stub on the newspage in front of him. Rub and scratch, scratch and rub.

Walsh checked his pocketwatch yet again: 19:58.

The owner stood up, stretched audibly, and then shuffled over to the doorway next to Walsh, holding an arm out to usher him into the street.

Walsh buttoned his coat and nodded his head towards the church across the street. *"L'église Notre-Dame, n'est pas?"*

The owner lit a cigarette, inhaled deeply, then exhaled with pleasure into the chilly night air. He nodded slowly before saying, *"Bien sur, Notre-Dame. Notre-Dame du Sablon."*

Walsh put a hand on the owner's shoulder. *"Notre-Dame du Sablon?"*

"Oui." The owner looked at Walsh's hand, which was swiftly removed. The wrong church!

"Mais où est Notre-Dame de la Chapelle?" Walsh stepped out into the street, while the owner lingered under cover of his doorway. The owner pointed towards the bottom of the Sablon, then curved his hand towards the left.

"En bas, dans la Place de la Chapelle. Vous prenez rue Joseph Stevens..."

But Walsh was off, running down through the Sablon, past the silent posh shops of the rue des Sablons, trying not to slip on the pavement. He paused at the entrance to rue Joseph Stevens, on his left, and sure enough, another large Gothic church could be seen further down the hill, at the end of the street.

He walked as swiftly as possible toward the church, without running, and found the main entrance. It was 20:05 and he could just make out a few figures loitering near the grand doorway of the building. Moving closer, he saw Ernst standing alone to one side, underneath a black umbrella. Walsh stopped in his tracks and waited for a few moments, until Ernst detected his presence.

After glancing around the Place de la Chapelle, Ernst came over and shook Walsh's hand.

"Thank you for coming, Mr Walsh."

Walsh took a second to compose himself. "It's no bother."

"Shall we go inside for a moment?"

Walsh held out his arm towards the entrance of the church, and they slipped inside. In the dim light Walsh could make out a few silent figures scattered here and there in the seats, and he followed Ernst to a quiet section near the remarkable carved pulpit located about halfway down the centre of the church.

After they sat, Ernst leaned over and whispered, "I come here for confession every week. On my own, of course. Tobias is…he's not a Catholic. He won't miss me."

Walsh nodded in understanding as he scanned the rest of the building. So Ernst and Tobias must live nearby, probably in the Marolles somewhere with the other, less well-off, inhabitants of Brussels. He turned back towards Ernst.

"So what can I do for you?"

Ernst clasped his hands together, as if in prayer. He bowed and looked towards the floor. He drew his breath in, and said, quietly, "Tobias is being difficult."

"How so?"

"He was…I mean we…we had agreed to ask only for five thousand pounds. Not ten."

"I see."

"Tobias thinks that he is in charge here. But I am the one with the secret. He can sell nothing without me."

"And do you think that five thousand pounds is fair?"

Ernst's thick lips spread into a rueful smile, and he cracked one of his knuckles. "Mr Walsh, believe me, I don't need the money. My family is wealthy enough."

Walsh nodded. "And what about Tobias?"

"He has a more…modest background than I."

"I see. So is he being greedy here, or just opening the negotiations with a high price?"

Ernst shook his head slowly. "I'm not entirely sure, Mr Walsh. We..."

Walsh cut him off. "Well, haven't you discussed this with him? Are you...hold on, Ernst, your nose is bleeding."

Ernst put a hand to his nose and saw blood on his fingers. "*Verdammen*," he said, under his breath. "Sorry, I get these from time to time."

Walsh fished in his coat pocket for a handkerchief but Ernst beat him to it.

"That's all right, I've got it, I've got it," Ernst said, holding up his own handkerchief. "Always prepared for these, you know."

"Are you sure you're all right?"

"Yes, I'm fine, I'm fine now."

"You were saying about Tobias?" Walsh asked, looking around the quiet church and feeling almost as awkward as Ernst.

Ernst dabbed at his nose and tilted his head back to stop the bleeding. He continued speaking with his head in that awkward position, making it somewhat difficult for Walsh to understand his hushed nasal voice.

"Yes. Tobias. Hmpf. My dear old friend. I've tried to discuss the price with him, you see, but he tells me to leave the bargaining to him." A pause. "He can be somewhat stubborn."

"But you think he will accept five thousand pounds?"

Ernst turned to look at Walsh, with his hand still closing his nostrils. "Mr Walsh, *I will accept* five thousand pounds. And that's all you need to know." Ernst's face became more determined. "Except for one other thing."

"And what's that?"

Ernst leaned closer. The bleeding seemed to have stopped. He checked his handkerchief before wrapping it up in a small ball.

"I need to finish our business as soon as possible," Ernst said.

"Why? What's the problem?"

Ernst paused for a moment, and cracked another knuckle. "I spoke with my sister recently. Maria. She's still back home, in Germany. With my parents."

"And?"

"And she told me that my father hired someone to find me."

Walsh grabbed his arm. "Hired who?"

"I don't know. A man called Retzlaff. She didn't have many details. Nothing, really. We were cut off..."

"Can you contact her again? Did she describe Retzlaff to you?" Walsh's voice was urgent.

"No, as I said, the call was interrupted. I don't know anything about *Herr* Retzlaff."

"And your father has the money to pay for that? For a professional investigator, if that's what he is?"

Ernst smiled and nodded. "Oh, most certainly, Mr Walsh. More than enough."

"Ernst, listen to me. I will pass your offer to my colleagues in London. The lower figure. As quickly as possible. But don't tell Tobias anything about it."

"Of course not."

Walsh looked around the church again to make sure no one was listening. Could Retzlaff be here already? In this very church? But the place was quiet; quiet and empty. Except for the two of them.

"I also need to know where you are staying," Walsh said. "I need to be able to contact you alone, without Tobias. And I need to know more about this Retzlaff."

"I am staying very close by. But I don't think I can tell you the address just yet."

"Ernst, you must trust me. Do you want Retzlaff to drag you back to your father? Or to the German authorities?"

Ernst's eyes grew wide. "No, of course not."

"Then I must know how to protect you. And where to find you."

"Very well. We have a shared telephone in our building." Ernst wrote the number on a scrap of paper. "Our flat is further down the rue Haute, near the Hospital St Pierre." Ernst continued writing his address, then folded the note and gave it to Walsh.

Walsh pocketed it. "And what about Tobias in the meantime?"

"Leave him to me. I will make him understand the situation."

Walsh thought for a moment. "He doesn't know about Retzlaff, does he?"

Ernst shifted in his seat, and shook his head slowly.

"Very well, Tobias is your problem. For now. But Retzlaff is *my* problem, *verstehen*? So can you contact your sister and find out more about him? His appearance perhaps? And can you find out exactly what she told him?"

Ernst drew in some air between his teeth, making a *pfff* sound. It was not an agreeable sound.

Walsh pressed on. "Well, does he know you are in Brussels?"

"I don't think so. Maria – my sister – doesn't know I am here, so she could not tell him that."

"But who else knows you are here?"

Ernst looked around before answering. "No one, Mr Walsh."

"Are you certain of that? What about Tobias and his family? His friends? If Retzlaff questioned your sister then he is sure to find out about Tobias."

Ernst shifted around again, and looked at his own pocketwatch. "Tobias would not tell anyone else. He doesn't have many friends, and his family…" Ernst shrugged his shoulders. "But he…he needs this money even more than I do. And his family could not possibly help Retzlaff, even if he did find them." A pause. "You asked me to trust you, Mr Walsh. Now you must trust me about Tobias. But we do need to conclude our business soon, for my own peace of mind."

"Yes, course," Walsh said. "But you realize that I haven't had a response from London yet, about any of this. I don't even know if they are interested in your secret, no matter what the price. So we could just be wasting our time again."

Walsh hated to admit that, but he knew it was true.

Ernst stared at him in disbelief. "How could your navy refuse a technological advance that could virtually guarantee them a steady supply of cordite?"

"I don't know, but my colleagues in London are…are handling that question right now. So I will need a little more time."

Ernst put his head down again and spoke in a small voice. "I suppose I have no choice but to wait. Could we possibly meet within a week's time?"

"Agreed. Assuming London gets back to me before then. Now here is how you can contact me."

Ernst left the church first, followed by Walsh a few moments later. As he made his way down the length of the church, back towards the Sablon, Walsh felt uneasy. He paused for a moment, as if to check his trouser pockets, then abruptly turned around and scanned the area back near the entrance. Yes, *something* had moved back there in response to his turning. Walsh was sure of it. Certainly Retzlaff could not have found them so quickly, could he? So was it Tobias?

Thoroughly drenched in the rain again, Walsh quickened his pace back towards the Sablon. Rather than re-trace his steps up rue Joseph Stevens, however, he kept walking and took the next street, rue de Rollebeek. It was darker, narrower, and quieter. Turning right into the street, he ran past a few shuttered shops and stepped into one of the deeper doorways on the right. He pressed his body against the side wall of the doorway, the one closer to the entrance of the street he was on. He unbuttoned his coat, reached his right hand into the left inside of his suit jacket, and kept it there. He looked at the reflections in the shop windows opposite him to see if there was movement down the street.

Sure enough, a moment later Walsh saw some motion in the window. This was followed by the sound of quick footsteps near the corner behind Walsh. The sound paused abruptly as the man stopped and looked up the street. In the window across the street, Walsh could see that the man was alone. Suddenly he was beside Walsh, who leapt out of the doorway, grabbed the man's upper right arm with his free left hand, and violently pulled him back into the shadows.

The man had no time to tear himself away. He lost his footing as Walsh swept his own right foot against the man's ankle while continuing to pull with his left arm. Walsh simultaneously removed his gun from the shoulder holster under his left arm after the man was completely unbalanced. As the stranger tumbled forward onto the pavement with a cry of pain, Walsh pushed him down face first. He pinned him easily with his right foot on the ground and his left knee on the man's back.

Walsh used his free left hand to pull the man's face up by his hair. Walsh did not recognize him. With Walsh's gun in his face, the man froze and held a hand up by each side of his head, indicating that he was unarmed.

"*Qui êtes-vous?*" Walsh growled.

The man shook his head.

Walsh pressed the end of the barrel against the man's right temple, hard, so that it would leave a mark.

"*Qui êtes-vous? Dites moi!*"

"*Long. Je m'appelle Dale Long...*"

An English accent! Walsh dropped his French charade. "You're British?"

"Yes! Now let me be!"

"Not just yet, my friend. Why are you following me? What do you want with me?" Walsh kept the gun against the man's temple.

Long shook his head.

Walsh pulled Long's head up a little further and the knocked the butt of his gun against Long's temple. Long cried out in pain.

Walsh leaned in close to Long's right ear. "Listen, Mr Long, I'm still prepared to shoot you right here, even if you are British. So you can start talking or you can start bleeding. It's your choice."

"Not so fast! Look here, I work for the British government."

"You work at the embassy here? With Major Bridges?"

"No, in London. I'm from London."

"And what do you do in London?"

Long hesitated again. Walsh cracked Long's forehead with his gun, again. And again.

"Stop that, please! I'll talk!" Long cried. "I work with the Secret Service in London. The Secret Service Bureau."

Walsh loosened his grip on the man's head, but only a little. "You work for Cumming?"

"Cumming? No, of course not, you idiot. Not Cumming. I work for Kell."

Chapter 25

The Maison du Peuple stood on an odd building site in Brussels: circular, wedge-shaped, and sloped, just around the corner from the majestic church of Notre-Dame de la Chapelle. It was covered with rectangular windows of various sizes, with a large curved façade looking onto the Place, and it made an awkward impression on many passers-by, who couldn't decide whether they admired or loathed the structure. It was certainly eye-catching, and seemed to be a major centre of action in this part of the city.

Having stared at the building for days on end now, as he was doing now on this sunny Monday afternoon in April, Retzlaff was sure of his opinion on the structure: he thought it was ugly. Hideous, even. Everything from the location to the proportions to the adornments was all wrong. But Retzlaff was not interested in the architectural significance of the Maison. Instead, he was here to observe the movements of the main occupants of the building: socialists, members of the Belgian Labour Party and related political groups. Political fanatics, Retzlaff thought.

Retzlaff had arrived in Brussels with no leads at all regarding Ernst's whereabouts, and had spent – that is, wasted – much time showing the young man's photograph around various cheap hotels and rooming houses in the poorer parts of Brussels, chiefly the Marolles. He had also nosed around the Free University of Belgium as well, with no luck whatsoever.

Eventually it dawned upon him that if Brussels was the final destination of Ernst and Tobias, and if they were involved in socialist politics, then perhaps they would have some contacts with the Labour Party here. As the Maison du Peuple housed not only the headquarters of the Belgian Labour Party but also the Secretariat of the International Socialist Bureau of the Second International – or the global network of socialist parties - Ernst and Tobias almost certainly would visit this building at some point if they had travelled here from Germany on a political mission.

Retzlaff knew better than to show Ernst's photograph around here, or to ask anyone within sight of the Maison about its inner workings, as he would be mistaken immediately for a police officer or, worse, a 'mouchard' - a police informant.

He was also tempted to stake out the large, always-busy café on the ground floor of the Maison, but worried that he might frighten off his prey if they caught sight of him too often. So Retzlaff sat in other cafés outside the building, hoping to catch sight of Ernst or Tobias. Fortunately there were enough socialist pamphlets, newspapers, books, and other printed materials to occupy his mind while he watched and waited.

From these publications he learned more than he cared to admit about the recent activities and problems of the Second International. In addition to his native German, Retzlaff was fluent in French and had a passable knowledge of English, so he was able to scan materials from a wide range of sources – *La Tribune Russe*, *The Labour Leader*, *Le Peuple*, *Vorwärts*, and such - as he sat, well within sight of the Maison du Peuple.

Yet the more he read, the more confused he became. On the surface, the movement seemed to be a formidable presence across Europe. The publications in front of Retzlaff described a growing network of worker's movements, supported by sympathetic parliamentarians and journalists, who were strengthening their communications linkages. With this network they were attempting to put forward a single unified message about the evils of industrial capitalism yet, to his way of thinking, international socialism seemed to be trying to be all things to all people.

Retzlaff believed this was inherently impossible, if international socialism really was attempting to reconcile the political goals of women's groups, unions, Zionist labour activists, Russian Bolshevists, national communist and socialist parties, sympathetic anarchist and anti-imperialist organizations, humanitarians, pacifists, on and on and on. And each group had its own particular spokesperson, so Retzlaff worked his way through the rantings of Jaurès, Lenin, Kautsky, Bauer, Adler, Luxemburg, and even the man who currently held the chairmanship of the ISB, housed in the odd building in front of him: the Belgian, Emile Vandervelde.

Underneath these larger political debates, Retzlaff could also discern in the writings a similar pattern he remembered from his time on the police force: unbelievably petty disputes about money and the rules of their organization. Money and rules, rules and money. Disputes over who paid their fees, who could attend the congresses, who could form national delegations to the ISB, who was authorized to publish and distribute information on behalf of the Second International, and so on. Most recently, the ISB had dealt with the difficult question of whether the British Labour Party should be allowed an affiliation with the International Socialist Congress, as it was not an avowed socialist party as such. After a heated debate at the ISB meeting in 1908, the Party was permitted such an affiliation, thanks in part to an intervention by Karl Kautsky, with the support of Vladimir Lenin.

All very interesting, thought Retzlaff, yet several questions nagged him. Above all, why were Tobias and Ernst on the run, and what were they doing in Brussels? Herr Hesse did not have an answer for that question. In fact, he seemed most annoyed when Retzlaff tried to speculate about it in his presence. The presence of Ernst in Brussels was especially puzzling, as the young man seemed to have a supportive family and a very promising career as a chemist back in Germany. So why give that up for Brussels?

Retzlaff was not especially worred about the logistics of bringing Ernst back to Germany against his will, even if Tobias was here to protect him. Hired help would be easy enough to find in Brussels, if you had the means to pay for it and you knew where to look. Retzlaff was already working on that problem. He was tempted to purchase an automobile for the journey but thought he could manage transporting Ernst by rail; the letter from Hesse should smooth things for him at the Belgian-German border, if anyone even bothered to question Retzlaff about his business. And after arriving in Germany at Aix-la-Chapelle, it would be an easy ride back to Leipzig.

Soon his brain became preoccupied with an equally important question: if he could find out their mission in Brussels, could he somehow profit from it before returning Ernst to his family? And if so, who was willing to pay, and how much might be at stake here?

These thoughts loomed large in Retzlaff's mind as he looked up from his table yet again and, across the crowded Place, saw Tobias and Ernst exit the front door of the Maison du Peuple.

Chapter 26

Walsh reached Cumming by telephone for the second time in four days after his meeting with Ernst at the church of Notre-Dame de la Chapelle. It took several calls for Walsh to trace him, as Cumming had finally moved his office to a new location in Ashley Gardens by the end of March.

"Well, my boy, I have some news for you about this cordite business," Cumming began. "It's taken some doing, but the Admiralty is interested. Very interested, in point of fact. So it appears that your man there might be on to something."

"Is that so?" Walsh tried to keep the edge out of his voice.

"Yes, apparently the Admiralty has several formulas for producing cordite, 'Cordite Mark I' and 'Cordite MD' and such, but they all involve acetone in one way or another. And it is time-consuming to produce, requiring lots of wood: birch, maple, beech. A hundred tons of wood to produce a single ton of acetone, they tell me. Apparently we import most of ours from America at the moment, since it has the wood. So it is expensive to make there and transport it to us for processing into cordite. But the best part, Walsh, is that we might be the only customers for this acetone deal."

"Are you sure about that?"

"Yes. I've been on the telephone with some experts at the gunpowder mills up at Waltham Abbey, and a man from the Royal Arsenal at Woolwich. They say that the French use a smokeless powder called 'Poudre BN3F', which is different from cordite. The Germans use something called 'RP C/12' which is similar to cordite but we must assume your man has a reason for not selling his formula at home. He probably doesn't think he will get a fair price for it there."

"Or any price, if he really discovered his acetone secret while enrolled as a PhD student. What about the Russians?"

"Woolwich believes they use picric acid and TNT," Cumming said.

"So we would be the primary market for this?"

"It would appear so. I suppose the Canadians are using cordite, but I don't think they would be playing this game."

"And is the Admiralty thinking of adopting an alternative to cordite?"

"Not that I've heard. Why do you ask?"

"Well, C, if they are moving away from cordite on their own accord, then the value of this secret would decline considerably, wouldn't it?"

"Yes, of course. Of course. I suppose it would. But for the moment the Admiralty is interested. There is no realistic alternative to cordite at the moment, as far as they are concerned. So you must pursue this thing," Cumming insisted.

"Right. That's all well and good, but what about the asking price?"

Cumming cleared his throat. "Yes, well, my boy. That could be a problem. Or I should say, it is a problem. Ten thousand pounds is more than we can afford right now. That's the simple truth."

Walsh had expected that. "Well, there's a chance that they might accept five thousand pounds. How would they feel about that?"

"Five thousand? Well done, Walsh! But how on earth did you manage that?"

"It's not important. But perhaps I can get them a thousand or two lower if I point out to them the facts we know about the acetone market just now."

"Walsh, it would take some doing over here, but I think we could meet that lower figure if you can manage it. But are you quite certain that your man can deliver the goods? You know we've had some…some fraudulent offers in the past. We can't afford to waste this kind of money on something that hasn't been tested. My credibility here would be in ruins."

"We're working on that over here," Walsh said, in a tired voice. "They've just offered to demonstrate the secret here in Brussels once we agree to pay. It would just take some basic laboratory equipment and they've agreed to allow one of our experts to observe the process."

"Splendid! Sounds like you have everything under control. If they can demonstrate this thing, then it can't possibly be one of Steinhauer's traps, can it? Anyhow, good work, my boy!"

"Yes. Well, that's why you sent me here, isn't it?"

"Of course."

"But just one other thing, now that I have you on the telephone," Walsh said.

"And what is that?"

"Who is Dale Long?"

A pause on the line. Walsh waited.

"Dale Long, did you say?" Cumming asked.

"Yes."

"Well, he...he is just one of our agents. Like you. Why do you ask?"

"Because he was following me for several days last week, C, while I was dealing with the Germans."

"Dale Long was following you in Brussels? Are you sure it was him?"

"Of course I'm sure. He told me his name."

Another pause on the line. Walsh waited.

"He also said he worked for Kell, not you," Walsh continued. "So who the devil is Kell? And why is he having me followed? Don't you trust me on this deal?"

"No, Walsh, wait, please! There must be a...mistake. A misunderstanding."

"I'm listening."

Walsh heard Cumming sigh on his end of the telephone before he spoke. "Kell is...is my counterpart in the SSB. He runs the business within Britain. I cover the foreign angle."

Walsh thought for a moment. "I thought you ran the SSB?"

"It's not that simple, my boy. We're still working out our arrangements here. Things have been difficult for us, you understand. This is still a...a young organisation. Kell and I have had some disputes, there's no denying that. That's why I'm in a different office now."

"So Long does work for Kell?"

"Long is supposed to work for both of us, I suppose," Cumming said, with another sigh.

"You suppose? But why is he following *me*, in *Brussels*, for *Kell*, if you handle the foreign business? Can you explain that to me, please?"

"Frankly, Walsh, I don't know why. Really, I don't. I need to look into this. Just give me some time. Didn't you ask Long yourself?"

"Of course I did. He said it was routine to check up on British nationals who might have some professional involvement with the Germans. He said it wasn't personal."

"Perhaps he was trying to recruit you for us."

Walsh nearly laughed at that. "I thought you had already done that!"

"Yes, of course, of course. Listen, Walsh. I will look into this. I promise. But how did you leave things with Long? Is he still there?"

"I think I frightened him off. I haven't seen him since."

"And did you mention what you were doing?"

"Well, I mentioned your name after he said he worked for the SSB. So the game was up by then. For both of us. But I didn't tell him what business I was working on. And he really wasn't...he wasn't in a position to question me. Frankly, it sounded like he was as confused as I was by that point."

Walsh heard Cumming shuffling papers on the other end of the line. "I need to sort this out with Kell."

"I would imagine so," said Walsh.

"Walsh, as I said, things are becoming complicated here. Kell has very good contacts with the Home Office and across the police. All over the country. He's also working closely with the new aliens sub-committee of the CID. With Churchill, the chairman. They've started to register foreigners here, mostly the Germans of course. The information comes in from the police and Kell has access to it all. I don't."

"The 'aliens sub-committee'? What the hell is that? And what does it all mean to me?"

"It means that Kell, and others here, are becoming more concerned about the Germans operating in this country, and more aggressive about handling them. Even if there is no clear evidence of a plot to invade the country. So Long is probably part of that effort. Remember I told you that we believe the Germans operating in Britain are being run from Brussels? By Steinhauer's group?"

"Yes, I remember," Walsh said.

"So even if your two Germans are not linked to this network, others there must be. We have to assume so. And so we, Kell and I, must take an interest in them."

"Fair enough. But obviously you two are not handling this well, between yourselves."

"No, I agree. Completely. And this...this is not the first time. I'll get it sorted here. As soon as possible. But you keep after your two Germans, agreed?"

"Yes, of course," Walsh said.

"In the meantime, I'll speak with Kell and try to make arrangements to see you soon in Brussels."

"That would be helpful."

"All right, then, Walsh. Keep up the good work, my boy. And I'll contact you very soon."

Walsh hung up the telephone, and wondered yet again whether he had made the right choice in coming to Brussels. But he supposed it was too late to worry about that now.

Chapter 27

Dewulf adjusted his field glasses slightly to bring the scene into better focus. Despite the bright sunshine on this April afternoon, the light in this part of the Marolles was as dim as most of the residents of this quartier. Tenements, shops, and warehouses crowded against each other in the small streets running off the main artery through the area, rue Haute, and the buildings effectively blocked the sun from reaching the street level. Dewulf put the glasses down, checked the target with his naked eyes, and put the glasses to his face again. After a few seconds he could see four, no, five, young men milling about in the small third-floor office of a large warehouse across the street from Dewulf's vantage point.

"Which one is your man?" he asked the oafish cop next to him, Inspector Gerold Kluskens of the Brussels communal police.

Kluskens had just finished lunch, some of which was still lodged in his teeth, and Dewulf could smell the garlic sausage on the man's grimy wool coat.

"Does the *Bourgmestre* know about this?" Kluskens asked, for the second time.

Dewulf kept his eyes on the warehouse. "I told you. It's all been approved. And it's only temporary, until the Exposition is well under way with no problems. That's less than two weeks from now, so I don't have time to argue with you." Dewulf lowered his glasses and glared at Kluskens. "Understand?"

"This will disrupt weeks of work, you know," Kluskens grumbled, just loudly enough for the other two policemen, more junior to him, to hear. "We've got him all set up with this gang already. It took some doing, inspector."

"I'm not interested in your problems." Dewulf put the glasses back to his eyes and turned away from the shorter man. "And I'm running out of time. Now are you going to point out your *mouchard* to me or do I have to ask one of your subordinates?"

Kluskens shifted his feet and avoided the gaze of the two younger men, police agents Remy and Goosens, behind him. He focused his attention on the view across the street. "He's the one in the grey cap and dark red trousers. With the beard, not the moustache. He was seated a moment ago." Kluskens put his own glasses to his eyes and aimed them across the street.

"That's Leysen?" Dewulf watched as the bearded young man across the street talked and gesticulated to the two men seated across from him. Their backs were to Dewulf and he could not see their faces nor guess their ages. Two other men, both older, wandered around the table with their hands in their pockets.

Kluskens nodded, and removed his glasses before turning his back to the window. "Dirk Leysen. He's good. Very good. Not like the other *ketjes* we've used around here." Kluskens used the old Marollien term for a young man who came from this area of Brussels. "He has a real gift for…for worming his way into these gangs. You remember the Weydeman case a few months ago? He actually managed to get the wife to admit…"

"Quiet!" Dewulf hissed. "Something is happening."

Kluskens turned abruptly, raised his glasses to his eyes, and took in the scene across the street. He and Dewulf watched in silence as the five men in their sights grew more animated. They all were standing; one of the chairs had fallen, or had been pushed over, onto the bare wooden floor.

"What is this?" Kluskens said.

"It looks like your esteemed Mr Leysen is getting himself into some trouble," said Dewulf.

The other two police officers behind Kluskens exchanged a look.

"Should we go over and break it up?" Goosens said. He was a few years younger than Remy, clearly the junior partner of the two, with a slim physique, small wire-rimmed glasses, and the face of an accountant. Full of nervous energy, unlike his morose senior partner, he bobbed his head back and forth to get a better look at the action unfolding across the street.

"No, just wait…" said Kluskens, as his eyes scanned the drama unfolding across the street.

The arguing continued in the factory, as Dewulf and Kluskens looked on, helplessly, without being able to hear any of it. Then one of the older men in their view, standing behind Leysen, drew a pistol from his coat pocket and jammed it into the side of the younger man's head. He clutched the back of Leysen's coat with his free left hand, just below the neckline.

Leysen raised his hands and froze his body, but his mouth was working overtime. He gestured as best he could with his hands in the air, obviously pleading his case to the others.

"Something has gone wrong," Kluskens helpfully pointed out.

"Do you really think so, Kluskens?" Dewulf said. "So what do we do?"

"We wait, inspector. Maybe he can talk himself out of it. He's usually pretty good at that."

"You should still put your men into position over there," Dewulf said. "Just in case Leysen doesn't convince them."

As Dewulf spoke, Leysen was being marched across the room, towards the office door that led into the larger warehouse space. Dewulf and Kluskens did not have a clear view of that section of the building.

"*Merde*," said Dewulf, through gritted teeth. "I'm going over." He put down his field glasses and raced out of the room, followed by Goosens and then Remy.

"Wait!" Kluskens cried. No one responded, so he followed them down the stairs and onto the street. He nearly bumped into a frail old woman, who batted him with her umbrella.

Dewulf had already instructed Remy to cover the main entrance and Goosens to work his away around the right side of the building. Dewulf took the left side, with his pistol drawn.

He ran down the side of the warehouse, expecting to find another entrance but none was in sight. He continued towards the back and paused at the corner, where he poked his head around. Leysen was already coming down the stairs of the rear loading dock of the warehouse, pushed by the man with the pistol. The two of them were followed by two others, neither of whom seemed to be armed.

Twenty metres away, Dewulf crouched at his corner of the building, took aim with his pistol, and was about to call out to the men when Goosens suddenly appeared on the other side of warehouse, at the opposite corner. He drew his own pistol and shouted, "Halt!"

The man covering Leysen took aim at Goosens and fired. The shot raised a small cloud of dust on the dirt ground and Goosens staggered back towards his corner of the building. He waited there, peering around the wall, and a second shot from the gunman hit the brickwork and shattered it, sending shards into Goosens's eyes. He screamed and disappeared from Dewulf's sight.

Right after the second shot, while the gunman behind him was still aiming towards Goosens, Leysen jerked his head violently backwards and into the nose of the gunman. Dewulf could hear the sickening crack of bone against bone, then saw blood gushing out of the gunman's broken nose. The gunman released Leysen with his left hand, which flew to his nose in a vain attempt to stop the bleeding. Then, before the gunman could take aim, Leysen jammed his right elbow into the gunman's upper ribcage and pushed backwards, sending the gunman into the two men crouching down behind him.

By this time Dewulf had moved closer to the action and Kluskens appeared, finally, right behind him, breathless and with his own pistol drawn. They both ducked behind a large wooden crate, watching as Leysen jumped down the rest of the stairs and ran towards them.

The gunman on the stairs stood up again, taking aim at Leysen's back. Before he could fire, Dewulf jumped up and shot the man in the neck, causing a spray of arterial blood to darken the front of his suit.

The other two men staggered backwards towards the rear doorway of the warehouse on the loading dock. It opened suddenly and Remy appeared, with his own pistol drawn. The two men put their hands up and stopped in their tracks. Remy moved further out onto the loading dock. The last man, the one who had remained in the office, was nowhere to be seen.

"Nice shot, inspector!" said Kluskens.

"Not exactly," said Dewulf. "I was aiming for his leg."

"Hmpff. Well, no matter. These boys are finished. And I suppose Leysen won't be needed on this case anymore. So you can have him now," said Kluskens, as he stood up and holstered his weapon.

"Shut up, you fool!" Dewulf whispered, holstering his pistol. "Don't let them hear you say that. Now go check on Goosens."

Chapter 28

Kiel, Germany. April 1910.

Kiel. Capital of Schleswig-Holstein, the main base of Imperial Germany's Baltic Sea fleet, and home of the renowned Kiel Regatta and the esteemed Imperial Yacht Club of Kiel, whose commodore was no less than Kaiser Wilhelm II himself.

Far away from the centre of the thriving city, a small group of German naval officers and civilians stood perfectly still on high ground above the harbour as the spectacle unfolded before them. The wind seemed to be cooperating for the moment, for once. Each of the men had a set of powerful field glasses, which were lifted whenever movement could be detected in the harbour. Their target today: the old rusted shell of a decommissioned destroyer, anchored and alone, out in the sea and well away from the many other warships remaining in the harbour.

Movement again. Time to look. As one man, the spectators on the hill lifted glasses to their eyes and watched as a small launch churned its way from the harbour to the silent destroyer. The launch was tied securely to the old ship and bobbed gently in the calm water next to it. Two men left the launch and made their way up a ladder to the main deck of the old destroyer, which had long ago been stripped bare of working guns and all other useful machinery. A few moments later, the officers on shore saw motion around several large wooden crates placed around the main deck of the destroyer. The two men on board the doomed vessel used hammers to knock away the sides of the crates, revealing a large iron cage within each one. Inside each cage were several live animals: dogs in two of the cages, sheep in another, and cats in another.

From shore, the spectators could just about hear the faint sound of the dogs barking, trapped and frightened in their iron cages. A few of the men watching from afar were surprised to see one of the men on deck reach into one of cages and scratch the muzzle of one of the dogs, as if he were simply leaving the animal for a few moments and would be returning to get him later in the day.

Once the cages were free of their crates, the two men left the ship and joined their companions on the launch, which headed back towards the docks. When they were safely away, the next stage of the experiment could begin.

This stage was marked by the sudden, horribly loud racket of shellfire coming from the main fortress at Kiel. As the noise broke the peaceful silence of this April morning, the spectators kept their glasses trained on the old destroyer, waiting for a few of the first volley of shells to hit their mark.

Soon enough, one of the shells scored a direct hit, but it did not burst in an explosion large enough to tear the vessel to bits. Instead, the shell broke up on the main deck, with a much smaller blast than one might otherwise expect. Once the correct range and bearing were known, several other shells managed to hit the vessel, some on the main deck, others tearing small holes in its side, also with very small explosions.

The spectators had expected this, and they were pleased. The animals on board the vessel were understandably terrified, however, and made horrible sounds as the shells slammed into the destroyer without actually killing anything. The dogs were the most violent, and they barked and clawed and chewed in vain at the iron bars of their cages.

The watchers on the hill now focused on the final stage of the experiment, as a thick discharge of greenish-yellow smoke poured out of various openings and settled around the deck of the destroyer following the volley of shells. The smoke, with its sickly unnatural hue, was just thin enough to allow the officers to watch the animals on the deck as they clawed frantically at their cage walls, howling and barking and coughing, surrounded by the relentless fumes. If the officers had been a hundred metres closer, they would have seen the doomed animals retching and vomiting whatever was left in their stomachs, the filth spewing over the bars and floors of their cages.

After just a few moments, the gas dissipated into the brisk sea air and the vessel was in full view again. Soon the launch appeared again, this time carrying a few naval officers and several men in white coats. The doctors, solemn and determined.

Wearing thick cotton masks and goggles, the small party boarded the old destroyer and swiftly checked the cages on deck. It was still too dangerous to go below to check the other cages, but even the officers watching from the shoreline could see that the experiment had been a complete success. All of the animals in their view were lying dead or dying in their cages, covered in their own filth, suffocated by the gas. Poison gas shells were supposed to be outlawed under the rules of war, but there were other ways to deliver the gas, now that they knew it worked.

The spectators congratulated each other and made plans to regroup at a restaurant later in the day, smiling and laughing as they walked back to their base. One of the civilians, however, remained behind for a few moments, watching the activity on the destroyer as the doctors prepared for another test, with a new set of animals. In his mind, the civilian observer was already composing a short note to be sent in secret, back to London. Back to Cumming.

He wondered exactly how much detail to include in his report, about the German navy's successful test of chlorine gas shells on this lovely spring day. It was a shame he was not able to take photographs of the dead animals, still reeking of the odd combination of pepper and pineapple-scented fumes, for that would tell C all he needed to know.

Chapter 29

Brussels. April 1910.

Walsh threw his newspaper, *Le Courrier de Bruxelles*, on the table in front of Ernst and Tobias, startling them both, and dropped into a seat across from them. The lunchtime crowd had not completely disappeared from Falstaff, so Walsh paused to look around the café to make sure no one was listening. Satisfied, he leaned forward to speak to them.

"Care to explain this, gentlemen?" Walsh said, as he pointed to a small advertisement in the petites annonces at the back of the paper.

Ernst and Tobias exchanged a glance before leaning down to read the tiny print at the end of Walsh's pointed finger. The page was crammed with notices offering or requesting a startling wide range of goods and services, and it took them a moment to find what Walsh was asking about.

Then they saw the advertisement. It was just a few lines, mentioning the offer of information, for a price to be negotiated, regarding a radically effective new technique for low explosives manufacture that might be useful to countries using propellents with a nitrocellulose base. Such as cordite.

The advertisement also mentioned a post office box in central Brussels, where bids and other enquiries could be submitted.

Ernst and Tobias exchanged another look before Ernst spoke up.

"I'm not sure..." he began.

"The same advertisement appears in other papers today. So now I understand your game. And I thought we were close to a deal," Walsh said.

"What do you mean, 'close to a deal?' What deal?" Tobias replied, his voice tight and edgy. "It's been over three weeks since we first contacted you. And we've heard nothing."

"You are asking for a lot of money. Far more than I normally require, mind you. And I told you this needed to be approved in London, which takes time. Don't you understand? I'm trying to establish your credibility with certain...certain authorities in my government, and this is not going to help."

"So you have agreed the full price?"

Walsh paused. "Not just yet. I'm working on it."

"Well, perhaps now you will work harder," said Tobias, barely concealing a smile.

"You really think you will have other bidders for this? At ten thousand pounds or more?" Walsh leaned back, motioned for a waiter, and ordered a coffee just for himself when the man appeared at their table a moment later.

"Mr Walsh, please. Do not be a fool," Tobias said, as coolly as he could manage. "The Exposition begins next week. It will run for months. And Brussels is now crawling with scientists, manufacturers, technicians, military officials, and other potentially interested parties. With many more to come. From all over the world. I would expect some of them would be interested in what we have to offer. Unless, of course, you are prepared to make a deal now."

Walsh looked at Ernst and raised an eyebrow at him. What was going on here? But Ernst's face was blank.

Tobias continued. "And, there are not just governments here. Private firms may take an interest. Nobel makes nitrocellulose-based explosives, you know. And perhaps an American firm will take an interest. Perhaps DuPont will attend the Exposition? Or Dow Chemical?"

Walsh's coffee arrived. He stirred some milk into it, returned the spoon to his saucer, and took a sip.

Ernst and Tobias waited.

Walsh took another sip of his coffee, and stared back at them.

"Well, Mr Walsh?" said Tobias.

"Get the hell out of my sight," Walsh said.

Ernst and Tobias exchanged a third look.

"Mr Walsh," Ernst began.

"I said, GET THE HELL OUT OF HERE!" Walsh bellowed the words, and everyone in the café turned to stare. Tobias's face reddened and he stood up. He put his hat on and stared at Walsh, who had returned to reading his newspaper. Ernst moved to follow Tobias, but paused at the side of the table for a last appeal.

"Mr Walsh, please," Ernst looked back towards Tobias, who was now waiting outside the café, buttoning his coat. "Let me handle this…"

But Walsh ignored him.

Chapter 30

Paris. April 1910.

Lefevre found Marchand drinking coffee in the officer's mess hall three floors down from their offices. The remains of a pain chocolat stained the dish in front of Marchand, who had his eyes glued to a copy of *Le Figaro*. Lefevre saluted and handed him a file, smiling broadly.

Marchand saluted. "Yes, Lefevre, what is it?"

"Just in from Berlin, sir. Pellé again."

Marchand raised an eyebrow. "Good news, I expect?" Marchand motioned for his adjutant to sit down.

"More from the Russians. Specific figures about the command of the German field army."

Marchand opened the file and flipped through the few pages within it. A moment later he, too, looked up and smiled.

"*Très interresant*, Levfre. *Merci.*"

The following day Marchand met again with General Regnault. He placed the file in front of his superior and took a seat across from the general.

"The Russians have arrived at similar conclusions, sir. Pellé has confirmed it in Berlin. The Germans can make use of cadets, retired officers, and one-year volunteers to make up the shortage of officers to command the reserves. The mixed divisions, that is. Plus they can use as many as twenty-four thousand non-commissioned officers who left the army with certificates of aptitude for wartime service. Twenty-four thousand, sir! So the Germans should be able to field and command an army in Belgium with the size we have estimated. And with mixed divisions fighting all the way."

"My congratulations, Marchand. It seems your analysis is holding up." Regnault did not look at up him.

"Yes, well, sir, should we think about revising Plan Sixteen now? To shift the focus more towards Belgium?"

Marchand was wary of being so direct, but he was also sick and tired of waiting on this matter. Besides, he had already made his play and it was time to follow through with it.

"Not so fast, I'm afraid. The situation has changed slightly since we met last."

"I don't understand, sir."

Regnault looked up now, and stared at Marchand with a blank look on his face. "You started at the *Ecole Supérieure de Guerre*, did you not, commandant? And came up through the ranks under André? General Louis André?"

"Yes, sir, I suppose you could put it that way."

General André had been the strongly republican French war minister during the country's centre-left government, from 1900-04. A reformer. Marchand's career had benefited from these reforms, after starting his military training during his school-age years, in the Cadet Corps that had been formed in every village, town, and city in France after its defeat in 1871. Marchand still remembered his first encounter with marksmanship training, the primary objective of the Corps, and the painful bruises the battered old Graz school rifle had left on his shoulder.

Regnault nodded. "And tell me, Marchand, how sympathetic were you to his ideas?"

"Which ideas, sir?" What was all this about?

Regnault leaned forward and put his arms on his desk, staring at Marchand. "You know the ideas I mean, Marchand. Purging the military of its more conservative officers. Controlling the promotions of those who remained, as long as they followed him. Discriminating against the more fervent Catholics in the officer class. Reforming the military justice system. *Those ideas*, Marchand!"

Marchand drew in a breath of air, audibly. There was no point in denying his views, not now.

"Considering the circumstances at the time, general, I think they were absolutely necessary," Marchand began. "I know what was going on. We all did. So I think a republic should not be allowing church officials to appoint its army officers. It should make more use of citizen-soldiers. And it should not be inventing intelligence estimates to suit its purposes, to suit the views of certain officers."

"And André's penchant for using informers in Masonic lodges to tell him about the religious views of officer candidates? Particularly *Catholic* ones? How did you feel about *that*, Marchand?"

"I don't know anything about that, sir." Indeed he didn't, though he had heard the rumours, like everyone else at the time.

"No, no one knows anything about that, Marchand. We only know that morale has gone steadily downwards, applications to St Cyr are down, and our dear old General André is gone. Now we have Brun in command."

General Jean Jules Brun, French Minister of War and one of the leading architects of the Franco-Russian alliance.

Marchand did not know how to respond. He waited in silence.

"I appreciate your honesty, commandant. Thank you." Regnault sat back in his chair. "You understand that sometimes we must spend as much time fighting each other at home as we do fighting our foreign enemies. Isn't that right, Marchand?"

"So who are you fighting, sir? Generalissimo de Lacroix?" The author of Plan Sixteen.

"No, Marchand. Not him. Or not him personally, I should say. I am fighting something else. Something much stronger, even. A way of thinking. An *idée fixe*."

"The conservatives."

"*Exactement*. Think about it, Marchand. We French think the *Boche* are far more conservative, more militaristic, than any other race in Europe. Certainly more conservative and traditional than we are, despite our own martial history. So if our own conservatives recoil at the idea of using reserves on the front lines, then they must think that the more traditional Germans, the *Junkers* and the *Prussians*, are even more opposed to this idea. To our conservatives, the thought of Germans allowing their precious army to be…to be defiled by unprofessionals is out of the question. Unthinkable. And even if the Germans did use reserves in such a capacity, they would be more likely to do so against the Russians, not in Belgium."

"Yes, I understand." Marchand sat back in his chair, deflated. "But…"

"But there is more to it than that, I'm afraid," Regnault continued.

"What is it?"

Regnault hesitated a moment to compose his thoughts. Marchand knew it was not typical of Regnault to explain everything so willingly, so he waited patiently.

"It is the more general opposition to the types of changes a new plan, what would become Plan Seventeen I suppose, would represent. The use of reserves in active forces. The idea of a democratic army, not a professional one." Regnault paused again. "The socialist idea."

Now Marchand understood. Defensive plans focused on Belgium versus offensive plans directed towards recovering Alsace-Lorraine. Reserves versus professional soldiers. Socialists versus conservatives, with the Catholics tending to side with the conservatives.

In other words, it was 'l'affaire Dreyfus' all over again, in a different form. The grand army must protect itself from all enemies, foreign and domestic. Including those who might dilute and weaken it with the extensive use of reserve forces. With the use of ordinary citizens and workers rather than highly trained soldiers. Soldiers who have always been used to the idea of protecting the French state at any cost, even if this means attacking its own citizens. So how could a citizen army take on that task?

"But what can be done?" said Marchand.

"Nothing, I'm afraid, for the moment. The forces we are up against will not be swayed by the accumulation of various scraps of intelligence, even if it all supports our point of view. Besides, this kind of evidence can still be interpreted in a more conservative fashion. And these views are not just held in the minds of a few individuals – de Lacroix, Brugère, General Donop, even General Dessirier to some extent. They are part of our doctrinal and planning documents, part of our history. They are promoted and taught to young officers by the war college. They are reinforced, are deeply *embedded*, throughout our system. Plus you have the question of recovering Alsace-Lorraine, which adds another dimension to their arguments."

Regnault paused and reflected on those various points for a moment, as if he had just realized the true course that France was on, and had been on, for years. The path that he and Marchand were now trying to change.

"No, Marchand," he continued. "I'm afraid it will take something more serious, more dangerous, to change this way of thinking. And not just a military crisis, you understand. A political one. A social one, even. Something far more *profond*."

In other words, Regnault might have added, but did not need to, it would take major changes throughout France that were far beyond Marchand's capabilities.

Back in his office, Marchand mulled over his options. He had survived the humiliating aftermath of the Dreyfus affair, which had especially discredited the Deuxième Bureau, and he believed the army's future required more support from the public rather than a retreat into the enclave of a privileged officer class that, in its view, could do no wrong against the French state. At home he had been reading an advance copy of Jean Jaurès's new 1910 book, *La nouvelle armée*, given to him by a colleague, and it only reinforced Marchand's views on the topic. The socialist leader Jaurès argued that a more democratic and liberal France required a more democratic and liberal army drawn from the masses, and Marchand found himself increasingly sympathetic to this view.

But what to do now? If Plan Sixteen could not be changed for the moment even in the face of new evidence about Germany's reserves strategy, then what options did Marchand have? He briefly thought about coordinating his efforts with his colleagues in the Troisième Bureau, the operations division, but his earlier encounter at the frontiers with Commandant Dupont indicated that working with them on this would be a serious mistake right now.

Certainly he and Lefevre could collect more intelligence on the German reserves situation, but that would not provoke the kind of radical change, the crisis, that Regnault had mentioned. So what was the point, really, of getting more information to support one's views when the views themselves would not be supported in the current political climate? What was the point, indeed, of 'pre-cooking the soufflé' when no one was willing to eat it?

Sitting in his office surrounded by his maps and plans and intelligence estimates going back decades in time, back to the Napoleonic wars, Marchand considered his problem from another angle: how to improve France's position in Belgium without actually changing its war plans against Germany.

And then he suddenly drew inspiration from an odd source. This problem with Plan Sixteen, he reflected, was all about conservatives against reformers. The old guard against the young. Those who try to prevent change, and those who will benefit from it. Perennial enemies, they were, no matter what the specific circumstances.

And then, another old saying popped into Marchand's head, like the old Russian aphorism about whores and soldiers that Regnault had mentioned during their first meeting. But the saying that Marchand remembered was not Russian. It was a Geman proverb, of all things, and it did not even involve the army.

Marchand could not remember where he had first heard it, but he realised that it could be applied to many problems, like the one he was now facing. A simple saying, really, but one with profound implications, just like Regnault had mentioned.

Die Alzen zum Rat, die Jungen zur Tat.

Age counsels, youth acts.

Chapter 31

Brussels. April 1910.

Retzlaff sat alone at a quiet side table at Le Café des Petits-Provençaux, on the rue des Bouchers, waiting for his late evening rendevous. He had been in many places like this one as a police detective, but had never become accustomed to them. It was a struggle for Retzlaff just to keep a distasteful look off his face. The wooden floors under his feet were stained and slimy with God-knows-what, and the stench of smoke, stale beer, cheap perfume, and burnt food permeated the place. The only thing the café lacked was a haze of opium smoke.

Even so, the place was crowded with an assortment of lowlifes who always crawled out at night in such districts, most of whom were dressed in tattered suits or soiled workman's clothes. A few patrons with military uniforms of the lower ranks were scattered about the place, though they hardly looked like they were fit to perform their martial duties. Retzlaff could also hear music and laughter from the cabarets outside, which just about helped to cover the strange, muffled sounds emanating from upstairs. The noisy clatter of Heirwegh's 'Danse Marollienne' also could be heard, faintly, although Retzlaff did not recognize the tune.

It had taken several inquiries at various drinking establishments over the past week for Retzlaff to reach this stage of his plan, and he was in no mood to hang about any longer than necessary in such a vile place. He tried to press closer to the wall behind him in a vain attempt to become more inconspicuous, but only called more attention to himself as his unbalanced stool shifted with a loud creak and nearly upended him. Then he lurched forward to catch his coat before it could fall onto the grimy floor, which also amused the Abschaum, the scum, at the table next to him.

Within seconds of gaining his composure, or so it seemed, a heavy-set and garishly rouged middle-aged woman appeared at his side. The top of her frock barely contained her ample bosom, flecked with freckles. What were those old lines from Baudelaire, about Belgian women?

> *The breasts of even the smallest women*
> *Weigh half a ton*
> *And their limbs are like sticks*
> *That remind you of a skeleton*

This one's décolletage would make Baudelaire blush but she certainly wasn't skinny. Someone was feeding her well.

The old hag leaned in closely and Retzlaff caught a whiff of what was supposed to be an enticing scent. It almost made him gag. At least it wasn't as nasty as butyric acid.

"Good evening, *monsieur*," she said, with a smile and a slight nod in his direction. One of her teeth had gone black, probably from gnawing at the chain they used to lock her up at night, Retzlaff thought. Charming.

"Good evening, *madame*." Retzlaff nearly cringed at having to use the word 'madame' with her, and tried to avoid looking in her eyes.

"All alone tonight, hmm? And such a well-dressed gentleman too. *Tant pis.*"

"No, I'm just waiting for my companions. Colleagues, I mean."

"Hmmm. Yes. Of course." She smiled again, more broadly this time. "Would *monsieur* care to see the layout of the upper floors?" she said, glancing upwards. "While you wait, perhaps?"

It took a moment for Retzlaff to realize what she was asking. Another look of disgust crossed his face: the wretched café also doubled as a brothel. Or perhaps the other way round.

"*Non, madame.* I am not here for that," he said. "But thank you for the offer," he added, too late.

"Hmpf," she huffed, before standing up. Smoothing her vast skirts, she added, "That is too bad. Too bad indeed. You look like you could use some time upstairs."

"My apologies, *madame*. Perhaps some other time." Retzlaff attempted his own smile.

"Yes, *peut être*." She turned to walk away, then suddenly looked back towards him. "In the meantime, *monsieur*, your...colleagues are waiting for you in the third room on the left, upstairs."

Fifteen minutes later, Retzlaff left the café, alone and very pleased with himself. He paused for a moment on the street to get his bearings. The rue des Bouchers was crowded with people at this time of night, most of whom were drunk and outfitted in the same way as the patrons in the café he had just left. He turned towards what he thought was the general direction of his hotel, back in the upper town near the Parc de Bruxelles.

After a few minutes he realized had gone the wrong way; the streets were darker in this area and the sounds of revelry could no longer be heard. He put his right hand in his coat pocket as a precaution and a moment later they were upon him. Two men in heavy overcoats appeared from an alley to his right and blocked his way. Their intention was perfectly clear.

"Inside here, old man, and be quick about it," the smaller one said, in guttural French. A slight accent to it, Russian perhaps.

The speaker held a knife in his right hand, pointed blade down against his trouser leg but plain enough for Retzlaff to see. The larger man sidled to the left of Retzlaff and pushed him into the alley. He had closely-cropped mutton chop whiskers and watery, bloodshot eyes.

"No, please, gentlemen, I will cooperate," Retzlaff pleaded. "Please don't hurt me. My wife is waiting at home…"

He staggered deeper into the alley, as if he had been pushed, moving several metres away from the entrance to the street. With a wicked grin and a quick glance at his partner, the smaller thief followed Retzlaff into the darkness.

The larger thief waited near the street, keeping his gaze away from the alley. A moment later he could hear another muffled cry of pain, again from Retzlaff.

"My heart!"

Retzlaff clutched his breast with his free left hand. He fell backwards in a heap next to a stack of empty vegetable crates, caked with dried mud and chicory leaves.

The larger thief remained on guard at the entrance to the alley while his smaller accomplice knelt besides the stricken older man.

"We're not interested in your heart, old man," the thief next to Retzlaff said. "Just give us your wallet. And my friend outside will take care of you soon enough."

The thief looked back at his partner again before moving next to Retzlaff, kneeling down by his left side. Retzlaff froze in apparent terror as the thief reached his free left hand into Retzlaff's inside coat pockets, holding the left side of Retzlaff's coat jacket open with his knife hand. The blade was pointed upwards just a few centimetres from Retzlaff's chin. Retzlaff could smell the garlic on the man's breath, which was still not strong enough to mask the stench of body odour he emitted. Retzlaff's left hand grasped in the air behind the thief's head at nothing in particular, his fist opening and closing as if he were attempting to pump blood into his veins.

The larger man standing watch looked back at them and hissed, "Quickly, now! What's going on back there?"

He looked back towards the street. Again Retzlaff cried out in fear and pain, as the thief next to him retrieved his bounty: Retzlaff's fat leather wallet.

"*Un instant!*" the smaller thief yelled towards his partner. Then to Retzlaff, he almost whispered, "Take it easy, *mec*. We're almost through here. And then my good friend outside will take care of you." A pause. "But what else do you have in there, old man?"

The thief used his free hand to put Retzlaff's wallet into his own inside coat pocket. He was crouched on both knees just to the left of Retzlaff, leaning in close, and unstable now. Retzlaff now had a perfect target area in sight: the thief's groin.

Retzlaff's right hand was still out of sight in his right trouser pocket. He slid the locking mechanism of his knife so the blade could be released. The weapon was a Schrade Presto automatic, imported from America through Retzlaff's contacts in the police force. The spine of the blade had been modified by Retzlaff himself, ground more narrow at the tip to pierce clothing and skin more effectively. Sharp as it was, the blade was wider than the stiletto carried by the thief and Retzlaff could not take the chance that his attack would fail to penetrate the thief's thick coat.

Soon enough, Retzlaff saw his chance. He put his thumb on the button of his knife and held it there for a moment, keeping the weapon in his pocket.

When the thief glanced towards his own chest to put Retzlaff's wallet in his inside coat pocket, Retzlaff bent his own left arm back towards himself, curling it around the thief's right forearm, which held the thief's knife. Retzlaff grasped the thief's own knife hand with his left hand while simultaneously retrieving his Presto with his right hand. The blade flicked open with a slight press of Retzlaff's right thumb.

Retzlaff then jerked the thief's knife hand away from his face before plunging his own blade deep into the femoral artery on the thief's right leg, very close to his groin, the side offering the clearest target. The blade was narrow but Retzlaff twisted it around in the wound to produce a thick stream of hot blood.

The thief produced his own cry of fear and pain, which was, surprisingly enough, indistinguishable from those Retzlaff had made a moment ago.

Retzlaff pulled his blade from the wound and pushed the unbalanced young man backwards, still holding the man's right knife hand in a strong grip. The thief instinctively used his free left hand to stop the gush of blood at his groin, which made it easy for Retzlaff to plunge his knife past the folds of the thief's open coat and deep into his heart.

A second cry of pain was cut short just before Retzlaff retrieved his wallet, and that of the thief, from the younger man's inside coat pockets.

"André, what is happening in there?" The big man spoke more urgently, peering into the alley, looking for his friend.

Silence from within the alley.

"André?"

The big man walked into the alley, moving cautiously as his eyes adjusted to the darkness. He looked at his partner lying there next to some crates, on his back, still and silent. André's eyes were open wide but there seemed to be no life in them.

The old man was on top of him, face down. Also still and silent. Two dead bodies. But how did André die while the old man was having a heart attack in front of him?

"*André?*"

The big thief leaned down to turn over the old man, who suddenly came to life and plunged a blade into the big man's carotid artery. There was no need to twist it this time. The blood splattered out in a violent gush and the thief staggered backwards, holding his hand to his throat. But the gesture was pointless.

Retzlaff carefully cleaned his blade on André's trousers and closed it with a click before slipping it back into his trouser pocket. He stood and watched for a few moments as the big man bled to death, crumpling slowly downwards, a few metres away. The man tried to speak but could only produce wet gurgles. Weak and garbled, his voice was useless.

When the man was still, Retzlaff took his wallet and slipped out of the alley.

Chapter 32

Cumming's foul mood nearly matched Walsh's own disposition when the two men sat down across from each other at a small café near the Palace Hotel in Brussels. So there was little time and no inclination for pleasantries on this occasion.

Walsh spent less than five minutes briefing Cumming on his last encounter with Ernst and Tobias. The tale did not please the older man.

"Walsh, are you completely sure about the game you're playing here?" Cumming said. "Suppose these two really have other buyers waiting? And the Exposition is to open this week! Won't that bring in more interest?"

"Possibly, if they were serious about spreading the word about what they have to offer."

"And you don't think they are?"

Walsh shrugged his shoulders. "Tobias perhaps, but not Ernst. And Ernst is the key here."

"Why is that?" Cumming quickly raised his hand to prevent Walsh from speaking. A moment later, a waiter appeared with their drinks.

After the waiter moved off, Walsh answered, "Because he alone knows the secret. And because he is the one under pressure from home. Not Tobias."

"What pressure?"

Walsh paused for a moment. "His family has hired a private investigator to find him. And it's possible that the investigator is now in Brussels. Or on his way here."

Cumming sat back in his chair, open-mouthed. "You can't be serious."

Walsh nodded. "Ernst has told me so, and he is obviously frightened about it. *Very* frightened, in fact. So I don't think he will be inclined to make his presence here known to anyone else. And he wants to conclude this business as quickly as possible." Walsh took a sip of his own coffee. "So I need to know if we can pay him what he asks."

"Five thousand pounds?"

"Yes."

Cumming shook his head. "You know, Walsh, I had an earlier meeting here with another of our agents on the continent. To look at a new German pistol. A Mauser, in fact. Have you heard anything about it?"

Walsh shook his head.

"Right. Well, we found someone who could smuggle it out of Mauser's shop so we could photograph it. Do you know how much we paid to have a look at it?"

"I have no idea."

"Twenty-five pounds."

Walsh smiled, but without humour. He got the message. "So what are you telling me, C? That we aren't going to pay?"

"Not quite. But it's going to take some time. I'm trying to put together a package of funds from several sources outside my normal budget. It will have to be approved by the CID, for a start."

"For the full five thousand?" Walsh raised an eyebrow.

"That's what I'm going to ask, but things would be considerably easier if you could get them lower."

"Well, I'm sure we could find ways to put some pressure on them. Or on Ernst at least."

"Any ideas?"

"For a start, I could make him believe that Retzlaff, the German investigator that is, is now in Brussels. It would almost certainly bring him back to the table."

"Is that possible?"

Walsh nodded. "Of course. Should be easy enough. But I don't think it will come to that. He's quite eager to make a deal right now, I think."

"You must be careful not to scare him into going back home," Cumming said.

"I don't think that's an option for him. I don't think he left home just to sell this one secret. There's more to it than that. But I get your point. He might have somewhere else to run. Though I don't really think so."

Cumming paused for a moment and stared at his coffee. "Walsh, I'm going to confide in you. I'm at a loss here. Really I am. If this business with your chemist falls apart, or worse, leads us to lose thousands of pounds over nothing, then our work here is through. It could be a nasty can of worms to open. We've had these problems in the past, even before I was appointed. Men promising things they can't deliver, even after we've paid. Or providing information that turns out to be completely useless to us."

"I can appreciate that, C, but..."

Cumming raised a hand. "Let me finish. On the other hand, I just finished my first six-month report on the work of the Secret Service Bureau. I must tell you that it was not impressive. Not impressive at all, in fact."

"It can't be that bad."

"Yes it is, I'm afraid. At least, I think so. I wouldn't be impressed with it." Cumming removed his monocle and rubbed his eye gently before replacing the eyepiece. "The first two months were completely wasted just getting things sorted out for my working arrangements. And now I still have just a handful of agents on the continent, such as yourself, keeping an eye open about German war preparations. Plus assorted 'volunteers' here and there, businessmen mostly, who offer to find information. Much of it is useless. Completely useless."

"And they, or should I say, *we*, are not finding any evidence to suggest a surprise invasion of Britain, correct?"

"Correct. And I've been looking into the topic myself. I've found two Admiralty papers, from 1906 and '07, and they concluded that it would be difficult if not impossible to mount such an attack. Probably impossible, I should think. The Germans can't possibly control the North Sea long enough to ferry enough men across to threaten us. Not in the face of our naval strength. And they won't be catching up anytime soon with their own Dreadnoughts. I mean, seriously! How many men would it take to invade Britain successfully? A hundred thousand? A quarter of a million? *Half* a million? And to shift them across the North Sea with our own vessels prowling around the entire time? Ridiculous. The Admiralty just doesn't think it is possible, and I'm increasingly inclined to agree."

"And there is no reason to believe otherwise, based on what I've learned here."

"Exactly. Speaking of which, did you follow up with those other sources? The mobilization calendar and the Zeppelin material?"

Walsh nodded. "I saw the calendar, briefly. The man said he *used to* serve with German forces, and the calendar itself was from around 1904, from their *Aufmarsch* against France at the time."

Cumming frowned. *"Aufmarsch?"*

"Sorry, I mean deployment plan. Anyhow, I thought it was fairly useless, being so old, and told him so. It specified a war against France alone, with sixty-seven divisions in total. But I know they are planning for a two-front war now, so this calendar won't help us."

"I see. Damn. What was he asking for it?"

"Five thousand francs," Walsh said. "Or two hundred pounds."

Cumming nodded. "Too much, you're right, my boy."

"But I also told him that more recent, more comprehensive information, would be helpful, and he said he would see what he could do. I specifically mentioned order of battle details. But I'm not hopeful about him. He just seemed to want to make a few fast quid and be done with it."

"And the Zeppelin material?"

Walsh took a sip of coffee. "That was from a *former* employee of Luftschiffbau Zeppelin. He wouldn't tell me where he works now. But after wasting my time with the mobilization calendar deal, I tried to keep this one talking as long as possible before we talked prices. He wasn't as jumpy as the army source; in fact, we had a long meal together, once I had agreed to pay for it."

"And his offer?"

"Well, he was a machinist in something called the 'Ring Shed' at Friedrichshafen, where the first assembly stage of a Zeppelin takes place. Anyhow, there's been a dispute between their army and navy about the use of these things in war. The army wants smaller, short range ships for missions over land, while the navy wants larger, longer-range ones for sea missions. A thousand-mile range, if possible, can you believe that? And so Zeppelin was trying to design something that would satisfy the navy. Satisfy Admiral Tirpitz. But Count Zeppelin wasn't happy about it all."

"Why not? And what did this employee have to offer?"

"Well, you remember the crash of their LZ-4 two years ago? The one that burned up near Stuttgart?"

Cumming shook his head. "I don't exactly recall…"

"I was in Stuttgart at the time, C, and still remember the photographs from the newspapers. It was having engine troubles, so they moored it overnight. But it came off the moorings in a thunderstorm and blew up in the air. It was totally destroyed."

Cumming nodded. "And so?"

"And so, after that disaster, Tirpitz insisted on paying on more attention to Zeppelin's works, while the Count himself was growing wary of building such huge ships. So Tirpitz assigned a naval architect, Felix Pietzker was his name, to help Zeppelin with this idea. Pietzker studied Zeppelin's works, and made designs for a huge ship, with over one million cubic feet capacity, more than twice as large as the LZ-4 that had crashed. According to my source, who was assigned to assist Pietzker, it was going to cost something around one-hundred and fifty thousand pounds, and Tirpitz doesn't want to pay that much. But my source says he has copies of the original designs if we want them. Including specifications for the six engines the ship would require."

"But they aren't building this thing?"

Walsh shook his head. "Not yet. And my source wants one hundred pounds for these drawings. I assume you are not interested?" He raised his eyebrow.

"I suppose not, if they aren't going to build it. And not at that price!"

Walsh leaned back in his chair, and held up his empty hands in defeat. "And so, more wasted time here."

Cumming leaned forward and spoke carefully. "Listen, Walsh, you are not wasting your time. Even with these…these missed opportunities, the lack of evidence of German aggression is still a kind of result, of a negative sort. So that could be helpful. But we can't just sit around confirming that point over and over. We need something else. Something more interesting. More useful, I suppose."

"And the acetone secret would be useful. A positive result."

"Most certainly. If it can be delivered. And it would help our budgetary situation for next year, undoubtedly."

Walsh paused. "Let me have one more meeting with Ernst, on his own, and I'll see where his mind is. Then I'll take the necessary next steps. If you think you can get the money, that is."

"The wheels are in motion, my boy. So let's try to mend some fences here, shall we?"

"Fair enough, C. Shouldn't be too difficult, if I read Ernst correctly. And he's fairly easy to read, from what I've seen." A pause. "Now what about the situation with Kell and Long?"

Cumming smiled a little now. "That's a more positive outcome. You remember I've been allowed to move my premises to another location separate from Kell?"

"Ashley Gardens."

"That's right." Cumming lowered his voice. "But there's more. I'm going to ask Blitz and Bethell for a complete separation of my work from Kell's."

"Because of what happened with Long?"

"That's just part of it. But all part of a pattern. Too much confusion over remits and directing our agents. Among other things. The details are not important. But, mind you, Kell still thinks that the Germans, the NA, might try to sow some false leads for us here. For you. Even if this acetone thing is legitimate."

Walsh nodded. "They have a point. But I'm being careful, C, very careful. Trust me. But will they agree to this separation from Kell?"

"Kell and I are coming to terms with it, so I don't suppose they will have much choice. Not if we both want the same thing."

"And what kind of division of labour are you seeking?"

"I will handle all foreign matters, and Kell will handle matters at home. Simple as that, really. Should've happened months ago."

"And each of you will handle both espionage and counter-espionage in your, your territories?"

"Yes, that's the idea," Cumming said. "But given the nature of these tasks, Kell will handle most of the counter-espionage work and I will handle the intelligence side. More or less."

"Of course. But this won't change what I'm doing here?"

"No, you are to stay focused on your current tasks. Unless directed otherwise by me alone. And you must let me know if Long or any other agent of the Bureau contacts you."

"Certainly. But I think Long got the message about that."

Cumming smiled. "I'm sure he did." He downed the rest of his coffee and stood to leave. "I'm afraid I need to catch a train soon. I'll be in touch through the usual means. And I hope to come back again soon. At least once again over the summer."

Walsh stood up as well. "Just let me know."

"Keep me informed about the next steps with Ernst, won't you?"

"Yes, it won't be long now, C. He'll come around at our next meeting. I'm sure of it."

"Good lad. And do be careful, won't you? Watch yourself. This business with the Germans could become complicated, especially if I do end up delivering thousands of pounds in cash over here."

Chapter 33

Agram, Croatia. April 1910.

Bogdan Zerajic, twenty-three years old, was not happy about meeting his contact from the east on his home territory, Agram University, but he knew he had little choice in the matter. A poor Serbian law student, Zerajic had been one of nine children born and raised on a kmet, or a peasant farm, in Nevisinje, eastern Herzegovina.

Raised in a filthy wooden shack, that is, with a thatched roof, packed earth floor, and no windows. He was not used to getting his own way, just like the rest of his family. Zerajic's feeble father was required to turn over one-third of the cash value of his annual output to his Muslim landlord, just one of the many indignities his people were forced to suffer under the kmet system condoned by the Austrian monarchy and controlled by local landowners throughout the Balkans.

Unlike his father, however, Zerajic was determined to make a brighter future for himself, hence his law studies at Agram University. Also unlike his father, he was determined to do something about the shame he and his fellow Serbs had to endure, and so his meeting with Mikhail Bukov.

If the man ever appeared, that is.

The streets of Agram were rapidly thinning out at this time of night, which only made this meeting more conspicuous. Zerajic, a lone bundle of nerves with bushy eyebrows, a full moustache, and thick, dark hair, sat on his bench outside of the main university entrance, pretending not to be waiting for someone.

But how does one do that, exactly? No matter what Zerajic's pretensions, fear still gripped his insides; he felt that if a policeman came upon him then he would instinctively run off down the street as if he had no control over his legs. That would be the end of this little scheme and, quite possibly, his life.

Zerajic crossed his legs again and tried not to fidget. In his pocket he fingered a small circular cardboard badge, a talisman of sorts. For him at least. It bore a portrait of a scowling man carrying a scythe, and was inspired by the cover of a book by Pyotr Kropotkin, the Russian anarchist.

Just as he was about to give up, Bukov was at his side. The small man sat down next to him and offered him a sweet from a crumpled paper bag in his hand. Zerajic quickly popped it into his mouth and waited. If only his heart would stop pounding so hard.

"Sorry for the late arrival," Bukov said, in Serbo-Croatian with a slight foreign accent. "A delayed train. The lines here are not so reliable, I'm afraid. I trust it didn't worry you?"

"It's no worry to me," Zerajic lied.

"Good. Excellent. You must maintain that attitude. No problems, no worries, no excitement. Just a typical student here." Bukov offered a grim smile and patted Zerajic on the back.

Zerajic almost flinched at the gesture, but held himself together. "I'm doing my best." The words were slightly muddled as Zerajic sucked nervously on his peppermint.

"Keep it up. Now listen carefully."

Bukov leaned closer. He stroked his beard and began to whisper next to Zerajic's ear. Zerajic could smell tobacco on him. Expensive pipe tobacco, earthy and masculine.

"Obviously the emperor is going to travel by rail," Bukov continued. "He's also going to stop at various places on the way to Sarajevo, to see as many loyal subjects as he can. Or to allow *them* to see *him*, the generous old fool! Isn't he a kind one? So, my friend, we expect him to stop in Bosna-Brod on the way to Sarajevo, sometime between May 29 and June 1. Do you know where that is?"

"Yes, of course. On the frontier with Bosnia."

"Yes, exactly. You need to be there for him. At the railway station. It's your best chance. Security will be much tighter for him in Sarajevo, you understand. The Ballhausplatz" - Bukov referred to the central administrative building of the Austrian State Chancellor – "is collecting information about supposed plots from its embassies all over Europe. Paris, Sofia, Berlin, Lisbon, Brussels, Budapest."

Something like a choked laugh escaped Bukov's tight little mouth; perhaps one of the sweets got caught at the back of his throat.

"Ha! See how many enemies they have!" he continued. "You think they would get the message by now. No matter. The point is that they will be ready in Sarajevo. Preparations are being made. But it is not the same in Bosna-Brod. Just a sleepy little village. Nothing ever happens there. A brief stop on the way to the main show. And there have been no changes to the route that we know of."

Zerajic nodded in understanding. "I can leave here a few days before that. It should be no problem. If you can pay for it, of course."

Bukov offered him another sweet. Zerajic declined.

"Yes, yes. We're working on that, comrade. Of course we are." Bukov paused, and looked off into the distance. It was dark; nothing to see there. "But there has been a slight delay."

"What delay?"

"Nothing to worry about," Bukov put a hand on Zerajic's shoulder. He was surprisingly strong for such a lithe man. "Only a slight one. We have things well under control. Revolution is not always such a exact business, you know."

"But a train timetable is," Zerajic protested. "And so is the emperor's schedule."

"Yes, certainly. We can pay for your ticket now. And I do have the other thing you need."

Bukov slipped a parcel, the size of a large book, into Zerajic's sweaty hand. It was wrapped in paper, like his sweets bag.

"Open this at your flat, and hide it well," Bukov said, with a wink.

Bukov stood to leave. As he looked around the silent streets, he continued talking, almost to himself. "We'll have more details soon. It won't be long now. Good luck, comrade. I will contact you again in two weeks."

Ten minutes later, alone and safe in his grubby flat, Zerajic ripped open the parcel with shaking hands. It was heavier than its size suggested, and contained only a single leather-bound book.

Inside the front cover of the book, whose title or author he did not even notice, Zerajic found a crisp new twenty-kronen note, enough to pay for a rail ticket to Bosna-Brod. He cursed under this breath; he had been hoping for much more than that, but perhaps at their next meeting. He threw the note aside, then flipped through the pages of the rest of the book.

In the middle of the book he found a large hollowed-out section. Inside the hollowed compartment was a Browning 9mm pistol, fully loaded.

Zerajic smiled, for the first time in a long while.

Chapter 34

Brussels. April 1910.

A crowd of thousands of visitors, exhibitors, and distinguished guests packed into the vast grounds of the Exposition Universelle to hear Albert I, King of the Belgians, officially welcome them to the huge spectacle organized so effectively by his small country. From his perch in the Belgian section of the Grand Palais in the centre of the Exposition grounds, the king took special care to note the noble aims of this peaceful celebration of the amazing achievements of modern international society.

"By its international aspect, the Exhibition has a human significance," he began, "for it appears as an imposing manifestation of the pacific struggle in the fields of labour and progress, in which the nations tend more and more to compete with each other. It is a work of peace and prosperity in which free competition has replaced the armed conflicts of former days."

After a few more lines of a similar nature, he concluded with another explicit appeal to the pacific natures of all those who could hear his words: "This, at least, is the wish which I have the right to express openly at the beginning of my reign, and before the representatives of the states friendly to Belgium. I do not doubt that it will find an echo in all hearts."

From the rear of that section the Grand Palais, where the Belgian section joined with British one, Dewulf watched as the young king gave his short speech. Gripped with nervous tension, Dewulf scanned the large hall with his bright grey eyes, searching for any signs of unusual activity. Anarchists tended to prefer pistols and bombs for their assassination plots, but Dewulf could not discount the possibility of a sniper equipped with a rifle.

A number of Dewulf's junior colleagues from the Sûreté mingled in the crowd, dressed in plain clothes, while dozens of uniformed men from the gendarmerie and the Brussels police watched the events from various positions around the room. They all breathed a sigh of relief when the king concluded his remarks and left the stage to join his wife, Queen Elisabeth of the Bavarian Wittelsbachs, named in honour of her aunt, the Austrian Empress assassinated in

1898. The dignified young couple waved to the cheering crowd and departed through the rear of the building, where a royal coach waited to collect them for the ride back to central Brussels. A few minutes later, Dewulf decided to follow their example and return by tram to his office, where he could collapse for a well-deserved nap. The king would soon be attending yet another public event, to open the new colonial museum – the 'Museum of the Belgian Congo' - in Tervuren, and Dewulf had to be ready for that.

Outside the Grand Palais, Walsh and Gisela watched the king and his wife depart before turning their attention to the guidebook and map Gisela clutched in her gloved hand. They were utterly overwhelmed by the range of entertainment possibilities open to them today. The Exposition was indeed a spectacular sight now that it was up and running, swarming with eager guests and fully-staffed shops, cafés, restaurants, and exhibitions. A narrow-gauge train line carried smiling visitors around the complex of buildings, and everyone was dressed in their finest spring outfits: handsome double-breasted suits and bowler hats on many of the men, strolling arm in arm with women adorned with feathered or ruffled bonnets and graceful lace dresses, parasols in hand. Even the children were turned out in their tidiest Sunday outfits: sailor suits and pretty pinafores.

In the distance Walsh could see a field of brilliantly-coloured hot-air balloons, a couple of which had already ascended into the blue spring sky. He could also hear the music of a dozen nations coming to his ears from various directions: squeezebox polkas, marching songs, dance hall tunes, folk guitar music, and even the sounds of an opera singer echoing across the huge spectacle laid out before him. He had to admit to himself that this was the most amazing event he had ever personally encountered, outside of a war zone, and he knew he would be spending as much time here as possible over the next few months, Cumming and the SSB be damned.

Gisela's gentle hand on his arm brought his mind back into focus. "This is unbelieveable, isn't it?" she gushed.

Walsh nodded in full agreement. "But where shall we start? '*Les Halles des Machines*' perhaps?" he asked, with no other possibility in his mind.

"There's so much to see!" Gisela said. "I can't believe there was nothing here just a few years ago. You really must give the Belgians some credit for this."

"I've never seen anything like it," he said.

They found an empty bench just outside the Belgian section of the Grand Palais. Once they were next to it, Walsh grabbed Gisela's waist in an awkward embrace just before she sat down.

"Wait!" he said.

"I beg your pardon, Mr Walsh?" She stood up abruptly and stared at him in confusion. But she didn't pull away from his embrace.

"Sorry, the paint might still be wet. This place isn't exactly finished, you know." He pointed his hand at the bench.

She gave him an amused look, and stepped back from him.

"Yes, of course. Wet paint. How careless of me! Can you check it please?" She held up her gloved hands in front of him – *I can't use these.*

He touched the seat and back of the bench. Dry as a bone. He wished he had a camera to take a photograph of the look on her face.

He smiled at her, then motioned for her to sit down. He sat after she did.

"Now let's get to business. How about the German section first?" Walsh said.

"Possibly. But let's make a plan, shall we? The German section is way at the back, but I want to see the *Palais des Travaux Féminins*. And it's closer." She pointed near the front entrance of the Exposition. "Just across there, I should think."

Walsh looked at the map, and yes, there it was: Le Palais des Travaux Féminins, off to the right after the main entrance.

"You can't be serious. A section for women's work? What does that even mean? Corsets and nappies?" Walsh tried to avoid scowling.

"Of course I'm serious! And why not? Am I not a woman?"

Now Walsh gave her a look. "Of course you are."

With her elegant shimmering spring dress, delicate wide-brimmed straw hat, white silk gloves, and light brown leather lace-up boots she could hardly be mistaken for a man.

"I just thought you were more interested in machinery, that's all," Walsh continued. "What about the automobiles and bicycles?"

"In good time, Mr Walsh, in good time. There is more to life than machines and trains and electricity." She smiled at him as she smoothed out the large map on the bench.

"Just call me Nicholas, if you don't mind."

"I suppose I can do that." A pause. "Nicholas. Now why don't we just start near the entrance and work our way back?"

"But we could have lunch at the *Münchener-Haus* in the German section. I hear it's very good. And there's an American bar at the *Alt-Dusseldorf* building."

It was also very close to the things he really wanted to see, conveniently.

"What, *Bier und Wurst*? I can get that anytime at home. And I don't even like it at home!"

"Well, the Nuremberg toy display is supposed to be really interesting," he offered. "Don't you want to see that?"

Gisela shook her head and waved her hand at him. "It can wait."

Walsh looked down at the map again. "Look, the *Pavillion de la Ville de Bruxelles* is right over there."

Walsh pointed down the avenue, towards a large building at the end. Constructed of brick and stone and adorned with many styles of carved figures, it was topped by a tall clock tower, making it an easy reference point for visitors to the Exposition. It also served as a kind of gateway to two other large Belgian pavilions.

"Suppose we compromise with some local cuisine?" he finished.

She followed his gaze and saw what he had in mind.

"Yes, I suppose we could eat while we plan. And it's a short walk from there to the *Travaux Féminins*." She smiled at him again.

Walsh knew this was the best he could do. Food first, then the bloody women's work after that. He stood up and he held his hand out to her.

"Shall we then, Miss Koenig?"

She took his hand, stood up gracefully, and then took his arm in hers. "Please, Nicholas, you might as well call me Gisela. Especially after saving me from that awful wet paint."

After a hearty meal – wild boar sausages smothered in dark-beer gravy for him, and a bowl of creamy waterzooi garnished with small chunks of lobster for her – they walked to the Palais des Travaux Féminins and spent as much time there as Walsh could stand. It was much easier for him on a full stomach, he decided. And perhaps it would distract her from wanting to see the Pavilion de la Fermière – the pavilion of the farmer's wife. He'd seen enough of that sort of thing as a youth.

Fortunately the building dedicated to the works of women was not especially large, when compared to the main pavilions in the centre of the Exposition. It was built in the style of a grand orangerie, complete with stone columns along the façade and large windows and glass-fronted doors to let in as much light as possible. Inside, however, rather than fruit trees, Walsh was treated to endless displays of lace-making, embroidery, weaving, tapestry, and painting. He followed Gisela around, nodding appreciatively here and there, barely able to conceal his boredom. Near the end of the displays, Gisela caught him blushing at the sight of the lingerie section, and he begged Gisela to take him out of there. Which she did.

Nearby they made their way into the Pavillion de l'Oeuvre Maternelle des Conveuses d'Enfants. Walsh easily recognized the cradles, cribs, examining tables, and other devices associated with the care of infants, but he and Gisela were both surprised to see a large, excited crowd moving along a row of tall, narrow machines. They moved closer to one of the devices for a better look.

It was about one metre wide and two metres tall, and resembled a steel and glass display cabinet on short steel legs, but with a kind of chimney coming out of the top. They peered inside and Walsh could see a child's baby doll lying nestled in some blankets.

Walsh knocked on the glass, playfully, pretending to wake up the 'child.' As they looked closer, suddenly the doll opened its eyes and moved its arm. It was alive! Gisela stifled a scream with her gloved hand, before smiling in embarrassment at Walsh.

They noted the sign above the display, announcing Dr Alexandre Lion's 'infant incubators.'

"An...oven for children?" Gisela said, as she tapped the glass and watched the infant move in response, like an animal in a zoo. "Can that be safe?"

"I suppose, if the heat is low enough. We used to put newborn lambs in a warm oven on my uncle's farm to strengthen them, if they didn't seem well enough to survive a cold night on their own."

"But to do that with a child?"

Walsh read the sign next to the incubator. "It's automatic. It constantly regulates air and temperature so the baby won't suffocate or overheat. Quite ingenious, I should think."

Gisela shuddered at the thought. "I can't imagine putting my baby in there. If I had one. It's inhumane! Suppose the regulator goes wrong? Suppose someone changes the dial by accident? Children in ovens – what next?"

"It says it's perfectly safe. I'm sure it's designed not to overheat, for any reason."

Why was he trying to convince her of his point of view again? After all, she did have a very valid point.

"I wouldn't trust it with my baby's life," Gisela insisted. "Not ever."

She sniffed again, and backed away from the line of shiny new incubators, each with a writhing infant trapped inside, behind the glass, in full view of a long line of fascinated spectators.

After the boxed babies and a few more, slightly less controversial, exhibits, they only had time for a quick drink at Moët et Chandon before Walsh abruptly left Gisela alone and confused, standing with her glass at the bar, still thinking about those imprisoned infants, he guessed.

It was nearly dusk when Walsh turned the corner from Chaussée d'Ixelles onto rue de l'Arbe, heading back to his flat in Ixelles. It has been the most pleasant day he had had in a very long time, even with the detour to admire the 'women's work'. Why had he put up with that? Of course, he knew perfectly well why he had allowed Gisela to drag him along, and he smiled at the thought of her.

On the corner, where rue de l'Arbe turned right onto rue Souveraine, he saw a lone figure. A man waiting, with his back to him. Waiting for Walsh perhaps?

Walsh paused at the small open area framed by the intersection of rue de l'Arbe and rue des Chevaliers. A tiny triangle of grass dotted with a handful of small trees, lit by a single gas streetlight.

What to do? No cafés here, no shops, no open doors, nowhere to hide. And he didn't want to enter his own flat if someone was watching him. He had just put his right hand in his coat to check his pistol, when the figure turned to face him. The man came running to him and suddenly Walsh recognized him: Ernst! Walsh kept his hand in his coat as Ernst reached him, breathless and haggard.

"Mr Walsh! Please!"

"What are you doing here? How did you find me?" Walsh grabbed the young man by the shoulder with his free left hand and pulled him to the nearest wall.

"Please, help me! It's Tobias!" Ernst said.

"Calm down! And lower your voice! What is it?" Walsh gripped the butt of his pistol, but kept it holstered. He looked into Ernst's eyes, wide with fear.

"He's disappeared! I think they've taken him!"

PART THREE

Chapter 35

Dewulf found Leysen alone in a holding cell at the end of a long corridor in St Gilles prison, the largest such facility in Brussels. Dewulf hated the place, although he knew it was necessary. He hated what it had done to the neighbourhood. And he hated what they, what he, had done to Leysen. But sacrifices had to be made.

The air in the place was sticky and foul on this late April afternoon. Dewulf struggled to resist the urge to douse a handkerchief with cologne and hold it to his nose to block the stench of piss and cabbage. He looked back into the holding cell, where Leysen reclined on his cot, staring at Dewulf but not actually looking at him.

The guard standing next to Dewulf caught his distaste. "You think this is bad, inspector? You should smell inside the solitary confinement wing. That should put anyone off crime for good."

"Well, it doesn't seem to be working, judging from the size of this place," Dewulf said.

St Gilles prison was indeed impressive to any observer, but it also looked completely out of place in its setting. The prison resembled a Tudor stone fortress, with multiple turrets crowned with merlons, thick stone walls, archaic arrowslits, and a massive wooden door, even though it had been completed only in 1884. From a central hub, five prison wings, each one three stories high, were filled with small tiled-floor cells and cast-iron rails. Dewulf could hear desperate sounds of shouting and clanging echoing off the high vaulted tunnels that snaked throughout the complex.

Dewulf motioned for the guard to leave. "Would you leave us alone for a few minutes, please?"

The guard nodded and walked back down the corridor.

Once he was away, Leysen spoke. It took a moment for him to register when he last saw Dewulf.

"I suppose I should thank you for shooting that bastard who tried to kill me."

"You're welcome."

Leysen sat up a little higher in his cot. He was not a convict, and so was able to wear his own clothes, which consisted of a dark brown suit with no tie, brown leather shoes with no laces, and a Borsolino-style fedora hanging on a hook on the wall.

"But I'm not thanking you," Leysen continued. "Not after I ended up in here. This wasn't part of the deal. So where the hell is Kluskens? And who the hell are you?"

Dewulf stepped closer to the bars of the cell, hands clasped behind his back. "I'm sorry, this couldn't be helped."

That was true; Belgium did not provide separate facilities for convicted criminals and those, like Leysen, merely awaiting trial. Or awaiting the appearance of a trial.

"I'm Inspector Dewulf. Your new boss. Temporarily."

"Is that so? And what about our dear Inspector Kluskens?"

Dewulf fished a packet of Piedmont cigarettes out of his pocket and offered one to Leysen. "How did you like working for him?"

Leysen hesitated a moment, then sat up abruptly and approached the bars to take the cigarette, which he put behind his ear. Dewulf got a better look at him now; about twenty-five years old, he seemed, with scruffy light brown hair and grey-blue eyes; an odd combination. A shade over two metres tall, with a physique that suggested he was comfortable with manual labour. A small scar on his left cheek. And a beard that needed serious trimming.

"I didn't," Leysen said. "But I didn't have many options at the time."

"You did after Kluskens magically exonerated you last year. On that counterfeiting scam, when he first caught you. But you stayed on with him."

Leysen smiled, showing a mouthful of dingy teeth. One of them was capped with gold. How had he managed that?

"What can I say? He paid me." Leysen rubbed his eyes. "And better than I could make on the streets around here. He also threatened to tell any new employer of mine about my past, so I didn't have much of an incentive to look for another job."

"Too bad for you. But the fact remains, as I see it: you have a taste for this kind of work. A real gift for it, if that means anything."

The smile faded. "I have a taste for money, inspector. I don't exactly care who pays me. But I do care when they double-cross me."

"You aren't being double-crossed, Leysen. This was just for appearances. Don't take it personally. We had to take you in on the street and now you've been seen in here, just like any other criminal."

Dewulf moved closer to the bars to get a good look at Leysen. "You're career is about to accelerate," he said. "Now get your things together."

An hour later, Dewulf tried to hide his disgust as Leysen slurped from a steaming bowl of lentil soup with a crust of bread in his hand. Their surroundings were considerably more pleasant now; an outside table at a large café on Place M. Van Meenen, a short walk from the prison. Dewulf decided to let the man eat for a few minutes before troubling him.

"God, the food in that place," said Leysen. "Not one day without mouldy bread! Not one in five! You people owe me more than a few good meals. Prison wasn't part of the deal."

"We'll do what we can. All in good time, my friend." Dewulf took a drink of his coffee. "So does this mean we have an agreement?"

"Not so fast, inspector! We're not there yet. I want to hear more about this case of yours before I decide anything. And as long as I'm eating, and you're paying, I'm listening."

Dewulf paused a moment. "It's not exactly a criminal case. In fact, it's not even a 'case' at the moment. If you want to use that term."

Leysen bit into his chunk of bread. "So what the hell is it then? Just a little hobby of yours?" A few crumbs flew out of his mouth; Dewulf managed to dodge them.

"You are aware of the Exposition in Brussels this year?"

"Of course I am. Who isn't? But I'm afraid I missed the opening. I was a little detained. Against my will, you understand." Leysen jabbed at the air with his bread to make his point.

"Yes, yes, I told you, we're sorry about that."

Leysen took a drink from his large goblet of Chimay. It dribbled down his chin.

"Ahh, that's good," Leysen said. "Couldn't get that in prison, I can tell you!" Another bite, another spray of crumbs. "But I still can't believe Kluskens is letting me go. He can't be happy about that. I broke four cases for him in less than a year. Plus the counterfeiting thing."

"Yes, we're aware of that. Now listen." Dewulf leaned in closer. "This Exposition is important to us, you understand? To Brussels. To Belgium. The entire world is watching us. And for such a small country, it is a great responsibility. A great opportunity. We are competing now with New York, London, Paris, Chicago, great cities."

"Yes, and so what? What does this have to do with me? What do I know about world's fairs?" Leysen stopped chewing for once.

"So, we are expecting millions of visitors over the next few months. It doesn't end until November, you know. And many foreign dignitaries. Very important people. People who need to be protected. Presidents and prime ministers. Royal families from across Europe. The Kaiser plans to attend, you know. And Roosevelt will be here very soon."

Leysen frowned in confusion. "President Roosevelt?"

Dewulf nodded. "He's doing a European tour and stopping here, just to visit the Exposition. The former president Roosevelt. It's President Taft in charge in America now. Remember Roosevelt's predecessor, McKinley, was killed at an Exposition. The Pan-American one."

Leysen stared across the table at Dewulf. "Wait just a minute. Who are you really? Who do you work for? What is this about?"

"I'm not with the police." A slight pause. "I'm with the Sûreté."

"The Sûreté?!"

Dewulf looked around the café with some alarm. "Yes, and keep your voice down, if you please."

Leysen looked down at his soup and put down his spoon. He put his hands to his face. He seemed to have lost his appetite. "And what does the Sûreté want with me?"

"I told you, these people need to be protected. And we need help with that."

"And is there a plot to harm them?"

"Nothing specific. But we must take no chances. It is going to be a long summer and autumn. We are doing the best we can to…to keep track of everyone. But it's not enough, I'm afraid."

Leysen put his head in his hands. *"Merde.* You want me to spy for you, is that it?"

"Something like that." Dewulf pushed a small piece of paper across the table. "And I want you to pay close attention to this."

Leysen shook his head. "That's not what I do." He opened the paper and looked at it, then shook his head again.

"Of course it is. Don't be naïve. You've been doing it for nearly a year now. And very effectively, it seems. You seem to have a real talent for this kind of work. Otherwise I wouldn't be here."

"No, that was different. That's crime. I was working against specific crimes, people who were up to something. The police were already preparing a case against them when I came in to help. But this is another matter entirely. This is not what I do. This is…politics!" Leysen practically hissed that last word.

Dewulf attempted a smile. "Crime and politics, what's the difference, really?"

"That's not funny. And I don't know how you expect me to get in here." Leysen held up the scrap of paper in front of Dewulf.

"I'm sure you'll manage. Now look, the chances are you won't find anything, right? We don't know of any specific plot. There may not be one. If we're lucky, it will be a nice and quiet Exposition. Fun and games for everyone and no harm done. So you just spend a few months keeping your eye on things, just to be safe. And if you hear something we should know about, then you tell us. Hopefully in time for us to stop it. It's that simple, my friend. In the meantime, you get to live your life normally. Without dealing with criminals."

"I think I prefer the criminals," said Leysen. "It's even *more* simple with them. I know what they want."

"Yes, they want money. And revolutionaries want power. And money is power. So I ask you again, my friend. What's the difference?"

Chapter 36

Walsh sat with Ernst at the same café in Place Fernand Cocq where he had met the two young Germans in March. The student chemist was still shaken up; he had not slept well. But Walsh had been even more uncomfortable, on the floor of his flat with a few thin blankets while Ernst had taken his bed.

"Steady on, now. Have some breakfast," Walsh said, as he munched on a croissant. "We'll sort this out soon enough."

Ernst looked deflated, as if the spine had been removed from his back. "I don't feel like eating. We need to do something."

"We are doing something. We need to think, and I can't think properly on an empty stomach." Walsh gulped down some of his coffee. "Now let's go through it all again, shall we? You were a bit incoherent last night."

"Can you blame me?" Ernst fiddled with a crusty roll. A moment later, a thin line of blood began leaking from his nose.

Walsh pointed to his own nose as a signal, and Ernst quickly understood, grabbing a napkin from the table and holding it to his nose. Then he tilted his head backwards.

Walsh looked around the room to see that a couple of patrons were looking at them. Or at Ernst, more specifically.

Walsh leaned towards Ernst and lowered his voice. "Well, we don't have all the facts now, do we? So let's not rush to judgement here. So Tobias went to meet a buyer. Someone interested in the acetone."

"I told you last night, we didn't place the advertisement. But Tobias thought it would put pressure on you so he let you think we had placed it." Ernst shook his head. "He can be so greedy sometimes."

Easy enough for you to say, Walsh thought, coming from such a rich family.

"But the advertisement had your correct contact details in it?"

Ernst nodded. "Yes, that's how they found us."

"So whoever placed the advertisement has been watching you. And who spoke to the buyer? You?"

"No, Tobias did."

Walsh nodded. "Of course he did. And did he know about Retzlaff?"

"Yes, of course!" Ernst looked around the small room. "I wouldn't let him go without telling him about that."

"And what did he say to that?

Ernst shrugged his shoulders. "He wasn't surprised."

"So Retzlaff found out where you lived and placed the advertisement to lure you out? Is that it?"

"I suppose. What else could it be?"

"Have you found out anything more about Retzlaff from your sister?"

Ernst shook his head. "I'm sorry, I haven't been able to reach her."

"Too bad. That would have been helpful. But the man on the telephone asked to meet both of you?" Walsh spread butter on his croissant. "Or only Tobias?"

"I don't know. Tobias didn't say much, on his end. He mostly listened to Retzlaff. Or the buyer. Whoever it was."

"And then Tobias said he was going alone, or what?"

"Yes, I think so. Well, not quite."

Ernst checked the napkin under his nose and saw that the bleeding had stopped. He tilted his head down to face Walsh and stuffed the napkin under his plate before speaking again.

"First I offered to come along but he didn't want Retzlaff to see me at all. He said it might be too dangerous for me."

"How kind of him to look out for you. So what was his plan, then? Tobias, I mean. If Retzlaff really isn't interested in your secret, that is. What was Tobias going to do?" Walsh raised an eyebrow at Ernst.

"I don't know."

"Of course you don't." Walsh paused for a moment to think. "But who else knows you're here?"

"What do you mean?"

"You heard me. Does anyone else know what you are doing here? Because there are only three options. One, this meeting could have been a real buyer lured by the advertisement, even if you didn't place it, and something went wrong for Tobias. Two, it was Retzlaff, and he has harmed Tobias or is going to use him to get to you. Or three, it is someone else we don't even know about. Another buyer monitoring your movements? Someone from the German government? And let's not forget that *Tobias* might already know about this third person, if that's what it was."

Walsh leaned forward. "So, *Ernst*, I need to know who else is aware of your task here. I need to know who you have been meeting here. And I need to know if you, if we, can trust Tobias."

"What do you mean?

"Because understanding who Tobias met, assuming he *did* meet someone, is only half the problem. We don't know what happened to him. And until then, we can only speculate. Suppose Tobias made some kind of deal with his contact, no matter who it was, and it involved leaving you on your own? To weaken your resolve, perhaps. Suppose he actually got paid by a buyer at this meeting and cheated you and the buyer? If he met with Retzlaff, suppose he earned some kind of reward for leaving you on your own? Or suppose he just got scared and left you? Without even going to the meeting. Have you considered that?"

Or suppose, Walsh thought but didn't say, the NA has been onto us all along, and arrested Tobias, and will use him to expose all of us?

A look of shock crossed Ernst's face. He instinctively put a hand under his nose to check if it was bleeding again. It wasn't.

"That can't be true! He wouldn't do that!" Ernst looked liked he was ready to cry, again.

Walsh reached across the table, grabbed Ernst's shoulder, and pulled his face closer to his own. "Then tell me what you've been doing here! Who else knows you are here? Is someone else helping you? Have you met with any other buyers or not? And there's something else, Ernst."

"What?"

"If this was Retzlaff, then how did he find out about your acetone secret, so that he could place such a specific advertisement? You said no one else knows about this, so how might he have found out, assuming he did place the advertisement and kidnap Tobias? Can you explain that, please?"

Ernst shook his head, then put his face down. He seemed very close to tears now but held his composure. *"Einverstanden.* All right. What the hell does it matter now?

I suppose you might as well know." A pause. "We are here for the socialists."

Walsh released his grip but stayed close to Ernst. "What do you mean? 'For the socialists'?"

"I mean they arranged all this. The party here. The Second International. It certainly wasn't my idea."

Walsh sat back. "The *International*? In Brussels?"

"Of course. The headquarters is here. Near the Marolles, where we stay now. You've probably walked right past it a few times."

"You mean they arranged for you to come here from Germany, and to offer the secret to us? To Britain?"

"Yes, it's that simple." Ernst gave a slight shrug of his narrow shoulders. "They need the money."

"Of course they do. And who is your contact there?"

"We meet only with one man, Hendrickx. David Hendrickx. He is one of the assistants to Emile Vandervelde, the chairman of the International Socialist Bureau, which organizes the international congresses and operates the Secretariat here. He's Belgian. He's also a member of the POB, the *Parti Ouvrier Belge*." The POB – the Socialist Party of Belgium. "But we never see Vandervelde. In fact, we are to avoid visiting the Maison if we can, until we have the money."

"The Maison?"

"The Maison du Peuple, the headquarters building. Off the Sablon. You know it, don't you?"

"Yes, of course," Walsh lied.

"The police watch it. Hendrickx gets nervous when we are there. So we have been there only a few times since we come to Brussels."

"And Hendrickx told you to ask for five thousand pounds?"

"Yes, he thought you would pay that price. But of course Tobias tried to get more."

Walsh took a sip of his coffee. "Was Hendrickx aware of that?"

"No, I don't think so. I met Hendrickx only once. Tobias deals with him. But I warned Tobias not to be greedy. He said it was just a bargaining trick."

"I see," Walsh said. "And did Hendrickx contact you in Germany? About arranging this scheme?"

"Tobias arranged it with him. After he learned of my acetone process."

"And that process works? This isn't a scam you've planned for us, just to get paid?"

Ernst vigorously shook his head. "No, of course not. Absolutely not! I could prove it to you quite easily, with the right equipment."

"And you found the secret on your own?"

"Yes. I told you so. And then I told my friend, Tobias, and he contacted his friends in the party, who led him to Hendrickx. They thought the Exposition would help to bring the right buyer in. They assumed Britain would send some representatives, like all of the great powers. And all the activity would help to cover our movements here."

"And Britain was always meant to be the buyer?"

"Yes, of course. Unless you refused to pay, and then we would try something else."

Walsh nodded slowly. "And all of the money, all of the five thousand, would go back to the party?"

"Yes, that was what we agreed. And then they would help us find a new life somewhere else. Away from Leipzig. Away from Germany, even. Anywhere we wanted. Paris even!" Ernst smiled at the thought.

"And what would the party do with the money?"

"Use it for political organization, I suppose. They are always needing funds. Everyone is complaining all the time."

"Yes, we all have that problem," Walsh said. "Now here is what we are going to do."

Two days later, Walsh sat with Major Bridges on bench in the Parc de Bruxelles, near the Palais de la Nation. Rain clouds threatened and Bridges clutched his umbrella with a tight fist, tapping it impatiently on the ground as they spoke. Walsh planned to tell him most of what he knew but Bridges soon stopped him.

"I've heard enough, thank you," Bridges began. Then he shook his head. "Christ, Walsh, this is precisely why we shouldn't be involved with these charlatans. It's like stepping into a swamp. Into quicksand. The game isn't worth the trouble."

Walsh drew in his breath before speaking. "He's not a charlatan, major. He's just a chemist. He has a legitimate offer about something that can help our naval defences. My office and the Admiralty have agreed to pursue his offer. And he will provide his secret if we help him find out about Tobias. We might not even have to pay him for it, if we can get Tobias."

"If *you* can get Tobias. Not me." A pause. "Do you know, Walsh, that Ernst even came to see me the other day? At our embassy! Can you imagine, a German civilian lurking around outside our front door? And he was in hysterics; wouldn't leave until I came out to see him. Do you know how that looks for me?"

"So you gave him my address?"

"I had to, Walsh. In fact, I took him to your flat myself. And believe me, I don't have the time to be escorting your, your *people* around town. That's not why I'm here! And we waited over two hours for you, but I had to go in the end."

"I was at the Exposition."

"It doesn't matter. I can't help you. And what about the socialist office?"

Walsh shook his head. "The building is watched. And their contact there is not likely to risk his own neck to find Tobias. As long as Ernst is alive, the deal can go forward, as far as he is concerned."

"So you met with this man?"

"No, Ernst explained the situation to me. Look here, major, I just need someone who works with the police here. Just one name. To help me check out the hotels where Retzlaff could be."

"*I can't help you*, Walsh. Do you understand? I don't work with the police, just the military. And even if I did work with the police, I wouldn't put you on to them. There are larger issues at stake here than your secret deals."

"Major, I'm very close to a deal with Ernst. It was all I could do to convince him to stay in Brussels a few more days. He was almost ready to turn himself in."

"He's still staying at his place?"

"At my flat. So if you think waiting with him for two hours was inconvenient, try living with him."

Bridges almost smiled at the thought of Walsh having to babysit the chemist. "Hmpf. It's not my problem. And I'm glad of that, let me tell you! And what about Cumming?"

"He has his own problems right now. And I don't think he has any other contacts here."

"Yes, I've heard about his problems. You know I have my own problems too. I tried to enlighten you about them. And now we have this Roosevelt business to attend to. It just never ends!"

"What Roosevelt business?"

"His visit here, of course. He's having a luncheon with us, among other things. The mayor of Brussels, dignitaries from the Belgian government, and others from the diplomatic corps here have been invited. Plus Minister Bryan, head of the legation here. And his wife and his sister! A real circus. Far too many people to impress, in one day. So the entire Legation has been roped in to help with that. So please excuse me if I don't have much time for your spy business just now."

"I wasn't aware of that," Walsh said. "But major, if Ernst and Tobias are working with the socialists here, then you are absolutely right: there are larger issues at stake here. Haven't you considered that they could be in the government soon? They are very close to a majority over the Catholics, if they join with the Liberals. It could be useful to show them that we are not adverse to working with such a government. By helping Ernst and Hendrickx, that is. It could make things easier for you here, especially if this Vandervelde fellow becomes involved in government."

Bridges offered a slight smile. "You've been reading the papers here, haven't you, my boy? Smart lad. But the socialists don't believe in joining a capitalist war between Britain and Germany, do they? Workingmen from around the world are supposed to live in harmony, not war with each other. Isn't that their argument? The socialists might even shut down all military cooperation with us, if they ended up in government, heaven help us! So your theory might not pan out. And I can't risk my time on it right now, quite frankly, even if I did think I could help."

Bridges stood up suddenly. "I've got another meeting," he said. "You got yourself into this mess, Walsh, and you need to clean it up. So don't contact me again, please."

Walsh remained seated, and kept his eyes away from Bridges. "Don't worry, major. I won't."

Chapter 37

Theodore Roosevelt, former president of the United States, arrived in Brussels with his wife and six children following a spectacularly successful visit to Paris capped by an aeronautical demonstration at Issy-les-Molineaux. A large cheering crowd met them at the station, to the accompaniment of a loud brass band. The American Minister to Belgium, Charles Page Bryan, was on hand to greet President Roosevelt, along with Mayor Adolphe Max of Brussels and other dignitaries.

The Roosevelt party then enjoyed a sumptuous luncheon at the American Legation in Brussels, attended by forty distinguished guests, including the Russian Minister to Belgium, the Government Commissioner of the Exposition Internationale, and the Belgian Prime Minister himself, Frans Schollaert of the Catholic Party.

In the afternoon, Roosevelt and his family visited the Exposition, travelling down Avenue Louise and then out to the Bois de la Cambre in a motorcade. The Avenue was lined with more cheering crowds and adorned with waving American flags, and the party eventually made its way to the Salle des Fêtes building near the main entrance to the Exposition, just around the corner from the Palais des Arts Féminins. The Salle was already packed with thousands of spectators, with many more waiting outside, ready to hear Roosevelt's speech.

Inspector Dewulf had followed the entire spectacle with intense interest, starting at Roosevelt's arrival at the train station that morning. He was amazed at Roosevelt's seemingly endless reserves of energy throughout the day, forgetting that the former president had left office a year ago at only fifty years of age, the youngest president in American history. Roosevelt had spent the past year hunting big game, yet an observer would never know that the ebullient American had just led a party that had killed or trapped over eleven thousand animals throughout Africa.

Today, Roosevelt was impeccably attired in a long black frock coat and a tall black silk top hat. He stayed in constant motion, waving and smiling and nodding and pulling at his moustache and shaking hands and patting admirers on the back wherever he encountered them. Dewulf watched in admiration as Roosevelt showered affection on his wife and children, especially his youngest son and favourite child, Quentin, just twelve years old. Quentin easily matched, if not exceeded, his father's energy level, and elicited many smiles in the audience by mimicking his famous father's gestures.

At the Exposion, Dewulf stood with his colleague from the Royal Palace, Ivo Massaert, to watch as King Albert arrived backstage at the Salle des Fêtes in a side entrance to the venue. The king wore his uniform as a Colonel of the Guards, and was accompanied by a single aide.

Dewulf and Massaert listened as the king and the president warmly greeted each other, like two old friends. Dewulf was surprised to learn that they had met before, during Albert's visit to America in 1898, and he felt somewhat embarrassed that their reunion today could not be a little more private.

The king entered the stage and was greeted by polite applause from the crowd, but the people erupted in wild cheers at the appearance of Roosevelt. Dewulf and Massaert smiled at each other at the sound, but their insides were churning. Surely no anarchist would mar this wonderful occasion with a spectacle of political violence? But how could one ever be certain?

As they had done just five days before, Dewulf and Maasaert scanned the vast crowd again as Roosevelt took his place at the podium, waving and smiling at the crowd. Dewulf rubbed his cold and clammy palms against his trousers to no effect, then jammed them in his pockets. He struggled to maintain his balance after being on his feet all day, and he wondered how many more occasions would he be required to work in this manner. How nice it would be when Belgium returned to its status as just another small, quiet European country and left its place on the world stage. But that time was still months away, Dewulf thought, with a slight shudder.

It took several moments for the cheers to die down enough so that Roosevelt could speak, after he was introduced by the President of the Exposition, Monsieur Wiart. He addressed the vast audience as 'his friends' and, speaking for about twenty minutes to the delight of his audience, paid tribute to his hosts.

"It has always seemed to me that the Belgian people offer one of the greatest examples of hope presented by any people of the world," Roosevelt proclaimed. "There has been much talk about decadence of race, but Belgium proves that a great past is not incompatible with a great present and a great future. Flanders was one of the greatest industrial centres of the Middle Ages. Now you are rivalling and surpassing the work of your ancestors."

No mention was made of Belgium's more recent colonial history in the Congo, which also pleased his audience.

After Roosevelt finished his speech and left the stage with the other dignitaries, Dewulf walked outside with Massaert. He updated his colleague about his surveillance of foreign visitors and other related activities, which prompted Massaert to shake his head in disbelief.

"You must be very careful here, Martin," Massaert said, as they walked along the Grand Concours near the main entrance of the Exposition. "I hope you are not getting involved in another Great Plot."

Massaert referred to a scandal in the Sûreté twenty years earlier, when its agents provocateurs had attempted to incite a general strike among the working classes in the Borinage and Centre regions of Belgium. In response, the Justice Minister, Jules Le Jeune, had slashed the budget of the Sûreté.

"I'm not intending to instigate anything, Ivo," said Dewulf. "I'm just trying to get a few reliable sources in place in case someone does try to devise a plot that could threaten the Expo. Suppose we could have stopped the killing of those two poor *flics* in Ghent last year, the ones shot by the Russian anarchist, if we had had the right information? Or the bombing in Liège a few years ago?"

"Yes, you know that sounds perfectly reasonable between us, of course, but infiltrating a political party with your own man comes dangerously close to crossing the line. The *Bourgmestre* would never stand for it. Not to mention the government. You would be ruined."

"If they found out."

"Yes, if they found out. But you know as well as I that these things have a way of becoming public. Eventually."

Dewulf shook his head. "I can't just rely on our filing system or collecting names from hotels, Ivo. That's too...passive. Ineffective, even. People lie all the time on hotel registers. Besides, this plan is only for a few months. Just until the Expo is finished. And the rewards are worth the risks." A pause. "Besides, this was your idea in the first place, wasn't it?"

"Yes, but to help keep an eye on foreigners at the Exposition, not something like *this*. And you really think you can get inside the Maison? Without raising suspicion? The gendarmerie have been sniffing around there for years, trying to find lists of its recruits who were secretly attending socialist meetings. Especially members of the Young Guards."

"I'm not trying to reach the POB's central committee, Ivo," Dewulf insisted. "This is not about their big political strategies. This is about discovering plots among the rank and file. Or information about new arrivals coming from outside the country, especially unexpected ones. New people, strangers, asking for help from the Maison, that sort of thing. I don't think it would hurt to have a man inside."

"Do you have someone in mind?"

"Of course. He's already working on it."

"I hope you know what you are doing, Martin. If this blows up in your face, then protecting the Exposition will be the last act of your career."

Chapter 38

The gentle sounds of Mozart's piano concerto No. 22 drifted up into the street as little Christina Hendrickx, age nine, worked on the Andante movement. Street traffic was fairly light at this time of day, and the piano lessons were conducted on an instrument situated near the front window of the basement flat. The two men outside therefore had little trouble following the contours of the lesson, though one of them listened far more carefully than the other. After a few moments the larger, and younger, of the two men moved further along the street and hid himself in an alcove while the other one remained in place.

At precisely 16:30 in the afternoon, Christina emerged from the building and said good-bye to her instructor, a young woman with two cats purring around her feet. Christina knelt to stroke the cats and then slowly climbed the stairs to the street, struggling to hold her schoolbag and music books. The door below slammed shut just as Christina reached the top of the stairs.

"Your left hand needs a little work," she heard, spoken in German-accented French, although she did not recognize the voice or the accent.

Christina turned to find an older, well-dressed man leaning against the wall a few steps away from the stairwell she had just exited.

"Excuse me, *monsieur*?" she said, as politely as she knew how.

"Your left hand has not yet caught up to your right hand," the man said, smiling at her.

Christina frowned. "I only started it a few weeks ago," she protested.

"Mozart's twenty-second concerto, is it not?"

"Yes."

"It still sounds beautiful. You have a great deal of talent."

The girl gave a slight bow. "Thank you, *monsieur*."

"You know, they say Mozart is much easier for children to understand than for adults." The man smiled at her again. "Isn't that strange?"

He came closer, and began to walk alongside Christina.

Five hours later, when darkness had settled over the Marolles, David Hendrickx went searching for his missing daughter. The man on the phone had insisted that he not contact the police, and that he come alone. The caller didn't need to say what would happen to Christina if these conditions were not met.

Hendrickx was not a rich man and he strongly suspected this was not a kidnapping for ransom. But if not that, then what? As he walked as quickly as possible to the meeting point, he reflected on the kinds of people, and the kinds of secrets they kept, that he encountered on any given day at work. And he had been working in his current position for a long, long time. Too many people with too many secrets. But which of these people would be foolish enough to take little Christina?

At 22:00, Hendrickx waited, alone and chilled, on a small grassy corner next the Porte de Hal, at the edge of his neighbourhood. The hulking dark mass of the medieval fortress gate loomed above him, black against the grey night sky behind it. A moment later another black object appeared, this one a formidable automobile Hendrickx did not recognize. It came up alongside his position and stopped next to the pavement. The vehicle was a Renault X-1, a type known as the Master's Car, with a fully enclosed rear carriage featuring large windows covered by lace curtains. Hendrickx could not see inside the passenger compartment.

The rear door of the vehicle opened. An arm beckoned from behind the lace curtains.

Hendrickx walked closer to the vehicle and bent to look inside. Before he could make out the features of its occupants, a dark sack came down over his head and he was pulled inside the vehicle. A strong hand pushed him back against the seat, facing him towards the read of the carriage.

"Don't move and don't speak," a voice growled.

A man's voice, one Hendrickx didn't recognize. Hendrickx felt the man sit next to him, and then he felt the barrel of a pistol pressed into his side. He could smell leather and cigarette smoke in the rear carriage of the automobile, along with the body odour of his captor. Or perhaps it was the sack cloth on his face.

The automobile continued its course away from the Porte de Hal, then began making a series of turns. The rapid succession of movements, from one direction to the other and then back again, only to repeat several times, left Hendrickx hopelessly confused.

After a few more moments of such confusion, Hendrickx sensed the automobile slowing to a crawl. Suddenly it turned off the street and rode over a rough pavement, or on dirt tracks perhaps.

Slower still, and over two slight bumps, then it stopped.

Hendrickx listened as a large door slid closed behind the vehicle. A few seconds later the carriage door next to him opened and another strong hand grabbed him from outside, pulling on his upper arm. Hendrickx flinched slightly as another strong hand dropped onto his head to keep it from hitting the door of the vehicle.

He was pushed against the vehicle and his hood was removed. The man holding it stood next to him, but was wearing his own mask, so Hendrickx could not make out his features. The man in the back carriage remained there, with the barrel of his pistol pressed against the small of Hendrickx's back as he leaned against the automobile.

Hendrickx blinked his eyes and started to look around the room. It appeared to be a garage for multiple vehicles, but details were difficult to determine in the dim light. He could just make out a Pneu Englebert sign, rusty and dented, tacked against one wall, and another advertisement by Dunlop.

Before he could effectively process this information, a new voice called out to him from the gloom.

"Look here, *Monsieur* Hendrickx, if you please. And only here."

Hendrickx watched as Christina appeared before him, with a blindfold and a gag in her mouth. Despite these coverings, Hendrickx could see that his daughter had been crying for hours and was paralyzed with fear. She was being held by a third man, standing behind her. Hendrickx looked closer and saw the blade of a knife held against Christina's throat by the man standing behind her. The shiny silver blade was pressed close against her pale skin, and the man was masked like his two partners.

"Oh, please," Hendrickx whispered. "What is this?"

"Quiet!" the man holding his daughter said. "Just listen carefully, understand?"

Hendrickx nodded. He recognized a slight German accent in the man's otherwise impeccable French.

"I'm going to say a name to you. Just one name. We've been following a man with this name for several weeks now. We know a lot already about this man. Possibly more than you do. But we need to make sure, you see? So you are going to tell me everything you know about the name I'm about to say to you. *Everything*. If you hesitate, or if I think you are lying, or if your answer does not match what we already know, then you will put your daughter's life at risk. Do you understand me?"

Hendrickx nodded again.

"Good. Excellent. Now you must think very carefully about the name I'm about to speak to you, otherwise your lovely daughter will bleed to death before your eyes."

Hendrickx watched in despair as Christina shuddered and began to cry again, helpless in the grip of the man with the knife.

"And then my colleague will shoot you in the back," the man continued. "And then we will find your wife, Alice, and put a bullet in her head. Do you understand me, *Monsieur* Hendrickx?"

Christina sobbed even more loudly at the mention of her mother. Hendrickx felt the gun barrel pressed harder into his back, just to make sure he understood. "Yes, please, just tell me what you want to know," he said.

"You have the right attitude, my friend. I'm very pleased that you have decided to see things the way we do."

The man holding his daughter removed the blade from her neck, then patted her head with the knife still in his hand. But he didn't let her go.

"The name that concerns us, *Monsieur* Hendrickx, is *Hesse. Ernst Hesse.*"

Chapter 39

Paris. May 1910.

Lefevre stood in his small vestibule outside of Marchand's own office, and held the telephone out to his superior. He had a very confused look on his face. Raising his own eyebrow, Marchand came around his desk to meet his adjutant.

"This is coming in through the outside switchboard, commandant," Lefevre said. "From Brussels, according to our operator. But the voice has an English accent. It's not our embassy there. I don't understand how..."

Marchand snatched the handset from Lefevre, then waved him away.

"That will be all, lieutenant. Go fetch yourself a coffee. And bring me one while you're at it."

Marchand waited a moment until Lefevre was gone before he spoke into the telephone. "Yes, this is Commandant Marchand. Who is this, please?"

Marchand listened for a few moments, then his face broke into a wide smile.

"I understand. At least I think I do. It's good to hear your voice. It's been a long time. But I would like to discuss this further in person, if you don't mind. Can you take down some information?"

Two days later, on a bright Saturday morning, Walsh made the two-hour train journey from Brussels to Lille, just across the border in French Flanders. From the Gare des Voyageurs at Lille he strode across the Place de la Gare and towards rue Faidherbe on the other side. The Café du Grand-Hôtel was just across from the Place, on rue Faidherbe, and Walsh headed straight towards it. Once inside, he scanned the near-empty room from the entrance.

Marchand sat at a table near the window, and he motioned for Walsh to join him. At the table, Marchand stood up and clapped Walsh on the sides of his arms. The two men shook hands warmly and Marchand clapped Walsh on the shoulder again, smiling broadly.

"What an unexpected pleasure to get your call!" Marchand said, in perfect English. "I never thought I would see you again, my friend. At least, not in France!"

"It's very kind of you to meet me at such short notice," Walsh said, as he took a seat. "I'm sure you must be very busy these days. And congratulations on your new appointment."

"Well, after the work we did before in Paris, how could they keep me down?" Marchand winked, then smiled again. "But it did not turn out so well for you, I think?"

Walsh nodded slowly at the memory. "I managed. It was worse for my boss, I suppose. Quite unexpected, in fact. But it gave me a chance to pursue other interests. For a while."

"Hmm." Marchand took a bite of his croissant. "Something to eat, Nicholas?" Marchand looked around for a waiter.

"No, Didier, thank you. I had a bite on the train. But I could use a coffee."

"Of course." Marchand gestured to a white-aproned waiter and made the order the way he knew Walsh liked it, a café crème.

After the waiter departed, Marchand looked closely at Walsh. "I thought you would be wearing black today," he said. "In mourning."

"What do you mean?"

Marchand frowned. "Haven't you heard? Your King Edward has died."

"Is that so? I haven't seen the papers today."

"Yes, it's true, quite true. Last night it was. Near midnight. My condolences."

Walsh nodded. "No great loss, as far as I'm concerned."

Marchand smiled. "I expected so. Always the republican, were you not? You should have been French. I suppose that's why we get on so well." A pause, then a slightly raised eyebrow. "And now you are back with the DMO, serving *Grande-Bretagne* again?"

"Something like that." Walsh offered his own odd little smile now.

The waiter returned with Walsh's coffee. Walsh dropped a teaspoon of sugar in it and gave it a stir. His Scottish sweet tooth.

After Walsh took a sip, Marchand smiled at him again. "Yes, Nicholas, I understand. Or at least, I think I do." He leaned forward. "But before we begin, could you please tell me who your shadow is, over there?" Marchand tilted his head, just slightly, towards the entrance to the café.

Walsh looked behind him, and nodded at Ernst a few tables away. With an awkward smile and slight wave, Ernst nodded back to him. At least the lad's nose wasn't bleeding.

"He's not my shadow." Walsh sighed audibly. "He's my problem."

"Of course. He looks a little too nervous to be a bodyguard. And young. Not that you need a bodyguard!"

Walsh smiled again, a little wearily this time. "No, I suppose I don't."

"Still keeping up with the *savate* training?"

Walsh shook his head. "Not as much as I used to."

"*Tant pis.* I never understood your fascination with that boxing nonsense, Nicholas. Especially when a pistol is so much more effective."

"When you have one, that is."

"Yes, I suppose so." Marchand took a sip of his coffee. "Now, my friend. I know we don't have much time. I did as you asked, as discreetly as I could, and a few names came my way. And I think your best hope is with someone from the Sûreté, in Brussels."

"That makes sense."

"Yes. They will have access to the information you need. Since the man you seek is a foreigner, that is. Of course, they are not so efficient as our own people in Paris, nor funded so well these days, but they should be keeping track of all foreign visitors. Especially with the Exposition going on. They will have lists of hotel guests from abroad, and other sources that might be helpful."

Walsh nodded. "That's what I expected. I really appreciate this, Didier. And who is this man who can help?"

Marchand now offered his own awkward smile, and raised his hand to caution Walsh. "In a moment, my friend."

Walsh sighed again. "I was wondering why you couldn't just telephone me with the information. So what do you want?"

Marchand looked over Walsh's shoulder to make sure Ernst was out of hearing distance. He was.

"Now, I know you can't give me details, Nicholas, but you are not in Brussels only for your business with your young friend over there, correct?"

Walsh nodded.

"*Bien sur.* You are based there, for a little while perhaps?"

Walsh nodded again.

"And if you have no contacts already with the Sûreté in Belgium or France, then you are not specifically working for state security in London. You are working under cover, correct?"

A third nod.

"So, we are in the same business again, but only for different…branch offices now, shall we say? But working on the same problem as before, correct?"

A fourth nod.

"As I suspected." Marchand smiled again, pleased with himself. "But you have some advantages that might be useful to me. To us. When the time comes."

"Such as?"

"I'm sure you know already that the Belgians don't exactly welcome the idea of military cooperation with us. I mean, with the French."

"Yes, their precious neutrality."

Marchand nodded. "We actually have a good relationship on the secret police side. A very good relationship. In fact, my contact in the French Sûreté works on a regular basis with his counterparts in Brussels. And with others in capitals across Europe. Fighting the anarchist element, you know. But on the military side, it is difficult."

Walsh leaned forward and spoke quietly after glancing around the room yet again. "Yes, I expected as much. But, listen Didier, the British have no advantages over you. The Belgians aren't cooperating with us either. On the military side, that is. And I'm not the only one in Brussels working on this. Besides, you must have your own people in Brussels."

"Of course we do."

"Well, I've been there for several months now and the Belgians are not interested. Believe me."

Marchand took another sip of his coffee. "Not *officially* interested, you mean."

Walsh leaned back in his chair. "Bloody hell, Didier. What do you have in mind?"

"Nothing too...dramatic. Just a sensible precaution, you could say. I simply think we need to prepare the soil, so to speak. And we don't necessarily need official Belgian cooperation to do that."

"It would help."

"Yes, but in the meantime, we can do other things."

"Such as?"

"Nicholas, we have been working on this similar problem for several years now, and it is time to get serious about it. Really serious, I mean. Not just planning but taking action on this matter. The fact is that we, that is, the British and French, have a common interest in defending Belgium against a German invasion. That's no great secret. But we also know that...political considerations make it difficult to plan effectively against that problem. With or without the Belgians."

"Yes, that's what got Grierson and me into trouble a few years ago."

Marchand nodded. "Exactly. And the situation has not changed too much."

"No. But we are paying more attention to Germany."

"Which is why you are in Brussels seeking the same information as I am, though I am still working at a desk in Paris. And I have my own political obstacles to contend with. Besides, I am not a field agent, like you."

"Actually, Didier, I don't know what I am right now." Mainly a child-minder lately, Walsh might have added, but didn't.

"You are skilled at reconnaissance. You are working on the same problem as I am. And you have some kind of cover that allows you to remain in Brussels. In Belgium. I don't need to know anything else."

"All right, just spell it out."

"Fair enough. We expect, or suspect, a German invasion though Belgium in the event of another European war. No surprises there. But we don't know the precise route or the number of troops."

"They will have to deal with Liège."

"Exactly. And I don't have the...authority or resources to look into that. At least, not very closely, that is," Marchand said.

"Look into what?"

"The rail lines into Liège. The choke points from Aix-la-Chapelle. From Aachen, I mean. From Germany."

"What about your precious maps and models?"

Walsh remembered his visit, years ago, to the Musée des Plans-Reliefs in Paris with Marchand, who proudly showed him a number of the models and explained their history and purpose to him. Walsh had been suitably impressed, as the models had revealed important details that no map could ever accurately convey.

Marchand shook his head. "We don't have a model of Liège."

"How could you not have a model of Liège? I thought you had modelled every fortified position around France?"

Marchand shook his head again. "They stopped making the models after our war with the Prussians. Our defeat, I should say. And the Liège fortresses were built twenty years after that. So we have no scale models of that region. We have a few others from Belgium, like Namur and Oudenaarde and Charleroi, among others. But not Liège."

Walsh nodded in sympathy. "Too bad for you. But I've been there already."

Marchand raised his eyebrows. "You have?"

"Yes, a couple of months ago. I've seen some of the fortresses."

"Well, Nicholas, the Germans won't attack those forts unless they have some way to destroy them. So we must assume they have, or will have, a gun large enough to do that. Then their troops will flood into the interior. To Namur, to Brussels, to Paris." Marchand paused. "By rail."

"If that's the plan."

"Well, we need to be ready to stop that. And we might have very little warning."

Walsh thought for a moment. "Didier, what exactly are you asking here?"

Marchand leaned forward. "It's very simple, Nicholas. Really. I just need to know the exact locations of the main rail lines leading from Germany into Belgium, and the main choke points: bridges, tunnels, and so on. And then I need to know if the Belgians have already prepared the rail lines into Liège for demolition. And if they haven't prepared them, could they be…*encouraged* to do so?"

He paused, then looked around the room again. "And if they can't be encouraged lay explosive charges as a precaution, then are you prepared to do it for us?"

Chapter 40

Brussels. May 1910.

Walsh arranged to telephone Cumming from his post office branch in Ixelles. He would have preferred to use Bridges's office at the embassy, but knew that option was likely to be rejected. Once the connection was made, Cumming answered his telephone at Ashley gardens after the first ring.

"It's me, C."

"Walsh, my boy. How are you?"

"Busy. Things are becoming more…complicated here."

"I can imagine."

Walsh briefly updated Cumming on the latest developments without going into too much detail over the telephone line.

Afterwards, Cumming took control of the conversation.

"Well, this is all very helpful. Very helpful indeed. But we've had a few meetings over here recently about these topics."

Walsh braced himself. "And?"

"And the feeling is that we simply cannot manage to pay anything close to what your man is asking." A pause. "So you may have to decline his offer, as sad as that is to report."

"I kind of expected that."

"We are still interested in his offer, of course. But not at that price. It's not possible."

"Why not? You said the costs would be shared by several offices over there. Certainly the Admiralty must still be interested in this."

"Not anymore," Cumming said. "We've split the agency in two, and there's barely enough funding to go round as it is. I've also got to justify everything in writing now, to the War Office and the Admiralty, before any funds are spent. And they are extremely wary of spending that kind of money on a single item. They did that once in South Africa a decade ago, for twenty-eight thousand pounds, and got nothing in return."

Walsh forced himself to refrain from bashing the handset into the wall of his cubicle. "So what can we offer? Anything? Or have I just been wasting my time all along?"

"Walsh, our priority in terms of the information we seek has not changed at all since our first meeting together. Not at all. Do you remember what that was?"

He did: early warning of an attack by Germany. "Yes, of course."

"Well, we can pay as much as one thousand pounds for that type of information," Cumming continued. "So I'm afraid to say that such an amount is your absolute limit. At the moment. I'm working with my paymaster here in the FO to see if that can be changed, but that will take some time. My people in the Admiralty are still very sympathetic to this opportunity you've found. But they will want concrete proof first. So in the meantime, I would not offer anything beyond one thousand pounds right now, unless you want to pay the excess with your own money."

Walsh shook his head in defeat. "How generous of them. But what about providing other incentives, like asylum? At least for Ernst; you can understand he's eager to stay away from Germany now. Very eager, in fact."

"Not possible. I'm sorry, Walsh, but there it is. There's talk in the Home Office that Churchill is preparing a new Alien Restrictions Bill to place more controls on foreigners here. Registering them with the police, removing them from sensitive areas, even deporting them if circumstances require it. No alien possession of firearms, explosives, motorcars, and such. That sort of thing."

"How convenient. So what brought that on?"

"Probably the row in the Commons last month. Over revelations of 'dirty tricks' on the part of the Home Office against Irish nationalists over the years. Haven't you heard about it?"

"Not specifically."

"It's a shame, really. Accusations about improprieties that occurred twenty years ago are causing the Home Office to close ranks today. Churchill is protecting his flanks as the new Home Secretary and trying to be a good Liberal at the same time. And the Liberals do not like the dirty work we have to do. So one answer is to come down hard on spies and aliens, easy targets for everyone. And so we have the talk about a new Restrictions bill. Plus a new Official Secrets Act soon. Among other things."

Walsh closed his eyes and leaned his head against the wall. "Unbelievable."

"Yes. So if that's the thinking right now, then I certainly don't think they would approve an offer of asylum to two German nationals, even if they had something important to offer. Heavens, man, they would lose their heads at such a request! Especially if the Conservatives found out about it!"

"Are you sure? Have you even asked?"

"Not specifically. But have you offered asylum?"

Walsh sighed. "It was just a thought. Since we can't pay what they want. But tell me, C, how does the Bureau expect its agents to convince people to work for us if we can't offer real rewards to them? Just ask them to do so out of the goodness of their hearts?"

"Walsh, I understand your frustration. Really I do. I'm experiencing the same kind of thing on my end. And not just with you! But until this gets sorted properly, just be careful not to promise what you can't deliver. And I wouldn't get my hopes up about this current deal you're working on, at least not in the current climate."

"No, don't worry about that, C. I've learnt not to get my hopes up about any of this. Not any more."

Disgusted, Walsh hung up the telephone with a slam.

A few hours later, Walsh sat with Gisela in a quiet area of the Exposition grounds, on a thick wool blanket, staring at the night sky. A half-eaten picnic, stale and cold, was spread before them, abandoned. He could tell she had sensed his foul mood but he couldn't think of a way to amend the situation. The fact that he might be in the process of ruining the surprise she had in store for him made him even more frustrated. And like a spoiled child, Ernst had protested at being left alone in the flat, at night, which also weighed on Walsh's mind. Among other things.

After a few minutes of uncomfortable silence once they had settled down on the blanket, away from the tired food, Gisela took his hand in hers. "You have rough hands. A mechanic's hands."

He watched her inspecting his hands, using her delicate lace-clad fingers to feel along the small calluses at the base of his own ungloved digits. "A farmer's hands, I should say."

She looked up at him. "Really?"

"Well, where I grew up you either fished or farmed. I don't like boats, so I've spent more years farming than working with engines. So you can't really call them a mechanic's hands, not just yet."

She frowned at him, yet again. "I don't believe you. Farming what?"

"Six main crops, in rotation, like most everyone else in Fife. The 'sair six' we called them. Oats, poats, wheat, neeps, barley, and hay."

She smiled at the speed with which he recited the crop names, as if they came from an old song. She mimicked him. "'Oats, poats, wheat, neeps, barley, and hay'. I know oats, wheat, barley, and hay, but what are 'poats and neeps'?"

"Tatties and neeps. Potatoes and turnips. Or swede."

"Tatties and neeps. It sounds like a children's song. Tatties and neeps, neeps and tatties. And did you like that kind of work?"

"I didn't have much choice."

Indeed he didn't; it was either his uncle's farm, or remaining at the industrial school for boys at Fechney, after one too many epic rows with his father after his mother died. Fechney wasn't as bad as some others, like Mossbank in Glasgow, where the deathrate was unusually high, but he was forever grateful to his uncle once he was out of that miserable 'school'.

She looked into his eyes, still stroking his fingers. "Do you miss it?"

"Not really."

True enough, for the most part, though now and again he thought of his uncle Callum, so kind and generous after Walsh's mother, Callum's younger sister, had suddenly passed away, throwing Walsh's family into turmoil. He thought of his sweet aunt Rose, Callum's wife, in her woollen shawl and sensible shoes, standing at the big Esse cast-iron cooker that dominated their farmhouse kitchen, frying up black pudding for breakfast, savoury yet sweet and flecked with specks of fat. After breakfast, the men dragged themselves into the cold, furrowed fields all morning, where you could watch the haar roll in from the Firth of Forth, with Bass Rock in the distance, and work while you waited, wet and desperate, for the urn of hot tea to be brought round.

Looking at the untouched smoked herring in front of him, Walsh suddenly recalled the pungent stink of fish-scented heron droppings smeared on the farm equipment he worked with six days a week before he left to join the Black Watch in 1899. Worked until his fingers were raw, especially during the freezing winter winds that stung bare skin. And he remembered his sheer boredom on every Sabbath, his one day off each week: no games, no sport, no newspapers, no fun, and no reading of any kind, except for the Bible and *The Pilgrim's Progress*.

No, perhaps he didn't miss his childhood back home so much.

"I have other things on my mind, things right here even," Walsh added, leaning close to her.

"Such as?"

"Well, you know." He moved his mouth closer to hers. "There's the Exposition of course, and my business opportunities here, and the food is better than I expected..."

She jabbed him in the ribs, but kept on smiling, and he pulled her back close to him.

"I'm sorry," he said, smiling for the first time tonight. How had she managed that? "You know what I mean."

As he leaned in again, moving his lips closer to her own, she suddenly pulled away and exclaimed, "Wait! There it is!"

She pointed up at the sky, smiling even more broadly now, her eyes sparkling, and he followed her gaze towards the heavens. Then he saw it too, an amazingly bright flash moving across the sky, with a long tail of light moving behind it.

Halley's Comet. Her surprise for him.

They sat and watched, transfixed, as the spectacle continued high above their heads. Walsh noticed that the crowds back at the main part of the Expo were still as well, watching the same sight that he and Gisela were enjoying. The entire park was stunned into stillness at the amazing light in the night sky.

"Isn't it fantastic?" she said. "We'll never see that again, I guess."

"I suppose not. The next one isn't until...until 1986, right?"

"Yes. Or perhaps 1985. It comes every seventy-five or seventy-six years." She continued to look at the sky for a moment, then turned to face him. "I wonder what kind of world it will be then."

He didn't have an answer for that, at least not yet, and so they sat in silence, watching the silver streak of light glide across the heavens, gradually fading from view, until it disappeared from their sight.

Chapter 41

Vienna, Austria. May 1910.

The Ballhausplatz, named for the indoor tennis courts originally built on the site by the Holy Roman Emperor Ferdinand I, was the nerve centre of the sprawling Austrian-Hungarian Empire. In a large office deep within the grand white and yellow coloured building, Count Alois von Aehrenthal, Austrian Minister of the Imperial and Royal House and of Foreign Affairs, worked through the papers on his massive desk. The architect of Austria's surprise annexation of Bosnia-Herzegovina in 1908, the count had found his tasks had grown ever more complicated since then, and now there seemed to be no end to the flow of paperwork coming into his office.

A knock at the door was followed swiftly by the entrance of his assistant, who placed yet another file in front of the count.

"This just in from Sofia, minister." The assistant departed quickly, leaving his boss alone again.

Aehrenthal sighed and opened the dossier, half-knowing what he would find inside. And indeed his instinct proved correct.

A second plot to assassinate Emperor Franz Joseph had been uncovered in the Bulgarian capital, by Austria's ambassador there. A journalist with leftist sympathies and connections to Serbia had informed him about talk of a plot conceived by the Slovenski Jug. It involved an assassination attempt to be made against the emperor during his upcoming visit to Bosnia-Herzegovina.

This information followed another report still buried somewhere on Aehrenthal's crowded desk, from Austria's embassy in Paris, which quoted information provided by an Austrian student. The student claimed that a South Slav anarchist group had already sent four members of an assassination team to Bosnia. They would attempt to kill the emperor in Mostar.

Aehrenthal read more of the file, observing that the informants in these cases had demanded money in exchange for their information. He also had a report from the Sarajevo police that the four-man assassination team could not be located in Bosnia, even though they had the names and physical descriptions of the men. He noted how curious it was that information about these plots, none of which ever produced a violent result, always followed new announcements about the royal family's travels throughout the empire.

Enough was enough.

Aehrenthal began to sketch out the draft of a note to be sent to Count Johann Forgách, Austria's minister in Belgrade. He worked the words over in his mind very carefully before committing them to paper. This was no time for diplomatic niceties. He would instruct Forgách to request an audience with Serbia's foreign minister. He would instruct Forgách to then inform the minister about these vile assassination plots against his emperor. And he would instruct Forgách to demand that Serbia take appropriate steps to monitor and then disrupt these revolutionary organizations operating on its soil.

Aehrenthal expected complete compliance with his demands. The emperor was already planning his journey through the Balkans. He would be leaving in less than a week. The emperor was an old and frail man, and Aehrenthal, like other senior servants of the empire, did not with to trouble his emperor with news that might upset him. Besides, the emperor was a master at prevarication, especially in the face of difficult decisions, where his most likely response would be 'I will have it thought about'. And Aehrenthal did not want to risk having to alter the tight schedule of visits, all linked by rail, which had already been devised by the emperor's staff.

Less than four hundred kilometres away from Aehrenthal, and almost directly south of him, Zerajic bought his rail ticket at Agram's Glavni Kolodvor station, valid for travel from Agram to Bosna-Brod later in the month. He left the station and cycled in a northeasterly direction, towards Maksimir Park. On his back he carried a small satchel of books, bread, cheese, and water. At the bottom of the satchel was the leather book with the pistol inside, resting next to several other books and one of Zerajic's law notebooks. A heavy wool blanket was stuffed into a wire basket on the front of his bicycle.

After an hour's ride, he found himself alone in a thick forest, on the edge of one of the park's many ponds. He spread his blanket and opened his satchel. He sat there for a long while, eating his bread and cheese. It was too dark to read, but he did not come to the park to read.

The sun sank lower in the sky and Zerajic's surroundings, already dim from the tree cover, became darker still. He listened carefully for any human sounds and could hear nothing but birdsong and the rustle of wind through the trees.

When it had become dark enough, Zerajic removed the leather book from his satchel. He removed his pistol from the leather book. For the hundredth time, he checked that it was loaded. It was.

Zerajic put the pistol in his belt and stood up. He gathered up the blanket, and folded it into a long narrow strip. He dipped one end of the strip into the pond, pulled it out, and wrung out the excess moisture. Then he held the pistol in one hand and carefully wrapped half of the blanket around the pistol, but loosely enough to allow the pistol's mechanics to work properly. The damp end of the blanket covered the pistol itself, so that the cloth would not catch fire from the explosion of gunpowder.

Satisfied that his makeshift silencer would keep the shots quiet enough during his practice, Zerajic took aim at a small log floating in the pond. His gun hand began to shake uncontrollably.

He lowered his arm and took a deep breath, then another. Calm now, Zerajic raised his gun hand again and fired his pistol. Then again. And again. And again.

234

Chapter 42

Brussels. May 1910.

The grounds at Tir National, in the Brussels commune of Schaerbeek, were quiet today, except for the sounds of Dewulf's pistol. That was how Dewulf preferred his occasional visits to the shooting range of the Belgian military; no distractions to break his concentration. And no forced conversations with gendarmes or, heaven forbid, Garde Civique amateurs who happened to be around.

Dewulf steadied himself and reloaded his pistol, ignoring the raw flesh on the thumb he had just used to press the cartridges into the magazine. With some irritation, he looked again at the silhouette of his target. His aim was steady enough when his weapon was already drawn and he had a few seconds to sight the target along the entire barrel of his pistol. That fact was confirmed by the tight grouping of head and chest shots on his target silhouette, ten metres away down the range.

Quick-draw firing, however, was another matter. Like most of his contemporaries, Dewulf used only one hand to hold the weapon as he fired it, and his outstretched arm was not always stable.

With his 7.65mm calibre FN M1900 fully loaded again, Dewulf re-holstered the weapon and stood facing his target. He suddenly drew his pistol, raised it to eyesight level, paused to aim, and then fired three times in rapid succession, hitting the target with the second and third shots.

He re-holstered his weapon and steadied himself. He drew again, aimed, and hit his target all three times, twice in the chest and once in the head. The shots were not as tightly grouped as compared to when his arm was already extended, but good enough.

He re-holstered his weapon and quick-drew a third time, firing twice. He hit his target both times, in the chest. But still not as tight a grouping as he had hoped. Dewulf frowned.

He re-holstered his weapon and turned to face the younger man standing a few yards behind him. He must have arrived during Dewulf's last shots. Or had he been there all the time?

"Mr Walsh, I presume?" Dewulf said.

"Yes." Walsh closed the distance between them with a few steps. "And you are Inspector Dewulf? Martin Dewulf?"

"Correct."

Walsh extended his hand. Dewulf shook it.

"Let's take a walk, Mr Walsh."

They left the range by a side entrance and walked towards Boulevard Auguste Reyers, the main thouroughfare next to Tir National.

"Do you practice here often?" said Walsh.

"I don't know. Once a month perhaps. Not often enough, I suppose. You saw the results, did you not?"

"Just at the end." A pause. "Do you mind a little friendly advice?"

Dewulf raised an eyebrow and turned to look at Walsh, walking on his left. Then he faced forward again, and smiled.

"Not at all," Dewulf said.

"Do you always attempt to aim so...so carefully along the sights when performing the quick-draw?"

They turned right onto the boulevard, heading towards the small Place at the end.

"As opposed to what, Mr Walsh? Firing crazily from the hip, like a cowboy?"

"No, but you can make a kind of compromise between those approaches."

"How do you mean?"

"Obviously there is a trade-off of sorts between speed and accuracy," said Walsh.

"Obviously. And shooting fast and then missing is not very effective."

"Of course. But you needn't aim so carefully, each time. You can only focus on one sight at a time, so just use the front sight alone. At the range you are practicing it will suit just fine. And don't bother with attempting head shots during quick-draw exercises. Always aim for the centre of the chest. Every time. Each time you change your aim, you reduce the chances of an effective shot."

Dewulf smiled. "I suppose that makes sense. Anything else?"

Walsh smiled back at him. "Well, and since you asked, I think you are tensing your thumb against the pistol sometimes.

That's probably why some of your shots go slightly to the right. And you also seem to have a tendency to look down at your holster when you put the pistol back. If that's a habit of yours, you must break it quickly. You should keep your eyes on the target instead, in case he gets up again."

"You seem especially well-informed about pistol technique, Mr Walsh."

"I had some good teachers, inspector."

A few minutes later, Dewulf waved Walsh into a small café on the boulevard. They took a seat near the window, away from the other few patrons in the room. Dewulf ordered coffee for the two of them; Walsh declined the offer of something to eat.

When the waiter had departed, Dewulf spoke again. "I'm not exactly sure of what you expect of me, Mr Walsh. And I'm busy as it is. Very busy, in fact."

"With the Exposition, I imagine."

"Correct. We are far too undermanned for such an undertaking. Perhaps if we were a larger country. But it is like a freight train for the past few years, this thing. Unstoppable. And no one has the courage to question whether we can really afford it. Or protect it."

"But this is precisely how you can help me, inspector. The man I seek is a foreigner. A German, in fact. I think he is involved in a kidnapping. Perhaps even a murder. And he has arrived here only recently. Certainly your office is keeping track of most foreign visitors?"

"Most of them," Dewulf admitted. "If they stay in honest hotels. And if they are honest when they fill in the registration cards. If they use a false name, then we might as well be chasing a ghost. And what is your man's name?"

"Retzlaff."

"First name?"

"I don't know."

"That makes things even more difficult for us."

Walsh nodded in understanding. "There's something else, inspector."

Dewulf raised an eyebrow. Their coffees arrived, along with a few spéculoos scattered on a small plate with a chipped edge. Dewulf stirred a cube of sugar into his beverage and Walsh bit into one of the hard biscuits.

"This…this *affair* I'm involved in, it has a political aspect to it," Walsh continued. "Our victim here, Tobias Stern, is involved in socialist politics. So is his friend, the man I'm trying to help find Tobias. I know they've been to the Maison du Peuple a few times. We believe Retzlaff has been there too. He must have been waiting there a number of times, in order to locate Tobias. So if your people watch the Maison, perhaps they have already noticed Retzlaff. Even if they don't know his name."

Dewulf stared at Walsh for a moment. "How do you know we watch the Maison?"

"Please, inspector. I am not a fool. I spent time in Paris with your office's counterparts there. Among other offices. I know you cooperate with each other. How do you think I found you? In the telephone directory?"

Dewulf took a sip of coffee. "Do you have a physical description?"

"No."

"Again, chasing ghosts, Mr Walsh. I don't have time to chase ghosts. Or the manpower to chase them, even if I had the time."

"Can we just examine the hotel registration cards for a start? If we locate Retzlaff's hotel, then we can get a physical description from the staff. Then we could match that to the files regarding visitors to the Maison. Maybe someone there talked to Retzlaff. Or just noticed him."

"Yes, but which hotels? There are too many to choose from, and thousands of new visitors here since the Exposition began. Plus boarding houses and rented rooms in private homes for visitors, all over the city. Most of which, I might add, are terribly overcrowded now. With foreigners. So where do we start?"

Walsh thought for a moment. "The man who hired Retzlaff is rich. Very rich. If he is paying, then perhaps we should start with good hotels. Expensive hotels."

"Possibly, Mr Walsh. But before we do that, you need to tell me why you are here. What is this business with the socialists? And why are you interested in it?"

Walsh drew a breath. "I have no interest in socialist politics, inspector. I am here simply as a representative of the

British government, to purchase a secret that would be useful to our national defences. Retzlaff is after the man who agreed to sell the secret to me."

"What man?"

"Hesse. Ernst Hesse. He is the friend of Tobias, who reported him missing."

"And what is the nature of this valuable secret?" Dewulf had a bemused smile on his face.

Walsh paused for just a moment before answering. "A new method for the manufacture of cordite."

"I see. And you represent the British government?"

"You could say that. Yes."

"Not through the embassy here?"

Another pause. "No," Walsh said. "Not exactly. I'm here on the behalf of the Admiralty. A temporary representative here. Only because of the Exposition, you see."

"I see." Of course he did. "And you trust this Mr Hesse, do you?"

"Yes. And we are very keen to hear what he has to say. But he will not cooperate unless we make every attempt to find his associate here."

"His associate is Mr Stern?"

"Yes."

Dewulf sat back. "Yet we don't know if a crime has been committed, do we? Has there been a demand for ransom? No? And we don't know the nature of Mr Retzlaff's involvement, assuming a crime has been committed. So, Mr Walsh, I'm still not sure what interest I have in this matter. Especially with so many other pressing tasks on my list." Dewulf removed a pocketwatch from his coat and looked at it.

Walsh leaned forward. "Inspector, listen to me. There is a great deal of money at stake here. I believe the socialists have some interest in that money. And so might Retzlaff."

"And so might Mr Stern."

"Yes, I've considered that. But he doesn't have it yet. Nor does Retzlaff. I control the money. But according to Ernst the plan was to give some or all of the funds to the socialist groups here. Now, why might they need this money? For a strike fund, perhaps? A strike specifically intended to disrupt the Exposition? And intended to embarrass Belgium, while the world watches her? Or for something else? Some other plot, something that requires new money, even secret money, to finance?"

Dewulf sat up a little higher, and seemed to be paying slightly more attention now. "What did Hesse tell you about this, this 'plot'?"

"He doesn't know. Stern might know, but only if we find him. He is the political activist. The Hesse boy is just a chemist."

Dewulf paused. "Do you have the money?"

"Not yet. But I can get it very soon, once we know what happened to Stern."

"How much is at stake?"

Walsh paused again. "Several thousand pounds, inspector." He sat back in his chair.

Dewulf nodded. "A very interesting tale. But frankly, Mr Walsh, this all sounds quite odd. Quite odd indeed. I don't know if can afford the time to help."

"Can you afford not to, inspector, if the socialists are planning something disruptive?"

Dewulf smiled. "But if you don't pay Hesse, then perhaps they won't act in such a manner. So by helping you, I could be hurting myself. Hurting Belgium. Isn't that so, Mr Walsh?"

Walsh leaned forward again, then looked around the room before turning back to face his interlocutor. He stared into Dewulf's eyes as he spoke.

"Inspector Dewulf, they could offer the secret to another buyer, a private firm perhaps. DuPont or Dow or Nobel; they're all here. But I promise you now, if you help me in this matter, then the socialists will still never get their hands on that money. Never. They will lose out. And I will get my secret. And you will improve the safety of those attending the Exposition by finding out what the socialists are up to before they can act. You have my word on this."

Dewulf thought for a moment. The man had a point. Dewulf suddenly realized that had not learned anything particularly interesting about threats to the Exposition despite all the eyes and ears he was putting into place. Squads of gendarmes, policemen, Sûreté officers, mouchards, and casual informers, paid and unpaid, operating throughout Brussels; none of these had exposed anything useful. So either there was nothing to expose, or the revolutionary brigades had managed to plan their operations with such effective secrecy that Dewulf and his colleagues have been in the dark all along. Where they remained to this day.

Walsh was correct. What a persuasive bastard! Dewulf could not afford to ignore the possibility, however slight it may be, that there was a link between the secret the British were buying and the political operations of the socialists based in Brussels. Perhaps he could look away under different circumstances, but not now. Not as long as the damned Exposition dominated the news headlines in Belgium.

"Very well, Mr Walsh. I will look into this. As a personal favour to you, based on everything you have told me. And what you have promised me. I will hold you to your word."

Walsh nodded in appreciation. "Thank you very much, inspector. I know you are taking a risk here."

"Exactly. So it must be done secretly at first, as no crime has been committed. But that's my problem. And I don't have much time during the day, so we will have to work at night. I assume you can manage that?"

Walsh nodded. Dewulf stood and found his overcoat. He pulled it over his shoulders and threw a few francs on the table. He donned his Homburg and turned to leave.

Walsh stood as well. "But begin where, inspector? With your files? Your hotel records?"

"No, Mr Walsh, with *your* Mr Hesse. I assume he is available in Brussels. I want to speak with him. I want to hear his version of how Mr Stern disappeared. Can you arrange that please? And tonight, if possible?"

Chapter 43

Infiltrating the socialist underground in Brussels was much easier than Leysen had expected. He simply began attending their meetings on a regular basis, and such events were advertised publicly throughout the city. No one paid any attention to Leysen the first time, but he began to notice the same faces in the audience here and there. And they began to notice him, once he was attending the meetings several times a week.

A nod of recognition between them at first, then a subtle effort made to sit next to each other when possible, and then an exchange of muttered, clever responses to whatever views were being inflicted on them by the featured speaker at each meeting. Leysen did not want to appear too eager to this crowd, so he adopted the demeanour of an unskilled labourer down on his luck who was just interested in the fellowship and, on occasion, the meagre bits of free food that were offered. This pose required virtually no acting on his part; the most difficult part of it, in fact, was having to avoid spending too much money on drink as this would lead to uncomfortable questions as to where he worked and what he did. And he could not afford to have his new comrades dig too deeply into his past. Better simply to tell the truth: he was a petty criminal who wanted some way to raise himself to respectability, and he wanted to know how the party could help him do that.

Soon he found himself challenging some of the claims he kept hearing about the solidarity of the working classes, about the inherent rights supposedly enjoyed by all workers, about the inevitable decline and crash of capitalism, and about the benefits he and his comrades would enjoy, eventually, when the POB – the Belgian Labour Party - gained power. Leysen's questions grew bolder as he became more familiar with the basic arguments underlying the socialist ideology. What about those, he asked, who did not yet belong to *any* economic class, thanks to too many past sins? How could the poor exercise their rights against a society that had already condemned them, again and again, to poverty and weakness and shame? And how could the POB ever hope to govern as a unified force in the face of the deeper social divisions –

religious, linguistic, geographic, and historical – that seemed to challenge the idea of class solidarity, at least in Belgium?

Once he found the courage to speak up, Leysen began to enjoy his time at the meetings, and he looked forward to them with unexpected eagerness. In listening to the speakers and the questions of other audience members, he learned to articulate his own views much more coherently than he could ever imagine. He also learned to tread a fine line beween ridicule and respect when questioning the speakers, and he always made a visible effort to mend fences when things seemed in danger of getting out of hand.

And, inevitably, he began to attract the attention of a few other young attendees at these meetings. One was employed as a furnace engineer in a small, struggling glassworks near Molenbeek. Leysen could still smell the smoke on his clothes at the meetings, and his hands were occasionally blackened with grease and soot. The other said he worked on the loading docks of the Bassin de Battelage in Anderlecht, though Leysen suspected this might not be true. No matter though, for his new companions shared their drink with him when he found himself, or claimed to be, '*sans le sou*', and they never tired of hearing his stories about life in the Marollien underworld. With extensive embellishment on his part, of course.

The breakthrough came during a meeting in the Brussels commune of Schaerbeek, at a large workingman's club near the Maison de Ville. Leysen never paid much attention to the names of the speakers, and he had arrived late to the meeting, which was already underway. Despite his ignorance about the proceedings, he found himself, yet again, questioning the dignified older man on the stage about his fervent belief that all men, and women, would be completely equal under socialism, no matter what their background. When the time for questions came, Leysen spoke up from the back of the room. He made it sound as if he, Leysen, had not even earned his status as a free man, thanks to his petty criminal background, which, apparently, society would never let him forget. This fact called into question the views of the speaker about equality and justice under socialism.

The speaker, ever so calmly, replied that Leysen obviously wasn't a child, nor a beast, so if he was also not a man then he must be claiming to be some kind of 'sub-human' or 'primitive' in the eyes of society. This caused an eruption of laughter in the room, and Leysen had to admit that things for him were not quite so bad, which prompted a knowing smile from the speaker and much of the audience. Besides, the speaker then replied, no one else in the room would allow any 'sub-human' to attend such a meeting and give him an equal chance to be heard, so things must be looking up for Leysen already. This prompted loud cheers from the audience and Leysen, chastened though he was, found himself applauding the speaker as enthusiastically as everyone else.

Afterwards, Leysen's two new friends joined him at the rear of the room while the crowd filed out. They clapped his back and smiled at him.

"Ha! That will teach you to think twice about opening your mouth next time," said Willem Debroux, the glass worker.

Debroux was still wearing his factory overalls; he had been working longer hours lately to prepare an order of laboratory equipment for the Solvay firm. But he didn't want to miss this meeting, given the reputation of the guest speaker.

"The old man sure put you in your place, didn't he?" This was from Bernard Meunier, the dockworker. Meunier rarely spoke up at meetings and took special delight in witnessing how the speaker cut Leysen down to size.

Leysen just shook his head and smiled.

"Seriously, Dirk, what made you think you could go up against him?" said Debroux.

They walked out of the building, shuffling along with the other audience members into the calm spring night.

"Who is he, anyway?"

"You must be joking!" Debroux stopped shuffling and pointed back behind him as he spoke. His mouth always seemed too small for the amount of teeth crowded into it, Leysen often thought, and when he started ranting the sight of his open mouth, crammed with teeth, and on such a gangly frame, appeared quite unnerving. "That was Emile Vandervelde! Chairman of the International Socialist Bureau! And he's been a lawyer for twenty-five years, the sharp-tongued devil! You're lucky he didn't take more offense at your questions. *Personal* offense."

They moved out into the street, away from the crowd, and paused again to look for a brasserie. Leysen struck a match and lit a cigarette.

"Well, I had to say something." Leysen dropped the match onto the ground and blew smoke into the air. "I've been to more than a dozen of these meetings now and I *still* don't see how this magical change is supposed to happen, all across society, and around the world. And all at once. Just because a new party has gained power. How will they make everyone treat each other the same? And with all the bad blood over the years between Catholics and Protestants, Flemings and Walloons, Liberals and Conservatives, young and old, rich and poor? How can the socialists wipe out those differences and impose equality on everyone?"

"Good point," said Meunier, lighting his own cigarette. He pulled his bowler tighter onto his balding head, and jammed his large hands into his coat pockets. He preferred to smoke without touching his cigarette, if at all possible, and preferred to speak without even removing it. And so he favoured short sentences most of the time.

"And besides, the socialists can't control all of the government, even if they get in good," Leysen continued. "No party can control all the seats. So they have to share with the other parties, right?" He spit a speck of tobacco onto the pavement. "So they'll have to compromise, and we'll be right back where we started."

"That's one possibility," said Debroux. He looked at Meunier, who nodded his head just slightly.

"And what's the other?" Leysen looked at Debroux. "Don't tell me you believe that some kind of 'world socialist revolution' is just around the corner!"

"No, but..."

Leysen wasn't finished. "And if you try anything more radical the police, or the gendarmes, will simply crack our heads open, won't they?" He shook his head. "No, thank you, I've had enough of that in prison."

"Listen, Dirk, there's another meeting in two days," Debroux said, more quietly now. He stopped walking and put his hand on Leysen's shoulder. "A more private one," he continued. "And the goal is to consider precisely that problem. Among other things."

Leysen looked at his two companions. Meunier nodded at him, the cigarette bouncing between his lips. The tip of it glowed and a puff of smoke curled from between Meunier's thick lips.

"You are both going?" Leysen pretended he wasn't convinced.

They both nodded again.

"It's just a small meeting, Dirk," Meunier added. "To discuss things, things you always mention at these meetings. It's just a few people who aren't exactly convinced that things are moving in...in the right direction."

This was quite a speech for Meunier, so it must be important, thought Leysen. He took a breath before answering. "I'm not sure I'm interested in more radical activities. I don't thing I have the stomach for it."

Debroux and Meunier exchanged another look, then smiled at each other.

"Look who's getting cold feet, all of a sudden," said Dubroux. "You like to complain but you won't do anything to help, is that it?"

"It's not a radical meeting, Dirk," Meunier added. Then another smile. "Trust us." He put his heavy hand on Leysen's shoulder, and patted it a few times. Leysen wasn't sure if the gesture was meant to be reassuring or intimidating. Or a little of both.

And so it was that Leysen, at the end of a lovely spring day in May, and with very little effort on his part, found himself accepting an invitation to meet in private with the Young Guards in Brussels.

Chapter 44

Walsh came in from the balcony of his flat after his stomach had growled for the third time. The smell of cooking interrupted his thinking about recent events. About Tobias Stern. And about the question of how to handle his relationship with Inspector Dewulf in case a dead body turned up once they set off to find Tobias.

"What is that?" Walsh asked, sniffing with pleasure at the unmistakable aroma of smoked bacon in the frying pan.

"You've never had a proper rösti before?" Ernst looked at him with an amused expression. "Then you are in for a treat!"

"That's just fried potatoes?"

Ernst nodded. "Not just any fried potatoes. Could you fetch those plates for me please? The secret is to boil the potatoes a little before you grate them. And a little goose fat helps. In Zurich they use raw potatoes, but what do they know?"

Walsh raised an eyebrow, as he handed Ernst the dinner plates. "Zurich?"

"My grandmother was Swiss. From Engelberg. She wasn't too impressed with those city folk from Zurich. Too much in a hurry about everything, including the raw potatoes in their rösti! She always cooked this for me when we visited her. Or when she came to see us."

Walsh watched in hungry anticipation as Ernst deftly stacked some fried bacon and poached eggs on the perfectly round, golden-brown rösti. Perhaps having a companion over the next few days, or weeks, wouldn't be so bad after all. And not only did Ernst pay for all the food now, he was much better than Walsh at cooking it.

"It's ready," Ernst said, smiling broadly as he motioned Walsh to the small table set on the balcony. "*Guten Appetit!*"

Two hours after dinner, Walsh and Ernst waited for Dewulf across from the Hospital St Pierre, on rue Haute in the Marolles. The Hospital was alive with activity, even at this time of night. A steady parade of vehicles, pulled by animals or powered by petrol engines, circled around the building and paused now and again to discharge or pick up passengers.

Walsh leaned against a wall and watched the spectacle while Ernst shifted his weight from foot to foot as if he was trying to keep warm. Walsh knew the motion was just a release of nervous energy.

"Steady now, lad. He just wants to take a look around," Walsh said.

"Or so he said. How do you know he isn't coming to arrest me?" Ernst stopped his rocking motion and turned to face Walsh.

"On what charge? You haven't committed a crime. At least, not in Belgium." Walsh smiled. "Or have you?"

"Of course not. This was meant to be a simple deal. And now look at it."

"The deal can still go through. Stop worrying about that. In fact, we need to think about the options if..."

"Is that him?" With his head, Ernst motioned down the street.

Walsh moved from the wall onto the pavement and saw Dewulf coming towards them.

"Sorry I'm late," said Dewulf, when he had joined Walsh and Ernst. "Couldn't be helped."

"No bother," Walsh said.

Dewulf looked Ernst up and down. "You must be Mr Hesse."

"That's correct, inspector." Ernst extended his hand. Dewulf hesitated a moment, then shook it.

"Very well. I would like to be home before midnight, gentlemen, so shall we proceed?"

The two older men followed Ernst further along rue Haute, away from the hospital. The streets became darker and quieter. And smellier, Walsh thought. He trod carefully as Ernst led them down a side street, crowded with a few small shops closed up for the night and several apartment buildings constructed of stone and brick. Some of these buildings had been converted from large houses that had lost their grandeur over the decades, while others seemed to be little more than a stack of narrow rooms held together by a stairway.

"You haven't been here since Tobias disappeared?" Dewulf called ahead of him.

"No, inspector. Except for when I came with Mr Walsh to pick up a few of my things, right after he disappeared."

A moment later Ernst stopped in front of a small opening between two larger brick buildings. The hole was not well lit and the end of it could not be seen from the main street.

Ernst held out his hand in front of the narrow impasse, with an awkward smile on his face. "Here it is. *L'impasse Bullinckx*."

Dewulf and Walsh exchanged a look, and Dewulf raised his eyebrows with a slightly amused expression. They entered the dark and fetid corridor, just ninety centimetres wide. Ernst led the way, followed by Walsh and then Dewulf. The rough ceiling was just inches above their heads, and covered with slime. As was the pavement beneath their feet. And the brick walls around them.

Walsh could hear the sound of water dripping into the drains cut into the rough stone pavement near the sides of the corridor. The stench was almost unbearable. The first time Walsh had been here it had been bright daylight outside, with more of a breeze flowing through the corridor. Now he could barely see his hand in front of his face. Suddenly he wished he had brought his pistol with him. Or at least a portable bicycle lantern.

Hopefully Dewulf was armed. To Walsh's surprise, Dewulf removed a small tube from his trouser pocket, a tube barely longer than a man's outstretched hand, and slid a switch on the side. The end of the tube glowed with light and it allowed them to navigate the corridor most effectively. Once Walsh could see the slimy filth on the floor, however, he wished they had remained in the dark.

Walsh made a mental note to see if he could obtain such a device. The last time he had seen a small electric torch, an American 'Ever Ready', it had been bulkier and the light flickered too much to make it really practical. But this one was smaller and the light was much steadier. He realized something like this might be even more useful to him than a pistol.

The closed corridor became an open alley after about thirty metres, which then opened into a small enclosed courtyard, with no other exit: l'impasse Bullinckx. The courtyard was dimly lit by a single streetlamp attached to one of the walls; the light revealed half a dozen doorways and the same number of small windows facing onto the impasse courtyard. Each of the doorways led into a small house converted into several small flats, the exact number of which depended on the height and layout of each individual building.

Ernst led them to a doorway in the far corner of the courtyard.

"Here it is," he said, before retrieving a key from his trouser pocket.

He had an awkward smile on his face; Walsh knew he was embarrassed to be here with them. It suddenly occurred to Walsh that Tobias must have been arranging this entire affair with the acetone, as Ernst most certainly would not have chosen to live in such disgusting accommodations. Not with his financial resources. He must have done it for the sake of keeping Tobias happy. Or of keeping them on an even footing. Or both.

Ernst led them inside and felt for a switch by the doorway. A moment later the corridor was lit by a bare bulb hanging from a wire running up the wall and across the ceiling. They moved into the small corridor and the stink of sewage immediately reached their nostrils, coming from the open door to the toilet at the end of the hall.

Two flights up a creaky wooden stairway and they arrived at the flat. Walsh could hear muffled voices from behind one of the rooms further down the corridor. The three men listened for a moment and could hear nothing from within the flat. The sound of a crying baby could be heard, faintly, higher up in the building. Ernst looked at Walsh and Dewulf to make sure they were ready to enter. Then he unlocked the door as quietly as he could and stepped aside.

Walsh and Dewulf each took a position by one side of the doorway with their backs to the wall. Dewulf handed his torch to Walsh, who aimed it at the doorway. Dewulf removed his pistol and held it across his chest, then pointed at the door. Walsh gripped the doorknob with his free hand, and waited for Dewulf to give him a nod.

Dewful nodded, just once, and Walsh quickly twisted the doorknob and pushed open the door. He flashed the light inside the opening.

Dewulf leaned into the doorway, in a slightly crouched position, with his gun in his right hand. No movement inside the room, from what they could see by the light of the torch.

Walsh reached in from his side of the doorway and found the light switch, which he flipped on. He turned off the electric torch and handed it to Dewulf, who slid it into his trouser pocket. Dewulf entered the flat first, with his pistol still drawn, followed by Ernst and then Walsh.

The flat was empty and, as far as they could tell, undisturbed. A faded and worn chintz sofa stood against one wall. Newspapers and books covered the entire surface of a large flat coffee table in front of the sofa. Two chairs, one wooden and the other covered in a patchwork of grey fabric, faced each end of the table. In one corner of the room a small kitchen area could be seen in an alcove; a curtain rod had been installed in front of the alcove and a thin panel of fabric hung limply from the rod, pushed to one side.

At the rear of the room a small window looked out onto an alleyway, across which could be seen the light from a similar window in another flat. A large bureau of drawers and a small desk stood side by side on the wall across from the seating area, and a doorway next to the sofa led into another room. The room had been fitted with cheap electric wiring, which snaked up the walls and across the ceiling to two hanging lamps, both of which barely illuminated the place.

Dewulf moved into the room and scanned the premises as quickly as he could. Still no movement or sounds from within.

"Bedroom in there?" said Dewulf.

Ernst nodded.

Dewulf moved into the bedroom, flipping the light switch with his free hand. Again, no movement or sound inside. The small room contained two single beds, both of which were unmade, two small wooden bureaus, and a large wardrobe in one corner. There was no window in this room. There was a dark stain on the edge of the pillow on one of the beds. Ernst's nosebleeds.

Dewulf poked his head into a small doorway leading from the bedroom and confirmed that the bathroom, which contained only a small sink and a tub, was also empty.

Dewulf joined Walsh and Ernst in the main room and holstered his pistol.

"Anything missing in here?" Dewulf said.

Ernst looked around the room and slowly shook his head. "No. Nothing."

Dewulf took a seat in one of the chairs. "Are you sure? Take a look in the bedroom. What about his clothes and personal effects? Did he have any valuables?"

Ernst shook his head at the mention of valuables, and stepped into the bedroom. Walsh sat on the sofa and began to look through the reading material on the table in front of him. He and Dewulf could hear Ernst opening and closing drawers, then handling the door to the wardrobe, which was stuck for a moment but Ernst forced it open.

Ernst came into the main room a few seconds later.

"Everything is as we left it," he said. "Exactly."

Dewulf nodded. Ernst sat down in the other chair.

Walsh spoke up. "We were in here the day after Tobias disappeared. It looks the same as it did then."

"You're certain?" Dewulf said.

Ernst leaned forward, over the coffee table. "Look at this." He moved some newspapers aside and revealed half a dozen or so books on the table. "These belong to Tobias. They are very important to him, you understand? *Very* important. They are his only 'valuables'. He wouldn't leave these behind."

Walsh took a look at some of the volumes: Kropotkin's *Memoirs of a Revolutionist*, Bakunin's *Letters to a Frenchman on the Present Crisis*, and Nechayev's *Catechism of a Revolutionary*. Among them Walsh also noticed numerous copies of something printed very amateurishly, with faded ink on cheap paper. The title at the top said *Ni Dieu, Ni Maître*. Walsh took a closer look and saw the usual revolutionary rantings.

"Interesting reading," he said, mainly to Dewulf.

Dewulf stood up and began pacing around the room. He proceeded to expertly interrogate Ernst about everything Walsh had already told him, starting with his flight from Germany with Tobias and ending at the moment he last saw Tobias. Dewulf asked the same questions several times, using different facts as if he had forgotten them each time, yet Ernst was able to maintain his composure about his entire story. As with his previous conversations with Ernst, Walsh heard nothing that would lead him to question the young man's motives.

Finally, Dewulf stopped pacing and sat down again. He folded his hands into a ball and placed them under his chin, staring directly at Ernst.

"And where did Tobias take the telephone call?" he said. "The one requesting a meeting?"

"From the number one flat downstairs" said Ernst. "Where the landlord stays. The telephone is available for use by the tenants, if they pay."

"And did you see him afterwards?"

"Yes, he came back upstairs to tell me he was going."

"Did he take a key to the flat with him?"

"I suppose so. He had his own set of keys and they weren't here when he left."

Dewulf nodded slowly. "Did you offer to go with him?"

"Of course."

"And?"

"And he said I should remain behind. He said he didn't want to put me at risk until he knew who he was dealing with."

Dewulf nodded. "I see. And did he tell you the name of his contact?"

Ernst shook his head. "No."

"So we don't know if it is Retzlaff?"

"No, I suppose not."

"And did Tobias have an address with him? A slip of paper?"

"Not that I could see."

"Did he have a weapon with him?"

"No! He's not like that..."

Dewulf nodded. "Did he seem frightened? Or excited?"

"No, I wouldn't say so. Just..." Ernst hesitated.

"Just what?" said Walsh.

"Just curious, I suppose. Like this was just another task to be completed in the course of our time here."

"I see," said Dewulf. "And you have absolutely no idea where he went?"

"No."

"Not even the general neighbourhood? Close by, or far away from here? Did he pause to check a map or did it seem like he knew where he was going?"

"He didn't check a map. Not in front of me, that is. But he said he would be back soon," Ernst said.

"How soon?" said Walsh.

"I suppose within an hour or two. As if he would be back before I turned in. Does that make sense?"

"*D'accord.*" Dewulf stood up again. "Now let's go speak to the landlord."

A few moments later, Dewulf interrogated the landlord while Walsh and Ernst waited in the courtyard. It didn't take too long, as Dewulf learned nothing useful. The landlord had not heard the conversation and did not know where Tobias might have ended up for his meeting. The caller spoke French fluently, but the landlord did not recognize the caller's voice and could not place his accent based on the few words he heard.

In the courtyard again, Dewulf asked Ernst about the advertisement that supposedly led the caller to request the meeting. His short answer led Dewulf and Walsh to exchange a glance.

The three men then left the courtyard through the long impasse corridor back onto the rue Haute. Once on the street again, Dewulf pulled Walsh aside and asked Ernst to excuse them for a moment.

"What do you think?" Walsh said, blowing the stench from his nose.

"Not much to work with, on this one." Dewulf looked back into the dark impasse and shook his head.

"But do you believe Ernst?"

"Who can say? But Tobias seems to have disappeared quite suddenly, if he left without his belongings and hasn't returned to retrieve them."

"Can you help us then?"

"*Peut être.* Perhaps. I suppose I can make inquiries on the name Retzlaff at the hotels. But there is something else."

Walsh nodded in agreement. "I know. The politics. The socialists. The Maison."

"Yes. The advertisement indicated a *poste restante* address in the Marolles, but not their address here or their telephone number. Whoever placed the advertisement must have followed them to this *impasse* to learn exactly where they lived, assuming Tobias did not place the advertisement himself, as Ernst claims. And as Ernst's flat number was not linked to a specific telephone number, the caller must have made inquiries to determine whether a telephone was available, and if so, what number to call."

Walsh finished Dewulf's thought. "Unless the person who placed the advertisement already knew their flat number. And unless the caller already knew the telephone number where they could be reached, because he already knew Tobias."

Dewulf yawned, and covered his gaping mouth with the back of his hand. *"Pardon,"* he said. "And are we dealing with the same person in both cases?"

"I don't know." Walsh shook his head. "But either way, it seems very odd. Ernst claims that neither he nor Tobias visited the post office after the advertisement was placed, but Tobias might have gone there on his own to investigate the matter. Without telling Ernst, I mean. And those books Tobias cares so much about?"

"What about them?"

Walsh made sure Ernst was still unable to hear them. "Not exactly standard socialist material, is it? More radical. More revolutionary."

"You're familiar with these books?"

"A little. I had some experience with that type in Paris. A few years ago."

Dewulf nodded. "I see. Well, we might need to look into this Hendrickx fellow soon. Do you know anything about him?"

"No, I've never seen him. And Ernst met him just briefly. Or so he says."

"I expected as much. I'll see if I can look into his background without raising too much trouble. Dealing with these groups here is a nightmare. They have rights in Belgium, you understand. Lots of rights. And I don't have enough evidence for a warrant just yet. But perhaps that is just as well for now, as we wouldn't want to frighten him away before we know what is going on here."

"I understand."

Dewulf leaned closer to Walsh. "But you must consider something else here."

"What?"

"Just this, my friend. I might have to treat this as a crime, you know, if something has happened to Tobias. A major crime, if something violent has happened. In which case your deal with Ernst might not remain a priority."

"What do you mean?"

Dewulf gave Walsh a conspiratorial smile. "I mean, do you *really* want to find out what happened to Tobias, before Ernst gives up his secret to you?"

Half an hour later, Walsh and Ernst entered their residence on rue Souveraine. The street was completely deserted, and the stairway to the flat was quiet and still. During the walk to the flat Walsh had attempted, without much success, to convince Ernst to get a list of laboratory equipment he would need to demonstrate his acetone process. Ernst was reticent to reveal the type of equipment he would need, as it might reveal the details of his secret, so Walsh had to reassure him, yet again, that Dewulf was going to help them find out what happened to Tobias as quickly as possible.

Walsh turned his key in the door to the flat and entered it. Before his own hand could flip the light switch another powerful hand grabbed his arm at the wrist.

"Run, Ernst!" Walsh shouted, before he was pulled inside the flat.

Ernst fled down the stairs, after crashing into the landing wall.

Inside the dark flat, Walsh was thrown onto the floor. He attempted to rise up but the barrel of a large pistol was pushed against the top of his head. A great bulk of a man held the gun; his silouhette nearly blocked all of what little light came into the room from the corridor.

"*Calme-toi*, my friend," the giant said, in rough French. He leaned over Walsh with his other hand tightly gripped on Walsh's shoulder. "And shut your mouth."

"What is this?"

"*Un instant.*" The giant kept his pistol against Walsh's head.

A moment later, Ernst appeared in the doorway. Behind him stood a second man, more normal in size, but also with a pistol jammed into Ernst's ribs. The second man smiled at his partner, who nodded in response.

"Now you see." The giant smiled at Walsh. "Together again. Just as it should be. Now, the important part." He leaned closer. "Do you have the money?"

"What money?" Walsh said.

The giant met this response with a very effective gesture, cracking Walsh on the temple with the side of his gun. If he had used the butt of the weapon Walsh would have been knocked cold.

Walsh fell to the floor again with a cry of pain. Ernst stood helpless in the doorway.

"You know what money, Mr Walsh. To pay this German *moustique*." A mosquito, he had called Ernst. "For his chemical secret. We know all about it, understand? The five thousand pounds."

Walsh quickly composed himself. "It's not here. It's at the...the embassy. The British Embassy is holding it for me. I can't get it right now."

"*Bien sûr*. We expected as much." The giant stood but kept his pistol trained on Walsh. "We'll be in touch. Tomorrow. So you should visit your embassy first thing in the morning, understand?"

"Yes, all right."

"And we'll take your friend here for insurance. I'm sure you understand."

And just like that, they were gone.

Chapter 45

Leysen almost expected to be blindfolded when Dubroux and Meunier met him for his introduction to the Young Guards, but the evening did not turn out to be so sinister. They took him by tram to the other side of Brussels from the Marolles, near the Bassin du Commerce where agricultural commodities and other goods arrived via canal, bound for the markets of Brussels. Dubroux and Meunier kept checking to see if they were being followed, and Leysen couldn't decide if their efforts were amusing, annoying, or prudent. Eventually, Leysen's two edgy companions seemed satisfied that they could proceed with the meeting, so they made their way through the market district to a row of small hotels and ramshackle shops on the rue des Commerçants.

The three men paused outside one of the doorways, glanced up and down the street, and slipped into the building. Leysen could tell what it was even before they entered; the door concealed a small 'hôtel de passe', with rooms rented by the hour for liaisons with prostitutes. Or for any other business that might not require a full night's charge.

"What is this, *mecs*?" Leysen said, with a wink and a leer. "Some fun and games before politics?"

"Not quite," Dubroux said, as he nodded to the bored young man at the registration desk, who barely registered their presence. "Just follow us."

They led Leysen through a door behind the desk, and down a dimly lit corridor covered with faded floral wallpaper, and turned down a second one, deeper within the building. Leysen tried to refrain from laughing at some of the sounds they heard in the corridor. Dubroux and Meunier seemed not to notice.

At the end of the corridor they waited for a moment. Waited and listened. Leysen struggled to maintain his composure against the sounds of muffled but enthusiastic moans coming from behind one of the doors. Someone was getting his money's worth.

A moment later a knock could be heard from the doorway to the corridor they had just entered. Then two more knocks. A signal.

At that Dubroux and Meunier opened another door, and led Leysen down a small passage, far more utilitarian in nature. A mop and bucket, worn bed linen stacked on a wire rack, threadbare towels, toilet tissue. Rough brick walls and a bare stone floor, so no need to wallpaper this area.

At the end of this corridor, a third door. Dubroux and Meunier paused for a moment, then Meunier slowly opened it. He held up his hand – *wait here* – and peered outside. Satisfied, he went through the doorway. Leysen followed, with Dubroux at his heels, and found himself around the corner from the main entrance to the hôtel de passe, in a large impasse. A black motorcar waited in the impasse, its engine running. A streetlamp high above their heads had already been extinguished, and the only light came from the night sky and the headlamps of the automobile.

They paused at the car, looking around the impasse and towards the exit to the street.

"*Bon. Allons-y,*" said Meunier. He motioned for Dubroux and Leysen to join him outside.

Once outside, Leysen looked back to the door they had just exited and saw that it was very effectively concealed against the side of the building, with no outside handle. He guessed, correctly, that there was a similar door into the hôtel on another street, so that patrons could enter and leave the premises through different locations without ever having to visit the main entrance.

The three men piled into the back of the car, then drove all the way back to where they had started. Back to the Marolles, safe now.

Half an hour later, Leysen found himself in a basement room crowded with a dozen other restless young men. Some of them were very young, perhaps fifteen or sixteen years old at most. They sat with greasy forelocks pasted on their foreheads, anxiously looking around the room to see if a flic or two had slipped in among them. The majority of the audience seemed to be around twenty years old, a few years younger than Leysen. He wondered what all the fuss tonight was about. Another political meeting, another leftist zealot, another evening of empty promises.

"We should be celebrating now, my friends," the speaker was saying. "Do you realise that?"

He was a tall man, perhaps forty years of age, and wore a faded but respectable grey suit that one might see on an accountant or petit fonctionnaire. As he spoke he passed his hand through his thinning dark hair now and again, as if to prevent it from falling out before he completed his speech. In the automobile, Dubroux had said his name was Penneman, Jan Penneman.

"Yes, celebrating!" Penneman continued. "Celebrating twenty-five years of Belgian socialism. Twenty-five years of the glorious POB. Twenty-five years since that first humble meeting of our party's founders at the Café de Zwaan, just a short walk from here. But do we feel like celebrating? Do you?"

He looked around the room, knowing the answer and seeing it in the faces before him.

"No? Well, then, let's take a look at our circumstances. Now, I will not disagree that we have made progress. We have extended the franchise to some degree. We have improved working conditions. And we are starting work on adopting a fair wage, a living wage, across the country. But that is not enough, is it?"

"No, it is not. Because these are modest, minimal, even *marginal*, reforms. These are reforms, not transformations. Simple changes that make an inherently inhumane system slightly more tolerable to its victims but do not fundamentally threaten it. Like putting a coat of paint and flowerboxes on the façade of a crumbling old house that actually needs to be demolished because it is unfit for human use. Is that not the truth here?"

Heads nodded around the room. Penneman nodded with them.

"Yes, of course it is. And I am not a mere decorator, my friends. I am not a painter or a flower-arranger. No, I want to be an architect. An architect of a new and more just, more *humane*, society. One that benefits *all* men, *all* women, *all* children. Not just those who can already afford to live like human beings rather than like animals. So that is why we do not feel like celebrating. Because the system persists and will continue to persist unless something more ambitious is done. Something more...persuasive."

Penneman began to pace back and forth across the makeshift stage. "Now, we also know why we cannot afford to take such action to radically reform the system into something equally beneficial to all workers. And this reason

260

for our inaction, our complacency, is simple: the armed forces. So let us think about this for a moment."

Penneman paused to take a drink of water. Like the rest of the audience, Leysen sat motionless and silent, eagerly anticipating the older man's next volley of arguments. Dubroux and Meunier sat on either side of Leysen, equally enthralled.

"The armed forces," Penneman said. "But Belgium is neutral, is it not? Ever since the creation of our tiny country, nearly eighty years ago, correct? Eighty years of Belgian neutrality. Eighty years of peace. Small and peaceful and neutral we are, and have always been. Eighty years now. So, another anniversary for us. Another reason for 'celebrating' tonight."

Penneman smiled at them. "So I ask you, my friends, how many soldiers does a small and neutral country need? How many thousands? And how should they be recruited and trained and organized? And for what purpose?"

"For the fact is, Belgium does not need so many soldiers. Instead, Belgium needs to provide real jobs, not guns and uniforms, for its young men. Does anyone here disagree with that? No? Of course you don't. But our problem does not end there."

"Now, we thought we had won with a more universal system of conscription. An army based on the broad structure of the society from which it is drawn is unlikely to turn against itself, is it? It would not attack the very society it is supposed to defend, would it? But the state solved that problem, in a very clever way. For now our standing army has been bolstered by two additional forces. These forces, the gendarmerie and the Garde Civique, these forces, can only been seen as instruments for dealing with internal unrest. And today the Garde Civique *alone* numbers over *forty thousand men*. Forty thousand! Nearly the same number as in the standing Field Army, in a tiny nation dedicated to neutrality and peace!"

Penneman's face glistened now. He pushed back his hair and moved closer to his audience, nearly in the midst of them.

"And worse, even worse, my friends, is that the rich can still buy themselves an exemption, while the poor and unemployed must wear the uniform in their place. Does any man here believe that this is a fair policy?"

"But worst of all, my friends, is that this, this…unholy system, this agglomoration of a bloated Field Army, a gendarmerie of equal size, and now even a Garde Civique, this *deeply* entrenched practice of substitutions and exemptions in the face of our supposedly universal conscription, this system leads you, the humble wage-earner, it leads you, it *requires* you, to take part in the violent oppression of your own class! In the subjugation of your own people! So that you and your kind, *our kind*, cannot enjoy a decent life! Have you ever heard of anything so absurd? This system causes you to raise your own fist in anger, if necessary, if required by the *state*, against your fellow workingmen! Against the brothers you see seated in this room! If they but only attempt to assert the rights they supposedly enjoy under the flag of our democratic republic!"

Penneman paced faster in front of them, slashing the air with his hands to make his points, and shaking his head.

"This is what we are dealing with. This singular evil: *embedded militarism.* This deep-rooted, state-sanctioned militarism directed at our own society and fuelled by the bodies, the blood, of the weak and poor when they are forced by the state to serve in the army, and cannot afford to pay their way out of it. This is what each of you faces, when your number comes up. Yes, when *your number* comes up."

Penneman glared at them, sweeping a pointed finger across the room. "Thirteen thousand of you will be called up this year. Thirteen thousand, at a minimum. And next year. And the year after."

Penneman paused to let that realization sink into his young audience. It certainly did; nearly every man in the room shifted in his seat at the mention of the thirteen thousand figure.

"And then, you too will one day face the order to beat down your fellow workers, as they did at Marchienne, at Charleroi, at Serainge and Borinage. Firing on unarmed workers! Firing without *mercy*! Sixteen innocents killed at Roux alone, and dozens more since then! Verviers, Jemappes, Borgerhout, the list goes on. Sending Flemish men to put down their brothers in Wallonia, and Walloons to attack Flemings, just to keep us all divided!"

Penneman smiled. "So I ask you again, do any of you feel like celebrating tonight? Or tomorrow perhaps? Or the next day?"

He looked around the room. Silence.

"No celebrations tonight? No?"

He stood at the center of the room. "Well then, my friends, my *comrades*" – the speaker gave them a knowing wink, producing laughter all around – "what is to be done? We may have brought in universal conscription and we may have extended the franchise, but has anything really changed? Hmm?"

"Of course not. Not at all. The rich have managed to claw back the rights we thought we had won, eighty years ago. So, then, we put our energies, our meagre funds, into our propaganda."

He picked up a handful of newspages and held them high.

"Our beloved *Le Conscrit* (The Conscript). Our respected *La Caserne* (The Barracks). For our friends in Wallonia, we have *La Jeunesse c'est l'Avenir* (Youth is the Future). For those in Flanders, *De Zaaier* (The Sower) helps our fight against militarism. And we have *Avante Garde*, and even the *Antimilitariste* now. Where the title says it all. And we have postcards and posters and pamphlets and bulletins. Reams and reams of paper. Yes, my friends, very admirable."

In a violent gesture, Penneman suddenly threw these papers into his audience, startling many youths in the audience as the pages fell upon them.

"But *we* fight with words while *they* fight with bullets and conscription laws enforced by the state. And *we* try to pull our nation together while *they* can all too easily pit us against each other with their recruitment and training methods. For just one example, they have taken control of the Garde Civique away from the municipalities and put it in the hands of the national government. What does that tell you? It tells me that that they can more easily use it to bash our heads anywhere in the country. They can use troops from one region to bash heads in another region, without fear that the troops will resist orders to avoid harming their own neighbours."

Across the room, those heads nodded all around.

"So, my friends, I'm afraid to tell you that our propaganda is not good enough. But we are also not a nation of bomb-throwers, are we? We are not assassins. No, my friends, we are a civilized people. Our party would never ask you to make such violence. I would never ask you to do such a thing. But at the same time, we cannot stand by while the state builds its military apparatus for the sole purpose of preventing the realisation of a more just society."

Penneman stopped pacing and looked directly at his audience. "So this then, is my appeal. This is why I am here tonight. To remind you of something. To remind you that when your number comes up, if your number comes up, you must remember your true loyalty. Loyalty to your fellow workers. Loyalty to your fellow citizens in a free democracy. To the POB. To world socialism. Can you do that for me?"

Again, heads nodded all around. Leysen found himself nodding as well, without even thinking about it. Dubroux and Meunier did the same.

"Thank you, my friends. I knew I could rely on you. And in remembering your true loyalty, even while doing your duty in our armed forces, you must do something else for me. For the party. You must help to spread the word. You must spread the message through the ranks. Our message of equality and justice."

"Now, we have provided some of the tools for you" – Penneman picked up the newspages and pamphlets once again and waved them - "but this is only a start. Only a small part of the effort."

"No, my friends. There is something else. You must help us organize. We might ask you to arrange meetings for us, among your fellow recruits. And you must send word back to us. Knowledge is power, is it not? So you must report to us about what is going on in your units. About what kind of strength these forces have across the country. About the places where they might be able to counteract our protests and strikes most effectively. Can you do that for me as well?"

Again, the nodded heads. An eager and willing audience tonight.

"Yes, I knew you could. But let us not forget that these acts will be seen as crimes in the eyes of the government. So this all must be done in *secret*. So you cannot be caught distributing our publications or organizing political meetings. Especially in groups, groups of five or more. If you are caught and convicted, you could face three to five years in prison. Three to five years of your young lives, gone in an instant. And if you think army life is difficult, wait until you experience the horrors of the *cachot*. Tiny cells, dungeons really, damp and unheated, and nothing but bread and water to live on. This is the punishment you face if you are caught."

Penneman took another sip of water, letting the image of life in the dungeon sink in. Then he gave them a ray of hope.

"So I will not lie to you about the risks. But I can also promise you this: that we will not forget you. No, that is not what we are about. If you tell us where you are, we will send help. We can provide some aid each month. A small allowance perhaps to help you forget the monotony of military service. Even as I speak, other meetings are being held tonight to help raise funds for this very purpose. Your fellow workers are giving what little they have to make your military life more bearable. So you will not be forgotten, I promise you that!"

Penneman pointed at them and then thumped his right fist to his breast when he said those last two sentences, with a loud but trembling voice, which caused some in the audience to applaud in admiration. Penneman came forward again and stared at them, to drive home his message.

"And finally, my young friends, this is what I mean to say tonight. The point of all my efforts tonight. The one thing you must take home from our short time together. Are you listening?"

Of course they were.

"What I mean to say to you is this: if you are called to serve, and even if you cannot do any of the things I have asked of you, you must be prepared to do this one thing, just one thing: to *deliberately disobey* any orders to fire upon or attack your fellow citizens. Did you hear me? I am asking you now, tonight, to disobey orders and face the consequences if you are forced to choose between us and them. If you do nothing else for us, can you do that for me?"

Of course they could.

Ten minutes later, the room nearly empty now, Leysen stood before Penneman along with Dubroux and Meunier.

"So this is the one who stood up to the great Vandervelde?" said Penneman, with a smile and a wink at Leysen. He extended his hand.

"Stood up and was shot down, I should say!" said Meunier, a cigarette bouncing between his lips.

"It was nothing," Leysen protested. He shook Penneman's hand with a firm grip.

Penneman shook his head. "I don't think so. Vandervelde means well, but I think he is losing touch with some of the challenges these boys face. Especially those who end up in the army. They need more specific direction from the party, and we try to give it to them. But the real point is this: we need people with the courage to speak up. People who can lead the younger ones. That's what this is all about, really, isn't it?"

Leysen shrugged his tired shoulders. "I suppose so. You were certainly persuasive."

"*Merci bien.* I've had some practice. But half the battle is getting them here. Once you have them in the room, then *c'est bête comme chou*, you know? Very easy."

"I suppose so."

Penneman put his arm on Leysen's shoulder and pulled him close. "Your friends here also tell me you have a slightly more...more humble background than our other recruits. A good story to tell, you understand? Something persuasive to help motivate these younger boys."

"I don't understand," Leysen said.

Penneman's face grew puzzled. He gestured towards Dubroux and Meunier. "Didn't they tell you why you were here?"

Dubroux and Meunier exchanged their own puzzled looks.

Leysen registered their confusion. "No. I thought it was just to hear you speak."

"Well, yes, for a start. For a start. But I can't do this all alone now, can I? And you seem to have found your voice recently, according to your friends here."

Leysen looked Penneman in the eyes. "What are you saying? What do you want from me?"

Penneman smiled again. "It's very simple. Really, it is. You've heard my little speech here tonight. You've seen how effective it is, even for someone like myself, someone who doesn't exactly look like most of these young boys. I think you would be even more persuasive."

"You want me to speak to them?"

"No, not to these ones. To other groups. I want you and your friends here to start organizing your own cell of Young Guards, and to hold meetings like this one. And for you" – Penneman put his finger into Leysen's chest – "for *you* to convince your audience about where their real duty lies, in the same way I just did. Can you do that for us?"

Chapter 46

Sarajevo. May 1910.

Early morning at the Konak building, the elegant personal residence of General Varesanin, governor of the province. Completed by the Turks in 1869 during the twilight of their rule over the city under Topal Serif Osman-pasa, the Konak towered over the Sarajevo neighbourhood of Bistrik as its three floors made it the tallest structure in the city. Varesanin was in a rush this morning, just leaving for work and striding through the large courtyard in front of the building, between the two stone lions, when his butler informed him of a telephone call.

Varesanin marched back to his house, and took the handset in a small alcove off the large foyer.

"Your personal secretary, excellency," said his butler, who bowed and quickly moved away from the governor.

"Yes, what is it?" Varesanin snapped.

"Another message from General Appel, sir," Varesanin's secretary replied, carefully controlling his stammer.

Appel, one of the senior officers of the Austrian army in Sarajevo, was helping to arrange security for the emperor's upcoming visit. Unlike Varesanin, Appel enjoyed a direct line of communication to Alexander Brosch von Aarenau, aide-de-camp to Archduke Franz Ferdinand, heir to the throne. Brosch was also head of the Archduke's Military Chancellery. Brosch had to be taken very seriously, and so therefore Appel must be taken seriously. But what was it this time?

"Yes, yes, what is it? And couldn't this wait until I arrived later this morning?"

"The general d-did not think so, sir. He's kept up with the correspondence between Minister von Aehrenthal and our minister in Belgrade. Minister Forgách. Regarding n-news of the assassination plots coming in here and there."

Not *this* again. "And?"

Varesanin tapped his foot on the tile floor. He did not want to keep his breakfast companions waiting too long. More time to talk about him without being present to defend himself.

"Well, sir, the general is not convinced that the Serbs are t-taking this very seriously. Forgách tells him otherwise, but the general does not believe him."

"And why not?"

"General Appel says he has his own sources in the Intelligence Bureau. In Vienna. They tell him that these Serbian p-plots are not just hot air. That opposition to the throne has grown considerably stronger than we suspect."

"Well, does he have specific evidence of a plot? A day and time perhaps? Names of the plotters?"

"Nothing very specific, at least n-not yet, but he is working on it. This is what he tells me."

"Then why the urgency? What does he want that cannot wait another hour this morning, hmm?"

"It's the...the emperor's route, sir."

Varesanin sighed. This could have waited a few more hours! "And what about it? What's the problem?"

"Well, the general thinks it might be unwise to publish the route in the newspapers. The exact route. It would make it too easier for any...any plots to be organized."

"Is that it?"

"Well, sir, the information goes to the presses this morning. The general thinks there is still time to stop publication. To eliminate some of the details, perhaps. Just a precaution."

Varesanin rolled his eyes. "Out of the question. Did you hear me? *Out of the question.* Is the general with you? No? Then tell him that this decision has already been taken and cannot be changed. Do you understand? The itinerary is already fixed. Preparations are underway. And we might also remind the general that the main reason the emperor is making this visit is to be seen by his subjects throughout the region. So they must know where they can see him, wouldn't you agree?"

"Yes, sir."

"And besides, how would it appear if the public was not allowed to know when to expect the emperor? If he just magically appeared here and there with no advance preparation for his welcome? After travelling all this way? How would that look for us?"

"Yes, sir."

"So do not stop publication of the schedule and route, understand?"

"Yes, s-sir, I understand, sir."

"Now is there anything else that cannot wait until I get there in a few hours? Hmm? Any other urgent business we have to discuss right now?"

"N-no sir. We have things w-well in order here."

"Good. I'm glad to hear that."

Varesanin slammed down the telephone and stormed out of the Konak.

Chapter 47

Brussels. May 1910.

Walsh found the note on the floor of his flat after he made his trip to the British Embassy, first thing in the morning after the two men took Ernst. He couldn't be sure if they were watching him so he had to go through the motions of getting the money. The note simply gave a time for a meeting the following night, well after dark. And it specified no weapons or police.

Walsh knew perfectly well that Retzlaff was unlikely to turn Ernst over to him if Ernst's father was still paying him. Assuming, of course, that Retzlaff was behind this sudden turn of events. Walsh briefly considered a telephone call to Inspector Dewulf, but thought against it. Obviously Major Bridges would be no help either.

The next day, the day of the meeting, Walsh killed time by catching up on his newspapers. They were full of stories about the lavish funeral of King Edward VII, the 'Uncle of Europe', and the uncle of Kaiser Wilhelm and Tsar Nicholas, among many other royals. Walsh wondered how much the funeral had cost, especially as he had had so much trouble squeezing a few thousand pounds out of the government to buy a secret that could dramatically improve Britain's naval preparedness.

Later in the day, Walsh bundled the 'money' in two secure packages and, after an interminable wait through the afternoon, made his way to his café on Place Flagey at the appointed hour.

At precisely 19:00 the telephone rang. The owner answered it, listened a moment, then held the handset out for Walsh. He listened for a moment, then handed the handset back to the owner. Walsh retrieved a map from his coat pocket, opened it, and checked the address. A minute later he fled from the building as quickly as he could.

Less than an hour later, Walsh arrived at the address in southwest Brussels, on rue des Fabriques near the abbatoir at the edge of Cureghem. The area was heavily industrialized, with large red-brick factories, smokestacks, and warehouses scattered throughout. Even at this time of day, when the majority of workers had disappeared for the night, Walsh could hear the throb of machinery behind the walls and could see smoke curling out of some of the chimneys into the clear night sky.

The building set for the meeting was a large industrial complex of stone and brick surrounded by a high wall. No one seemed to be around so Walsh made a quick circuit of the structure before hiding his parcel in a stack of empty wooden boxes he found down a dark alley next to one of the walls.

Back at the main entrance, on rue des Fabriques, he approached the main gate, which was slightly ajar. Walsh pushed the heavy iron door open and slowly entered the complex. Across the way, at the other end of a loading area where two small lorries were parked, Walsh saw a light coming from a window above a door. The door was the entrance to the largest building in the complex, and Walsh could see a large brick chimney, at least fifty metres tall, rising from the top of it. No smoke came from the chimney and Walsh could hear no machine noises in the area. Nor were any other doorways or windows lit in the complex.

A moment later Walsh knocked at the door, and it quickly opened to him. The same man who had pistol-whipped him at his flat stood there.

"Right on time. Good for you," he said.

The giant stepped aside and Walsh entered the building. Before he could proceed much further, he felt the man's huge paw on his shoulder.

"*Attendez*," he growled.

The man put his hands under Walsh's arms and pushed them up, away from his body. He roughly patted his hands along Walsh's body, feeling for a weapon. Walsh could feel the strength in the hands as they grabbed along his arms and legs.

The man spun him around and felt inside Walsh's coat. Nothing was there, except for Walsh's streetmap of Brussels. Walsh got a better look at the man now, and first noted a long scar across his left check. He had a few days' growth of beard on him, with some grey in it, and looked older than Walsh had originally thought. Closer to forty rather than to Walsh's own age. Or even older perhaps. He had dark bushy eyebrows that nearly grew together into a single line, the color of which matched the hair poking out from under the stained cloth cap perched on his head. Walsh tried to avoid cringing at the stench coming from the man's mouth as he leaned forward to feel around Walsh's beltline.

Finally the giant stood back.

"Satisfied?" Walsh said.

"Hmpf. *Allons-y.*"

The giant pushed Walsh down a short corridor, then through another door and into a large open factory floor. One area of the room was covered with short stacks of dingy-grey coloured metal bricks. Walsh could also see some type of conveyance mechanism in part of one of the side walls, and piles of empty sacks made of thick white fabric. Along another wall, a row of stout wooden pegs held heavy canvas masks with dark glass faceplatess, many stained black with carbon dust. In a large hallway leading from the room, he saw wooden pallets stacked a metre high with the same fabric sacks, all full now, and placed in a cross-wise pattern to distribute the weight of the bags. In the very center of the room he saw a huge vat of liquid, still and deep.

After a moment Walsh realized the purpose of the factory, and he stepped towards the centre of the room to confirm his suspicion. He looked up, and peered into what he originally thought was the tall chimney he had seen from the outside. It was centered exactly above the vat of liquid in the middle of the room. Walsh could see now that it was not a chimney; it was an open structure leading to a small platform at the top, reached by a narrow staircase curving along its inside walls. The tower, fifty-five metres tall, was in fact a structure for making lead shot. A furnace at the top of the tower melted the lead ingots stacked along the wall here, and the liquid metal fell through a large sieve and down the tower, cooling and forming into shot pellets in the process before they splashed into the tank.

"Welcome to the Tour à Plombs, Mr Walsh," he heard, in German-accented French. The voice was crisp and precise, but one he had never heard before.

Walsh turned from the tower and saw a tall, well-dressed man approaching him from one of the side corridors.

"Quite impressive, isn't it? A crude but effective method," the man continued, looking up into the tower void. "You should see it in operation. And hear it! Tons of molten lead raining down from above, and landing as perfectly-formed spheres in this tank."

The man held up one of them for Walsh to see, rolling it between his leather-gloved fingers.

"The devil's rain, some of the men here call it." He looked up again, into the dark tower. "You can just imagine how this substance was used as a weapon in medieval times, to keep the hungry hordes at bay. And you could put it through a small hand-held sprinkler too, to torture rather than kill. Or to kill more slowly, I suppose. Burning hot lead splashed onto sensitive, delicate human skin? The effect must have been too horrible to contemplate."

"Very interesting." Walsh said. "And you are?"

"Yes, forgive me. Retzlaff. Klaus Retzlaff, at your service." The man touched the brim of his black Homburg and bowed to him, ever so slightly.

"And where is Ernst?"

"Oh, we have have him, don't worry about that. Yes, he is very safe. And you've been a very busy man, Mr Walsh, haven't you? Trying to set up this little exchange with poor young Ernst. Trying to negotiate with his socialist *scum*."

"What business is it of yours?"

Retzlaff ignored him. "Do you have the money?"

"Of course."

"And where is it?"

"It's close by." Walsh looked over at the giant, who was now holding a pistol. "Very close by. And when I get Ernst, when I see that he is safe, then you get the money."

Retzlaff smiled. "Of course. Or we could just...force you to hand over the money, couldn't we?" He threw the small lead pellet at Walsh.

Walsh ducked and narrowly avoided being hit by it. Then he shook his head. "No, you won't. Don't be stupid, *Herr* Retzlaff. My colleague in the Sûreté already has your name. If your men have been following us, then you know about him. And he knows about Ernst. If I don't contact him tonight, he will begin a search for you and Ernst. He also has a detailed physical description of your two accomplices. The scar on this one is an especially helpful distinguishing feature. His police record probably mentions it. And his size, of course. You should hire men who are a little more *inconspicuous* next time, don't you think?"

The giant shot a hard look at Retzlaff, raising his one bushy eyebrow.

"You won't even make it to the border, let alone back to Germany," Walsh continued. "So let's just make this a simple trade, shall we?"

"I see." Retzlaff walked over and stood next to his gunman, giving him a quick soothing look. "Yes, there is no need to complicate things. They are complicated enough, wouldn't you agree?" Another smile.

"And what about Tobias?" Walsh said.

"Tobias?"

"Ernst's friend. The one who brought him to Brussels."

"Ah yes, the Jew. The poor furrier's son. The one nobody cares about. You think I have him?"

"He's missing."

"Yes, I know that. But I don't have him. What would I want with him? He's worthless to me."

Walsh considered that. He couldn't afford to press the issue just now. "Fair enough. And what about Ernst?"

Retzlaff came forward, next to the vat, and peered up into the tower. He looked at Walsh again, and smiled. "Gerwyn!" he suddenly shouted.

"*Oui?*" came a voice from above.

"Show Mr Hesse to us, *s'il vous plaît.*"

"*Oui, un instant, monsieur.*"

A moment later, Ernst's voice could be heard. "Mr Walsh?"

"Yes, Ernst," Walsh said, in a loud voice. "I'm down here. Are you all right?"

"Yes, I'm all right." His voice was faint in the tall chamber. Walsh wondered how many nosebleeds the lad had had since Retzlaff took him.

"That's enough!" Retzlaff said. "Now, Mr Walsh, the money please? So we can finish this business?"

"It's outside. I'll bring it here. You bring Ernst down from there. And he better be unharmed."

"Go with him, Hugo," Retzlaff said, to the large man with the pistol. "Be careful. And make sure you aren't being watched, *d'accord?*"

"*D'ac,*" said Hugo. He motioned to Walsh with his pistol.

Walsh followed Hugo back outside the building and through the courtyard into the main street. It was mostly quiet up and down the street; a few motorcars passed at the end of the street and a couple of very small groups of workingmen passed them by. Hugo kept his gun hand in his coat pocket. When they had passed, Walsh led Hugo around the building and into the alley with the boxes.

Walsh moved closer to the boxes and leaned to reach inside a small opening between two of them. He took a deep breath. "It's in here."

"*Arrête!*" Hugo said, pulling the pistol from his pocket. "I'll get it."

Hugo held the pistol, and his eyes, on Walsh while he reached his left hand a few inches into the opening. His eyebrow went up as he found the parcel, which he removed from the small space. He clutched the parcel to his chest with his left hand, and clumsily attempted to unwrap the edge of it with the two small fingers of his gun hand.

"Wait!" Walsh said, suddenly. "Where's the other one?"

Hugo looked up in confusion, but did not let go of his parcel or raise his pistol. Before he could react, Walsh reached into the opening, deeper this time, and quickly retrieved his own pistol. He put the barrel against Hugo's huge head, knocking off the man's cap. Hugo froze in shock.

"Drop your gun!" he said to the large man.

Hugo did as he was told, dropping the parcel as well. Walsh smacked him against his head, just to get his attention.

"Doesn't feel too good, now, does it? Now move." Walsh pointed his pistol back towards the main building.

Walsh pocketed Hugo's gun and marched him back into the Tour à Plombs complex, leaving the worthless parcel on the ground. They made their way inside, where Retzlaff was waiting next to Ernst and Gerwyn, who held a pistol on Ernst. Ernst looked slightly more shaken and tired than normal, but otherwise seemed unharmed.

Walsh kept his gun against the back of Hugo's huge head, and stood behind him.

"What is this?" Retzlaff said. "Where is the money?"

"There is no money, you numpty," said Walsh. "Ernst! Come over here."

Before Ernst could move, Retzlaff raised his hand and spoke up. "Hold him, Gerwyn!" Then to Walsh, "You can't think we'll just let you walk out of here?"

"Of course you will," Walsh said.

Gerwyn put his pistol to Ernst's temple.

"He'll kill him," Retzlaff said.

"I don't…"

Suddenly Hugo shoved his huge body backwards, easily unbalancing Walsh. The next few moments were a blur. Hugo spun around to his right, fast for a man his size, and grabbed Walsh's right wrist with his left hand. He now had total control of Walsh's gun hand. Hugo forced the gun to point upwards, away from his body, and grabbed for Walsh's throat with his right hand. Walsh backed away and ducked down to avoid Hugo's grasp, and just missed the big paw coming at him. But he couldn't shake the grip on his gun arm, so Walsh viciously kicked his leg up and slammed his shin into Hugo's groin as hard as he could. As big as Hugo was, he couldn't ignore the pain between his legs and he relaxed his grip on Walsh's wrist just enough for Walsh to break free.

Walsh moved back a few feet and shot Hugo in the leg. The big man cried out in pain a second time and collapsed on the ground, clutching his shattered knee.

Walsh quickly trained his pistol onto Retzlaff, holding it with both hands.

"That's it. Ernst comes with me or you die right now," Walsh said to Retzlaff. "Or we can just wait here for the police to arrive. I'll fire this pistol a few more times to make sure they do. It's your choice."

Gerwyn had trained his own pistol onto Walsh by now, while still clutching Ernst's shoulder with his free hand, but Walsh kept his own weapon aimed at Retzlaff's head.

"Your man might be a good shot," said Walsh, slowly moving away from the crumpled, moaning Hugo and towards Retzlaff, who held his hands in the air in front of him. "Maybe even fast enough to kill me before I kill you. But do you want to bet your life on that?"

Retzlaff stared at him.

"If you leave quickly, you might even get out of the country before the Sûreté finds out about this," Walsh added.

"Enough," Retzlaff said, finally. "Gerwyn, let him go."

"But *monsieur*!" Gerwyn protested.

"*Genug*! Let him go!" Retzlaff turned and began walking down the corridor behind him. "And get your friend."

Gerwyn looked at the back of the swiftly departing Retzlaff, then back at Walsh. Then, with a growl of *merde* under his breath, he suddenly released Ernst and crept over to Hugo, with his gun still on Walsh. Once next to Hugo, Walsh lowered his own weapon, which prompted Gerwyn to holster his own pistol. Gerwyn knelt close to Hugo and pulled one of the big man's arms over his shoulder. With a grunt from Gerwyn and another cry of pain from Hugo, who hopped on one knee, the two men staggered down the corridor after Retzlaff.

Walsh and Ernst watched them disappear into the gloom.

"*Auf Wiedersehen, Herr Retzlaff!*" Walsh called after them.

Chapter 48

Agram. May 1910.

The railway station, Glavni Kolodvor, was throbbing with activity as Zerajic walked through the heavy crowds in front of it. He moved slowly, taking his time. Bukov was late again.

This time, Zerajic was much calmer; having so many people around for his meeting with Bukov, their final encounter, made Zerajic feel as if they would not be so conspicuous. Glavni Kolodvor was the largest railway station in Croatia, and its huge neo-classical façade concealed numerous places for clandestine liaisons. Besides, here Zerajic could see that several of the trains would be late, although he did not know which one would bring Bukov. Or whether the old man would even arrive by train.

So, just two friends having a quick coffee before one of them departed. Zerajic had just sat down with his beverage – he could not afford something to go with it – when he spied Bukov walking over from the platforms.

Bukov entered the station café from another direction and sat alone at a table. He looked around the room and, satisfied, gave a slight nod to Zerajic, who picked up his coffee and book and came over to sit with Bukov.

"My friend," Bukov began, in a gentle voice. "How are things these days?"

"Not so bad. How are things with you?"

Bukov ignored the question. He looked around the room again. "Have you been...practicing with your new toy?"

"Yes, a few times."

"It works well? You are comfortable with it?"

"Yes, I suppose so," Zerajic said. "We had a similar...toy on my father's farm. A much older one, of course. Not so...effective as this one."

Bukov gave a small nod. "Good. Just be sure no one finds you practicing."

"Of course not."

"And don't...waste too many resources with the practice, understand?"

"I only need a few."

"Yes."

"And how is your father? Your family?"

Zerajic took a sip of coffee. "My father is not well."

"Sick?"

"No, he cut his arm in the fields, trying to repair his plow. It won't heal now. He can't work so well."

"I'm sorry about that. They should not have to live that way. No one should. But then, that is why you are doing this, my friend, isn't it?"

Zerajic looked Bukov in the eye. "You will help them, won't you? When this is over?"

"Yes, of course we will. *Of course* we will." Bukov reached over and patted Zerajic on the arm. "That is already agreed. You are doing a very brave thing for them. For everyone in your country, suffering under the emperor."

"And the money you promised now?"

Bukov looked down at his hands. He sucked in some air across his teeth, and shook his head very slowly. "I'm afraid things are still delayed. I'm sorry, Bogdan. One of our...sources has run into difficulties."

Zerajic swore under his breath and shook his head. "What delay? What is it this time?"

"Not to worry, my friend, I have some of it now." Bukov lowered his voice again. "Five hundred." He retrieved an envelope from his coat pocket and passed it across the table to Zerajic. "That should help them, no?"

Zerajic put the envelope in his pocket without looking inside. "And the rest?" he asked. "I thought this was our last meeting. How are you going to get it to me?"

"We will send it to your family. I promise you that," Bukov said.

"See that you do."

"I promise, Bogdan. Trust me. You must trust me."

Zerajic sighed, then drained the rest of his cup. He wasn't doing this for the money, not entirely, but it would help his family. He looked outside the café, towards the mingling crowds. People getting on with their lives. Enjoying themselves. At a nearby table, a striking blond girl with shiny crimson lips was nuzzling against a young man who looked very pleased with himself. No wonder, thought Zerajic. She caught his glance and smiled at him.

He quit his reverie and looked back at Bukov.

280

"My uncle will be upset," Zerajic said. "Even more than my parents, I think."

"Your uncle?"

Zerajic nodded. "He's a doctor. With the medical service. He was the one paying for my studies here. Until I quit, that is."

"I see."

"He won't understand this."

"Perhaps he will. In time." Bukov's hand reached out again, and gripped Zerajic's wrist. Tightly. "You are doing an *amazing* thing, Bogdan. Amazing! Just think about it. This emperor, his family, has a lineage going back over a thousand years. A thousand years, Bogdan! And you are going to put an end to it, an end to their tyranny, with one daring act! You, Bogdan! Just days from now! And afterwards your name is going to be written, is going to be carved in stone, in the history of your people. Forever! Now, how can your family not understand this, hmm? How can they not? I think you should give them more credit. And if your uncle is an educated man, as you say, then he will certainly understand the sacrifice you are making. For him. For your parents. And for the Serbian people, for generations to come. Think about it!"

Zerajic allowed himself a smile. "You are very persuasive, Mikhail."

Bukov shook his head. "It's not me, Bogdan. It's the simple truth. You know it is. But sometimes we need reminding of it. At times like this, when difficult choices have to be made."

"Very well. And thank you for reminding me. But I need to go now. I need to get this to my family."

Zerajic patted the front of his coat, where the envelope was.

Bukov nodded. "Yes. I understand. Then we must say good-bye."

Bukov removed his hand from Zerajic's arm, and held his palm out. Zerajic shook it. They smiled at each other.

"Good-bye," Zerajic said.

"Good-bye, my friend. And *Sretno*! Good luck!"

Chapter 49

Brussels. May 1910.

Two days after Walsh rescued Ernst, he met with Major Bridges in a small park near the British Embassy. Ernst waited in a café nearby, tending to his nosebleed.

"Why are you here? I can't help you," Bridges said, by way of greeting.

"I'm here to help you. Or warn you, I suppose," Walsh said.

Bridges motioned for Walsh to sit down on a bench. "What warning?"

Walsh gave him the short version of what had happened with Ernst over the past couple of days. Then he added, "So just know that you've been watched. Retzlaff knew everything, even my name and the amount Ernst was asking for the acetone secret. So they must have been following you, or watching the embassy at least. Hopefully I scared him away, but we can't be sure."

"All right, then, thanks for letting me know. I'm sorry about before, but you must understand my position."

"It's no bother," Walsh said, in a flat voice. "I won't be disturbing you any more."

Bridges leaned closer to Walsh. "Listen, old boy, since you're here, I'll give you a warning of my own. Things have not progressed on our commitment to Belgium, you understand? The FO is still confused about what to make of Germany. And I'm getting no help from the Belgians here, or the Dutch, for that matter. It seems as if everyone concerned simply wants to keep their heads in the sand."

"And what does that mean for me, Major Bridges?"

"It just means that if I were you, I wouldn't risk my life to make these kinds of deals you are working on. Or even risk prison, for that matter! Christ, man, this little transaction has turned into kidnapping and extortion and attempted murder! Do you really want to be a part of all that? And when the information you *might* collect turns out to be useless in light of our problems with these neutral countries? Is it really worth the trouble, old boy?"

Walsh shook his head. "How the devil should I know, major? I'm just following orders."

The next day, Walsh met Dewulf near his flat in Ixelles. Walsh told him about the events at the Tour à Plombs, except for shooting Hugo in the knee. After he finished, he could see that the inspector was not happy.

"I'm sorry, but what did you expect me to do? I had to go alone," Walsh said. "They insisted on it, and threatened Ernst's life."

Dewulf glared at him. "And without even having the money to trade?"

"I had to take a chance. I thought he might have Ernst and Tobias."

"Suppose they had found your pistol? Or had taken you to another location? What then?"

"Listen, inspector. Retzlaff is only in this for the money. I know that now. I confirmed it. He would not have done anything to jeopardise that, if I didn't have it with me."

"And you told them about me. About the Sûreté."

"Not your name. Nothing particular. It was a gamble, understand? Besides, if they've been watching, then they knew about you already."

"And you still want my help? After all this?"

Walsh nodded. "Please, inspector. I still want to keep track of Retzlaff, if at all possible. I'm not sure that he will give up so easily. And he might still know about Tobias."

"You think so, hmm? After this debacle?"

"Ernst thinks so. He insisted that I tell you about this. We both think that it would be a good idea to put some pressure on Retzlaff, now that he's made a move to take Ernst against his will. And I...I need to keep Ernst's hopes about Tobias alive. For a little while at least. You understand?"

Dewulf sighed. "Where did they keep Ernst?"

"He doesn't know. He was blindfolded in a car and did not see anything until the Tour à Plombs. He said the walls echoed and it smelled of smoke. Burning. A furnace or some type of factory."

"That doesn't help us." Dewulf paused for a moment. "And you didn't get the last names of the two men with him?"

"No. I had a good look at them, though."

"Well, that's a start. We have some photographs you could look at. And if Ernst was taken against his will then we could arrest Retzlaff for kidnapping. If we find him, that is. If we can just find him, we could end this thing right now. No more troubles with these Germans."

Walsh thought for a moment.

Dewulf spoke the thought for him. "But then all this would become public knowledge, wouldn't it? And you don't want that."

Walsh shook his head. "Not just yet, inspector. If you don't mind."

"Ha. If I don't mind. You English are so polite."

"I'm not English. I'm Scottish."

Dewulf nodded at him. "My apologies."

"It may require an arrest, if Retzlaff tries again, but can we keep all this just between us for now?"

"I suppose so. Less work for me, for once!" Dewulf paused again. "But Retzlaff already knew about the five thousand pounds before they took Ernst? The exact amount?"

Walsh nodded. "Yes. They mentioned that figure at my flat, before they took Ernst away."

"So they knew the exact amount before they attacked you. So if that information did not come from Tobias or Ernst, then how did they know?" Dewulf raised an eyebrow.

"The Maison. Hendrickx. It must be Hendrickx."

Dewulf nodded. "I think it might be time to have a talk with him."

"I agree." Walsh thought about this for a moment. "But can you do that? I mean, officially? Without raising suspicions?"

Dewulf smiled. "It's going to be...delicate."

Walsh looked Dewulf in the eyes. "Inspector, if the socialists know you are investigating these matters, then my deal with Ernst will collapse. All of this effort will be for nothing. And the German government will almost certainly find out, which would greatly complicate things for me. Not to mention for Ernst!"

"Well, there are...formal investigations. And then there are...informal inquiries. And then there are...other methods." Dewulf stood up. And then he smiled, oddly, at Walsh. *"Comprenez-vous?"*

Chapter 50

Agram. May 1910.

In the last week of the last month of spring, Bogdan Zerajic packed a worn leather suitcase with his meagre belongings, checked his secret stash of newly-acquired kronen notes and his Browning pistol, and left his miserable university flat for the last time. He did not pause to say goodbye to any of his fellow students at Agram; they had no time for him, and the feeling was mutual. Zerajic was more upset at having to leave his precious books rather than his fellow law students behind. But he also forced himself not to dwell on such disheartening thoughts when they surfaced in his young mind. After all, the time for reading and studying was over; it was now time for action.

He did manage to say goodbye to Vasily Grdjic, a leading Serb intellectual he knew, but that farewell was just a happy accident. Grdjic was a member of parliament and secretary of the cultural society Prosvjeta, based in Sarajevo; he often met with Serbian students throughout the Balkans. He happened to be passing through Agram during the last week of May and made the effort to see Zerajic. They had little time for more than a few pleasantries over coffee near Zerajic's flat. It was just as well the encounter did not drag on, as Zerajic seemed to be greatly preoccupied. Grdjic also thought it odd that Zerajic said he was returning home before his term at university had ended, but he did not ask him about this.

During his preparations for leaving, Zerajic also occasionally reflected on the curious path that had led him to take his decision to abandon his studies, after all of his hard work to get to university. These thoughts he found it more difficult to control. So he thought of his parents, back on the kmet, and his poor father struggling to work with an injured arm that would not heal. He thought of his generous uncle, surprising Zerajic and his family with an offer to help pay for law studies once they all could see that Zerajic might have a future beyond the farm. And he thought of his friends back home, some of whom remained on their filthy plots of land they did not own with no real future ahead of them, while others managed to find their way out of the kmets by entering university or, more often, the Serbian Army.

Above all, Zerajic thought of Vladimir Gacinovic, his close
friend from secondary school during their youth in Mostar,
where they both belonged to a schoolboys' secret society.
While Zerajic had ended up at the University of Agram thanks
to his uncle, Gacinovic had had the amazing luck to win a
stipend from the Serbian government. This windfall took him
all the way to the glorious University of Vienna, the oldest
university in the German-speaking world and the most
important centre of learning in the Austrian-Hungarian
empire. During his studies he made frequent visits to Bosnia
and stayed in close touch with his old friend Zerajic, who
shared his passion for the cause of Serbian nationalism.

Gacinovic joined another secret society of Bosnian
students in Vienna, one of several at the time dedicated to the
liberation of the Balkans from Austrian rule. Some of these
groups were small satellite organizations under the direction
of Narodna Odbrana, and had local branches throughout the
Balkans. As student societies, they were largely unknown to
General Varesanin and his security team in Sarajevo, who
tended to focus on more prominent organizations, such as
Narodna Odbrana, and respond to rumours of other militaristic
secret societies, such as Crna Ruka, the Black Hand. They
had little time to deal with small student groups, which did not
seem to pose a threat when compared to those organized by
the army.

It was through Gacinovic's link to his secret student
society that Zerajic first met with the old man from the east,
Bukov. Bukov, in turn, was eager to meet with other
passionate students who shared Gacinovic's views about
Austria's rule in the Balkans, and therefore he was deeply
grateful to Gacinovic for giving him the name of Bogdan
Zerajic, a young law student.

After all their years together, it troubled Zerajic greatly that
he would only have time for a quick goodbye to Gacinovic,
his dear old friend from Mostar. But this situation could not
be helped, and he had a very important train to catch. He was
sure Gacinovic would understand.

Chapter 51

Brussels. May 1910.

Leysen met Dewulf and Walsh at midday in front of the massive Halles des Machines complex at the rear of the Exposition, well away from the scheming socialist masses of the Marolles. The crowds had thinned out somewhat since the grand opening of the Expo, but there were still plenty of visitors to help conceal this brief rendevous. Leysen took the precaution of keeping his fedora brim pulled down over his eyebrows; Walsh thought it made him look even more suspicious. But at least he wasn't wearing a false moustache, and his suit was clean.

"And who was it who asked you to organize these Young Guard groups?" Dewulf said, after introducing Leysen to Walsh.

"Penneman," said Leysen.

"First name?"

"Uhh...Jan. Jan Penneman." Leysen kept his head down as the three men slowly navigated their way along the rear exhibition halls of the complex.

"And he simply wants you to spread socialist ideas among these young men? Especially those who might end up in the army? Is that it?"

Leysen made a negative sound. "I don't think it's that simple. He wants me to help them spread socialism in their regiments, if they are called up. And inform Penneman about where they are sent, what kind of strength they have around the country, that sort of thing. In case the socialists want to plan a strike, I suppose."

"I see," said Dewulf.

"And...something else."

"What is it?"

Leysen paused for a moment while a small group of Asian visitors passed them. Then he continued.

"He...he wants me to help convince the recruits to disobey any orders to fire on protesters or strikers. If their regiments are asked to respond to such events."

That prompted a sound from Walsh, a kind of choked laugh.

"What?" said Dewulf, to Walsh. "You know something about this?"

Walsh sighed, then looked over at Leysen, on the other side of Dewulf.

"What is it?" said Leysen.

Walsh nodded, just slightly. "Next he's going to ask you to help prepare for a military strike in the event of war," Walsh replied.

"How do you know that?" said Dewulf.

"They're doing the same thing in France," said Walsh. "Or have been, for years. It's in the *Manuel du Soldat*, circulated by the French socialists throughout their army. I'm sure there's a Belgian version of it floating about. Or they might even circulate the French version."

"And how do you know *that*?" said Leysen.

Walsh paused for a moment. These two trusted him with their secret work; he would have to trust them. Then again, there was that great line from one of the socialist rags he came across in Paris, years ago: *Three people can keep a secret if two of them are dead.* What the hell.

"Because I...I encountered the same thing when I worked in Paris," Walsh continued. "A few years ago."

"I see," said Dewulf.

"What does that mean for me?" said Leysen. The fear was evident in his tone. "What am I supposed to do?"

"It's all in the *Manuel*," Walsh continued. "They'll try to call for a general strike in the event of war. Disrupt the railways, the coalmines. Docks and harbours. That sort of thing. Of course, I could be wrong. They might just ask you to speak to the new recruits, nothing too serious. But once you show a...a talent for that kind of work, you could be asked to do anything. They'll keep asking more of you until you start to resist." Walsh made sure he looked Leysen in the eyes. "Just be ready for it."

"What about that?" Dewulf said, to Leysen. "Have they mentioned anything violent? Anything about the Exposition?"

"No, no, nothing like that," said Leysen, who turned to face Dewulf. "*Merde*, inspector! What are you trying to do to me? Get me accused of treason? This has nothing to do with the Exposition! They haven't even mentioned that to me, not in any of the meetings I attended!"

Dewulf shook his head. "Nothing to worry about right now. You are simply attending meetings at the moment; don't agree to anything else right now, understand?"

Leysen nodded, but didn't seem so sure. They turned left, and continued walking slowly in front of the Galerie Française. A juggler was in front of it, throwing coloured balls into the air. A small crowd had gathered. Nearby, a group of visitors was having a picture taken with what looked like a smiling pair of Pygmies, dressed in little more than rags despite the chill in the air.

After they had passed the show, Dewulf lit a small cigar. "And you haven't told this Penneman that you will work for him, correct?"

"Not exactly. I said I needed a few days to think about it. I wanted to ask you first. This is not what interests you, correct?"

Dewulf blew a puff of smoke. "Well, you need to stay close to them until this is over." He waved his hand around, indicating the Expo. "Very close. And they must continue to trust you."

"And so?"

"And so, this Penneman fellow, he is working with the big man there, with Vandervelde? At the Maison?"

Leysen nodded. "I expect so. He mentioned his name."

"Excellent. So my friend," Dewulf put his gloved hand on the back of Leysen's neck. "I want you to go to the Maison, and meet with Penneman. Tell him you would like to help but want some more details about it."

"What details?" said Leysen.

"Oh, just think of something. Some excuse. Ask him for some assurances. Can he give you a specific text to help you prepare your meetings? What happens if you get into trouble, if you get arrested? Remind him of your past trouble with the police, so you want him to be clear on what kind of protection he can provide. How will you maintain contact and receive their publications for distribution, and keep it all secret? That sort of thing. And you can appear to be as nervous as you want; he would expect that."

Leysen nodded. "I suppose I can do that."

Dewulf nodded and blew a puff of smoke into the air. "Of course you can. All very innocent. These are political types, not the criminals you've dealt with before. So don't worry. And when you are in the building, do something else for me."

Leysen stopped walking. Dewulf and Walsh stopped as well. "What now?" Leysen said. The irritation was clear in his voice.

"Nothing too difficult. Not for you," Dewulf said. He put his hand on Leysen's back and pushed him along. They started walking again.

"Ask about someone named Hendrickx," Dewulf continued. "David Hendrickx. He is close to Vandervelde."

"Ask Penneman?"

Dewulf shook his head. "No, no, of course not. Just keep your eyes open, if they have a directory or something. Try to find out his title and office location. His normal working hours. That sort of thing." He smiled. "Nothing too difficult, correct?"

"Who is he?"

"Just someone who might be able to help us. But keep it secret, understand? Don't spread the word that you are looking for him. We just want to know if he is around there."

Leysen nodded. "All right then."

"Excellent."

Walsh left Dewulf and Leysen a few minutes later, as his business with them was concluded. Ernst was waiting for him at a café in the Belgian section, but Walsh quickly made his way back to the automobile exhibition. He searched the area for Gisela, hoping to explain why he wouldn't be able to see her for a little while, until this business with Ernst and Hendrickx was sorted out. But she wasn't there.

Chapter 52

Bosna-Brod, Bosnia-Herzegovina. May 1910.

The special royal train carrying Emperor Franz Joseph I of Austria-Hungary and his family made its way southwards from Vienna as scheduled on the last weekend of May, stopping at railway stations large and small throughout the Balkans.

Bosna-Brod, situated on the frontier between Croatia and Bosnia-Herzegovina, was still on the emperor's itinerary. The tiny village, on the Bosnian side of the river Sava, had belonged to the Turks until they lost control of the province after the Congress of Berlin. It was still very much frontier country, sparsely populated and surrounded by large oak trees and rolling meadows.

Bosna-Brod itself was little more than a rough main road anchored by a small railway station outside of the village and a larger hôtel-guest house within it. The village was surrounded by a bend in the river Sava and prone to flooding, so the rough wooden houses filling in the gaps between the larger buildings were perched on raised foundations. A small mosque, also constructed of wood, could be seen at one end of the main street, topped by a minaret painted in very faded red, yellow, and green colours.

Zerajic waited at the railway station, hidden within a small crowd of local residents. A detachment of Austrian soldiers from Slavonski-Brod, the fortress town across the river in Croatia, was on hand to help protect the emperor.

Zerajic kept his eye on the soldiers, and his damp palm around the cold butt of the pistol in his right front trouser pocket. He thought he was waiting as patiently as possible, but his legs told him otherwise. He kept bouncing on his knees, just slightly, as if trying to warm himself despite the late May sunshine, and he resisted the urge to pace around the crowd. Perhaps it was the coffee working on him; Zerajic had probably downed too many cups of it earlier that morning while he spent several hours waiting in one of the few Turkish cafés remaining in the village. The coffee had been made in the traditional Turkish manner and he could still feel the grit of coffee grounds in his mouth.

Just a few more minutes now. Surely there was no chance that the emperor's private train would be late?

Zerajic waited and rocked on the balls of his feet. A mounted soldier from the Austrian regiment seemed to be taking an interest in him, but before either man could act, they heard a train whistle from across the river. The sound grew louder, and within a few moments the train itself came into view, from the bridge over the river Sava.

The crowd surged towards the railway station and closer to the platform, waiting expectantly. Zerajic joined the spectators and watched the train slow to a crawl before stopping in the middle of the short platform.

Two dozen or so soldiers worked their way in front of the crowd, between the citizens and the train, and held up their hands to keep everyone back.

Zerajic gripped the butt of his pistol and gradually shuffled his way to the front of the crowd, near to where several local dignitaries were waiting to see the emperor.

Now he was ready.

The door to the train opened, and a step-box was placed on the ground by a station agent. A train conductor appeared next, and he stepped onto the platform and then waited at one side of the train carriage doorway.

Zerajic readied himself; he got into position and put his finger on the trigger of the pistol in his pocket. He kept his eyes on the door to the train carriage and watched, mesmerized, as the emperor appeared on the top step. Franz Joseph was nearly eighty years old and Zerajic expected to see a frail old man, but the emperor was a formidable presence in person. He wore his dress military uniform, as always on such occasions, and a massive display of coloured plumage adorned his helmet. The feathers were even larger than the size of his head, which itself seemed quite large thanks to the bushy whiskers and sideburns he kept. The breast of the emperor's crisp white jacket was vividly decorated with just a few of his major honours: the Order of the Golden Fleece, the Royal Hungarian Order of Saint Stephen, the Order of the Garter, the Order of the Black Eagle, and the Order of Leopold.

The emperor waved to the small crowd and Zerajic found himself paralyzed in fear and awe. In his mind he knew he had the means to destroy the powerful figure standing just a few metres away from him, and yet he could not move. He simply watched as the emperor moved down the small stairway and into the crowd, shaking hands with whatever assorted dignitaries tiny Bosna-Brod could provide today. The emperor stayed for nearly half an hour, and did not move far from the platform, so Zerajic had more than enough time, and opportunity, to put a bullet in the old man's heart.

And still, and with utter amazement, Zerajic found that he was frozen in place as the emperor moved among the crowd. He simply could not bring himself to remove the gun hand from his pocket. He could not lift his weapon.

He could not shoot. He could not kill.

With growing frustration, yet still unable to act, Zerajic stood in shock as he watched the royal party board their train, wave to the crowd, and leave the station as swiftly as they had arrived. As the crowd rapidly thinned out, Zerajic found himself alone on the platform.

His mind whirled in confusion. What had he done? How could this happen?

Zerajic sensed a slight feeling of panic spreading in his consciousness. It very nearly turned into dizziness, and he almost felt light-headed. He quickly composed himself and then, with some of the money left from Bukov's largesse, he bought another railway ticket for the next train to Sarejevo.

In the Bosnian capital, Zerajic saw the emperor again during the second day of his three days in Sarajevo, during which time the security forces were out in full force. All of Bosnia's ethnic communities were represented in the emperor's audience, and it seemed that no group could escape the attention of the massed security forces during these few days. They also took the precaution of removing all known local political agitators and similar undesirables. Zerajic, however, was not known to the authorities and could move easily among the thousands of policemen, soldiers, and plain-clothes detectives keeping an eye on the crowds.

He therefore was able to watch, along with many other surprised spectators, the highlight of the emperor's visit to Sarejevo: when the supposedly frail old man, riding a large stallion, galloped onto the parade ground in Sarajevo and rode with pride and skill in the colourful parade organized in his honour.

Zerajic watched and waited, his pistol always at the ready. And yet, for the second time, he simply could not bring himself to raise the weapon from his pocket.

Following the visit to Sarajevo, the emperor made the final leg of his journey, to Mostar now, just over seventy kilometres to the southwest. Again, Zerajic followed his train, arriving soon after the emperor. The emperor spent only a few hours in Mostar, and although Zerajic was close enough to touch the emperor during his brief stop at the railway station, he could not find the courage to raise the pistol from his pocket and shoot the old man. Zerajic was close enough, almost, to smell the stench of the emperor's favourite lunch on his breath - sauerkraut and boiled beef – and yet he failed, again, to draw and fire his weapon, the one he had practiced with so many times.

That was Zerajic's last chance. From Mostar, the emperor went directly back to Vienna, with no more public stops. His security advisors throughout the region, from Vienna to Mostar, breathed a collective sigh of relief that the visit had been so successful. And so safe.

Zerajic had missed three chances to make his mark on the world. Three chances to perform a bold deed on behalf of his fellow Serbs. He returned to Sarajevo in shame, disgusted with himself. When would he ever get another chance such as the ones he missed with the emperor? *When?*

Chapter 53

Brussels. June 1910.

On the first Friday in June, Walsh received an unexpected telegram stating that Cumming wished to meet him two days later, in Brussels.

At the appointed time and place, Sunday evening, Walsh and Cumming sat together at a café in central Brussels, near the Bourse. Cumming began by saying that he hoped the telegram didn't alarm Walsh; he was in Brussels for another meeting with one of his agents, involving something about the forts in Wilhelmshaven, and he thought that he might try to reach Walsh during the same visit. Once Walsh was more at ease, the two men caught up on recent events involving Ernst and Tobias.

After hearing the details about the encounter with Retzlaff, including the shooting of Hugo and Dewulf's involvement, Cumming drew a sharp intake of breath and shook his head.

"I must say, Walsh, I'm growing ever more inclined to have you cut your losses and move on from this. Things are becoming too complicated. Even if we do find the money for your man."

Walsh held his tongue, but only just.

"And Kell still thinks this is all a trap," Cumming continued. "He might be right, you know. Suppose Retzlaff is a German agent, sent here to make us believe Ernst's story about being an innocent chemistry student? Suppose Steinhauer has been involved all along?"

Walsh shook his head. "Damn it, C, Ernst *is* just an innocent chemistry student! His sister confirmed that his father hired Retzlaff to find him. And I've been living with the lad for a month now! You think he could fool me that entire time?"

"How can you be sure? Absolutely sure?"

"Because I am. Because I know." Walsh stabbed his index finger on the table top, punctuating his words. "Ernie hasn't asked me anything about our methods or our agents or our defences or anything involving the intelligence game. He just doesn't care, not a whit. His problem is not that he is guilty, guilty about lying to us all this time, but that he is innocent. He's totally, utterly naïve about his involvement in this mess, with Tobias. With those socialists or whoever Tobias is working for."

Cumming frowned. "What do you mean by that? Who is Tobias working for?"

"I didn't mean anything by that."

Cumming voice's was urgent. "Come now, my boy. You've let the cat out of the bag! Are they or are they not working for the socialists?"

"Of course they are. Dewulf and I are attempting to make inquiries at their offices here. Discreet inquiries, mind you. Nothing official, so don't worry about that."

Cumming leaned forward and looked Walsh in the eyes. "Walsh, listen to me. Think about this, will you? Even if Ernst is being completely truthful with you, all this time, Tobias might be up to something else. Have you considered that?"

"Well, even if he is, I don't think it matters anymore. He is out of the game now. And Ernst has the information we need, not Tobias."

"As far as you know."

"Yes, as far as I know. But C, if Tobias is working for Steinhauer, then they've known all along about me. And what could they hope to gain by it? They can't expect to trick us into giving up that five thousand pounds and just disappear. They won't have their money unless Ernst can prove his secret to us. And he's agreed to do that."

"Yes, I've been thinking about that. How to prove all this and get Kell off my back."

"How so?"

"You remember I can pay a thousand pounds for really important information; Blitz and the others have agreed to that."

"And so?"

"Well, Ernst's secret probably involves a process. A set of steps, you understand? To convert some type of raw materials into useful acetone."

Walsh nodded. "I understand. You want him to tell us part of the process in exchange for part of the money."

"Exactly." Cumming smiled. "So you need to ask Ernst how much of his secret one thousand pounds would buy. Just to keep us all...honest."

"I'm not sure he would agree to that." Walsh took a long drink from the glass of bitter lemon in front of him.

"You might be surprised. Try to get him to explain, without actual details, how many steps are involved. What kind of...sequence is involved in his method. From raw material to the finished product. Then see how much of that method you can buy with one thousand pounds. Who knows? We might even be able to put together the rest by ourselves, and save four thousand pounds in the process."

Walsh nodded. "Fair enough, C. I'll ask him; that's no bother. Maybe he could tell us the type of equipment he needs as well. Maybe that could provide some clues."

"Yes, by all means." Cumming consulted his pocketwatch. "I'm afraid I must run. I need to get back to London tonight."

"Well, thanks for taking the time to contact me."

"No bother at all, my boy." Cumming leaned over the table again. "And one more thing, Walsh."

"What's that?"

Cumming lowered his voice, almost to a whisper. "If Ernst really is a chemist, then you are right about trying to keep him on our side. Trying to keep him in their chemical works, in some fashion, if we can manage that. We've had word from one of our agents in Germany. He witnessed a poison gas test at Kiel and sent us the details. It's pretty grim, Walsh. Ernst should be asked to look into that, once we get past this acetone business. So you might start preparing the field for that now, if you understand me."

Chapter 54

Sarajevo. June 1910.

After Emperor Franz Joseph left the Balkans for home, General Appel of the Austrian Army in Bosnia composed a letter to his colleague in Vienna, Alexander Brosch von Aarenau, aide-de-camp to Archduke Franz Ferdinand. Appel thought it unnecessary to consult General Varesanin about his communication to Brosch, which was intended as a personal one. He began by informing Brosch about the triumph of the visit, but then attempted to explain the lack of crowds in certain places as a consequence of fears about disturbances during the emperor's visit, fears which proved to be unfounded in the event. Appel kindly pointed out that the 'oriental' peoples of the Balkans were not in the habit of cheering for their leaders, which is why the emperor's subjects seemed somewhat subdued compared to the receptions he always enjoyed closer to home.

General Appel also mentioned how the emperor's horsemanship skills had greatly impressed the locals; he didn't need to add that they had expected to see a frail monarch who could barely walk, let alone gallop on a horse. Overall, then, the visit had made a 'deep and lasting impression' on the emperor's subjects throughout the Balkans, and had 'captured their hearts.' Appel closed his eight-page letter by suggesting that Brosch should visit the region himself to confirm these views.

Once Brosch had made such a confirmation, the letter continued, he should then propose to the heir to the throne, Archduke Franz Ferdinand, that he, too, should visit Bosnia with his wife Sophie and their children. Such a visit would 'give the population great joy' and help to strengthen the bond between the heir to the throne and his people in the region. Franz Ferdinand and his family could also relax in comfort at the spa town of Ilidze, just a few kilometres outside of Sarajevo. It would be a visit to remember, certainly.

Appel closed his letter by reassuring Brosch about the Archduke's safety if he came to Bosnia, pledging that 'I will vouch for the security of such a visit with my head.'

A few kilometres away from Appel, in a tiny hotel near Sarajevo's railway station, Zerajic sat on his bed and tried to keep thoughts of Bukov out of his head. To distract himself, he methodically stripped and cleaned his pistol. As he shifted the cold metal components in his hands, coating them with a light film of oil, he felt his courage, and his anger at Austria-Hungary, gradually return. True, he had missed his chance, his most important chance, with the emperor. The thought of coming so close but failing to complete his bold act haunted him to no end, especially as he struggled to find sleep each night. Bukov was not likely to forgive that mistake.

Zerajic soon realised, however, that there were other targets available in Bosnia. Other ways to demonstrate Serbia's resolve to the world, if the courage did not elude him next time. And now, after several days of torturing himself at his failure with the emperor, Zerajic was sure that it wouldn't. Absolutely sure.

Chapter 55

Brussels. June 1910.

On the balcony of his flat, Walsh sat with Ernst and looked out over the rooftops of Ixelles. The day was warming up nicely, for once, and the skies were very clear and still. On days like this, Brussels wasn't half bad. Unfortunately they were all too rare.

Walsh sipped at his coffee and pondered his next move. Since his meeting with Cumming, he had spent several days attempting to tease Ernst's technical secrets out of him without resorting to the offer of one thousand pounds. Ernst seemed to have accepted the fact that Tobias might not be found very soon, but he still was not inclined to give up his information without seeing some money on the table. Walsh attempted to reassure him that Dewulf was helping to investigate goings-on at the Maison, in hopes of learning more about Retzlaff and Tobias, but these measures would not convince Ernst to open up.

Sod it, Walsh thought.

"I met with my people from London a few days ago," Walsh began.

Ernst nodded. "Good news, I hope?"

"I think so. We've managed to get some of the money released for you."

"How much?"

"One thousand pounds. For a start. But they want to have something in return before they release the rest."

Ernst frowned, and looked down into his coffee cup. "What do you mean?"

Walsh turned his chair to face Ernst. "Your secret, your process, involves several steps, does it not? To convert some type of raw material into acetone?"

"Yes, of course."

"Well, they want to know some of the process in exchange for the rest of the money."

"I see. Before or after the thousand pounds?"

Walsh hesitated. "After. We will pay you the one thousand, then you tell us part of your process, to reassure us that it works, and then they will exchange the rest of the money for the rest of your secret. Does that make sense?"

"Do you have the money in Brussels?"

Walsh shook his head. "Not yet."

"So you lied to Retzlaff? About the five thousand?"

"Of course I did. I had to find out what happened to you."

Ernst thought for a moment. "That was quite a risk," he said, in a small voice. "If you hadn't managed to find your pistol, who knows what they would have done to you? To us!"

Walsh shrugged his shoulders. "You've thanked me already about that. So forget it. And at least Retzlaff is out of the way now, probably back to Germany. I just need to know if we have a deal to get this exchange back on track."

Ernst sipped at his coffee, and looked over to the Palais du Justice in the distance.

Walsh watched him. "Well?" he said. "Should I contact London about releasing some of the money?"

"I'm thinking. You are very clever, Nicholas. May I call you Nicholas now? And you know that if I give you part of the secret then you might be able to determine the rest without having to pay me the full amount."

Walsh shook his head again. "That's not what we're doing. Trust me, Ernst. It's a simple matter of bureaucracy. Office procedures. We can pay one thousand pounds far more easily than five thousand. And my office has been deceived before, you understand. So this is simply a question of good faith on your part. If your information turns out to be legitimate, then they will release the rest of the money. Nothing more than that."

"And if I refuse?"

"Then we have no deal." And you can go back to your own stinking flat, Walsh didn't need to add.

"I see."

Walsh lost patience now, and slammed his mug on the small table in front of them. "So what's your answer then, lad? Hmm? Do we have a deal or not? We need to bring this thing to an end, and get you out of Brussels, don't you agree? Because, frankly, I'm getting a little tired of looking after you."

Ernst drew back. "I'm sorry, Nicholas. I was never meant to handle the money side of things. That was Tobias's job."

"Well, he's not here. You need to decide. Right now."

Walsh sat back in his chair and fixed his eyes over the rooftops again. Thoughts of Gisela kept creeping into his mind and it was a struggle to maintain his interest in this acetone business. He had never been able to bring her to his flat, with Ernst around all of the time. He supposed he should be grateful for that, now, as Retzlaff might have seen her here and might have used her to get to him. But Retzlaff was gone, and once this business with Ernst was out of the way...

Walsh's thoughts were interrupted by Ernst's tiny, almost hushed, voice. "All right, Nicholas. I think I can do what you want. But not a demonstration, correct? I can just tell you some of my process."

"Yes, that's correct. But they are likely to want a demonstration..."

Walsh was interrupted by the sound of knocking at his door. Hard knocks, insistent.

He and Ernst froze, staring at each other.

A voice, male, coming from behind the door to his flat. "*Monsieur* Walsh? Open the door! This is the police!"

Walsh stood, then pointed to Ernst. "Wait here."

Walsh briefly wondered if the two of them could leap to safety from the balcony, then decided again it. The small garden behind his building was surrounded by a high courtyard wall, with no easy way out. He left the balcony and moved to his door. He thought, also just briefly, about getting his pistol, but heard several more voices outside his door. Too many men, too risky. Too late.

Again the voice, more urgent now, and another series of knocks. "*Monsieur* Walsh!"

Walsh opened the door. He found three uniforms in front of him, men garbed in dark blue and red, with flat kepis atop their heads: Belgian gendarmes. Behind them stood another man, older, also in military uniform. To Walsh it looked like a German army uniform, and that of an officer, though he could not detect the rank. But the polished Pickelhaube on his head was unmistakeable. Behind the German, back near the stairwell, nearly out of sight, stood a second German: Retzlaff. With a tight smile on his bearded face.

Walsh was just taking this in when the gendarme closest to him spoke, in English.

"You are Nicholas Walsh?"

Walsh tried to avoid Retzlaff's gaze. "Yes, that's me. What is this?"

"You have Ernst Hesse here with you?"

Walsh considered a lie, but knew it was pointless now. "Yes, I do."

The gendarme smiled. "Would you be so kind as to bring him to me, please?"

Ernst appeared now at the door of the balcony, but Walsh stopped him with a wave of his arm. "Not just yet. Who are you, and what is this about?"

"I am Major Jacquard of the Belgian Gendarmerie. These men are my adjutants." Jacquard indicated the two other men at his sides. They both wore sidearms and each man kept a hand on the butt of his pistol. They watched Walsh with steady eyes.

Walsh pointed behind Jacquard. "And the Germans? What business do they have with Mr Hesse?"

"This is Lieutenant-Colonel Moench. Of the Imperial German Army. He is attached to their embassy here. He has come into the possession of important information regarding the activities of Mr Hesse, here in Brussels. Illegal activities, I might add, in the view of the Imperial German government."

Jacquard suddenly pushed his way into the room, followed by his two adjutants. Walsh could do little to stop them. Moench and Retzlaff moved to block the doorway. Retzlaff was still wearing that damned smile of his.

All of the men could now see Ernst cowering near the balcony.

"Mr Hesse?" Jacquard said. "Ernst Hesse?"

Ernst nodded; his hand was under his nose to stop the bleeding that had already started.

"Would you please come with me?" Jacquard continued, beckoning with his arm. "You are wanted for questioning."

Walsh moved in front of Ernst, just as the young man dropped his coffee cup on the floor. It shattered into a dozen pieces.

"Wait!" Walsh said. "Is he under arrest? Whose authority are you under?"

The two adjutants moved to restrain Walsh, one on each side, holding his arms. He refrained from breaking free, and breaking their necks, but only just.

"Mr Walsh, this matter does not concern you. We are interested only in Mr Hesse. And we do not answer to you, understand?"

Walsh would not give up. "Where are you taking him?"

"That does not concern you either."

The adjutants held Walsh as Jacquard took Ernst by the arm. Ernst's nose continued to bleed but Jacquard ignored it.

"Nicholas! What is this?" Ernst cried. He kept a hand to his nose as the blood streamed out of it, while Jacquard began to pull him towards the door.

"This man has business with the British Embassy here!" Walsh said, in desperation. "They will hear about this!"

Jacquard now had Ernst at the door. Moench was out of sight now, but Retzlaff kept in sight, smiling at the proceedings.

"Yes, we know all about his business, *Monsieur* Walsh. That is precisely why we want him," Jacquard said, with a smile, just before he and Ernst disappeared into the hallway outside the flat.

The two adjutants released Walsh and swiftly followed their leader out of the flat.

Retzlaff was the last to leave. He remained in the doorway, staring at Walsh standing alone in the room, and the two men could hear the sound of footsteps descending the stairs as Ernst was taken away. Fading footsteps, heavy boots, tromping down the stairs.

Retzlaff spoke, finally, still smiling. "I didn't get a chance to say goodbye the last time we met, you remember. How rude of me."

Retzlaff tipped his hat and gave a little bow. *"Auf Wiedersehen, Herr Walsh."*

Then he was gone.

Chapter 56

Leysen thought the Maison du Peuple was the oddest building he had ever seen. It was fronted with several crowded shops open to the public, where he wandered for a few moments to gather his nerve. There was no security at the main entrance to the building, at least not on the rez-des-chaussée, or the ground floor, and Leysen moved about freely, looking in the large, airy grand café, packed with noisy visitors. In the vicinity of the café he saw a boucherie opening onto the rue des Pigeons, and an epicerie opening onto the rue de la Samaritaine. Like the café, they too were busy with patrons, most of whom wore working class clothes, rough and functional but otherwise clean.

Leysen himself was dressed in the best suit of clothes he owned, recently purchased with money provided by Dewulf. He made his way to the stairs, and found a convenient directory on the wall. The first floor of the building contained the main offices of the Maison. The second floor consisted of a large hall and several other small meeting rooms. The third floor contained more offices, and the fourth and final floor housed, Leysen was surprised to learn, a cathedral *cum* theatre, which could accommodate three thousand people. From other signs here and there, Leysen saw that the Maison even offered its members free medical care, a death benefit, a pension benefit, and emergency food provisions to its members thanks to a system of paying modest membership fees on an instalment basis.

Impressive.

Leysen walked up the stairs and onto the first floor. A reception desk faced the stairwell, and Leysen told the girl at the desk that he was here to see Penneman. The girl smiled and asked him to wait for a moment, indicating some chairs against the wall next to the stairs. Before he sat, Leysen asked her, as casually as he could, if Mr Hendrickx might also be about. A look of concern crossed the girl's face.

"Mr Hendrickx?" she asked. "Do you...do you have an appointment with him as well?"

"No, I do not," Leysen gave her a smile. "I just happened to speak with Mr Vandervelde at a meeting a few weeks ago, and he said that Mr Hendrickx might be able to assist me with the work I'm doing for Mr Penneman. Since I'm here, perhaps I might see him as well."

She nodded. "I see. Well, I'm very sorry but that won't be possible. Mr Hendrickx has been very ill lately. He has not been in the office for several weeks. The doctors insist that he stay at home for a while."

Leysen replaced his smile with a frown. "Oh, I'm sad to hear that. I was looking forward to meeting him, finally. It must be something serious, if he has been away so long."

"I'm afraid I can't say. I don't know the details myself."

"So you cannot say when he might return?"

"No, I'm sorry I can't."

"Very well. Perhaps Mr Penneman can enlighten me."

"Perhaps. He will be with you in a few moments. Won't you please take a seat, Mr Leysen?"

Chapter 57

Sarajevo. June 1910.

Still delighted by the success of the emperor's visit to Bosnia-Herzegovina two weeks earlier, General Varesanin was in a pleasant mood, for once, during his attendance at the opening of parliament. Following the ceremony, he left for his ride back to the Konak in a carriage accompanied only by his aide-de-camp. As they rode towards the centre of Sarajevo, Varesanin listened, only partially, as his aide informed him about the rest of the day's commitments. Another series of boring formal rituals, Varesanin thought, with disdain.

The carriage soon approached the Miljacka River, and Varesanin could see the Kaiser Bridge directly ahead of him. Further up the river he could see the Latin Bridge as well. A few children were running along the Kaiser Bridge, kicking a ball. This was a school day, Varesanin thought, with irritation. Why weren't they in school? Didn't the people of Sarajevo care about educating their children?

The carriage turned onto the bridge. The wheels made a loud rumbling sound as the vehicle slowly moved along the structure. As the carriage crossed the centre of the bridge, Varesanin heard another loud sound. A pistol shot! He instinctively ducked forward, just as he heard four more shots fired in rapid succession – *pop, pop, pop, pop*!

Varesanin's mind raced. What was this? How many of them were out there?

Then a sixth and final shot, and then silence.

Varesanin slowly raised his head, as his aide did the same, and looked back towards the riverbank, at the Appel Quay they had just left. People were running about, shouting, pointing, looking around in great confusion. Someone across the river was screaming now, a shrill and terrified howl.

Varesanin ordered his carriage to stop at the end of the bridge, then he walked back across the bridge, alone and alert, but oblivious to the possibility that another gunman might strike. In the middle of the street he saw a young man lying on the road, with blood streaming from his mouth and a horrible gunshot wound to the head, which also now lay in an expanding pool of blood. The young man was dead; an obvious suicide following the failed assassination attempt against the general.

Varesanin paused by the side of the body, taking in the sight and wondering how close to death he had come on this old bridge. His aide joined him, breathless.

"I d-don't believe it," said his aide. "How could this happen? Who is he?"

Without a word, Varesanin knelt next to the dead man and felt through his pockets. He retrieved an identification card from Agram University, which named the would-be assassin: Bogdan Zerajic. Varesanin also found a little more than one hundred kronen in paper money, and an odd circular cardboard badge, faded and worn. The badge showed the traced image of a man carrying a scythe.

A policeman joined Varesanin and his aide on the bridge. Varesanin gave Zerajic's belongings to the policeman, and beckoned his aide to join him. The two men started walking to the Konak, leaving their carriage by the end of the bridge. In his mind Varesanin was already attempting to draft the official report he would have to send to Vienna. He feared it would be the last such report he would ever send.

Chapter 58

Brussels. June 1910.

Walsh found Dewulf at his flat in Schaerbeek, very close to the Tir National shooting range where they had first met. Walsh had already spent, or wasted, nearly two hours at the British Embassy, first waiting for, and then arguing with, Major Bridges about their options regarding Ernst. Bridges calmly told Walsh that they had no options and could not get involved. This was now a bilateral Belgian-German affair, and Britain would have no part of it. Besides, Walsh was not in Belgium in any official capacity, and Bridges advised that he should avoid pursuing Ernst for fear of disclosing the nature of his true business in Brussels.

Walsh knew that Bridges was correct, at least in an official sense, but found himself now arguing with Inspector Dewulf about the same topic.

"I can't do that," Dewulf was saying, with a shake of his head. "This is not my business anymore. And I would advise you to stay out of it as well, Mr Walsh."

"How can you say that, inspector? You've been involved for weeks now!"

Dewulf raised his hand in protest. "Don't be absurd. That was unofficial and you know that. Now it is something else entirely. It is a…a diplomatic affair. It doesn't concern me."

"Now wait, inspector. Listen to me. Please." Walsh struggled to make it sound like he wasn't begging, but he was. "It's not that simple. There is still the matter of Tobias. He is still missing. You can say Ernst is a witness, or even a suspect, in that matter, can't you?"

Dewulf shook his head again. "No, I can't. I don't handle routine police matters. Even if there was a crime involving Tobias, and even if the gendarmes would agree to keep Ernst in Belgium for the moment, I wouldn't be the one to handle it."

"I can't just leave him, inspector. We were just about to make a final deal, and he was taken away. I can't believe Retzlaff could manage this."

"He must have made his own deal with the German authorities here," Dewulf said. "The German Army gets Ernst's secret, and Retzlaff gets to take Ernst back to his father. Or something like that. Unless Ernst has to go to prison first, that is."

"I can't leave him, inspector. Not after all this, damn it! And his secret could be very important, critical even, in the event of a war with Germany."

Dewulf considered that, but said nothing.

Walsh looked him in the eyes. "Inspector, can you at least let me know what is happening with Ernst? Perhaps my contacts with the British government can help with this."

A lie, Walsh knew perfectly well, but worth a try.

Dewulf sighed. "All right. I know someone at the Brussels gendarmerie. At the Special Brigade. I'll just see what is happening with the boy. But I don't believe anything will come of it."

"Thank you," Walsh said. "Tell them about Ernst's connections with the socialists here. That you've been monitoring him because of potential threats during the Exposition. That he is a potential witness or informer, something like that. Whatever you can use, use it."

Dewulf smiled and shook his head again. "Are you mad, Mr Walsh? Are you even hearing yourself? You want me to tell them I've been monitoring the Maison's political activities even though the Burgomeister has expressly forbid it? Are you trying to get *me* arrested?"

Chapter 59

Sarajevo. June 1910.

Varesanin completed his official report for Vienna regarding Bogdan Zerajic's assassination attempt just days after the event took place. As with all of his work, it was very thorough, produced in triplicate, and covered with the official Austro-Hungarian mark of 'K. u. K.' throughout – for 'Imperial and Royal'.

The document included diagrams showing the trajectory of the shots, and Varesanin reported that, based on these diagrams, he would almost certainly have been killed by a bullet in the head if he had not ducked forward after hearing the first shot. What amazing reflexes he had!

Varesanin also suggested that the assassination attempt was part of a 'carefully orchestrated anarchist plot,' even though the authorities in Sarajevo had not discovered any accomplices who might have assisted Zerajic. Instead, the police had determined some details about Zerajic's personal background, such as his secondary schooling in Mostar from 1900 to 1907 and the assistance provided by Zerajic's uncle for him to attend Agram University.

Vienna would require more information eventually, of course, so Varesanin ordered the police to begin a thorough investigation of Zerajic. He demanded that they interview Zerajic's acquaintances in Bosnia and Herzegovina, and that they send agents to do the same in Croatia and Serbia. Varesanin also requested extra assistance from authorities in Vienna, Budapest, and other 'known anarchist centres in Europe' to determine the extent of Zerajic's plotting.

The investigation was expected to take several weeks.

Varesanin completed his report by pledging that he would not rest until he had determined the full story of how a poor young law student had transformed himself into a failed but cold-blooded assassin. He also hoped that Vienna would be patient during this time.

Chapter 60

Brussels. June 1910.

Walsh's time at the British Embassy the day before had not been spent entirely in vain, as Bridges had reluctantly allowed him to arrange a private telephone call with Cumming. On the second day after Ernst's arrest, and still with no word from Dewulf, Walsh stood alone in Bridges's office and reached Cumming at his office in London at the appointed hour.

After hearing about the latest turn of events, Cumming was adamant: Walsh had to avoid all contact with Ernst.

"But C, there may still be time for you to intervene," Walsh said. "If we can keep him in Brussels for just a few days, and I can get in touch with him, we might be able to get some details about his secret."

"Out of the question, my boy."

"But…"

"Now listen to me, Walsh! What you ask is not possible, do you understand? My office has no official business, no official standing, in Brussels. And neither do you, remember! I think it is remarkable that you've managed to get the inspector to help you, in an unofficial capacity, over the past few weeks, but that's where it ends. Ernst is still a German citizen and his country's government wants him, now. And Belgium is cooperating with them. So we can't possibly intervene now and turn this into a…a *diplomatic* incident!"

"I just need some time with him."

"Walsh, stay out of this, do you hear me? Inspector Dewulf is correct; it is beyond our control. Do you understand?"

"All right, C."

Walsh hung up the telephone, disgusted yet again.

Bridges was silent as he walked Walsh to the main entrance of the embassy, and watched him walk away in the June sunshine.

An hour later, Walsh was with Dewulf in the centre of Brussels, near his office at the Justice Ministry. Dewulf motioned Walsh to a bench and the two men sat.

"I don't have much time," Dewulf said. "I'm afraid things are moving more rapidly than we expected."

"How so?" Walsh asked.

"Ernst has been with the German Embassy since the arrest. But now they believe he is going to be moved very soon. I should stay in my office."

"Who believes he is going to be moved?"

"The gendarmerie." Dewulf sighed, and looked down the street, away from Walsh. "They are working with the Germans. Facilitating things."

"I see," Walsh said. "But moved where? To Germany?"

"Most likely."

"When?"

"I don't know. Tomorrow, perhaps the next day."

"Should I wait with you?"

Dewulf shook his head. "No, you shouldn't be here. It would…complicate things. Can I reach you at your flat?"

"Yes, I'll go there now and wait."

"All right. I'll check again and get back to you if I hear something."

Walsh went back to his flat at the end of the day, worn and angry after the conversation with Cumming. After his meeting with Dewulf he had fought the urge to visit the German Embassy in search of Ernst, convincing himself, finally, that such a stunt might have done more harm than good.

He entered his building and found the concierge seated near the front door, as if waiting for him. In fact, he was.

"*Ah, Monsieur Walsh*," he said. "*Un message pour vous.*"

Walsh waited while the old boy fished in his pockets, and retrieved an envelope.

Walsh thanked the man and walked back into the street, where he tore open the paper.

It merely said: "Ernst leaving for Germany tonight. Etterbeek station, 19:30." And initialled at the end, "MD."

Dewulf.

Walsh checked his pocketwatch: it was already after 19:00. But Etterbeek station was not too far away. He ran along rue Souveraine and reached Chaussée d'Ixelles less than a minute later, searching for a cab. None could be found, but he quickly spied a young man parking a motorbike on Place Communale. Walsh ran up behind the man and pulled him off the machine, climbed aboard, and started it.

19:10.

Oblivious to the lad's anguished protests, Walsh raced through Place Communale and headed down Chaussée d'Ixelles, away from the centre of Brussels. He turned left on a side street and found Avenue de la Couronne a moment later. He turned right on the avenue, barely missing a cab parked at the corner, and drove along the thoroughfare, running parallel to the railway line running between Ixelles and Etterbeek. He kept watching on his left, as the side streets flew by: one of them, he knew, led to the Gare d'Etterbeek.

A second later, Walsh found it. The station was there on his left, just off the Avenue. Walsh left his motorbike at the curb, checking his pocketwatch again as he crept closer to the small railway station.

19:21, still time to make it.

The station was built directly above the railway line, perpendicular to it, with just four tracks running underneath the station. The tracks were in two sets of two, with a single wide platform between the two sets and a narrower platform outside each set. All four tracks were in full view from the open waiting area behind the station office built above the tracks, and reached by three sets of stairways, one to each platform.

Walsh crouched low and approached the centre of the open waiting area, near the main stairway. He looked over the railing and saw, among the crowds on the platform furthest to the right, a man who looked very much like Retzlaff. Walsh kept low and moved further to the right, closer to the platform. It must be the eastbound line, for the border. For Germany.

Walsh stood up again to take a closer look and heard the whistle of an approaching train, coming from the city centre. The crowd on the platform moved closer to the track, and Walsh could plainly see Retzlaff, standing somewhat apart from the others and watching towards the approaching train. It looked like he intended to board the train in one of the front carriages, in first class perhaps.

Next to Retzlaff, Walsh could see, was Ernst, with his hands clasped together and his head down. He seemed to be in a kind of daze and did not look towards the approaching train. Walsh dropped down again behind the railing as the train began to come directly under the station.

Walsh popped up again for a second look and caught sight of a third man, in a German army uniform, standing with Ernst and Retzlaff. He didn't look like Moench, but Walsh was too far away to make sure.

The main part of the train was now moving directly underneath the platform, and Walsh noticed several people running down the stairs. He joined them, and followed behind them as they stepped onto the platform and spread out along its length, as the train slowed down next to it.

Passengers lined up much closer to the edge of the platform, jostling against each other, waiting to board the train once it stopped. Walsh threaded his way through the crowd, keeping low, with his cap pulled down over his forehead.

Thirty metres away, he could see Retzlaff shaking hands with the German officer. The two men smiled at each other like old friends, and the officer clapped Retzlaff on the back.

Twenty metres away now. Retzlaff stepped away from the officer as the train slowed to a crawl, then stopped.

19:28.

At ten metres away, as people started to board their carriages, Walsh broke into an open run towards Ernst and Retzlaff. The German officer saw him first but did not act, as he did not recognize Walsh. Too late, then; Walsh easily brought him to the ground with a sweeping kick against his ankles, and knocked him out with a single hard blow to his left cheek.

Retzlaff had already forced Ernst onto the train and he stood in the carriage doorway, blocking it. As Walsh stood up from the German, he saw that Retzlaff had a knife in his hand, and was firmly planted on the top step of the carriage. Another figure was moving behind Retzlaff; Walsh assumed it was Ernst.

The conductor blew his whistle and Walsh could hear the carriage doors start to slam shut along the length of the train.

Retzlaff shook his head and gave Walsh that odd smile again.

"Think about it, my friend," he said, waving the knife blade at him, with his other hand on a handrail next to the carriage door.

Retzlaff leaned forward slightly and glanced down the platform to see if the conductor had boarded. Walsh chose this moment to charge forward and grab Retzlaff's knife hand with both of his hands. He slammed Retzlaff's hand against the hard edge of the doorway, again and again, expecting Retzlaff to relax his grip on the knife, the handrail, or both.

The train started to move, and Retzlaff dropped the knife before Walsh could break his wrist. The knife clattered into the space between the train and the platform. Retzlaff fell backwards into the doorway, deliberately, and attempted to push his way back into the train with his feet on the stairs.

Walsh grabbed Retzlaff's legs, both of them, and pinned them with his arms. Retzlaff kicked frantically while pulling himself back into the carriage. Walsh held on as best he could, trying not to fall onto the track between the train and the platform.

At that, someone shouted for the train to stop and Walsh could hear the squeal of brakes again. The train slowed.

"Ernst!" Walsh yelled. "Jump off the train!"

Ernst appeared in the doorway behind Retzlaff, but couldn't make his way past him.

"Get off the train, Ernst!"

Walsh pulled harder, twisting his upper body, and forced Retzlaff to release his grip on the handrail. Retzlaff fell onto the platform in a heap, hitting the back of his head on the stairs on the way down. He cried out in pain.

With Retzlaff out of the way, Ernst jumped onto the platform next to Walsh. He was handcuffed and pale. His nose began to bleed but he ignored it. Walsh pushed him away from the train and turned his attention to Retzlaff again, who was attempting to stand up.

Before he could do so, Walsh kicked him in the head, knocking him over again. Walsh slammed the door of the train and saw the conductor approaching him from the front car.

"What is going on here?" demanded the conductor.

He knelt down next to Retzlaff, who was trying to recover from the blow he had just received.

"Let's go, Ernst," Walsh said.

He grabbed Ernst by the upper arm and they dashed away from Retzlaff and the conductor.

Walsh looked back one last time, still holding onto Ernst's arm, and saw Retzlaff sitting up now, holding his head, staring back at him with rage. The conductor started to help Retzlaff to his feet.

At that point, while Walsh was still turned towards Retzlaff, he heard the unmistakable crack of gunfire, just a single shot. Ernst jerked away from him, and collapsed onto the platform with a loud groan. Walsh had heard that pitiful sound many times before, many years ago, in South Africa.

Walsh looked back towards Retzlaff, who had not moved and did not have a weapon in his hand. The few people remaining on the platform scattered away from them, screaming in terror.

"Ernst!" Walsh cried.

"Nicholas..." the boy sputtered, just before he lifted his hand from the centre of his chest. It was covered with blood.

Walsh heard more screams from the train, as the passengers saw the blood.

A couple of doors opened and some men left the train. They approached Walsh, asking what happened.

Walsh could say nothing; he glanced around for signs of a gunman but without success.

"Nicholas..." Ernst said again, with a very weak voice. He shuddered a little, and died.

The crowd moved closer around the stricken man, and Walsh stood, then slowly backed away from Ernst. He looked back towards Retzlaff but did not see him. As he turned to face Ernst again, he saw Dewulf approaching.

"What happened?" Dewulf said.

"He's been shot," Walsh said, holding his bloody palms before him, pointing at Ernst's still body, crumpled on the platform. "He's dead."

Dewulf looked down at Ernst, then at Walsh, then towards the front of the train.

"Was it Retzlaff?"

Walsh shook his head, and kept staring in disbelief at Ernst, with his bloody nose and his hands still cuffed in front of him. "No. No. The shot came from the other direction."

Dewulf put his arm across Walsh's shoulders. "You better come with me, Nicholas," he said, quietly. "We need to get you out of here."

A policeman had now arrived, and Dewulf showed him his identification. He spoke to the policeman, just briefly, before leading Walsh away.

PART FOUR

Chapter 61

Sarajevo. July 1910.

Through the rest of June and into July, the investigation into Zerajic's assassination attempt against General Varesanin continued. Authorities in Sarajevo, Mostar, Agram, and elsewhere in the Balkans located and interviewed everyone who had even the slightest links to the dead law student from Nevisinje.

And so they spoke with prominent figures such as Vasily Grdjic, of the Serbian cultural society Prosvjeta, as well as some of Zerajic's more humble peers, such as his old friend Vladimir Gacinovic of the University of Vienna. They found other friends of Zerajic's, such as Pero Slijepcevic and Jovan Starovic, who, in the end, added very little to the official understanding of how Zerajic planned his pathetic gesture on the Kaiser Bridge. They could not explain why Zerajic had left Agram, and his studies, on May 28 - more than two weeks before his attack on the general. They could not explain why he had stopped in Bosna-Brod, Sarajevo, and Mostar during the emperor's earlier visit to Bosnia and Herzegovina. And they could not explain how Zerajic, a dirt poor student, had acquired the money found on him after his death, and how he had paid for several rail tickets prior to his attack on the general.

As days grew into weeks after Zerajic's suicide, these questions became less urgent, once Austrian authorities in Vienna had released their own official explanation long before the police report was concluded. They had asserted, quite confidently, that Zerajic was simply an unhinged, desperate young man. He had acted alone in his assassination attempt, and was not part of a larger conspiracy. There was, therefore, no general threat to the emperor and no extensive plot against his regime, and his authority in light of the attack on General Varesanin was still secure.

This view was published in newspapers throughout the Empire and beyond, and unless the police could find evidence to the contrary, Varesanin and his deputies had little incentive to challenge that official view.

Chapter 62

Aix-la-Chapelle, Germany. July 1910.

Late summer in the Rhineland, the manufacturing centre of Imperial Germany, where Aix-la-Chapelle lies only about sixteen kilometres from the Belgian border. Weavers, coal miners, leather workers, iron workers, glass blowers, office workers, and visitors crowd into the city centre for a midday drink or meal, or both, happy to sit outside in the warm sunshine and watch the world go by.

The leading restaurants and cafés of Aix-la-Chapelle are full today: the Kurhaus, the Lennertz, the Grand Monarque, the Elisenbrunnen, the Am Knipp, the Karlshaus, the Eulenspiegel, and, of course, the ubiquitous Kaiser-Café, on the ground floor of the majestic Hôtel Nuellens on Friedrich-Wilhelm-Platz. Not many leatherworkers or coal miners to be found at the Kaiser-Café, however, considering its prices. And its dress code. And the attitude of its old Prussian managers.

At the restaurant Spatenbräu, on the Theater-Platz just a short walk from the Hauptbahnof, Walsh sat with a glass of bitter lemon and a newspaper, waiting for his train to Liège. On a plate before him were the remnants of his lunch, along with most of a small Printen cake. Its taste reminded Walsh of gingerbread. He hated gingerbread.

Outside in the street Walsh could see the crowds passing by the pretty Drei-Fenster façades on the houses, on their way to work or play or a little of both. He turned again to his three-day old copy of *The Times* and read about the recent 'fight of the century' in which African-American boxer Jack Johnson had defeated James J. Jeffries in Reno, Nevada, making Johnson the first black heavyweight champ. In Britain, aviation pioneer Charles Rolls became Britain's first aviation fatality when he crashed a Wright biplane near Bournemouth.

The news about Rolls made Walsh reflect upon how much training would be necessary to fly an airplane. How similar is it to driving a motorcar, he wondered? He looked up from his newspaper just then and noticed a waiter clearing a table nearby. Upon closer inspection, the man had what looked to be a Schmiss on his cheek. Or perhaps he had just cut himself shaving.

Without even realizing it, Walsh touched his own forehead scar and thought back to his time in Stuttgart. It had been over a year now since he had left Germany for home, for Scotland, intending to start his own machinery firm. He cringed at the memory of the Mensur duel with Horst, the eldest son of his old landlord in Stuttgart. A student at Heidelberg University. He hoped the boy had borne no grudges after Walsh had defeated him with that cheap kick of his. But Horst had insisted on demonstrating Mensur to Walsh, in front of his university friends, and what did he expect, after he had first scarred Walsh's own skin so expertly? And so surprisingly?

Thoughts of his last encounter with Trommler naturally led Walsh to think about his time with another young German – Ernst Hesse - yet again, even though he had done his best to avoid dwelling on the terrible shooting at Etterbeek. It had been difficult, though, during Walsh's trip on the express train from Brussels to Aix-la-Chapelle two weeks earlier, when he felt as if he was abandoning his mission in Brussels. Watching the fields go by on his nearly four-hour train journey, Walsh had realized that Ernst would have taken the same route back into Germany, and then on to Leipzig. If only he had been allowed to leave Germany with Retzlaff.

If only Walsh had not interfered.

Dewulf, though, had been supremely effective in helping to arrange Walsh's swift departure from Brussels, just two days after Ernst was killed. Of course, the dozen or so witnesses at the shooting, all of whom completely exonerated Walsh given their excellent vantage point from the train carriages, helped to keep suspicion away from him, while Dewulf himself had a personal interest in keeping the case from turning into a drawn-out public spectacle. It also was not in Belgium's interest to turn the drama at Etterbeek into an Anglo-German diplomatic incident, as everyone involved knew. Especially during the all-important Exposition.

Walsh assumed it would all be wrapped up by the time he returned to Brussels, later in the month. It was odd, though, that Dewulf had not been in touch with him during his two weeks in Aix-la-Chapelle, in case Walsh needed to add details to his official statement. He had told Dewulf where he would be staying in Aix-la-Chapelle, at the modest Hôtel Düren on Bahnofplatz, but no message arrived for him.

He did manage to reach Cumming in London by telephone before leaving Brussels, who was shocked to hear about the latest turn of events. But Cumming also agreed that it might be a good idea for Walsh to stay away from Brussels for a little while, until the case with Ernst had been solved. Or at least forgotten.

Cumming was also adamant that Kell had not been involved in Walsh's dealings with Ernst, but he would check again just to make sure. Walsh promised to get back in touch with Cumming after a few weeks away, and assured him that the troubles with Ernst and Tobias would not distract him from his original mission: to find evidence of German designs against Britain, or Belgium, as the case may be.

Entering Gemany was easy enough, via the express train from Brussels. He was not required to show a passport at the German border, although his luggage was examined at the German customhouse at Herbestal. On arriving in Aix-la-Chapelle, Walsh intended to take his mind off the last few months with Ernst and Tobias, and so had played holidaymaker for a week or so. He was also troubled by his failure to see Gisela before his abrupt departure, although it was just as well; he wouldn't know how to explain things to her if he had had the opportunity.

He quickly learned, however, that Aix-la-Chapelle was a small town and had few amusements. The baths and casinos did not interest him, and he could not afford to lose any money at the tables even if he had been partial to gambling. He was, however, greatly fascinated by the cathedral, the resting place of Karl der Große, or Charlemagne, the greatest Holy Roman Emperor of them all. Walsh explored the treasury and the archives of the huge Kaiserdom, and was very impressed by the recently restored marble throne of Charlemagne. The massive copper-gilt chandelier, thirteen feet wide and donated by Holy Roman Emperor Frederick I - Barbarossa – in the 12th century, also caught his eye.

Walsh also visited the Rathaus next to the Cathedral, to see the statues of fifty emperors of the Holy Roman Empire, on the north wall. Charlemagne's own statue in bronze could be seen on the Kaiserbrunnen fountain in the centre of the Markt-Platz. A half-day was also spent in the Suermondt Museum, although Walsh was not exactly a connoisseur of fine art. He did, however, appreciate the fine craftsmanship on display in the metalwork section, in Room XIV on the first floor.

Eventually, Walsh forced himself to remember the real reason for his trip to Aix-la-Chapelle: to pay his debt to Marchand. So he spent his second week in the region in the countryside between Aix-la-Chapelle and the frontier with Belgium, thanks to a rented bicycle and the excellent network of electric tramways traversing the area. Two rail lines also led from the city centre into Belgium, and Walsh would take note of possible chokepoints as he travelled from Aix-la-Chapelle to Liège.

After paying his bill, Walsh left the Spatenbräu and walked, suitcase in hand, down Theatrestrasse, towards the railway station. At the Hauptbahnhof, while waiting for his train, Walsh again noted the long disembarkation platforms at the new central station. They seemed nearly empty given the size of the platforms relative to the small number of passengers waiting on them. An attendant had told him that the new Hauptbahnhof had only been finished in 1905; it was intended to replace the traffic bound for the older station at Aix-la-Chapelle, which had been built outside the city walls. Walsh also noted, during a previous walk around the station, that a large Kazerne, or army barracks, was situated directly east of the Hauptbahnhof, along the Kaiserallee, along with a Bezirks Kommando, or district command, headquarters at the end of Pariser Strasse.

On board the train for the short trip to Liège, Walsh noted a railway tunnel near Herbestal, about thirty kilometres east of Liège, where two railway lines from Germany converged. Blowing up this tunnel should slow the German advance, and Walsh made a note of it. It might also be necessary to destroy railway tunnels and bridges at Belgium's border with Luxembourg, to the south of Liège, if the Germans invaded through that country as well as through Belgium.

Walsh's train stopped briefly at the first Belgian station after the border, at Welkenraedt, then at Dolhain, with its ancient fortress nearby at Limburg, then at Verviers, where Walsh waited more than an hour to have his luggage routinely inspected by Belgian custom authorities. Much less efficient than when he entered Germany, in fact. From Verviers the train crossed the narrow Vesdre River at several points before arriving at Liège, twenty-five kilometres from Verviers. In fact, Walsh counted more than a dozen short railway bridges over the Vesdre that could easily be demolished between Verviers and Liège, and therefore most effectively stop any train on this route from Aix-la-Chapelle.

Walsh spent nearly two weeks in Liège and its environs, starting with a few days in the heart of the city. He noted its excellent defensive position, with steep slopes rising nearly one hundred and fifty metres up the left bank of the Meuse, and the river nearly two hundred metres wide at some points. It was easy to see why this was considered one of the most impressive fortified positions in Europe. Walsh thought it should be able to hold out for months given its ring of twelve fortresses, but Marchand was taking no chances. And so, Walsh's agreement to explore the area on his behalf. As he wandered around, taking photographs and making drawings wherever he would not attract attention, Walsh grew more determined to see if there was any substance to the Frenchman's fears about the prospects of a successful German invasion in this area.

The German First, Second, and Third Armies were the most likely to move through Belgium, based on what Walsh had learned from the DMO before he left for Brussels. The First Army would be concentrated north of Aix-la-Chapelle, and would make for the five bridges of Liège, their first major objective. Liège was also the junction of four railway lines linking Belgium, Germany, and northern France, which would supply the German forces as they moved across Belgium and down into France. Above all, the central railway bridge in Liège would have to be destroyed, along with two tunnels, one on each side of the city. Walsh wondered how quickly this could be done in the event of a crisis. Would the Belgians wait until the Germans were at the eastern fortresses before destroying the Meuse crossings? Or would the Belgians even resist at all, in the face of a massive invasion by German troops?

The most critical area was north of Liège, stretching to the border with the Netherlands, which led to an open plain between Hasselt on the north and Namur on the south. Between them was the way to Brussels. South of Liège was the thick and hilly Ardenne forest, as it was known in Wallonia, which would act as a natural barrier to the German advance. So Walsh paid special attention to the fortresses and approach routes on the right bank of the Meuse. He started at Visé, a village of just over two thousand souls on the right bank of the Meuse above Liège, very close – less than a kilometre – to the Dutch border. If the Germans did attack Belgium without invading the Netherlands, this would be the very northernmost limit to their advance into Belgium. Visé was unfortified and provided a road crossing over the Meuse, which could be blown up in the event of a German attack if the charges were prepared in time.

From there Walsh worked his way down the right bank of the Meuse, by bicycle and rail, from Argenteau and then on to the six fortresses on this side of the river. He wondered how much attention would be given directly to the twelve fortresses of Liège, ringed around the city in a fifty-kilometre circumference, each one roughly seven kilometres from the city centre. The Krupp works at Essen were not too far away from Liège, about one hundred kilometres or so northeast of Aix-la-Chapelle. If Krupp's engineers were working on heavy guns to use against the fortresses, the weapons could be brought into place by rail fairly quickly from Essen or Aix-la-Chapelle. It beggared belief, however, to think that the Germans could devise a gun large enough, but also mobile enough, to blast through the fortresses Walsh had seen with his own eyes in Liège.

Walsh wondered if Cumming had managed to find a source in their factory. Again, he regretted wasting so much time with his chemist.

At the fortresses, Walsh started with Barchon, then worked his way to Evegnée, Fléron, Chaudfontaine, Embourg, and Boncelles. He crossed the Meuse near Seraing, and continued his reconnaissance of the six fortresses on the left bank: Flémalle, Hollogne, Loncin, Lantin, Liers, and Pontisse. From his previous visit to two fortresses at Liège, Walsh had remembered no trenches or fences or barbed-wire lines or any other defensive barriers between them. He now confirmed this fact for the other fortresses ringing the city, which were about four kilometres away from each other. So the Germans could move between them at will once they had control of the area, if the Belgians chose not to fight.

If Belgium did resist, its defensive plan was likely to involve no more than six divisions, according to Major Bridges, to be deployed along the Meuse. But Bridges had also mentioned that these forces were currently spread out all across Belgium, at Ghent, Antwerp, Namur, Charleroi, Mons, and Brussels. Only the Belgian Third Division remained at the ready for the defence of Liège at all times. Like the lack of barriers between the fortresses, this dispersion of forces was also in keeping with the country's doctrine of strict neutrality. Walsh began to appreciate Marchand's thinking on the matter: if the Belgian forces remained dispersed, then by the time they converged around Liège and Namur, assuming this order was actually given, the Germans would already be on their way into France, if the Liège fortresses did not hold and if the bridges were not destroyed.

On his last day in Liège, Walsh decided to take a risk on behalf of Marchand. He returned to the fortress at Fléron, the one he had visited in February. He found some soldiers at a café near the fortress. They wore the uniform of the Belgian cavalry: funny, old-fashioned uniforms, with wide crimson trousers and Polish lancer caps. Walsh asked if they knew Captain Delfosse. The men had never heard of him, but they said he could ask at the fortress itself.

On their advice, Walsh went to the gatehouse at the entrance to the fortress, where two older soldiers sat playing cards. They looked as if they were off-duty but Walsh found that that was not the case. One of them noticed Walsh and asked if he could help. Walsh asked about Captain Delfosse and the guard here also replied that there was no one posted here by that name. Walsh waited patiently while the guard called his commanding officer in the fortress; certainly he would know about any Captain Delfosse serving in this sector.

But that was not the case. The commander also had never heard of such a person during his past two years on duty, at this very location. He was sure of it. Quite sure, in fact.

Chapter 63

Brussels. July 1910.

Leysen could barely suppress his joy as the raucous cheers filled the small room. Cheers for him. Cheers for his words and gestures. For his ideas and his beliefs.

The low ceiling and stone walls in the room greatly amplified the racket, but there was no mistaking the enthusiasm of Leysen's audience. As he stepped down from the makeshift stage, a few planks of pine laid across empty beer crates, he noticed Dubroux and Meunier at the back of the room. They were smiling and nodding in approval at his performance.

Good thing, too, as they had arranged the secret meeting in the first place, and had encouraged the young men in the area to attend it. Young men who were prone to boredom when forced to listen to socialist dogma spouted by wrinkled intellectuals, but who listened with rapt attention to Leysen's words. Stories about his time in the army, with no hope of advancement given his background. About his career as a petty criminal in the Marolles, living day-to-day and dodging bullets, les flics, and hunger with equal enthusiasm. And about his time in prison, where he began to pay attention to ideas about how the world *really* worked, and about how supposedly insignificant men, such as himself, could help to change things for the better. For everyone.

After Leysen's speech, he spent twenty minutes in the room with Dubroux and Meunier, taking names and other details from some of the men who lingered next to them while others filed out into the street. This always happened; tonight was Leysen's fifth time as a speaker and he could almost predict, when surveying his audience, which boys would stick around afterwards for more chatter about the Young Guards, and about what they could do to help.

Often two or three of these boys would express a willingness to use violence, especially those whose older male relatives had passed down knowledge of Belgium's strike-breaking actions. But Leysen, together with Dubroux and Meunier, assured them that the Young Guards were fervent but peaceful, and did not support the use of violence in their cause. Except in self-defence, of course.

After the last of the young men had left for home, or for the local brasseries, Leysen helped Dubroux and Meunier collect the remaining copies of their leaflets and other socialist publications. They were careful to avoid leaving any evidence that the meeting ever took place, just as they had been careful in gathering the audience in the first place.

Unfortunately, they had not been as careful in choosing the venue – a large storeroom behind a shuttered café, near the Gare du Midi and the École Vétérinaire - as they had in choosing their audience. As Leysen, Dubroux, and Meunier left the building, with bundles of publications in hand, and made their way up the narrow impasse towards the main street, they were set upon by five masked men armed with rubber truncheons.

Meunier saw them first, and managed to cry *"Attention!"* to his companions just before dropping his papers in time to raise his thick forearm in front of his face. His arm absorbed the blow, which was still powerful enough to send him reeling backwards against a brick wall. A second thug joined the first, and the two continued to beat Meunier as he struggled to get to his feet.

"Fucking troublemakers!" the first thug hissed at Meunier, before poking the end of his truncheon in the young man's ribs. "Why don't you learn to behave?"

Two other thugs set upon Leysen, and he managed to stay on his feet for only a few moments. It was impossible to defend himself effectively against his attackers, and eventually a hard blow against the back of his left knee brought him to the ground next to Meunier. His leaflets and other papers scattered around them on the dark, wet street.

As the smallest man under attack, Dubroux suffered the attention of just one assailant, but he was as large as his four companions. Dubroux was no match for the man, even if he had not been armed with a club, and collapsed to the ground after a single blow.

After Dubroux pulled himself into a tight ball and stopped moving, his assailant turned his attention to Meunier, who was still attempting to fight back from his position on the ground. He writhed around and dodged the blows as best he could, occasionally throwing whatever he could grab – papers, a stone, a piece of wood – up at his attackers. But eventually he too gave up and curled into a tight ball, until it was over.

Leysen opened his eyes and removed his hands from his face when things were silent again. He was rewarded with a handful of crumpled newspaper, from his own copies of *Le Peuple* brought to the meeting, crammed into his mouth by one of the thugs.

"That will teach to you keep your mouth shut!" the masked man said, before running out of the impasse and into the night along with his four partners in crime.

Leysen spit out the paper and attempted to sit up. He could taste salty blood all over his mouth. He heard Meunier's moans behind him and looked back at the larger man, who was curled in a ball and holding his stomach with both hands.

"Fucking bastards," Leysen heard Dubroux say, or rather spit, from a split and bloodied lip. Bloody saliva hung from Dubroux's lip in a long strand, almost to the ground, as he struggled into a sitting position and gingerly felt inside his mouth with an index finger.

Dubroux nodded towards Meunier, so Leysen slid over to the large man and pulled him to a sitting position.

Meunier moaned in pain, but only a little, and otherwise kept silent behind gritted teeth.

"What the hell was that?" Leysen said.

"Rubber batons. Hard enough to hurt but soft enough to avoid serious damage. Very smart," Dubroux said, before spitting blood again.

"The police?" Leysen said. "In plain clothes?"

"Probably not *les flics*," Dubroux replied. "If they were, they would have just arrested you. Us."

Leysen felt above his eye and saw blood on his hand. He wiped it on his sleeve. "Then who?" he said.

"Who knows?" Dubroux said. "It happens sometimes." He moved next to Leysen and the two men got Meunier to his feet.

"*Merci, mecs*," Meunier said.

"Are you all right?" Dubroux asked him, with an anxious voice. "Can you walk?"

"Yes, just give me a minute." The big man leaned against the wall and smiled weakly at his companions.

"You big ape," Dubroux said, placing Meunier's dented bowler on his big head.

Meunier smiled again and put his hand on Dubroux's shoulder. Dubroux feigned a look of pain at the touch of his friend's huge hand, and smiled back at him.

Then after a moment or two, Meunier said, "We're very lucky, you know."

"Lucky how?" Leysen asked.

Meunier looked him in the eye while rubbing his own head. "They were just sending a message. That's all. If they had wanted to kill us, we'd be dead already."

Chapter 64

On his return to Brussels in late July, Walsh arrived at his flat to find a note from Dewulf. He rang the inspector at his office, using his concierge's phone, and they arranged to meet two days later at Dewulf's office in the Justice Ministry. Dewulf would not say anything further over the telephone.

Two days later, Walsh sat in Dewulf's office in the former Hôtel Engler building on the rue de la Loi. Dewulf looked haggard and he was not in a pleasant mood. He updated Walsh on the progress, or lack thereof, in the Ernst Hesse murder case. Hesse had been killed by a 7.65mm pistol round, most likely a Browning, widely available throughout Europe. The Belgian authorities had no firm leads so far.

"We've had word the Kaiser is coming to visit the Exposition," Dewulf said, after Walsh sat down. He rubbed his eyes. "This is going to cause too many headaches. On top of the ones I already have."

"When is he coming?" Walsh asked.

"September or October. That's what they tell us, in any event. So we have some time but it doesn't really matter when we lack the men to stay on top of things. Even without visits from so many dignitaries." Dewulf paused, then picked up a file in front of him. "And now this."

"What?"

Dewulf opened the file and removed a photograph from it. He looked at it briefly, as if he wanted to change his mind about sharing it, then slid the image across the desk to Walsh.

Walsh leaned forward to take a closer look. It was a photograph of a young man lying on what looked to be an autopsy table. He was naked from the waist up; his lower body was covered by a sheet. The face and body of the man were marked with dark purple bruises, and a number of small cuts that had been cleaned of blood.

Walsh looked closer at the photograph, and recognition set in.

"Is that...?" he began.

Dewulf nodded slightly. "Tobias Stern."

Sangster put the photograph back on Dewulf's desk and sat back in his chair, dumbfounded. "Bloody hell, inspector. What happened to him?"

"'Bloody hell' is right, Mr Walsh. That's certainly what he suffered in his last moments. Anyhow, his body was dumped the day after you left Brussels. After Ernst was killed."

"Dumped where?"

Dewulf looked at him closely before answering. "At the entrance to the Maison du Peuple. In the middle of the night. No one saw anything, of course."

"Hold on, inspector," Walsh said. "You don't think I had anything to do with this?"

Dewulf shook his head. "No, I don't. I know you were out of the country when the body was dumped. I called your hotel in Aix-la-Chapelle and they confirmed you had arrived."

Walsh held up his hands in frustration. "Why didn't you speak to me then? Why haven't you been in touch with me? Don't you need my help on this case?"

"There was no point, really. And this is not my case in any event. So it could wait until you came back."

"And why are you telling me now?"

"As a courtesy. I thought you would want to know what had happened to him."

Walsh nodded. "I see. And what about Hendrickx?"

"He has been on sick leave for three weeks. Away from work. But he returned after Ernst was killed."

"And?"

"And his wife confirms that he was home when Ernst was killed. Ill in bed, she said. And he was home the night that Tobias's body was dumped. So we are satisfied. But we are also keeping a closer eye on him now, just in case."

Walsh looked out the window for a moment, out at the Parc de Bruxelles in the sunshine. "And it couldn't be Retzlaff?"

Dewulf shook his head. "No, he left the country right after Ernst was shot. The railway confirmed it. Then he came back a few days later with Ernst's father to claim the body, Ernst's body, and they left the country again right afterwards."

"What about Tobias's family?"

"We reached them in Leipzig. We offered to ship the body to them if they would share the expense, but his father refused. So Mr Stern was cremated here two weeks ago. The autopsy confirmed that he was beaten to death. Most effectively, I might add."

"So the same person killed Ernst and Tobias? Is that what you think?"

Dewulf shrugged his shoulders. "We assume so. I don't know much more than that. It's not my case."

"Why not?" Walsh asked.

"I'm not a criminal investigator, Mr Walsh. That task falls under the responsibility of the Public Prosecutor."

"Can I speak to the man running the investigation?"

Dewulf shook his head. "I don't think that would be a good idea."

"Why not?"

"Because the Public Prosecutor does not want to add any…any complications to this case. It's complicated enough as it is, wouldn't you agree? Even without you inquiring about it."

Walsh leaned forward and stared at Dewulf. "The prosecutor is not interested in the truth?"

"Mr Walsh, the Public Prosecutor, like me, is interested in keeping things calm and safe during the Exposition." Dewulf paused as he retrieved the photograph of Tobias's broken body and placed it in his file. He flipped the cover over the documents and tossed them aside. "And in maintaining friendly relations with other powers."

"I see. Inspector, if Tobias was dumped at the Maison, in public, then someone is sending a message. Especially since he was beaten so badly, rather than simply shot in the head. Doesn't that mean anything to you?"

Dewulf nodded. "So it would seem. But that's one interpretation."

"Then what did you tell Ernst's family about all this? His father?"

"The German Ambassador here explained things to him, with the help of the Public Prosecutor." Dewulf sighed. "*Herr* Hesse was satisfied that justice will be served in this matter. He understands that it was an internal socialist affair. And you know how emotional young radicals can be."

"*Herr* Hesse does not want a scandal involving his son," Walsh said, without bothering to conceal the edge in his voice. "A scandal involving radical politics and the sale of German technical secrets to Great Britain. Isn't that right?"

"I suppose so," Dewulf said, his voice small all of a sudden. "He is satisfied that the case will be resolved in good time. And that justice will be served for his son. But it might take some time. So you see, Mr Walsh, everyone is satisfied."

Walsh stared at Dewulf. "Are *you* satisfied?"

Dewulf smiled, but without humour. "Mr Walsh, please. I am far too busy to worry about being 'satisfied.' *Comprenez-vous?*"

After his time with Dewulf, Walsh arranged for a telephone call with Cumming, and reached the man himself two days later. Once they had connected, Cumming listened in silence as Walsh explained the past several weeks to him.

When Walsh had finished speaking, Cumming remained silent for a moment.

"Tough luck, my boy," Cumming said, finally. "I didn't see that one coming."

"Neither did I," Walsh admitted.

Cumming sighed. "Well, no choice but to put all that behind us and move on to new business. Call it a learning experience."

"But...don't you want me to look into it?"

"Into what?"

"The murders, of course. Ernst and Tobias."

"Whatever for?" Cumming said. The exasperation was clear in his voice.

Walsh considered whether to continue, and decided to press on. He had nothing to lose, really.

"Because something is going on here," Walsh continued. "Someone must know what Ernst and Tobias were doing here, and killed them because of it. And that means someone must know what I'm doing here. Wouldn't you agree?"

"Walsh, I'm sure a number of people know what you are doing there, especially now, so it may be that the rest of your time in Brussels will be somewhat unproductive. Think about that. And if you start sticking your nose into these killings then I'm sure you won't have a future in Brussels. It would be more trouble than it's worth. Best thing, my boy, is to cut your losses and move on. And don't stick your neck out too much next time. Heavens, man, you could have been shot instead of Ernst! Have you considered that?"

"Yes, I have, C, and that's partly why I want to look into this. I'd rather stay on top of this rather than have Ernst's killer come after me when I least expect it."

"I have another idea. Perhaps we should just bring you out of there now. Now wait, listen to me. Please. You've been into Germany already, you speak the language, so perhaps there's more work there for you. We're trying to get more information on their North Sea defences. The Admiralty is organising a recce team for that right now, in point of fact. Could be very important to us, to the Admiralty. Maybe you could join them, or serve as a kind of support unit for them, in Wilhelmshaven. Or Bremerhaven perhaps. I'm sure you could be very helpful to them. What do you say?"

Walsh thought for a moment. Then he said, "C, I don't want to go to Germany. Not yet."

"Are you absolutely sure?"

"I told you about that phantom captain from Liège. Delfosse. The one I can't find now."

Cumming sighed again. "Yes? And what about him?"

"Suppose he was a German agent? Suppose the NA has been involved in this thing all along, once they knew I was here, thanks to Delfosse? Suppose they helped to set it up, just to expose me?"

Cumming thought for a moment. "I don't know, Walsh. It doesn't sound right. Steinhauer doesn't work that way. He's not an assassin, for heaven's sake! He's just a naval intelligence man, like me. Besides, why would he kill his fellow Germans, when he could simply arrest them? Does that make sense?"

"That may be true, but something is not right here. I'd like to find out what it is, before I leave."

"You're grasping at straws, my boy. It's time to move on to something else."

"I will, C, but I need to keep an ear to the ground about this business with Ernst. Can I do that?"

Silence from Cumming again. Then: "Walsh, do you remember when we first met? For lunch?"

It seemed like ages ago. "Yes."

"Then you remember I told you that you have no official status with us over there. You are not working for the British Government in any capacity, as far as we are concerned. Do you know what that means? You have no cover, no diplomatic immunity, no help from the embassy there. Nothing. If you get into trouble, with the police or the NA or anyone else, then there is nothing we can do for you, understand?"

"I understand."

"So do you want to stay in Brussels or go to Wilhemshaven? Or come home?"

Walsh hesitated for just a moment. "I'll stay in Brussels, C. For now. It's no bother, really. Besides, the Exposition is over in a few months, and then we can talk about next steps."

"Fair enough, my boy. But tread lightly, understand? You're only still alive because Ernst's killer wanted you to stay alive. Wouldn't you agree? So maybe you aren't a threat to him at the moment. But that would change if you get too close, correct?"

"I understand, C."

Walsh hung up the phone, and stood in the booth for a few moments. Then he picked up the phone again, paused for just a second, and called Gisela.

Chapter 65

Sarajevo. August 1910.

The official report by the Provincial Government of Bosnia regarding the assassination attempt against General Varesanin was sent to Vienna during the first week of August.

As everyone expected, the report identified Bogdan Zerajic as the sole conspirator of the assassination attempt, although it also briefly indicated that anarchist literature had been found in his flat in Agram. The police attempted to find evidence of contacts between Zerajic and other known anarchists or anti-Austrian movements but were unsuccessful. His Browning pistol was of a type found throughout Europe, exported from Liége along with thousands just like it, and the police could not say precisely how Zerajic, a poor student, had acquired it.

Interviews with Zerajic's friends, family, and acquaintances also suggested that Vienna's original assumptions about the young man where correct: his act was that of a deranged young man, acting alone. After six weeks of investigation, the police could find no evidence to the contrary, and in the end they officially concurred with Vienna's views. General Varesanin was pleased that Zerajic, whom he often referred to in private as 'scum', was not part of a larger conspiracy.

During the summer of 1910, progress of the investigation had been reported in newspapers throughout the Balkans, and Zerajic's bold act, although it failed in the end, captured the fervent imaginations of his fellow Serbs. Stories of his courage in the face of such great odds began to circulate among various student and nationalist groups. His dear old friend Vladimir Gaconovic, from their days as secondary school students in Mostar, began to compose and publish essays in honour of his dead companion. One of them described Zerajic as a 'man of action, of strength, of life and virtue, a type such as opens an epoch, proclaims ideas and enlivens suffering and spellbound hearts, preaching the new ethic of dying for an ideal, for freedom.'

Copies of the essays were smuggled throughout the Balkans, and they slowly built up the legend of Zerajic's suicide, of his sacrifice, of his martyrdom. And above all, of his inspiring example to other young Serbs.

Chapter 66

Brussels. August 1910.

Walsh met Gisela at the Bruxelles-Kermesse, the cheerful carnival section of the Exposition, as she had requested. She had been angry with him on the telephone, for leaving her without an explanation, but he quickly worked up a lie for her about his abrupt trip away from Brussels. At the Expo, Walsh wondered why she wasn't busy with her automobiles in the mechanical section, and learned the answer soon enough.

"I want to have some fun before I leave," she said, taking his hand. She offered an awkward smile in response to the look of surprise on his face. "I need a break from the machines."

"You're leaving now? Before the closing?" Walsh said. He tried to mask the disappointment on his face, with little success.

They were wandering along the rue de la Senne, leading through the Kermesse. The street led them through an odd mish-mash of architectural styles represented by the buildings on either side. Ponderous public buildings of grey stone and slate stood next to modest, and more modern, replicas of houses and cafés constructed of wood and brick. The crowds were thick and animated in the August sunshine, and Walsh walked in his shirtsleeves with his suit jacket draped over his back, hanging on his index finger. He left his wool cap back at the flat.

"My father has decided to go into business for himself," she said. "There's talk of a merger between Hansa and Lloyd and he wants no part of it. And he's made some useful contacts here over the past few weeks. Very useful. He thinks he can use them to get a loan for his own factory."

Walsh's head swam, though he couldn't tell whether it was from the heat or the events of the past month. Or both.

"A factory?"

"Yes, his own factory! Back home in Bremen! Isn't it wonderful?" She clapped her hands together, then maneuvered in front of him, walking backwards and smiling up at him. "And he wants *me* to help run things! Can you believe it?"

Back to Bremen. Close to Bremerhaven, where Cumming had asked him to go. Perhaps he should reconsider staying in Brussels, now that Ernst was dead and Gisela was going back to Germany.

"You must be very pleased."

She nodded. "We're going to build taxicabs at first, for a firm in Hamburg. But then maybe we sell to the public, if things go well. There is so much to be done!"

"Well, what do you want to do here?"

There was no mistaking the edge in his voice. She ignored it.

"Let's have some fun, Nicholas. Enough with the mechanics and exhibits. How about the Luna Park? Yes, the water chute!"

She motioned down the street towards a large basin, filled with water, into which a long ramp deposited screaming riders on carts attached to two rails.

"A water chute? You can't be serious. What about your clothes?"

She pulled him along, towards the Luna Park. "I'll buy some new ones. After I start my new job!"

Three days later, he saw her off at the Gare du Nord. She was all business now, in her suit again, ready with business papers and company catalogs to read on the train. To read and then report to her father. Her new boss. Her new job.

Walsh lifted her case and handed it to the porter. Other luggage would follow, along with her father, a week later. She would be visiting factory sites for him while he wrapped up business in Brussels. Back to Bremen, via Cologne. So much to do!

She extended a hand. Walsh shook it. So long, old chum!

"Maybe we do some business together," she was saying to him. "Some day soon perhaps?" That wicked smile again. "You can be our distributor in Scotland. How about that, Nicholas?"

"Yes, wouldn't that be something."

"I'll send you a letter, Nicholas. Once I get settled at home. I'd like to hear how you get on here."

He nodded. "Just send it to the post office branch in Ixelles. *Poste restante*, I mean. I'll be taking post there for a few more months."

He had never taken her to his flat, since Ernst had been there much of the time. And her father had prevented him from visiting her residence in Brussels. Now it was too late for anything, unless he told Cumming he changed his mind about going to Bremerhaven.

The conductor blew a whistle. Carriage doors began to close up and down the length of the train. The hiss of steam surrounded them.

"It was very nice to have met you, Nicholas. Promise me you'll write!"

"I will," he lied.

The train began to move. Suddenly she stood on tip-toe and kissed him on the cheek, before jumping up into her carriage.

She held the handle next to the carriage door, and leaned out towards him. "*Tchüss*, Nicholas! *Bis bald!*"

Walsh waved to her, as the train gathered speed and left the long platform stretched out ahead of him. After a few moments she was lost to him, and he stood alone next to the empty track.

Another departing German, Walsh thought. Another train back to Germany.

He stood still for a minute, watching the train disappear into the distance. Suddenly his mind shifted to another train departure, from another railway station.

Then he walked quickly to the line of cabs outside the station and asked the first driver in line to take him to Etterbeek.

The next day Walsh waited for Dewulf outside his office, at the building on rue de la Loi. Dewulf did not appear happy when Walsh approached him.

"Mr Walsh. What is it now?"

"If you could just spare a few moments, inspector. Please," Walsh said. "And why don't you call me Nicholas?"

"Very well. Nicholas." Dewulf checked his pocketwatch. "I'm due across the park in a few minutes." Dewulf nodded at the Royal Palace on the other side of the park. "Walk with me then."

They crossed rue de la Loi, then entered the Parc de Bruxelles. Dewulf walked swiftly and Walsh hurried to keep up with him.

"Inspector, I've been to the station at Etterbeek again."

"And?"

"And I was wondering when you found out about Ernst's train."

Dewulf looked over at Walsh. "Why? What does it matter?"

"Because the killer was either extremely fortunate to be in the right place at the right time, to make a perfect shot and get away so easily, or..."

"Or?"

Walsh paused as they passed a group of three men smoking together. "Or it was not luck."

"What do you mean?"

"I mean, he was waiting for us. For Ernst. The shooter had to be in place at the station, even before I arrived. He already had a place to get a good shot and where he could be concealed and get away quickly, in a public area. That sounds like some degree of planning. And so he knew when we would be there."

Dewulf waited while Walsh finished his thought.

"And so, inspector, how did the killer know about that train? Don't you see? Someone at the embassy must be involved. The German Embassy."

Dewulf sighed. "Ernst wasn't at the German Embassy that day."

"What do you mean? Where was he?"

"He was moved in the morning, to be closer to the station. Apparently."

Walsh grabbed Dewulf's arm and stopped his progress. They stood in the pathway as others walked about them, oblivious to their conversation.

"Moved where, inspector? To the station itself? Did he wait there all day?"

"There are several *casernes* near the station at Etterbeek, you know. Just along the boulevard in front of the station, across the railway tracks."

"*Casernes*? Barracks, you mean? Military barracks? For what forces?"

"Various forces, the artillery services, the cavalry." Dewulf sighed again, and looked over towards the Royal Palace. "And some gendarmerie. Ernst was being held by the gendarmes and the German authorities while he waited for his train."

Walsh looked at Dewulf, into his eyes. "You mean the gendarmes who helped to arrest Ernst at my flat? When did you find this out?"

"Soon after you left me. I sent you a message."

"Yes, I got it right when I arrived at my flat. So the person who killed Ernst must have found out around the same time that you did, or very soon afterwards. If Ernst was being moved just an hour or two before his train."

"So it would seem."

"But inspector, how did you know about his train?"

"I have a...a colleague in the gendarmerie. We work together to protect the royal family, you understand? The Special Brigade protects the king, and I, the Sûreté I mean, we protect the state. But it's the same thing, sometimes."

"Inspector, what are you saying?"

"Nicholas, if you are correct about how...how *efficiently* this murder was executed, and if the Germans did not want Ernst to be killed, and if I was the only one in the Sûreté who knew anything about this, then..."

"Then we need to speak to your friend in the gendarmerie, don't we?"

Dewulf shook his head, with a tight smile on his face, and resumed his pace towards the Royal Palace. "What do you mean, 'we,' Nicholas?"

"Inspector, when I was in Liège earlier this year, I spoke with an officer in the Belgian army. I thought he was with your army intelligence. Or so he said. But I tried to find him last week and no one there has heard of him. Suppose he was involved in this? Suppose he was with the gendarmerie? Or working for the Germans?" Or the NA, Walsh might have added.

"And so?"

"And so I am involved in this, and have been since the beginning." Now it was Walsh's turn to sigh. "It's because of me that Ernst was killed. I tried to rescue him from Retzlaff, and I might have told the wrong person about my role here, back in Liège, months ago. I put him in danger. Not you. So this is my fault. And so I need to know who killed him. My government needs to know."

Dewulf stopped walking and faced Walsh directly, with anger in his eyes. "Your government? Nicholas, you have no official status here. We both know that. I could arrest you now for spying if you've been attempting to get information from our forces in Liège."

"Yes. And you would only implicate yourself in all this, inspector. If you arrest me, then the entire story becomes public knowledge. Including the bit about your informer in the Maison."

Dewulf considered that for a moment.

"Inspector, we can still do this secretly. You know that something isn't right here, don't you? If your job is to protect the state, then we need to find out what's going on here. With Ernst and Tobias. Don't forget about Tobias; that's two murders in this affair!"

Dewulf checked his pocketwatch again. "I'm nearly late for an appointment."

Walsh grabbed his arm. "Inspector! I'm not going to let this go, *comprenez-vous*?"

Dewulf tensed for a moment, as if he was going to strike Walsh. Then he relaxed just as quickly. "*D'accord*, Nicholas. Very well. I'll contact you at your flat, later today. All right? Just don't do anything until then, understand? This must be handled carefully. Very carefully. Because I'm just as much at fault as you are in all this."

Walsh frowned at him. "How do you mean?"

"Well, I gave you the secret information about the train, didn't I?"

Chapter 67

The next day, after making a plan of attack the evening before, Walsh rode with Dewulf in an official car out to the barracks at Etterbeek, along the Avenue de la Couronne. Dewulf was not a very good driver and Walsh cringed now and again as he heard the gears grinding as Dewulf mishandled the lever. During the ride, Dewulf's complaints were almost loud enough to drown out the wretched sounds of his bad driving. Almost.

"My job is to supervise foreigners, you understand. That's all," Dewulf was saying. "And *live* foreigners, my friend, not dead ones! But it's not so simple these days, is it? No, all the communes in Brussels insist on maintaining their own local police forces to deal with subversives. Along with the central Brussels Police, of course. Then the gendarmerie has a special brigade for monitoring anarchists and terrorists, plus their own intelligence service, which is distinct from the army's service, even though gendarmes are part of the army! Can you believe it?"

"This is why you sent me away, isn't it?" Walsh said. "After the killing. Not to protect me, but to protect yourself. To protect Belgium. Isn't that right?"

Dewulf shook his head. "It was to protect both of us. You need to maintain your own secrecy here and I certainly couldn't afford to have you investigated too closely while I'm trying to maintain security at the Exposition *and* do my normal duties. Because the problems don't end there, Nicholas, do they? No, of course not. Because the gendarmerie also insists on helping to protect the Royal Family, which conflicts with my usual responsibilities. Isn't that useful? And now we have a special passport section in the Ministry of Justice to keep an eye on things, just in case. And lots of returning Force Publique soldiers, from the Congo. They need to be kept busy as well! Plus there used to be an investigations bureau in the Brussels city police charged with surveillance of subversives, but it ran into difficulties years ago."

"What happened?" Walsh stifled a howl as the vehicle bounced over a pothole.

Dewulf barked out a laugh and shook his head again. "You wouldn't believe it."

"What?"

"The Chief Superintendent was charged with operating a white slavery ring between London and Brussels."

Walsh shook his head. "You're right, I don't believe it!"

"It's true. He was helping to support the very brothels he was supposed to be policing. Supplying them with alcohol and other favours. When that scandal broke, centralized surveillance was broken up as well. And so now our approach is more…fragmented."

"And so less efficient."

"Yes, but apparently that's how we like it. Or so they tell me. And the various mayors of Brussels and the communes have all the control, really, in the city. The idea is that if we avoid centralized authority, then we will more easily retain our liberties. That's the theory, anyway. But in the meantime, we are invaded by every subversive and radical group in Europe. Invaded, I tell you! And remember, we've had it all here: Italian anarchists, Dutch Orangists, Russian revolutionaries, British Chartists, German socialists, Spanish Carlists, French Communards and even *ultramontains*. On and on and on. Plus our own internal problems. Flemish and Wallon nationalists, Catholics and Protestants, you name it. Impossible to keep track of them all. And that's before all this business with millions of visitors to the Exposition!"

Walsh looked at him. "What the devil are '*ultramontains*'?

"It's an old French term for Catholics who assert that the ultimate authority in their church, and even in the public life of their country, is vested in the man who lives 'beyond the mountains'. Beyond the Alps, that is. In Rome."

Walsh understood. "The Pope," he said.

A few moments later, the vehicle arrived at Etterbeek station, where Dewulf turned left and drove past the station. Then he turned left again and Walsh could see the large barracks buildings on his left and his right, tall walls of red brick capped with barbed wire.

Dewulf parked in the street and the two men walked into one of the barracks. At the guardhouse next to the main gate, two men were standing watch. Dewulf told one of them about his appointment inside, and the guard checked his visitor list. A second later he telephoned inside for confirmation.

A few moments later, Walsh saw a uniformed man approach them from the entrance to the barracks building. He spread his arms and waved them over.

"Martin, Martin! So good to see you!" the man said.

He was in his late fifties or early sixties, Walsh guessed, and was perhaps the most elegant uniformed man Walsh had seen since his arrival in Belgium. His dark red and blue, high-collared coat was fully buttoned, his kepi was set firmly upon his head, and the aiguillettes hanging from his shoulder were a brilliant white against the dark tone of his uniform. His muttonchop whiskers were well-trimmed, and Walsh smelled the faint aroma of cologne on the older man, along with cigar smoke.

"General Smet," Dewulf said.

The general — major general, to be specific - put his hands on Dewulf's shoulders in an almost fatherly gesture.

"And who is this?"

"This is Mr Walsh. Nicholas Walsh. He's...he's with the British Embassy here." Dewulf almost cringed as he spoke the lie.

"How do you do, general?" Walsh asked, extending his hand.

General Smet smiled and shook his hand.

"How do you do?" he replied, in perfect English. "Now, my dear inspector, you were very cryptic on the telephone. So what brings you all the way out here?"

In the general's small but tasteful and extremely tidy office, Dewulf and Walsh waited in silence for a response to their query, sipping their tea. A minute later, they had it.

"Here it is," Smet said as he returned to the office, with a piece of paper in his hand, which he kept in front of him. "But I still don't see the point of this. I thought this was a matter for the Public Prosecutor?"

"Yes, of course," Dewulf said. "But you see there is also the matter of the Stern murder. Tobias Stern. I think there may be a...a political connection with Ernst's murder. Something to do with the socialists perhaps. As I told you before, we, the Sûreté I mean, we have been keeping an eye on them since the Exposition. Merely as a precautionary measure, of course."

"I see. Always the intrigue with them, isn't it?" Smet smiled at them. "And what interest does the British government have with this, if I might ask?" He kept smiling, and waited for a response, with the paper still in his hand.

"Mr Walsh is here in an advisory capacity. He is investigating similar...conspiracies in London. With the socialists."

"We call them the Labour Party," Walsh said, shooting a glance at Dewulf. "We think there may be a connection between the socialist organizers here and in London. There's been...problems since the British election in January. Problems in the government," Walsh lied. "These groups are all linked through the Maison du Peuple, where the body of Tobias was found. Dumped. And he was in Brussels with Ernst, so we just want to make sure we've looked into all the possibilities."

"I see. How very interesting. And you believe someone on this list is involved?" Smet held up the paper again.

Dewulf replied to his query. "General, we both...we *all* know this is probably some internal socialist dispute." Dewulf looked over at Walsh. "This kind of thing goes on all the time. You understand me, don't you? But the fact is, someone may have, *may have*, told the killer that Ernst would be at the Etterbeek station on the day he was shot. We merely want to stay...stay aware of various possibilities. You can understand that, can't you?"

Smet nodded, very slowly. "Yes, I suppose so. I suppose so. But, my dear inspector, you must understand that I have my own responsibility. To my service. And to the men under my authority here. They have rights, as do I. Wouldn't you agree?"

"General, we are not here to arrest anyone. Or even to accuse anyone. But if someone here may have *accidentally* spoke about Ernst being here, right before he was killed, then we do need to know about it. And we all would prefer to look into this as quietly as possible, believe me. But if we have to bring our concerns to the Public Prosecutor, rather than handle it discreetly, *today*, then it could be difficult for all of us."

Smet sat back in the face of Dewulf's threat. He looked ready to concede defeat.

"If I give you this list, then I have one condition that must be respected before you act on this information," he said. "To protect their rights."

"Of course. That is understood. We do appreciate your assistance, general. Very much."

Smet smiled at them. "My pleasure, inspector. As always. And it's not like I have a war to fight right now, is it?"

Two hours later, Walsh and Dewulf rode back to the centre of Brussels after having had little success with their excursion to Etterbeek. Smet's list had given them only four names, besides his own, of gendarmes who knew about Ernst's transfer from the German Embassy to the barracks and then to the railway station. But his one condition was firm: before Smet would allow Dewulf to question any of the men directly, he insisted that Dewulf and Walsh investigate the possibility of a leak at the Maison itself.

As Dewulf's automobile sped down the rue du Trône, he shook his head in admiration of Smet.

"The general is no idiot, that's for sure," Dewulf said. "If we can't find out who the gendarme might have leaked this information to, then this investigation stops now. If it is a real investigation."

"You said that it was the general who told you about Ernst?" Walsh said.

Dewulf nodded. "Yes, I had told him some of that socialist business you heard in the office just now. Only to get him to tell me about what was happening with Ernst. I asked if I could interview Ernst and Smet told me he was leaving on the train the day Ernst was killed. But all that was before Tobias was killed. Now there is, or may be, some connection with the socialists at the Maison. And so now the general is even more nervous about his role in all this."

"So he could run into some trouble if the Public Prosecutor found out that he was giving out information to you and cooperating with the Germans."

Dewulf nodded. "Which is why he agreed to help us so readily with the list, but then not allow us to question those men unless we had more proof that one of the gendarmes leaked this information."

"So it's back to the Maison," Walsh said.

"I suppose so."

"But we need to avoid scaring Hendrickx just now, isn't that right? So you can't go in yourself and try to question him about this?"

Dewulf shook his head. "Not at the moment. And he has no reason to cooperate with me. You know how much legal help they have now. The POB, I mean. In fact, their main leader, Vandervelde, is a lawyer. A very good one. He helped to write their constitution. Who knows, he might lead the government here one day."

"Perhaps I could talk to him. Hendrickx, I mean."

"Perhaps."

"But I don't trust him," Walsh said, after a moment's thought. "Not from the beginning."

"Neither do I."

"No, too much has happened since I met those two German lads. Disagreements about the real price for Ernst's secret, and Hendrickx doesn't want them around the Maison for some reason, and he doesn't want to meet with me in person, then he doesn't offer to help Ernst after Tobias disappears, then he disappears when I'm trying to reach a final deal with Ernst. And then both Ernst and Tobias are killed. So Hendrickx is at the centre of it, somehow. Or at least some of it."

"You don't think Hendrickx had them killed?"

"No, I don't think so, not after taking the trouble to bring them to Brussels, in secret. And certainly not if he needed the money I was going to pay. And not if Tobias was dumped on the steps of the Maison itself. But we still need to make a connection between Smet's list and the Maison, or otherwise completely rule out such a connection. And Hendrickx is the man in the middle. So we need to deal with him in... in some other way."

Dewulf nodded. "I was afraid you would say that."

Walsh nodded as well, then he looked over at Dewulf. "Yes. I guess there's no other way right now. We have to risk it." Walsh thought for a moment, then added, "Can you leave it with me, inspector? I think we may be able to handle this without revealing ourselves."

Dewulf glanced at him. "What do you want to do? Break into the Maison after dark and search his office?"

"No, nothing like that. At least, not yet." Walsh smiled at Dewulf. "Too crude, wouldn't you say? No, that's not the way to proceed. But we'll need a favour from our friend Leysen. Can you arrange a meeting with him?"

"I suppose so. I want to hear your plan first."

"In a moment. I'm still thinking it through. But, inspector, there's something else I still don't understand. I need to ask you before we proceed with Leysen."

Dewulf glanced over again. "What is it?"

"Why is the Belgian Gendarmerie cooperating with the German authorities in the first place? Why were they so eager to help deport Ernst? It all happened so quickly. It was almost as if they couldn't wait to get rid of him."

Dewulf avoided Walsh's eyes, and shook his head before replying. "You can guess, I'm sure."

"Don't tell me. Something about your blessed neutrality."

Dewulf nodded again. "And they don't want to have any trouble, any *embarrassment*, during the Exposition, remember that."

"But neutrality doesn't mean doing dirty work for the Germans," Walsh said.

"No, it doesn't." Dewulf smiled at Walsh, then looked back at the road ahead of him. "It means doing dirty work for *everyone* around us, sometimes. To keep things fair. Like Smet just did for his Germans. And like I'm doing with *you*."

Chapter 68

Walsh and Dewulf found Leysen at a café on the Place du Jeu de Balle, directly across from the Église Nôtre Dame Immaculée. Walsh remembered his first meeting with Tobias and Ernst at the Église and felt another twinge of regret.

At the café, the young man in front of Walsh and Dewulf did not seem especially happy to see them. He sat across from the two government agents with a morose look on his face. His battered face.

"What happened to you?" Dewulf said, by way of a greeting.

"You've haven't heard? Of course not," Leysen said. "What do you care about me now? I was beat up by some government bullies. Government bullies! And I'm supposed to be *working* for our government!"

"Keep your voice down!" Dewulf scanned the room for eavesdroppers. The place was nearly empty; the market in front of the café had finished hours ago. "What do you mean, 'government bullies'?" he continued. "Police?"

Leysen shook his head. "I don't think so. I don't know. They didn't identify themselves. They had masks on. No uniforms. And they didn't stay around to answer questions."

Dewulf and Walsh exchanged a glance.

"You're becoming more effective," said Walsh. "With your socialist friends. So someone is starting to pay attention to you."

"They're not my friends," Leysen protested.

"And he was not attacked by the police or the Sûreté," said Dewulf. "I would've heard about it. And we don't...we don't normally operate that way."

Leysen made a negative sound. Dewulf leaned closer to him.

"Listen, Dirk," Dewulf began. "I'm sorry about this. Really I am. But chin up, my friend. It could have been worse. At least you weren't arrested. Or killed!"

Dewulf attempted a smile, but Leysen did not seem to appreciate his good fortune at failing to get arrested. Or killed.

Dewulf leaned closer to Walsh and spoke close to his ear.

"Do you still want to go ahead with this?" Dewulf whispered. "If he is being watched now…?"

Walsh nodded. "We have to try." Then he lowered his own voice, and practically whispered to Dewulf. "Besides, if he was just beaten up, he has more credibility at the Maison. For the moment. In fact, he could say they now owe him some…some consideration. So they'll believe him. Don't you think?"

Dewulf and Walsh moved apart and looked at Leysen. The young man shifted in his seat.

"So what are you going to do about this?" Leysen said, indicating the bruises on his face.

Dewulf smiled. "Promote you. You're now a foreign intelligence agent. Working for the British government on behalf of the Sûreté." Dewulf nodded at Walsh. "Meet your new temporary boss."

Dewulf left a moment later. He could not allow himself to listen to Walsh's instructions to Leysen, in case things did not go as planned.

Leysen glared at Walsh. "What is this?"

Walsh leaned forward, and spoke carefully and plainly. "I know what you've been doing at the Maison. I'm very familiar with that kind of work. Understand? I know it can be difficult at times. Your head gets mixed up with clashing loyalties. You get confused. You don't know if you are coming or going, moving forwards or going backwards."

"Or just standing still, waiting to take another fucking beating!" Leysen said.

Walsh nodded in appreciation. "That was too bad. But that's the nature of this work, sometimes. And you have to balance the risks with the rewards."

Now Leysen showed some interest. "What rewards? Do you know what the inspector pays me? Hardly enough to feed myself! And certainly not enough to risk having my jaw broken next time!"

"Yes, well, now I will add to whatever he is paying you."

Leysen raised an eyebrow. "How much?"

"Let's say, one thousand francs."

Leysen nodded. "Let's say, I'm still listening. But I want to know what I'm supposed to do now."

Walsh explained the situation to him. Leysen listened carefully.

"I don't know," Leysen said, after Walsh finished his story. "And if I can do this, I need more money from you."

Walsh sighed. Here we go again. "How much more?"

Leysen raised an eyebrow. "Double your previous offer."

Walsh thought for a moment. This money would be coming out of his own pocket; Cumming certainly wouldn't pay for it. It had better be worth it.

"All right," Walsh said. "Two thousand francs. But you must do exactly as I say."

Leysen leaned forward and looked Walsh in the eyes. "But how can you be so sure about all this?" he said. "Suppose you're wrong?"

"I told you, I'm familiar with this kind of work. I know how these groups operate. And if I'm wrong, there's no harm done."

"Unless I get caught."

"You won't get 'caught.' You aren't working with the inspector now, not directly, and I'm just a Scottish businessman here for the Exposition. And I've never been to the Maison. So if you can't get what we want, or it doesn't exist, then we'll have to try something else."

"And I'm supposed to deal with Hendrickx?"

"If you can."

"But they told me he was sick at home."

"I have a feeling that he has recovered. Miraculously, you might say."

Leysen shook his head again. "But I've never met him. I've only been dealing with Penneman. He's in charge of the Young Guards."

Walsh shook his head. "Listen to me. You've just been beaten up, right? Doing some work for Penneman? So now you don't trust Penneman, understand? You're scared and angry and want someone to confide in at the Maison. You want protection. You tell all this to Hendrickx, in secret. You tell him that Vandervelde gave you his name. And then you give Hendrickx the name I mentioned."

"You mean, Jacquard?"

"Yes, that's it. Major Jacquard, of the Belgian Gendarmerie."

354

The very next day, Walsh had his answer. Leysen was actually smiling when they met at Falstaff, and Walsh decided to treat the young man to lunch. They both ordered large slabs of beef, with a mound of hot crispy frites between them. Leysen's eyes grew as large as the steak when it was put before him.

"Hendrickx was there. And he didn't look sick to me," Leysen began, with a mouth full of beef, after the waiter had moved off.

Walsh cut into his steak, and saw that it had been perfectly cooked. Rare. "Of course he wasn't," he said. "He was just staying out of sight while this business was Ernst was winding up."

"But he did look nervous when I came in, I have to tell you! Oh my, when I said that someone from the gendarmerie was threatening me!" Leysen waved a chip in front of Walsh as he spoke.

"Major Jacquard."

"Yes, yes, of course. Major Jacquard." Leysen gave a mock salute, and took a long drink from the glass of Rodenbach set before him. He wiped his mouth with his sleeve.

"Did Hendrickx seem to recognize the name?"

Leysen shook his head. "Not that I could tell."

"No matter. We had to risk that. If he checks on this, he will find there is a Major Jacquard. That's all we need to worry about right now."

"But I was nearly shaking when I sat down with him," Leysen continued. "Petrified. I kept expecting Penneman to come in. And they kept me waiting outside Hendrickx's office for half an hour! But it is on the third floor of the Maison, and Penneman works two floors below that."

Walsh stirred a dash of cream into his coffee. "It's good that you were nervous. Makes you more believable."

"Well, then, I was very believable!" Leysen smiled, with his cheeks full.

"And what did you tell him, exactly?"

"Just as you told me. That I was scared of Penneman. That I didn't trust him since I was beaten up. And that Jacquard wants me to work for him, against the socialists."

"And what did Hendrickx say?"

"He told me that if Jacquard approached me again, I should ask what he wants me to do. Specifically. And to report back to him about it. To Hendrickx."

Walsh raised an eyebrow. "And without telling Penneman?"

Leysen shrugged his shoulders. "I suppose that was understood. He didn't say it explicitly."

"But he also didn't ask you to contact Jacquard?"

"How can I? I have no way to reach him."

Walsh nodded. "Good then. So Tobias and Ernst were both killed while they were involved in the deal Hendrickx was trying to set up. A deal that might have been unknown to others at the Maison. That's how these people operate. Then you were beaten up, probably by the gendarmes. And now you've told him the gendarmerie wants you to work for them. To spy on the Maison."

"You're trying to squeeze Hendrickx?"

"In a sense. But what else did he say, once you gave him Jacquard's name?"

"Well, he wrote it down. He thanked me for being so honest. And brave." Leysen rolled his eyes. "He also said this kind of thing wasn't unusual, in his experience."

"It's happened before, then?"

Leysen nodded. "That's what it sounded like."

"So then he keeps track of these contacts. With the gendarmerie, or any other authorities. And we need to get that list."

Chapter 69

Two days later, Leysen again sat outside of Hendrickx's office at the Maison, sweating profusely. This time, however, he didn't have to wait more than a minute or two.

Standing at his office door, Hendrickx beckoned Leysen inside and pointed to a chair in front of his desk. And this time Hendrickx sat down right next to Leysen, rather than behind his own large desk. He had black button eyes and a bushy moustache; the combination of these features reminded Leysen of a walrus.

"So, my friend, they've been in touch again?" Hendrickx said.

Leysen nodded. "Yes."

"I see. Good. And what is it this time?"

Leysen removed a small piece of paper from his coat pocket, and handed it to Hendrickx.

Hendrickx unfolded the paper and read it. Just a list of fifteen names. Names and ranks, of junior officers in the Belgian Gendarmerie.

"And what is this?"

Leysen took a deep breath. "Jacquard suspects these men of working for you. For the socialists. Gendarmes are not supposed to be involved in socialism," he added quickly, without actually needing to.

"And he wants me to confirm this? Just like that?" Hendrickx snapped his fingers in Leysen's face, and the young man flinched. Then Hendrickx stared at Leysen. "Or were you supposed to…steal this information from me? From the Maison?"

Leysen answered quickly. "No, no! It's not like that. He…he has something to trade. That's what he said."

Hendrickx stared at Leysen, without blinking, for a moment. A long moment. Then he spoke. "You must be joking."

"No, he says there is an informant here. A mouchard, you understand? Someone who can be very damaging to us. He can provide the name. In exchange for helping with this list." Leysen indicated the paper clutched in Hendrickx's hand.

"A police informant?"

"He didn't say."

Hendrickx put his hand on Leysen's shoulder. It was not meant as a friendly gesture. "Someone from the gendermerie? The Sûreté?"

Leysen shook his head. "He didn't say! But..."

"But *what*? Tell me this instant!"

"He said...he said this informant helped to cause the deaths of those two men working for you."

Hendrickx grabbed Leysen's shoulder again. "What two men? What are you talking about?"

"I don't know who they are. I don't, I swear it!" Leysen flinched at the pressure from Hendrickx's hand. "He...he said they were two Germans, two young men from Leipzig, and that you would know what I was talking about."

"He wants to do it," Leysen said to Walsh, two hours later. "He wants to meet with Jacquard. In secret."

"Very good," Walsh said. "That's very good work."

"But..."

Walsh looked Leysen in the eyes. "But what?"

"But I'm not sure he'll bring what you want."

"Possibly not. But you did see him write down this information, didn't you? In his office?"

Leysen nodded. "Yes, of course."

"Don't worry. He keeps records. They always do."

"But...I don't understand all this. He's probably as interested as you are in finding out who killed Tobias and Ernst. Why don't you just ask him for this information?"

"Three reasons," Walsh began, holding up three fingers. "First, I don't trust him. Second, I'm not sure if the socialists are infiltrating the gendarmerie, or if the gendarmerie is infiltrating the socialists."

"Or both!"

Walsh nodded. "Yes, or both. All we know is that they are interested in, and worried about, each other. So perhaps we can use that to our advantage."

"And the third reason?"

"The third reason, my friend, is that I've learned at least one thing since I arrived in Brussels. No one provides anything for free. Isn't that right? Everything has a price. And Hendrickx already knows a lot about me. Too much, in fact. He knows I can't pay as much as he wanted for Ernst's secret, and he knows I don't have any information of my own to trade. And he probably knows that I'm not an official agent of the British government. So we need to pretend otherwise. We need to pretend that I can give him something that he really wants. Now do you understand?"

"Yes, I think so. But why would he trade a long list of his socialists for the name of just one informant from you?"

"Well, you leave that to me."

"It still seems like a lot of effort when he might just give you the information."

"I can't count on him doing that, and if I ask him in person before we...before we play our little game, then he won't cooperate with anyone about this information. For any reason. He'll be far too suspicious. Or at best, his price for it will go way up. And I'm not about to get into another damned bidding war over something I need. I've had enough of that already."

"I suppose you're right."

"It's what my instincts tell me. And sometimes you have to tell a lot of lies to find the truth. Now listen carefully. Here's what I want you to tell Hendrickx."

The meeting was arranged the following night, near midnight. Walsh expected Hendrickx to come on his own, but was surprised to find Leysen next to him on a dark platform at the Gare du Luxembourg, in the Quartier Leopold. Otherwise the small station was practically empty, as Walsh had expected.

Walsh wore a coat with a high collar and pulled his hat down over his eyes so that most of his face was covered. In the near darkness he was virtually unrecognizable. He had never met Hendrickx but could not take a chance that the man had seen him before, which would threaten his plan tonight.

Walsh stood in the darkness as Leysen and Hendrickx moved closer to him. Once they were within speaking distance, Walsh called out to them to stop. In German. Then he switched to French and said the same thing: *that's far enough*.

Hendrickx froze at the sound of Walsh's German words, and looked quickly at Leysen. "What is this? Is this Jacquard?"

Leysen nodded. "That's what he told me."

"This is the man you've been meeting with?" Hendrickx said. "But why is he speaking German?"

Leysen shook his head in confusion. "I don't know. He never spoke German to me before."

Walsh spoke again, in French. "No, I'm not Major Jacquard."

Hendrickx stood frozen. "Then who are you?"

"My name is unimportant. Do you have the list of socialist gendarmes as Leysen requested?"

Hendrickx nodded. "Yes, but I came to trade with Jacquard."

"I have the information you want."

"But you are not with the gendarmerie?"

Walsh shook his head.

"You're not even Belgian!"

"Of course not."

Hendrickx looked at Leysen and saw a blank face. Then he asked, "But then how do you know...?"

"Because we work together. Sometimes. Us and the Belgian security services. Like with many other countries. Not so often with the gendarmerie, though it does happen now and again. But now they are not so eager to help me, I've recently learned. So I've come to you."

Hendrickx looked at Leysen, who looked as confused as he did. "What are you talking about?"

"They are refusing to help investigate the death of my agent. So I need your help."

"What agent?"

Walsh paused for a moment. "His name was Hesse. Ernst Hesse."

"Ernst was *your* agent?"

"Of course. We told him to cooperate with Tobias. We gave him the secret of the acetone, and told him to sell it here. You don't think a simple student would come up with that on his own, do you?"

"Why did you send him here?"

"Why do you think? To expose the extent of Britain's espionage network in Brussels, of course."

Hendrickx shook his head. "I knew it. I never trusted that boy. He never would tell me his special formula."

"Of course not. He was told not to tell anyone until payment was offered, although his 'secret' would not have worked so well for the British, you understand. The acetone formula would have made the cordite quite unstable, in time, and therefore useless. But now Ernst is dead, our little game with him is over, and I need to find out what happened. I know the British agent didn't kill him, and I know that *we* didn't kill him."

"And who is 'we'?"

Walsh paused for a moment, as if he was deciding whether to tell. "You may as well know. I'm with the *Nachrichten Abteilung*."

Hendrickx looked confused. "The what?"

"The intelligence department of the Imperial German Navy. It's our job to find out what Britain's navy is doing, and what her spies are doing, so we set Ernst on this little mission for us."

Hendrickx smiled, but without humour. "And it went wrong. Very wrong."

"Yes, which is why I'm here. Now may I see that list?"

"Not yet. I have some questions. For one, Ernst was killed weeks ago. Why are you looking into this only now?"

"Our original intention was to leave it alone," Walsh said. "Ernst was expendable. But we've lost agents in the UK and France since then, and there may be a pattern. And all paths lead through Brussels these days, or so it seems. So we need to reconsider what may have happened here. To Ernst. And then to Tobias, although he wasn't working for us directly. I want to know if Tobias was also killed just to send a message to us."

Hendrickx frowned. "But Ernst was arrested by one of *your* agents. Taken from the flat of the British agent. To be sent back to Germany."

Walsh shook his head. "Not an NA agent. Not one of ours. The German military attaché, Lieutenant-Colonel Moench, was not aware of our operation here. He is with the army, which does not always…cooperate with the navy. He thought he was doing Germany a great favour by finding Ernst here. And so he acted too quickly for us to intervene, thanks to the stupid cooperation of your gendarmerie."

Hendrickx relaxed. The explanation of these facts seemed to convince him of Walsh's lies. "Hmpf. It's not *my* gendarmerie," he said, finally.

Walsh moved a few steps closer to him. "Fair enough. But you can see that I have no interest in your politics or your relations with the internal security services here. I'm only interested in my primary enemy: the British Admiralty. So I expect you won't mind letting me have a quick look at the names on the list."

Hendrickx removed the paper from his coat pocket. He looked at it, then at Leysen, then at Walsh. "I have it here. Just as you asked. But perhaps we should negotiate a new price, now that I know who you are."

Walsh had suspected that possibility. "Is that so?"

"Yes. You see, from my point of view, I've lost five thousand pounds because this deal of yours didn't go as planned."

"Yes, because someone in *your* organisation leaked the information. So I need to see that list."

Hendrickx shook his head. "You don't know that."

"There's only one way to find out."

Hendrickx hesitated. "I still want my five thousand pounds, plus the name of the informer in our organisation. If you have it, that is. Or was that another ruse?"

"You can have the name, once I see your list."

"Is it Penneman?"

Walsh shook his head again. "After I see the list."

"And the five thousand pounds?"

Walsh moved closer to Hendrickx and made sure he had his attention. "Mr Hendrickx, listen to me very carefully. I came here to meet with you in person and I told you the truth. The truth about an important secret regarding Imperial Germany, because I believe we have a shared interest in finding out how the Belgian Gendarmerie may have caused the death of Ernst Hesse. So I expect you to live up to the bargain that we have agreed. The name I have in exchange for the name you have. That's all."

Hendrickx hesitated. "And if I refuse?"

Walsh unbuttoned his coat and revealed his holstered pistol. He could see that Hendrickx was properly impressed. "Then you will be killed, Mr Hendrickx. You and your family as well. And I will get my list some other way, while you rot in your grave."

Hendrickx glanced at Leysen, who said nothing. Then Hendrickx came closer to Walsh, and opened the paper still clutched in his hand. He looked at it. Leysen stood still, watching the two men complete their transaction.

"What name do you suspect?" Hendrickx held out the paper to Walsh.

"Let me see."

Walsh looked closely at the list in Hendrickx's hand, and then back to his own, much shorter list. The list Hendrickx gave up had names, ranks, service dates, service locations, brief physical descriptions, and home addresses of about two dozen gendarmes, all of whom were in the Young Guards and/or the POB. After just a second Walsh circled a name on his own list, then looked up at Hendrickx with a smile.

"That's it," Walsh said.

"Who?" Hendrickx said.

"I can't tell you. But what do these marks mean on your list?" Walsh pointed to marks beside a few of the names.

"First give me the name of the Belgian informer," Hendrickx said. "Is it Penneman?"

"All right. And no, not Penneman." Walsh pocketed his slip of paper. "It's Beckers."

Hendrickx was surprised. "Beckers? *Frank* Beckers? I don't believe it!"

"Who is Beckers?" said Leysen.

The other two men ignored him.

Walsh nodded. "It's true. He works for the Special Brigade of the gendarmerie in Brussels."

"Not the Sûreté?"

"No. Now explain these marks to me." Walsh pointed to the paper Hendrickx was holding.

Hendrickx sighed. "Frank Beckers. Of all the people."

"The marks, please, Mr Hendrickx?"

"The marks refer to gendarmes who are not to be trusted."

"Why not?"

Hendrickx looked at Walsh, who was suddenly afraid that he would be recognized. But Hendrickx merely smiled and said, quietly, so that Leysen could not hear: "Because we suspect them of being informers. *Mouchards*, understand? And it seems that may be the case here, does it not?"

Chapter 70

Walsh updated Dewulf on his meeting with Hendrickx as they walked from Etterbeek Station to the gendarmerie barracks, where General Smet was waiting for them.

"So who is Beckers?" said Dewulf, as soon as they left the crowd at the station.

"He's one of the men directly under Vandervelde at the Maison. A senior party member, someone with power. I asked Leysen to get some names after his first meeting with Hendrickx."

"And how did you know Hendrickx would agree to a meeting with Major Jacquard?"

Walsh shrugged his shoulders. "I didn't. But if Hendrickx is as ambitious as most political types, then he would be eager to help ruin someone above him. Like Beckers. And I believe Hendrickx is the security officer in the POB, so he would be unlikely to pass up a meeting with one of his adversaries."

They crossed Boulevard St Michel and entered the barracks complex.

"But then why the ruse with the German agent?"

"Well, a few things occurred to me after Hendrickx agreed to the meeting. One is that information is often more trustworthy when it comes from an independent third party. Someone without an interest. And I thought he would be more likely to trust a German NA agent than someone from the Belgian Gendermerie."

"I suppose that makes sense."

"And there was a slight chance that Hendrickx might have known Jacquard. Or met him or knew his face. Which would have made things difficult if I had attempted to impersonate Jacquard. There is no way he could have known the German NA agent. And finally, if I had to threaten him, I thought he would be more afraid of a foreign agent than one of his fellow countrymen."

"And did you have to threaten him?"

Walsh looked at Dewulf, then smiled ever so slightly. "Only a little. I think he wanted to believe me, especially as I knew all the details about the Ernst's arrest and his mission here."

They stopped briefly before going in to see Smet. Dewulf wasn't finished yet.

"But how did you know Ernst wasn't part of this? Actually working for the Germans, or working on a scam with Hendrickx to cheat you?"

Walsh shook his head. "Ernst was innocent. I know that. He was just a pawn."

"And Hendrickx had never met you?"

"No. Of course, if we had met, then I would've thought of some other ruse. But he insisted on keeping away from me, apparently, according to Ernst. To protect himself. But odd how measures taken to protect oneself can create other problems. Other risks. Isn't it?"

Dewulf nodded. "Hmmm. But then suppose Hendrickx was working with the Germans in some fashion?"

"That wouldn't make sense, as the Germans acted to arrest Ernst as soon as Retzlaff informed on him, so they could not be aware of his mission here. Not if Germany works the way I think it does. So I gambled that Hendrickx wouldn't know about that, and that he might believe the Germans were as disorganized as you are. And that he would be eager to hurt the gendarmerie while raising himself up in the ranks of the Maison, once he had Becker's name."

Dewulf frowned. "We're not *that* disorganized."

Walsh put a friendly hand on his shoulder, and smiled again. "Of course you aren't. And I could tell you a thing or two about disorganization back in Britain. But there's something else, now that I think about it."

Dewulf put his hand on the doorknob and paused before turning it. "What's that?"

"Hendrickx didn't ask or say anything about Tobias. About why he was killed."

Five minutes later, they sat before Smet and told him they had confirmation about a name, someone linked to the gendarmerie and the Maison. And someone who most certainly knew about Ernst's train departure. Before Smet could answer, however, Dewulf interjected.

"There's something else, general."

"What is it?" Smet's frown had increased in intensity since they began speaking, and Walsh was afraid he would shut down the proceedings at any moment.

"According to Hendrickx, at the Maison, the man we seek is suspected of being a *mouchard*. I know he isn't working for the Sûreté, but I can't speak for other services. He may be with the gendarmerie, or the police."

Smet looked at them both. "But he is a gendarme. So let's start there, shall we?"

"So we have your permission to question him?"

"In front of me. I will have him brought to me, and we will speak with him here."

The gendarme's name was Bosmans. Captain Willem Bosmans. As he was currently attached to the Etterbeek caserne it took only a few minutes to bring him in. Walsh watched from the window of another office as they led him into Smet's quarters. The man looked a little old for a captain, in Walsh's opinion; he seemed at least fifty years of age. His uniform was unkempt and he walked with no military bearing at all, like he had the weight of the world on his shoulders. Even his moustache was slightly askew, making his entire mouth seem crooked.

Smet would not allow Walsh to attend the interrogation, so he waited nearby, well out of earshot. Another captain, a much younger one working as Smet's ADC, offered coffee to Walsh, but he declined. Walsh could tell the young man wanted to ask about the little drama Smet was running, but he kept his mouth shut. Good lad, Walsh thought.

Less than thirty minutes later, Dewulf emerged from Smet's office, shutting the door behind him. He threw an odd look at Walsh, kind of a confused frown, as if he was making up his mind about something, but declined to speak about it in front of Smet's ADC. Then he grabbed his overcoat and strode towards the exit.

"Let's go," Dewulf said. "You might as well come with me."

Walsh grabbed his own coat and followed Dewulf.

Outside a car was already waiting for them, a shiny black Minerva open tourer. It gleamed in the sunshine. Smet's personal car perhaps. A driver opened the door for them, and Dewulf and Walsh settled quickly in the back seat.

Once the driver had started the car, Dewulf said, simply, "To rue Bréderode. And quickly, please."

They were underway a moment later, and the noise of the engine and the street traffic on the way back into Brussels effectively drowned out the following conversation, spoken by Dewulf and Walsh with their heads leaned close together, so that the driver could not hear.

"What's on rue Bréderode?" Walsh said.

"Are you sure you've never met this man? Bosmans?" Dewulf said.

"No, never."

"You've never seen him around? Following you? At the Exposition perhaps?"

Walsh shook his head. "No, I'm sure of it. Quite sure. What did he tell you?"

"Not much."

"Well, did you confront him with the two lists?"

The automobile turned right onto the Avenue de la Couronne and gathered speed. Dewulf and Walsh had to raise their voices a little to understand each other.

"Yes, after he admitted he knew about Ernst being taken back to Germany on the evening train. But we knew that already. Then once he saw we had evidence of his involvement in the Maison, he said he could not tell us anything more until he had permission from someone else. The general threated him with a court martial, and I threatened him with arrest, but he wouldn't say anything further."

"Who is supposed to give him permission to speak to us?"

"The man we're going to fetch right now."

The vehicle stopped briefly where rue du Trône meets the Boulévard du Régent, then crossed over the boulevard. Right in front of the vehicle Walsh could see the huge Royal Palace, with its white stone brilliant in the August sun, and for a brief moment he thought they were going to stop there. But the Minerva quickly turned towards the left and entered the street right behind the palace, then parked at the curb.

The driver said, "Rue Bréderode, sir," before stepping out of the vehicle and opening Dewulf's door.

"Wait for us here, please," Dewulf replied.

Walsh could see what looked like government buildings along the narrow street, some of which were constructed in the similar imposing stonework as the Royal Palace. They seemed very tall and cramped relative to the size of the street, as if they had been originally built on more modest foundations and then added to over the years, if not decades. These imposing edifices were interspersed with far more modest structures, most of which were wooden, and Walsh could make out the name of one firm posted on a sign in front of its office: the *Société Anversoise du Commerce au Congo*.

"What is this?" Walsh said.

Dewulf hesitated, but just for a moment. Then he sighed audibly. "It's our colonial offices. What's left of them, I should say. For the Congo."

Dewulf walked into one of the larger buildings, through an archway and past a large open wooden door. The place was eerily quiet for such a large office building, and Walsh could see open doors leading into empty offices. Many were lined with tall wooden shelves reaching nearly to the ceiling. Empty shelves, mostly, except for the occasional file or book standing alone and unneeded. Some of the offices were in complete disarray, as if they had been ransacked, and even in these rooms Walsh could see the occasional placid fonctionnaire, working on determinedly at his desk as if it were perfectly normal to conduct government business in a rubbish dump. Windows were open throughout the building to let in fresh air, causing loose papers to rustle around everywhere, even on the floor, though no one seemed to care.

Dewulf checked the numbers on the doors as they moved through the building. Some of the walls were decorated, if that is the correct word, with posters and maps of the Belgian Congo. Walsh also noticed a poster for the Anglo-Belgian India Rubber and Exploration Company, lying on the floor, ripped and dirty with footprints. Then Dewulf found room 46 and stopped before it. He entered the room without knocking and practically ran into another older man, also in his fifties like Captain Bosmans. And he was dressed exactly like Bosmans, in the uniform of the Belgian Gendarmerie. But this man was far tidier in appearance, and held himself with a proper bearing.

"*Excusez-moi*," the man said to Dewulf, then politely tipped the brim of his kepi.

Dewulf gently put his hand on the man's chest to prevent his leaving. The man kept smiling.

"Colonel Geerts? Victor Geerts?"

368

The man kept smiling. "Yes, I'm Colonel Geerts. And you are?"

Dewulf smiled back at him. "I'm Inspector Dewulf, of the Sûreté. Martin Dewulf."

Dewulf extended his hand. "And I don't believe we've had the pleasure, sir. I'm happy to meet you."

Confused, but still smiling, Geerts extended his hand. "Yes, yes, likewise. But, inspector, I'm on my way back to work. I just stopped here to...to see an old friend."

"Yes, Colonel. I understand. But General Smet said I could find you here."

"General Smet?"

"Yes. He and I are working on a...a very sensitive matter at the moment, and we believe you can assist us. I have a driver waiting outside for us."

Dewulf extended his arm, pointing the way.

"I see. And who is this young man, may I ask?" Geerts nodded to Walsh. He was no long smiling. Neither was Walsh.

"This is Mr Walsh, with the British Embassy. He is assisting us with this matter as well. Now if you please sir..."

Geerts held up his hand. "Just a moment, inspector. I really should telephone my office to inform them of my whereabouts. It won't..."

Dewulf practically blocked Geerts's way back into the office he had just left. The colonel glared at him.

"That won't be necessary, sir. General Smet has already informed your office. That's how we found you here."

"I see. Very well."

The colonel composed himself and extended his own arm towards the dark corridor.

"After you, inspector."

They left the building, in a line of three, with Walsh following closely behind the colonel. Without even thinking about it, Walsh made sure his gun hand was free at all times, and kept it close to his holster.

Less than fifteen minutes later, after riding back to Etterbeek in complete silence, Walsh again waited in an outer office while Dewulf and Smet met with Colonel Geerts.

Bosmans also remained in another office, under guard, while his three countrymen conferred.

A few moments later, Dewulf came out and took Walsh aside, away from Smet's ADC.

"We think we have most of the story," Dewulf said. "Enough to start with, at least."

"What is all this?" Walsh tried to keep the irritation out of his voice.

"He's agreed to help with Bosmans."

"Who is Geerts?"

"He's with one of the special gendarmerie brigades in Brussels." Dewulf sighed again. "One I wasn't aware of."

"What special brigade?"

Dewulf shook his head. "Internal security, just like my office. A temporary assignment. He says Bosmans was working for him. As a *mouchard*, an informer, at the Maison."

"You didn't know about this?"

"Of course not. If it's true."

"Can you check Geerts's story?"

"I'm about to. Come with me."

They returned to Smet's office, where Geerts sat with a cup of coffee, in front of Smet's desk. Geerts didn't seem particularly annoyed to be there now; in fact, he seemed quite pleased with himself.

Smet, however, was frowning even more severely than when Walsh had last seen him. He stood up and waved Walsh to a chair next to Geerts, who ignored him. Walsh sat down, while Dewulf leaned against the windowsill, with an angry look on his face.

"Thank you, Mr Walsh," Smet began. "I thought you should hear this, before we bring Captain Bosmans back. I understand you have an interest in the conduct of certain inquiries at the Maison du Peuple."

"I suppose you could say that," Walsh replied.

"Yes, indeed. Indeed. And we are doing our best to help you. Please believe me. Now, we are all grateful to Colonel Geerts for his assistance today. Very grateful. So, colonel, could you please tell us, again, about your relationship with Captain Bosmans."

370

Geerts put his empty coffee cup on Smet's desk before he spoke. "Yes, but first, we are all agreed that my assistance with your inquiry must remain secret. Can we agree to that?"

Geerts looked around the room. Silence gave consent.

"Very well. And you must understand too, that my orders to Bosmans were very specific. *Very* specific, gentlemen. As all military orders must be. In fact," – Vermuelen suddenly looked over at Dewulf – "I imagine my orders were, are, very similar to those you operate under, inspector."

"What are you talking about?" Dewulf said.

"Orders from Massaert, of course. I beg your pardon, inspector, but Mr Massaert doesn't exactly give 'orders' now, does he? Only 'suggestions' and 'instructions.' But they function in the same way, do they not?"

Dewulf stepped away from the windowsill and stood before Geerts.

"Ivo Massaert? What instructions did he give?" Dewulf demanded.

"I told you, inspector, the same as you received. Months ago. Special instructions to help secure the Exposition. To keep track of subversive elements operating in the capital region. Nothing unusual in that, is there? Hmm?"

Dewulf glared at him. "And so you infiltrated the Maison? With Bosmans?"

Geerts nodded. "Of course."

Now Smet spoke up. "Bosmans is one of *my* men, Colonel Geerts. He is supposed to take orders from *me*."

"Yes, of course," Geerts continued. "And I apologize for that. But I couldn't very well ask all the members of my Special Brigade to do this job now, could I? That would expose all of us to those scum. And put us all at risk. This was unacceptable to me."

Geerts shifted in his seat before continuing. "So I had to use other men, under other commands. Men I could trust, completely."

"And how did you choose Bosmans?" Walsh asked. "Why do you trust him?"

Geerts looked at Smet, then at Dewulf, then back to Walsh. "I think your friend here" – he indicated Dewulf – "can answer that for you. And it's nothing sinister, I assure you. I have no regrets. I have nothing to hide."

Before Dewulf could speak, Smet broke in.

"Inspector, why don't you take Mr Walsh outside again, *s'il vous plait*? I would like to speak alone with Colonel Geerts for a few moments."

Again in the ADC's office next to Smet's, Dewulf and Walsh stood together, waiting. Before anyone could speak, they suddenly heard Smet shouting at Geerts. From what little Dewulf and Walsh could hear, General Smet didn't seem particularly pleased with some of the things he had just heard from his fellow officer.

Pretending he didn't hear anything, the ADC smiled at them, awkwardly, and held out his arm. His forehead glistened with sweat.

"Won't you gentlemen please come this way? You'll be more comfortable in the officer's lounge."

Dewulf and Walsh followed the young man into another room, furnished with more comfortable fittings and a small drinks bar. The window looked out onto a small parade ground, which was as empty as the room they were in.

"Please help yourself to anything," the ADC continued. "I'll come to get you when...when the colonel is finished. I'm sure it won't be too long."

"What was Colonel Geerts talking about?" Walsh began, after the ADC had left. "What do you know about all this?"

"Did you see the medal on his chest?" Dewulf asked, shaking his head. "I can't believe he still wears it."

"What medal? What are you talking about?" Walsh suppressed a strong urge to throttle the inspector.

"An Order of the African Star, of the *Commandeur* class. Why is he still wearing that trinket?" Dewulf could barely contain the disgust in his voice.

"So he served in Africa?"

Dewulf nodded.

"With the Force Publique?"

"Yes, of course, of course," Dewulf said, in an irritated voice.

He walked over to the window and looked out at nothing in particular.

Before Walsh could ask why Dewulf was so annoyed with Geerts's decoration, the inspector spoke again.

"They served together, Bosmans and Geerts. In the Congo. Years ago. And then stayed in touch once they returned here, along with others in their unit. That's why they trust each other."

"I see," Walsh said.

"Yes, I'm sure they shared a lot of interesting experiences, from all their time out there. And interesting secrets as well." Dewulf paused for a moment, then spoke in a smaller voice, as if he was talking to himself rather than to Walsh. "But some of us are...are not so proud of the Force Publique. Of course, it was different when we were young. Back then, it was all about honour and glory for our empire. Our wonderful Belgian empire. We were going to civilize them, like you were doing in India, correct?"

Dewulf turned and smiled at Walsh, who said nothing.

"Build bridges and roads and railways and schools and bring our modern ways, our Christian faith, into the dark heart of Africa," Dewulf continued. "All well and good, until they found the rubber trees. Those damned rubber trees. My God."

Dewulf shook his head.

"I got out right after that," he said. *"Right after that,* you understand?" Dewulf turned to look at Walsh again. Walsh understood.

"But most...lots of my...my colleagues stayed on. They had nothing here to come back to. And they lived well enough in Leopoldville and Stanleyville and all along the river, I suppose, if you stop to think about it. But I didn't go to Africa for that. Before I left I asked one of them how he could continue to do it. Collecting severed hands from workers who failed to meet their rubber sap quotas? Beating naked children with a *chicotte* to make their terrified parents work harder? Can you imagine?"

"What did he say about that?" Walsh asked. "Your...colleague?"

"He said it didn't bother him. Obviously the Africans, well, they just needed to be motivated to work. Motivated in quick and simple ways, ways that they would easily understand. And they were not civilized, you know, and one could beat them like beating a stubborn donkey. No difference, for him. So for him it was just another part of the job. Besides, the Church was there too. Isn't that convenient?

All he had to do was confess every week and his sins would be wiped clean. Magically. Assuming, of course, that he even felt sinful, doing the things he did."

"I had my...my time in Africa too. For our Empire," Walsh said.

"Well, that was a long time ago. I try not to think about it these days."

Walsh nodded. "Me too."

Chapter 71

Ten minutes later, Captain Willem Bosmans sat before General Smet's desk, with Colonel Geerts sat next to him. Inspector Dewulf stood to the side of Smet, while Walsh remained in the corner of the office, behind Bosmans and Geerts.

"Now that we are all here, it's time to clear up this matter once and for all," Smet began. "Because, quite frankly, each one of us has better things to do at the moment."

Smet looked up from his papers and met the eyes, briefly, of every man in the room, before staring directly at Bosmans. Then he continued.

"So, captain, I've spoken at length with Colonel Geerts about his instructions to you, and we understand the nature of your mission at the Maison du Peuple. Your clandestine mission. We also understand that you were acting under the colonel's authority, and that Colonel Geerts *himself* was acting under the instructions of the Royal Palace. And we further understand that these…these extraordinary efforts were meant to be undertaken as a…as a preventative measure, as a *temporary* preventative measure, I might add, to help enhance the safety of our International Exposition this year. Now, captain, do you disagree with any of those understandings?"

Bosmans shook his head. Smet looked at Geerts, who nodded for him to continue.

"*Bon.* Very well. Now, captain, given the nature of your mission at the Maison, we are further agreed to treat this matter as an internal affair, an informal inquiry, if you cooperate fully with us. If you tell us everything. But this is only a courtesy. If you do not cooperate, then we have no choice but to turn the matter over to a court martial, and your colonel here will *not* be in a position to protect you, as he is *not* your commanding officer. *I am your commanding officer.* Do you understand?"

Bosmans looked over at Geerts, who avoided his gaze. Then he nodded again, ever so slightly.

"So, then, captain, we are all aware that you were in a position to share information about the movements of Ernst Hesse on the day that he was killed. You were at the *caserne* here helping to guard him for a few hours, and you knew he was scheduled to leave on the evening train. So I must ask you now, with whom did you share this information?"

Bosmans looked at Geerts, again, then up at Dewulf, and back to Smet. The three faces he searched were impassive. He opened his mouth slightly, but still did not speak.

Smet's frown grew far more severe. "Captain, I am growing very impatient. Two young men are dead. Foreigners. Murdered here in Brussels. These cases are still officially unsolved. If you do not assist us here, *right now*" – Smet pounded the desk, and everyone in the room flinched – "then you may be charged with these murders. Do you understand me?"

Bosmans lowered his head, and shook it slightly. "I told you, I had nothing to do with the murders."

"But you did tell someone about Ernst? Isn't that right?" Smet demanded.

Bosmans nodded, finally. Geerts shook his own head, and avoided Smet's glaring eyes. Dewulf and Walsh exchanged a glance.

"And who did you tell?"

"Just one man. But he couldn't possibly be a part of this. It's just not possible."

"Why not?" Geerts said. "Who did you tell, captain?"

"Listen to me, he knew about this already. About the Hesse boy. What he was doing in Brussels. I didn't get that from the Maison, you understand. I never met with Hendrickx. I was keeping track of Penneman, and the Young Guards. And the...the man I told said my information would help the boy, after the Germans took him. You see? I didn't...inform about this. I only, I only...confirmed what was going on. So this is not my fault. I was trying to help the boy! It's not my fault!"

"Give us the name, captain," Smet said, in a calm voice.

"And besides, this man must be innocent. He must be!" Bosmans added.

"Who is it, captain?" Smet shouted. "Is he a gendarme?"

"No, not a gendarme." Bosmans looked around the room again, at all of them. "He's a priest. Father Devos. Father Alain Devos."

The other men in the room exchanged glances before turning their attention back to Bosmans.

"So he must be innocent. He must!" Bosmans continued.

Smet sat back in his chair and looked up at Dewulf, as if to say, *Do you still want to pursue this?*

Before anyone else could respond to Bosmans, Walsh stepped forward from his place near the door.

"So you are Catholic, captain? Isn't that correct?" Walsh asked him.

Bosmans nodded.

"And confession is good for the soul, is it not?"

Bosmans nodded again.

"And you confessed your recent activities to Father Devos. About your lies at the Maison as a *mouchard*. About deceiving your commanding officer here. About having some of the Young Guards beaten up by masked men, after one of their meetings."

Bosmans nodded a third time. Smet shook his head again before aiming another glare at Geerts, who seemed to shrink into his chair.

"And the Father already knew all about Ernst, didn't he?" Walsh continued. "And he asked you to look after the boy, and to let him know what was happening after the Germans took him. Isn't that right?"

"But why?" Smet asked. "And how did the Father know?"

"Because Ernst had already told him," Walsh said. "Long before Bosmans was involved. Because they attend the same church, don't you, captain? You and Ernst?"

Bosmans turned and looked at Walsh.

"The Eglise Nôtre Dame de la Chapelle. That's where you confess, isn't that right, captain?"

Walsh walked over to Bosmans and leaned down slightly, looking into his eyes.

"And that's where Father Devos can be found, correct?"

Fifteen minutes later, they had the entire story. Dewulf and Walsh decided to walk back into the centre of Brussels, as Walsh's flat in Ixelles was on the way. Smet and Geerts had decided not to discipline Bosmans for the moment, unless new information was uncovered that implicated him as the murderer of Ernst. Or Tobias.

After Bosmans admitted his confession to the priest, Geerts admitted that the priest had also served with them in the Congo Free State, along with Major Jacquard. Jacquard, however, was not a mouchard like Bosmans, just a 'friend' to them all. Geerts said they had lots of such friends in Brussels, all loosely connected from their time in the Congo. Friends in the military, the police, business, the government, the universities, the clergy. But it was all purely social for them, not sinister, and Geerts continued to insist that he was acting under the full authority of Ivo Massaert, who served King Albert himself.

These four particular friends – Geerts, Bosmans, Jacqaurd, and Devos - had forged their own bond when serving under Commander Guillaume Van Kerckhoven in the Congo, during the late 1800s. But Geerts claimed that these connections leading to Ernst's death were a mere convenience for them all, just a way of helping fellow officers once they returned to new lives in Brussels. They were not involved in a secret plot to kill Ernst and Tobias. Or to help Imperial Germany's defence planning. Or anything else.

And unless Dewulf and Walsh could find firm evidence to the contrary, Smet was happy to treat the affair as internal matter for the Belgian Gendarmerie, and it would end there. You couldn't arrest a man for confessing to a priest, after all.

"So, my dear friend Ivo told others to do the same job he asked me to do," Dewulf said, as they walked along the Avenue de la Couronne in the bright sunshine. "What a surprise. What a friend."

"Or so Geerts says," Walsh said.

"Yes. Perhaps I should talk to him now. Massaert, I mean. Just to make sure about what orders he gave to Geerts. And to tell him how his secret orders to protect one thing ended up causing someone else to be harmed. To be killed, in fact. Not to mention the fact that Geerts and I have almost been working against each other for months now. And that our old idiot Bosmans and his men even beat up my own *mouchard*!" Dewulf shook his head. "Isn't life grand these days?"

"So who is Commander Van Kerckhoven?" Walsh asked.

"Just a thug. A sadist, you might say," Dewulf said. "He used to offer the native soldiers under his authority a payment in brass rods for every human head they brought back to him during a military expedition. Among other creative rewards. And punishments."

"You must be joking."

"No, it's true. Completely true, I'm afraid. In Africa they called him *Boula Matendé*. It means 'the hurricane' in their language, because people would clear out of their homes in panic simply on a rumour that Van Kerckhoven was heading their way. And he would leave nothing standing after he departed, just like a hurricane had been through. He led expeditions to find ivory in the north of the country, while everyone else in the country was hunting rubber. Or I should say, stole ivory from the local hunters. Millions of francs of it."

"Sounds like a charming man."

"I never met him. But I know his type. He wasn't the only one enriching himself back then."

"And you believe Geerts? About the lack of a conspiracy among these men?"

Dewulf shrugged. "Bosmans seemed like he was telling the truth. And Geerts, he also looked surprised by the story. We also know Bosmans was at the barracks when Ernst left for his train, so he could not have killed the boy. I can ask about Geerts and Jacquard at their own barracks. But I really don't think it's necessary."

"Why not?"

"Nicholas, if Geerts really was acting under orders from Massaert, orders to simply keep track of subversives during the Exposition, like I've been doing, then I just don't think he would allow himself to be a part of some foolish assassination conspiracy while Massaert is watching him. It would be far too risky for Geerts. And Jacquard, he helped to arrest Ernst in the first place. Simply to get him out of the country as quickly as possible, to keep the Germans happy. So this was all about deporting Ernst, not murdering him. Now, it would be easy enough for me to check their alibis, once I talk to Massaert, but like Smet said, we all have other business to attend to these days."

"I see." Walsh stopped walking, as he needed to turn left off the main street to go back to Ixelles. "And what about the priest?"

Dewulf stopped as well, then sucked in some air across his teeth, and shook his head slightly. He looked around the busy street, then back to Walsh.

"I don't know about that."

"Inspector, listen to me. The killer was an expert shot. Someone told him to be there, at the station. The right place at the right time with the right target. If the priest knew about this, and told the killer, then we need to talk to him. *Right now*."

"Nicholas, first I will look into these alibis. And then I will ask about Massaert's exact orders to Geerts. We need to confirm these claims. But that's all for now, understand? And then we can decide, I will decide, what to do about the priest. Is that clear?"

Walsh looked at Dewulf with a blank face before answering, in a flat tone. "Certainly, inspector. I'll leave it to you."

Walsh turned on his heel, and walked away.

Chapter 72

Leysen waited in an alcove, outside, just across the street from the main entrance to the Eglise Nôtre Dame de la Chapelle, and tried his best to blend into the scenery. The darkness helped a little, but he was still wary of lurking so close to the Maison du Peuple, just up the street behind the church, after Walsh's little charade with Hendrickx. But Dewulf had insisted that he remain here all evening, so here he was.

At least it wasn't raining tonight, and the mid-August temperature was pleasant enough. He was tempted to duck into the café behind him for a coffee, or something stronger perhaps, but he was not allowed to leave his 'post' until he heard from Dewulf.

The church bells were just ringing for eight o'clock in the evening when Leysen spied Walsh walking down the street next to the church. He seemed to be in a hurry. Leysen quickly turned away but continued to watch Walsh in the reflection of the café window. He lit a cigarette and kept his eyes on Walsh as the older man entered the church, then closed the huge door behind him.

Leysen threw down his cigarette and raced across the street, then paused for a minute at the door. What next? Dewulf hadn't been clear on what he should do if Walsh arrived; he said only to keep an eye on him and to make sure he didn't get into trouble here. But what the hell did *that* mean?

Leysen cursed under his breath, then shook his head in exasperation after realizing where he had just taken the Lord's name in vain. He opened the door slowly, and listened for a moment. He could hear a voice echoing off the ancient stone walls inside. Walsh's voice. Angry and insistent.

With the door closed behind him now, Leysen crept along the nave of the church, staying close to the line of massive columns leading to the altar. Suddenly Walsh was there next to him, with a pistol in his hand, aimed at Leysen's head. Behind Walsh stood, or rather, crouched, an old priest in a black cassock, holding his hand to a gash in his head. Walsh's free hand was gripped on the priest's upper arm.

"What the devil are you doing here?" Walsh growled at Leysen. His eyes flashed at Leysen, cold and hard. He kept the pistol aimed at Leysen's head.

"I…I was told to be here," Leysen stammered.

"Who told you to be here?"

Leysen paused for a moment, then spoke up when Walsh pressed the pistol to his skull. "Dewulf. He told me to wait here."

Walsh shook his head. "Unbelievable. And where is Dewulf now?"

Now Leysen shook his head. "I don't know. At his office, I suppose. He left a telephone number to call if I needed him."

"Well, then, you go call him now. *Right now*, understand? And you tell him that the priest, Father Devos here, is going to take me to Ernie's killer."

"Take you where?"

"To the Exposition. The electrical section next to the central gallery, just inside the main entrance."

Walsh forced Devos up the hill behind the church, along rue Joseph Stevens and into the Sablon. As Walsh had expected, several cabs were lined up along the side of the Place. He led Devos to the first one, and forced him into the back of the vehicle.

"The Exposition," Walsh said to the driver standing next to the vehicle, who nodded without comment as Walsh climbed in next to the priest. The driver held the engine choke closed with a pull cord attached to the carburetor and started the vehicle with a hand-crank. After the engine sputtered to life, the driver climbed into the front seat, adjusted the spark lever and the throttle, and turned the cab around, heading towards the rue de la Régence.

"Please, *monsieur*, you are making a mistake," the priest said, with Walsh's pistol poked into his ribs. "There is still time to stop this madness!"

"Quiet!" Walsh hissed. "I'm not interested in anything you have to say."

The cab turned right onto rue de la Régence, passing in front of the Royal Conservatory and the Grand Synagogue of Brussels, both of which were dark and quiet.

"This does not concern you, young man," Devos continued. "And you must stop interfering!"

Devos seemed to be in his late fifties and had the physique of a wrestler, with a low centre of gravity and short, thick limbs. His black cassock ballooned around him in the back of the cab, making his head look absurdly small for his body.

Walsh glared at the priest for a moment, then whispered, "Why was Ernst Hesse killed?"

Devos shook his head. He held stubby fingers to each side of his silver beard, as if deep in thought, then put his hands out in front of Walsh, empty and pleading. "I told you before, I don't know! I can't answer that! I had nothing to do with it!"

Walsh forced himself to refrain from striking the priest again, then said, "Then how do you know this doesn't concern me?"

The priest looked away from Walsh, as the cab turned left at Place Poelaert, crossed Boulevard de Waterloo, then picked up speed on Avenue Louise.

"And you were the one who kept track of Ernst, and told the assassin where to find him," Walsh continued. "Isn't that right? So how can you say to me that you don't know what happened?"

The priest stared straight ahead, his jaw set. "I am a man of honour. I have done my duty. I don't need to answer to you."

"Not yet. But you will."

There was little traffic at this time of night, especially on a Sunday, and the cab reached the Bois de la Cambre a few moments later.

"Take us around to the side entrance, driver," Walsh said. "By the *Kermesse*."

The driver did as he was told and stopped the vehicle at the entrance to the Kermesse, in front of a large iron gateway leading into the attractions. It was much quieter here compared to the main entrance to the Exposition around to the right, and the evening crowds were already thinning out.

Walsh paid the driver and pulled Devos out of the vehicle, keeping his pistol out of the driver's sight. Walsh and the priest stood for a moment as the cab quickly turned and drove away, back towards Avenue Louise.

"Let's go," Walsh said, dragging the priest towards the gate. "And keep your mouth shut or I'll silence you myself with this, understand?"

Walsh held up his pistol quickly for Devos to see, then put it in his front jacket pocket, where he kept his hand on the weapon.

They entered the Kermesse and walked quickly along the rue de la Senne, past the main attractions, with Walsh keeping a firm grip on the priest with one hand and the other on the pistol in his jacket pocket. He could feel strength in Devos's shoulder and hoped he would not have to get more physical with the man, with a *priest*, especially in front of a crowd. Walsh continually scanned the surroundings to make sure he wasn't about to be ambushed, and saw that the scenic railway at Luna Park was still running, although he could see only a few riders on it. The puppet theatre and the water-chute had closed for the evening, however, and the absence of screaming boat-riders in the now-still waters gave Walsh an odd sense of unease after seeing the pool so crowded and lively during the daytime.

They walked further along the boardwalk in the Kermesse, past the restaurant Chien Vert and the cabarets and cafés along the rue de l'Escalier. They stomped across an arched wooden bridge, and through a large open gateway, which led into the main Exposition. At the gateway, Walsh pushed Devos to the side and stopped.

"Just a moment," Walsh said.

He peered around the gateway, towards a small building on the left, which was attached to the front left corner of the much-larger central gallery. Walsh knew that the small building housed the offices of the executive committee of the Exposition. He could see that the lights were still on but he could see no one about the place, other than a few patrons entering the central gallery next to the executive committee offices.

Walsh motioned for Devos to follow him and they entered the central gallery at the far left entrance, where the Belgian section – running to the right along the front of the building – intersected with the British one, which ran perpendicular to the Belgian wing and parallel to the electrical exhibits. A single gendarme seated at the entrance to the pavilion stood up as they approached, holding out his hand to stop them.

"I'm sorry, the exhibit is closed for the evening," said the gendarme, shaking his head.

Walsh removed the Exposition identity card from his coat pocket and handed it to the gendarme.

"I need to check something in the British section," Walsh explained. "There's a problem with one of our exhibits."

The gendarme checked Walsh's face against the image on the card, then handed it back to him. Then the gendarme looked at the priest with an odd smile on his face.

"It must be quite a problem, *monsieur*, if you need a priest tonight!" said the gendarme, with a wide grin.

Walsh smiled at him, and shook his head. "No, no, nothing serious. It won't take a moment, if you don't mind, sir. We just want to be ready for tomorrow."

The gendarme stepped out of the way and waved his arm towards the interior of the building, allowing Walsh and Devos to pass.

"Thank you, sir," Walsh said.

The gendarme tipped the brim of his kepi. "My pleasure, *monsieur*." Then he gave the priest a quick second glance, and went back to reading his *Petit Journal*. Walsh and Devos moved quietly into the building, which was only dimly lit with electric lights and empty of visitors now.

The British section was directly ahead of them, while the French exhibition was at the other end of the British wing, across a courtyard behind the Belgian section. Together, the three main parts of the central gallery, which stood just inside the main entrance to the Exposition, formed a kind of squared-off 'C', with the Belgian section at the bottom of the C, the British/electrical section along the side, and the French section at the top, separated from the British one by a paved path.

"Where's your man?" Walsh said, once they were inside the massive structure, and well past the guard.

Walsh kept the priest in front of him, and made sure he could see along the Belgian corridor to the right and the long British wing in front of him. From here Walsh had a view of thousands of pounds' worth of antiques, pottery, jewelry, and artwork around them, just ahead in the British section. A massive display of old China from the South Kensington museum was along one side of the gallery, near some paintings by the Scottish artist William Orchardson, who had died just before the opening of the Exposition.

"He said he worked in the electrical section. At the back," Devos said, indicating the rear of the electrical gallery, parallel to the British one.

"All right, let's go."

Walsh followed Devos towards the left, through a large archway and into the massive electrical gallery. The high-powered arc ceiling lights in here were already off, although some illumination filtered in from the nearby Kermesse through the high windows along the left side of the gallery. The place was completely empty of visitors, as this was not the time to be looking at generators and dynamos and other electrical machinery. It was the time to be enjoying a last drink at the American bar or frolicking in the cafés along the Kermesse.

Walsh checked his pocketwatch. Just before 21:00 now. The galleries would be locked for the night soon.

"Let's move closer to the wall," Walsh said, pulling the priest back with him.

Once inside the electrical section, they began walking slowly along the right side wall, separating the electrical gallery from the British one. The electrical gallery was about half the length of the British one, but it was still impossible to see the entire place at once, especially with such little light.

Walsh's skin felt slightly tingly as he considered the situation. He could smell the heavy machinery around him, a slight metallic odour combined with the strong scent of diesel fumes. Too many hard surfaces, too many places for a gunman to hide. Too many ways for a misplaced pistol shot to ricochet. So they moved quickly past a large turbine and could see long rows of multicoloured incandescent lamps, all dimmed now, of various styles and from various manufacturers across the globe. Walsh could just make out the name of Carel Brothers, a workshop in Ghent, on one of the silent steam generators along one wall. It was coupled with a large electrical generator to power some of the exhibits here.

At the middle of the exhibition was a display of various types of illumination devices, for the purposes of comparison. Walsh could see electrical lamps, gas lamps, acetylene lamps, and high-pressure gas and oil lamps. Wires and tubes snaked all over the tables, providing various types of energy to the lights, all of which were dim.

Walsh paused now, and pulled Devos next time. "So where is he?" Walsh demanded.

"There is an office here, at the back."

Devos pointed towards the end of the room, where several doorways could be seen along the rear wall. Two were slightly ajar and three were closed, but Walsh could see no light or movement nearby.

"What's his name?" Walsh said.

Devos shook his head. "I told you, I don't know his full name. Just his Christian name. His forename."

"Call out to him." Walsh pulled his pistol out and held it on Devos, pointed at his head.

Devos shook his head again. Walsh cracked the butt of his pistol against the back of the priest's head. Devos cried out in pain, staggered forward a step, and reached to feel behind his head.

Walsh hauled Devos back upright. "It's not bleeding. Yet. Now call out to him!"

"Renaud!" Devos hissed.

"Louder!"

"*Renaud!*" Louder this time, in full voice, but not quite a shout.

No answer or movement from the end of the gallery.

Walsh cursed under his breath. He held his pistol against Devos's head, and hissed in the priest's ear, "If your man isn't here, then I'm holding you personally responsible for Ernst's murder."

"Perhaps he didn't hear us. Let's move closer," Devos said.

They continued along the gallery, toward a bank of electrical controls on display, followed by a range of small electrical motors and household appliances.

Walsh was just registering some of the brand names he saw, Edison and the Electrical Supply Companies of London prominently among them, when he heard a loud *clang* behind him. He turned around, as did Devos, but they could see nothing moving back at the front of the gallery. They quickly turned their faces back towards the doors, one of which seemed to be more open now.

Walsh realized that Renaud must be nearby. He held his pistol on the priest, and they inched towards the doors. A moment later the strong smell of petrol began to fill the air.

Walsh looked around him but still could see no movement of any kind.

The smell of petrol grew stronger. Where was it coming from? One of the displays? Was something damaged in here?

"Call out to..." Walsh began to say, when the sound of a pistol cracked loudly and Walsh felt a sharp pain in his right shoulder. He lurched backwards, letting go of Devos and dropping his own pistol at the same time.

Devos ran off, leaving Walsh exposed in the gallery. Walsh threw himself on the ground and scrambled underneath a table, clutching his injured arm. He reached to retrieve his pistol, just a few feet from his outstretched arm, and another shot rang out. It hit his own pistol, which clattered far behind him, well out of reach.

Walsh was helpless now. His shoulder was bleeding freely and he sat up underneath the table, his head just inches from the tabletop. He pushed with his feet and worked his way backwards, until he reached the end of the table. He leaned out slightly and looked towards the door at the end of the gallery. He thought he saw movement there, and then it stopped.

A second later flames erupted all around the gallery. The petrol!

Walsh could hear distant shouts now; the gendarmes must be on the way in from outside. Walsh lay on his back and pushed against the side of the tabletop with his legs, the side nearest to the wall. He grunted with the effort and felt the blood from his shoulder running freely through the fingers of his left hand, which gripped his upper arm.

The table began to lift up, slightly at first, and then it gave way completely, toppling over to one side. Broken glass from a dozen large lightbulbs shattered all over the ground as they slid off the table. Grunting with effort, Walsh kicked the tabletop again so that it turned on its side, with the long, thick tabletop taking up most of the space between the side wall and the middle of the gallery. It gave him just enough cover to duck and scramble to the middle of the gallery, as two more pistol shots were fired at him. They missed Walsh, and he hid behind one of the large generators positioned in the center of the space.

Flames and smoke surrounded Walsh, and he could hear small explosions and more glass shattering as other pieces of small equipment blew up. Crashing sounds, then more shouts and screams, from outside this time. Firelight was reflected in the large windows along the side of the gallery, making the entire room seem like an inferno. In a few moments, it really would be an inferno. Coughing and choking now, Walsh thought he should be able to maneuver his way back to the entrance of the gallery, away from that damned Renaud and his pistol skills.

Still clutching his shoulder, Walsh leaned slowly around the generator to take another look. He wanted to make sure Renaud was not aiming at him before he worked his way back to the entrance of the gallery. Or he could attempt to jump through one of the side windows, if it came to that.

After another spasm of heavy coughing from the smoke filling the gallery, Walsh leaned out to take his look, and Devos cracked him on the skull with a wrench.

PART FIVE

Chapter 73

Paris. August 1910.

"*Incroyable!* Have you seen this?" Lefevre put the front page of *Le Monde* in front of his boss.

Marchand glanced at the newspaper and gave a slight nod. He had already guessed what Lefevre was excited about.

"Of course I have," Marchand said. "I read it at home."

Lefevre sat down across from Marchand's desk. "What a catastrophe! It looks like a bomb went off in there!"

Marchand looked at the photograph on the newspage. It showed what remained of the main Belgian, British, and French sections of the Brussels International Exposition: nothing. Just a massive pile of charred, smoking rubble. Only a bare skeleton of some of the façade's steel girders remained upright; the central gallery was stripped of its stone-clad covering, except for the two large columns on either side of the main entrance to the central gallery. The image was reproduced on newspages around the world.

Not exactly the kind of publicity the Belgians had been planning for over the past four years.

"Perhaps a bomb did go off," Marchand said.

Lefevre gave his boss a look. "You don't mean that?"

"Of course not. I'm sure it was just an accident, like the story says."

Lefevre summarized the story, more to himself than to Marchand, shaking his head slowly the entire time.

"The City of Paris exhibition: destroyed. The French restaurant: destroyed. The Executive Committee offices. The race track. The wild animal enclosures. Parts of the Brussels *Kermesse* burned to the ground. The entire British, French, and Belgian sections of the Central Gallery: completely gone. *Mon Dieu!*"

"Yes. It took several hours to extinguish, apparently. And did you read that little bit about how the lack of standardized equipment among the different communes of Brussels made it even more difficult to fight the fire?" Marchand grunted to himself. "Nothing like kicking a man when he's down."

Lefevre sat down and shook his head again. "The Belgians must be devastated. All that work. Millions of francs' worth of damage."

He put down the paper and picked up his coffee.

"Yes, lieutenant," Marchand said. "Now *we* must get to work, wouldn't you say?"

"The Picardy maneuvers."

"Yes, lieutenant. Only a month away now."

"Yes, sir. I'll get the files."

"*Merci*, Lefevre. I would appreciate that."

After Lefevre left his office, Marchand picked up the newspaper lying in front of him. He gazed at the photos in the Exposition fire story, for the dozenth time this morning. What the hell had happened there? And where was Walsh? Did he make his trip to the Belgian frontiers, as he had promised?

Marchand had half a mind to get on the next train to Brussels, and try to find his friend. But the damned Picardy manuevers, scheduled for the second week of September, demanded his full attention now. Besides, without the information Walsh was going to provide he didn't have any compelling new evidence to make a case for writing a new plan to replace Plan Sixteen.

Those poor Belgians! And their precious, elaborate, doomed Exposition.

But what to do about it right now? Perhaps Marchand could make some enquiries at the French Embassy in Brussels about all this. Discreetly, of course. At least there were no fatalities at the Exposition, at least as far as anyone could tell at this stage. No charred bodies pulled out of the rubble, except for a number of exotic, but terribly unfortunate, caged animals.

Chapter 74

Brussels. August 1910.

Fortunately for Walsh, there was a small hospital located almost directly across from the main entrance to the Exposition, right off Chaussée de Waterloo, on Avenue de Fré. He awakened there, two days after his 'accident', in a private room. His right shoulder was bandaged but still ached from the gunshot wound; the doctors told him that the bullet had only grazed the skin and muscle of the top of his right bicep so there would be no permanent damange. Just a nasty scar. Yet another one.

The doctors were more worried about his concussion, and decided to keep him in hospital a few more days for observation. His lungs had suffered only a very slight amount of smoke inhalation, which had been relieved by oxygen treatment for several hours after his exposure, followed by deep breathing and gentle coughing exercises. So there was no danger of pneumonia now, and his respiratory condition would improve once he was more ambulatory.

More importantly, he had suffered no burns in the fire. Miraculously.

Dewulf came to see him on his third day in hospital. The inspector stood at the foot of his bed, looking him over with a slight smile. Dewulf was dressed casually today, with no jacket and tie, to stay cool in the August heat and humidity. Dewulf also carried a folded newspaper under his arm.

"So it looks like you'll recover," Dewulf said.

"I suppose I'm lucky to be alive, thank God."

"Hmpf. Don't just thank God. Thank young Leysen. He pulled you out of that inferno."

"He did?"

Dewulf nodded and sat down in an armchair, after pulling it closer to the bed. He started to light a cigarette, but then remembered where he was. And where they had found Walsh.

"I suppose I should be angry with him for not coming to get me right after he found you at the church. But then, he did save your life."

"Is he still working with you?

Dewulf nodded. "For now. He's turning out to be quite useful, don't you think?"

"In more ways than one."

"Yes. Indeed." Dewulf paused. "In fact, they've asked him to travel beyond Brussels now, to other gendarme groups across the country. Young Guards groups, I mean."

"Is that so?"

"Yes. We're still not quite sure what to make of it. But you needn't concern yourself with that."

"I suppose not. But could you thank him for me, please?"

Dewulf nodded again. "Certainly."

Walsh looked Dewulf in the eyes. "So you knew I would go after the priest."

Dewulf shrugged his shoulders. "I suspected it."

Walsh sat up higher in bed, and coughed a little. "Then why didn't you come with me?"

"You know I couldn't do that. At least, not officially. And this, this *incident* has gone far enough, wouldn't you agree?"

Dewulf unfolded the newspaper and placed it on Walsh's bed. It was *Le Soir*, the main Francophone daily in Belgium. Walsh picked it up and looked at the photographs inside, still very prominent in the headlines several days after the fire.

"Oh my God."

"You haven't seen this yet?"

Walsh shook his head. "No. They haven't said anything about it. Not the most attentive service here, I have to say. I think they are short of staff now."

Dewulf nodded. "Probably so. It's just a very small hospital, next to a very big Exposition. But you're lucky it was here."

Walsh read some of the story, then looked over at Dewulf again. "But how did the fire spread so far? And so fast? We were only in the electrical section…"

"Well, there will be inquiries about that, I can tell you. But, also good for you, right now they are far more concerned about keeping the Exposition open for business rather than looking into your, your *visit* there on Sunday night."

"What about my gunshot wound?"

Dewulf smiled again, much wider this time. "What gunshot wound? You cut your arm when you fell against that table, didn't you?"

"And Devos? And the killer, Renaud was it?"

"Both disappeared. No dead bodies in the fire, anywhere. No sign of Devos since the fire, and there was no one named

Renaud in the records of those managing the electricity exhibition. Or with the firms exhibiting there. We're still checking with them. And we have no record of Devos leaving the country, so he may still be about. We'll keep an eye out for him. But Renaud? Who knows? We can't keep track of all the visitors to the Expo here now, can we?"

"And what about me?"

"I told you. Everyone is happy to call this an accident right now. A sad mystery. Take a look at the story." Dewulf pointed to the *Le Soir* in Walsh's hands.

"And that includes you? Are you happy?"

Dewulf smiled again. "Especially me. I'm always happy, can't you tell by now?" Then he stood and stretched. "Yes, I'm always satisfied. But now I have some more work to do in the office. No rest for me, my friend!" He raised his hands and rolled his eyes in mock awe. "The Kaiser is coming!"

"To the Exposition?"

"Yes, of course."

"So they are going to open again?"

"*Bien sur.* With all the work we put into it? How could we close three months early? They're already working on a new façade to the central gallery, and building new galleries, just temporary ones, to replace the burned ones. So we will manage."

Dewulf paused at the foot of Walsh's bed. He looked out the window, which would have a view of the Exposition if another building was not in the way. He shook his head again.

"All that work chasing revolutionaries and terrorists, to protect the Expo," Dewulf said, almost to himself. "And it gets destroyed by a simple fire."

"I don't think it was so simple," said Walsh.

Dewulf looked at Walsh again. "Yes, it was, Nicholas. Anyhow, that's what the world is going to believe."

Walsh nodded, and put down the newspaper.

"Back to work now. Remember Balzac, my friend. 'Governments pass, societies perish, but police are eternal.' But can I bring you anything next time? Something to read? To eat?"

Walsh could kill for a few slabs of fried black pudding and a couple of eggs but doubted Dewulf could manage that. And there was the rösti Ernst had cooked for him, once.

"How about an English-language newspaper? And a fresh sandwich from outside? I'm supposed to be in here a few more days, or so they tell me."

Dewulf nodded. "Certainly. I'll add it to your bill. I'll stop by tomorrow, all right?"

Walsh nodded back.

Dewulf affected an odd little smile before speaking again. "And so, Nicholas, tell me the truth. You didn't even get off one shot, with your pistol?"

Walsh shook his head. "No. And where is my pistol, by the way?"

"Leysen found it. I'll bring it to you once you're out of hospital. Does that suit you? And I've stationed an officer outside for your protection. But I don't think Renaud will be around to see you. Or Devos."

"I would appreciate having the pistol back. I paid for it myself."

"Yes, it is a very handsome weapon. Much nicer than mine, in fact." A pause. "So you didn't even get to fire back at the assassin? Not one little shot? And you lost your own pistol? Tsk tsk. What a pity. Perhaps you need some time on the range? Perhaps I could give you some instruction? A few lessons in how to control your weapon, during a gunfight?"

Dewulf's smile grew into a grin, and Walsh, smiling as well, shook his head.

"Good-bye, inspector."

Dewulf tapped his hat, and bowed slightly. He moved towards the door, then paused again, his hand on the handle.

"I almost forgot. We informed your embassy about your injuries. I hope that doesn't complicate things for you."

Walsh shook his head again.

"I told *Monsieur* Bridges, Major Bridges. The name you mentioned before. Is that correct?"

Walsh nodded, and settled down in his sheets again. "That's no bother, inspector. I suppose they need to know. Thanks for telling them."

"Well, they sent someone to see you. Someone from England."

Walsh frowned. Would Cumming have travelled so far just to visit him in hospital? Or was it Grierson, perhaps?

"Who is it, inspector? Someone named Cumming?"

"No, not Cumming. He said his name was Kell. Vernon Kell. He's outside now. Shall I let him in?"

Chapter 75

Sarajevo. August 1910.

Bogdan Zerajic, the would-be assassin of Emperor Franz Joseph and his representative in Bosnia-Herzegovina, General Marijan Varesanin, was buried secretly in Sarajevo, in the section of St Mark's Cemetery reserved for paupers, vagrants, suicides, and other social undesirables. The decision for a secret grave was taken because Austrian authorities hoped to prevent Zerajic's martyrdom among Serbian nationalists. There was no reason, after all, to call the public's attention to the desperate last act of a fanatical young man by giving him a decent burial and a prominent grave marker. Especially during these volatile times.

The decision to remove Zerajic's skull before he was buried was a more personal one, as the chief of detectives in Sarajevo, Viktor Ivasjuk, thought it would be very useful as a threat during his interrogations of other young Bosnian Serbs who might want to imitate Zerajic's act. Other police officials thought the skull would be useful in demonstrating the relationship between criminal tendencies and physiognomy, such as high cheekbones and large jaws, in keeping with the theories of the respected Italian criminologist Cesare Lombroso. And so the skull would sit on display for years on Ivasjuk's desk, facing any poor soul who happened to end up on the wrong side of the law. It also made a handy inkpot.

Yet the secret burial of Zerajic, and the defilement of his corpse, could not prevent the rise of an underground cult devoted to his memory. During the days and weeks following Zerajic's death, young Bosnian Serbs began removing their caps as a sign of respect to the young failed assassin when they passed the spot were he died by his own hand. In time, they would also discover his modest grave in St Mark's Cemetery, and mark it with a cross and flowers.

Fervent young men, these were, and true believers, like Nedjo Cabrinovic, who carved Zerajic's sacred name in the cross on his grave so that others could find it. And Vladimir Gacinovic, who wrote a pamphlet, *Death of a Hero*, in which he paid tribute to his dead friend by claiming that Zerajic's revolutionary example made him an artist and a conspirator, as well as a martyr and a plotter. A pamphlet that closed with a desperate plea, spread among Gacinovic's fellow nationalists, "Young Serbs, you who are rising from the ruins and foulness of today, will you produce such men?"

And young men such as Gavrilo Princip, who helped to maintain the flowers on Zerajic's gravesite with great devotion, even if he had to steal them from other graves. Who came from a humble kmet like Zerajic himself, and who shared Zerajic's obsessive hatred of Austro-Hungarian authority. Who would very soon become an instrument of the most important secret society in Sarajevo, the Black Hand. And who would do his very best to help their sacred cause, in his own time, by succeeding where Zerajic had failed, but with a different target in sight.

Chapter 76

Brussels. August 1910.

Walsh waited in silence and confusion as Kell took the seat vacated by Dewulf, who left them alone. Kell looked younger than Cumming by at least a decade, and his eyes fell upon Walsh with a steady gaze. He wore a smart dark suit with no hat and a pair of small rimless spectacles, which somehow made his stern expression seem even more severe, even though his thin lips were shaped into something like a smile underneath his trim moustache.

Seated now, Kell extended his right hand.

"Major Kell," he said. "Vernon Kell. Pleased to meet you."

Walsh shook Kell's hand. The man's grip was firm. "And you, major."

Kell settled back into his chair, and crossed his legs. "I'm with 'The Firm,' as Cumming so eloquently calls our little organization. Cumming with his clever little nicknames and green ink. I prefer the term 'counter-espionage bureau' where my work is concerned. But I expect you know all that."

Walsh nodded. What was this?

"Yes, I'm very pleased to meet you, finally, Mr Walsh," Kell continued. "And I hope you don't mind this intrusion. Major Bridges was kind enough to contact us once he heard from your Inspector Dewulf."

Walsh sat up a little higher in bed. "Where's Cumming?"

"He's a bit under the weather lately, poor chap. He desperately wanted to see you, but simply couldn't get away right now."

"Nothing serious?"

Kell shook his head. "No, I don't think so. But he's been advised not to travel for the moment. He's been under some pressure lately, what with that damned fiasco in the Friesian Islands."

"What fiasco?"

"Those two men the Admiralty sent. They were caught by the Germans. Earlier this month, it was. We've denied all knowledge since then, of course, but it won't work. The Germans know what we're playing at. Our chaps were caught breaking into a restricted zone, and they actually had the plans of German defences at Wangerooge on them. Damn fools!"

Walsh suddenly felt very grateful that he had decided to stay in Brussels rather than help with Cumming's recce mission – and pursue his romance with Gisela - in northern Germany.

"Will they be returned?"

Kell reached into his pocket for a cigarette, then suddenly remembered Walsh's condition. He paused and put the cigarette back before speaking.

"Not bloody likely. I don't see any way out of it. They'll go on trial soon, and they'll likely be convicted. And so they'll be out of action for a while, but we don't know how long just yet. Nothing we can do about it. They don't have diplomatic immunity, of course."

Walsh shook his head. "Cumming must be in a rage now."

"Yes, if he weren't so ill. All just casualities of this spy business, I suppose," Kell went on. "And I hear you've had some interesting adventures here of your own, Mr Walsh. Or so Major Bridges tells me."

"That's one way to put it." Walsh wasn't sure how much to share with Kell, so he kept his answers short.

Kell nodded slightly. "Hmmm. Yes. Well, I expect you also know we've been…keeping an eye on you here, so to speak."

"Who's been keeping an eye on me?"

"My half of the Firm. The really important side."

Walsh frowned. "What do you mean?"

"We have our own agents, of course. Not here permanently, mind you. But able to come in from London as necessary."

"You mean Mr Long, is that it?"

Kell nodded again. "Yes, Mr Long. And Mr Melville. And a few others, now and again."

"I don't understand."

Kell pulled his chair closer and leaned forward slightly. He looked back at the closed door again, then towards Walsh, before he spoke.

"You see, Mr Walsh, we had to make sure this acetone business was not part of some scheme by the NA to flush out our resources here, so to speak. Steinhauer doesn't operate like this, normally, but we weren't going to take any chances.

So we simply kept an ear to the ground about these two young Germans you've been dealing with. Nothing too...too intrusive, mind you. No direct contact with you or the Germans; Cumming insisted on it. He trusted that their secret was legitimate. Based on your information, of course. Your somewhat limited information."

Walsh tried to keep the anger from his voice. So Cumming knew about this. "And what did you learn, if I might ask?" Walsh said.

Kell looked down at his legs, and removed a bit of fluff from his creased trousers.

"Well, the NA was not involved here, at least at first. They've had nothing to do with it, as far as we can tell. But since the German Embassy became involved, they are certainly aware of you now, and of your mission here. And the acetone secret, of course."

"Which was lost with Ernst."

"Yes, it seems so. They've made inquiries at his university, Leipzig, and they've no knowledge of this process. Knew nothing about it, in point of fact. Seems he came up with it on his own, smart chap."

"And so?"

"And so, I've made some other inquiries, and it seems that Tobias was taken by the Okhrana. And killed by them, of course," he added, almost as an afterthought.

Kell's cold manner was starting to grate on Walsh, but he kept his voice even. "The Okhrana? Why? How do you know this?"

Kell looked at Walsh as if he was daft. "Because the Russians told me, Mr Walsh. It's just that simple. You see, unlike you and Cumming, and those two unfortunate Admiralty spies, I can make official inquiries into these matters, and speak directly with individuals across Europe who know what is going on amongst these radicals. We cooperate as much as possible, once an official contact is made."

"But why was he killed? Tobias, I mean?"

"St Petersburg thinks this was part of some scheme by their Warsaw branch. The Warsaw Defence Station of the Okhrana. St Petersburg wasn't even aware of it until I asked them about it. So they've looked into it now. Seems their man in Warsaw somehow became aware of this acetone mission after your two Germans arrived in Brussels. So he wanted to help move things along so that we could have the secret in the end. I'm sure you know that the Russians are increasingly eager to...to cooperate with us. And with the French, of course.

"I don't believe it."

"It's a fact, Mr Walsh. And the Okhrana's man in Brussels also placed the advertisement to put pressure on you. And then they took Tobias once they found that he had asked for twice as much as the socialists initially wanted. They...interrogated him in Brussels about this, and eventually learned the truth."

Walsh glared at Kell. "What truth?"

"That young Mr Stern was acting on behalf of another group, a more radical one, based in southern Europe. He was going to send half the funds to them. Half of the ten thousand pounds. Or so he told the Okhrana here."

"What radical group?"

Kell shrugged slightly. "He didn't say. Wouldn't say. Couldn't say."

"So they killed him."

Kell nodded. "Yes, it seems so. Right after Mr Hesse was shot. Killing Mr Stern wasn't part of the plan, of course. But things got a little...out of hand. The Russians are somewhat more aggressive with their methods than we are. And they are becoming very nervous about developments in Germany."

"And what about Ernst? Was that part of the plan too?"

Just then the door opened and a white-aproned nurse came in. *"Bonjour, Monsieur Walsh,"* she sang out, with a tight smile.

She carried a tray of pill bottles with her, and a small pitcher of water. Her face was shiny with perspiration in the heat of the afternoon.

"Plus tard, infirmière, s'il vous plait!" Walsh practically shouted at her.

"Mais, monsieur, j'ai..." she began.

"Pas maintenant!"

The nurse shook her head in irritation, turned on her heel, and left.

Walsh looked back at Kell. "What about Ernst?"

Kell shook his head. "He wasn't part of this. Just an innocent pawn."

"But then who killed him?"

"The Okhrana doesn't know. They'll keep after what Tobias was doing, of course, and something may turn up. But they didn't want the chemist dead any more than we did."

"But his murder also wasn't an 'accident.' Someone wanted him dead."

"Yes, it would seem so. But not the Okhrana, certainly not."

"And you don't know who?"

Kell shook his head again. "No. But not us. Not the Russians. Not the Belgians. And not the Germans."

"His own radical group?"

Kell nodded. "Possibly. Who knows what they are up to down there?"

"But why didn't the Okhrana contact me directly? Or you? About all this?"

"I told you, this little scheme was being run out of Warsaw. They didn't want it to become broader knowledge in case things went wrong. Warsaw and St Petersburg don't always see eye-to-eye, you understand. And they may have thought that one or both of your young Germans were linked to the NA. And besides, their man here didn't..."

"Didn't *what*?"

"Didn't want to scare you, Mr Walsh."

Walsh shook his head in disbelief.

"Yes, apparently he thought you were being kind of amateurish about this," Kell continued.

"Is that so?"

Kell nodded again, more purposefully this time. "Yes, wasting all that time negotiating with them. I suppose the Okhrana would've handled Mr Hesse differently."

"Yes, I'm sure. He would've wound up dead with them."

"As he did with you."

Walsh lost his patience. "I was trying to save him, major! Who knows what would've happened to him back in Germany?"

"Yes, you were trying to save him so that he could betray his country for us. So don't pretend you are just being noble about all this."

Walsh glared at Kell again, but knew he was right.

"Yes, well, that's all very interesting," Walsh said. "So do you expect me to thank you for looking out for me? Is that it?"

"No, Mr Walsh."

"And so you came all the way here to tell me what the Russians think of me?"

"Among other things. As I said before, Mr Walsh, your effectiveness here is quite limited now. The NA, and the rest of the German intelligence services, they know that you are here, and that makes you a target for their schemes. And the Russians don't think very much of you, so I'm not sure how helpful they might be to you here."

"So what are you saying? Give up?"

Kell shook his head. "Of course not. What I'm saying is, come back to London."

"London? Why?"

"To work for me, of course. With me." Kell smiled again, slightly, with just a hint of charm.

Walsh stared at him, not knowing what to say.

"I've told you where I stand in this business, Mr Walsh," Kell continued. "I have more resources than Cumming. I have an official status in His Majesty's Government, which you will have as well, in my side of 'the Firm.' Cumming cannot offer you that. I also have cooperation with police departments and interior ministries, with postal offices and customs offices, throughout Europe. Official cooperation, mind you, so no lurking about in the shadows all the time, chasing after phantom spies and snippets of useless gossip, wondering if you'll be arrested at any moment. And I've been more effective than Cumming, you must admit, far more effective, in point of fact. We've already rounded up a number of German spies across Britain, with more to come. They are the real threat to Britain right now, and we have a system to expose them. A good system, as you'll see. We've already collected the names of over ten thousand foreigners to monitor. And you've seen what happens to amateur spies on the continent. You don't want to end up like those Admiralty spies, do you?"

"What about Cumming?"

Kell smiled again. "You probably have the impression that we are great rivals, but that's not the case. Not anymore, now that we have a clear understanding regarding our effective responsibilities. I handle things at home, and Cumming handles things abroad. That's it. And we share agents, of course. There's no harm in working for both of us, as long you take instructions from just one of us at a time, that is! And I'm sure he'll understand you want to come over to my side for a while once he hears all the facts. About what little you can still do here, in Brussels, in light of your recent adventures."

"I don't know. I suppose I'll have to think about it. I'll be stuck here for a few days, anyhow."

"Certainly, Mr Walsh. There's no rush to decide. Take all the time you need."

Kell stood up, but remained in place. He paused, and leaned down to Walsh, and spoke close to his ear.

"Forget about the Hesse boy, Walsh. Understand? Nothing can be done about him now. And he is not important to us, not any more. This is a long game, not a short one. A very long game. And you can't be worrying about each casualty along the way. Otherwise you'll be useless to us, and drive yourself round the bend in the process. So what do you say, Walsh? Do you want to come back to London? And do you want to work for me?"

Chapter 77

Three floors below Walsh's room, William Melville stood outside of the hospital and watched the parade of vehicles moving around the wreckage of the Exposition. The scene of the disaster was enormous; much more impressive than it had appeared in pictures in the newspapers Melville had read over the past few days. Melville had had long experience with reading about disasters in the newspapers. Sixty years old in 1910, and for years a legend in various British security services – the Metropolitan Police, the Special Irish Branch, the Special Section (MO5) in the War Office, and now the Home Section of the Secret Service Bureau under Kell – Detective Melville had cracked some of Britain's highest-profile cases, including the Jubilee Plot against Queen Victoria in 1887.

At the moment he found himself wondering how many of his counterparts in other countries actually believed the ridiculous stories about the Expo disaster planted in the papers by the Belgian government. As he debated whether to visit the site again before leaving Brussels, Kell suddenly joined him. The two men walked back towards the tram stop near the main entrance to the Exposition.

"So, major?"

"He'll join us," Kell said. "I'm quite sure of it, Mr M. Cumming said Walsh would be a team player when he had to be, if he had to be, and everyone knows he has no future in Brussels at the moment. After all that."

Kell tilted his head upwards slightly, indicating the vast Exposition rubble across the street in front of them. Parts of it were still smoking. Postcards of the wreckage were already appearing in newsagent shops. *Greetings from Belgium!*

"So we'll leave Brussels alone?" Melville spoke with a slight Irish lilt, having spent his early childhood in County Kerry before moving to London. He adjusted his straw hat to block the sun from his large bald spot.

"Not exactly. Cumming is going to put someone else on it, once he's on his feet again."

Melville shook his head. "You should have brought me in on this sooner. I don't trust Walsh. All that time with the German lad, without ever learning his secret, and fraternizing with a German girl at the same time? And then the Admiralty's two scouts in Germany get picked up near where she lives, right after she returns home? It doesn't smell right to me, major. Doesn't Walsh know who the enemy is here?"

They paused at the tram stop on Chaussée de Waterloo, taking care to continue their conversation well away from the other waiting passengers.

"It could be just a coincidence. What about his flat?" Kell said, keeping his face away from the people around him.

Melville smoothed his moustache as he spoke, hiding his lips. "Nothing important that I could see. The usual maps and books. Some basic field equipment. There is some film in his camera but obviously I couldn't take that."

"Was the girl ever there?"

Melville shook his head. "Not as far as the concierge or his wife knew. And they didn't recognize her photograph. A mechanic at the Exposition saw them together a couple of times, but they always talked about automobiles."

"A mechanic?"

"In the German section." Melville paused. "A German mechanic."

"Another German. Well, Walsh does know how to engage with them, doesn't he? Perhaps that will be helpful to us."

A tram appeared and slowed down in front of them, ringing its bell. Kell and Melville joined the crowd to board the vehicle, keeping to the end of the queue until they finished speaking.

"So you're going to take him on? Despite these…these misgivings?"

Kell nodded and motioned for Melville to board the tram.

"Best to keep him close to us, in London," Kell said, standing very close behind Melville. "That way we, or you, that is, can keep an eye on him. To see if he hears from the German girl again. Or from any other Germans we should be investigating. Wouldn't you agree, Mr M?"

Melville nodded, and they boarded the tram. It was time to find a quiet lunch somewhere, and some shelter from the summer storm expected later that day.

THE END